P9-CLJ-358

NOAH WARENESS

MEAT HEADS

OR, HOW TO DIY WITHOUT GETTING KILLED

ChiZine Publications

FIRST TRADE EDITION
Meatheads © 2016 by Noah Wareness
Cover artwork © 2016 by Erik Mohr
Cover design © 2016 by Samantha Beiko
Interior design © 2016 by Jared Shapiro

NOAHWARENESS.COM

This work is released under a Creative Commons BY-NC-SA 2.5 license: you are encouraged to share and redistribute the text in any way you like, and to build on it with other works (such as shared-world stories or adaptations) so long as you release them under the same Creative Commons license. Under these terms you have to give credit to Noah Wareness, and you can't use the work for commercial purposes without prior written permission from the publisher.

Noah Wareness does not use government funding for his work. All the money he makes from this edition of *Meatheads* goes to the Red Door, a family shelter in his neighbourhood.

This book is a work of fiction. Names, characters, places, and incidents are either a product of the author's imagination or are used fictitiously. Any resemblance to actual events, locales, or persons, living or dead, is entirely coincidental.

Distributed in Canada by
Publishers Group Canada
76 Stafford Street, Unit 300
Toronto, Ontario, M6J 2S1
Toll Free: 800-747-8147
e-mail: info@pgcbooks.ca

Distributed in the U.S. by
Consortium Book Sales & Distribution
34 Thirteenth Avenue, NE, Suite 101
Minneapolis, MN 55413
Phone: (612) 746-2600
e-mail: sales.orders@cbsd.com

Library and Archives Canada Cataloguing in Publication

Wareness, Noah, author
    Meatheads, or, How to diy without getting killed / Noah Wareness.

Previously published by the author.
Issued in print and electronic formats.
ISBN 978-1-77148-388-9 (paperback).--ISBN 978-1-77148-389-6 (pdf)

    I. Title. II. Title: How to diy without getting killed.

PS8645.A7567M43 2016   C813'.6   C2016-901766-4
                                               C2016-901767-2

CHIZINE PUBLICATIONS
Peterborough, Canada
www.chizinepub.com
info@chizinepub.com

Shelfie
A free eBook edition is available
with the purchase of this print book.

CLEARLY PRINT YOUR NAME ABOVE IN UPPER CASE
Instructions to claim your free eBook edition:
1. Download the Shelfie app for Android or iOS
2. Write your name in UPPER CASE above
3. Use the Shelfie app to submit a photo
4. Download your eBook to any device

Edited by Brett Savory
Proofread by Tove Nielsen

Canada Council   Conseil des arts
for the Arts   du Canada

We acknowledge the support of the Canada Council for the Arts which last year invested $20.1 million in writing and publishing throughout Canada.

ONTARIO ARTS COUNCIL
CONSEIL DES ARTS DE L'ONTARIO
an Ontario government agency
un organisme du gouvernement de l'Ontario

Published with the generous assistance of the Ontario Arts Council.

Printed in Canada

*N*oah's not my name. I live in a toner cartridge in a copier on a painted wood desk next to a bed in a little room at the top of eighteen stairs in a house of friends in the middle of a big city. I've never made anything like this before.

In the order we met, this is for Melanie Lambrick, Nathan Garfat, Jessica Yeandle-Hignell, Emese Boyko, Justine Sawyer, Simon Frankson, Anthony Crage, Andy Anderson, Alexis Hogan, and Caela Butt.

I only know LA's founding punk scene through printed histories. Mostly that's *Lexicon Devil* by Brendan Mullen, *Wild-Eyed Boy* by Lori Wiener, *American Hardcore* by Steven Blush, and *We Got The Neutron Bomb* by Mark Spitz. I should have read them better, too.

Writers owe their supports and sources, but a story owes the stories behind it. Some of this one's closest links are called *Cruddy, Peace, Riddley Walker, Blood Meridian, The Troika,* and *Nine Hundred Grandmothers.* The last two are nearly forgotten, and you need to go find them. That's actually the most important thing.

∧∧∧

MEAT HEADS

OR, HOW TO DIY WITHOUT GETTING KILLED

CIRCLE ONE OF THE OUTER KALIFORONIA BOOK OF THE ALIVE

Don't owe your mind. Mind's the first tyrant.
Don't owe your band. You are your friends.
Don't owe your songs. You'll never meet.
Don't owe your gear. None of it's yours.
Don't owe your space. Can't hold the past.
Don't owe your heroes. They were just moments.
Don't owe your oaths. What transcends is worthless.
Don't owe your hardcore. It's like . . .
Like, I guess this is sposed to be my death song,
I just don't know how to sing this part.
But if you act like you owe something to your hardcore?
That's just your mind thinking it's hardcore.
Then you're getting hungry to start the really fucked up shit.
That shit doesn't need you.

—Arco's death song

THE AAAARGH YOU MEANT

Before my parents were born, Saint Phil was writing about teenagers who spiked their hair, put bones through their noses and threw out all their inherited rules of space and time. You can't ever tell what comes true. Hardcore punk was a real thing that really happened and continues to mutate in the modern underground. Its shockwaves are still remaking people's understanding of genuineness, ethics, and craft. When I was a teenager I was too scared and lazy to do more than put up my hair. This book is an attempted work of thanks.

Hardcore's also young enough that most of the original kids who built it are still around. That means in the real world they're people first, historical persons second, and myth persons third. I got the order backward and I hope this is okay with everybody. In particular, some of the myth people in the streets and stories of Lost Angeles are distortions of real historical people. Punks name themselves, mostly, and I didn't change those names, but when they do horrific or stupefying things, I don't mean to suggest the original people were capable of those actions.

That goes hardest for Darby Crash, who led the band Germs. During his quick life in the real world he pulled all kinds of manipulative stunts and positioned himself as this kind of messy teenage cult leader, but never anything like this. I know he was your friend, and you loved each other. I'm sorry to be one more clueless traveller pissing at his grave. Darby Crash really did invent hardcore. He invented consciousness, too. Both those parts are true.

3 9222 03192 0585

THE RECLINE OF WESTERN CIVILIZATION // WE GOT THE NEURON BALM

An escalator can never break. It can only become stairs.
—**Mitch Hedberg**

If you cut a face lengthwise, urinate on it, and trample on it with straw sandals, it is said that the skin will come off. This was heard by the priest Gyojaku when he was in Kyoto. It is information to be treasured.
—**Yamamoto Tsunetomo**, *Hagakure kikigaki*

We wouldn't of played if I knew there was a barricade.
—**Jerry A**, intro spiel at the last Poison Idea show

—Back before all that shit went down and the punks had to take it to core, a crew we all know found a cheap house on the edge of the park, and they lived there for a couple of years. And it was the House of the Unfinished Basement, right, and the House of All Ways In. This is the joke of how it all began, and the house was called Anything Goes.

They stood sticks in the dirt til tomatoes grew. They pulled down a wall in the basement and did shows. Punker'd jump from the washer and dryer into the crowd. They had a dumpster copymachine they fixed with the guts from a lamp, and they'd truck it around in a sideless shopping cart, back when the roads were flat as your hand, so if your crew wanted to do zines they'd bring it out. They had to flush the parrot when it broke its neck fucking the windowpane, and then they got wasted on sugar cider and packed eight kids into the shitter, stuffing the corpse down with a mophandle and watching the feathers float up. They put the sofa up on phonebooks, punks sleeping underneath, and in the bathtub they made chowder and smokebombs.

You weren't there.

When things broke down they'd get together at the kitchen table and spread out some library books, or trade favors with somebody who knew the trick. So the wind never got in under the windowframes, and the power never jumped off the wires and cooked anyone, and whenever somebody's elbow broke the plaster, they both got patched. Spaces kept going under, but they kept it together at the House of Anything Goes, and the shows got really hard. On Groundhog Labor Boxing Day somebody went assfirst through the only wall standing in the basement and left a hole shaped like a dirty punk.

Couple nights and they had a wall fixing party. Everybody was broke so they pried twobysixes off a halfbuilt pizzahut. They took bikes out to the desert and dug around for gyprock to mix a bucket of plaster. When the patch was up they stuck their fingers in the wet plaster and carved FEAR and GERMS CIRCLE ONE. They carved AGNOSTIC FRONT, MDC, BAD BRAINS. Then somebody took a hammer and beat a nother hole in the wall. Said this patch we made, it's the only diy part of this whole fucking wall. And somebody else grabbed the hammer. They were like, what's wrong with your hands?

So the wall fixing party crew shoved their hands up the house's asshole. They used their knees and headbutted and jumpkicked the framing apart and in their chaos laughter bit chunks off the drywall till nothing stood but one plaster patch like a gutter punk's gray soul flying backward. Then the ceiling caved in. They fucked off to the backyard and had a lot more shine, and everybody slept that night with their drunk jackets on.

Spaces kept going under. There's no good times for hardcore, and Angeles was an oldschool city, with laws instead of hands. They'd come by a hall and say this doorway's too narrow, we're shutting you down. Or they'd say, your backyard's got too many old mikeywaves and your shower water's piss. We're pushing it down with a backhoe. Don't ask us bout it. We're actors of the law.

But their hardcore stood all around them in the House of Anything Goes, under the couch cushion stains and under the sink and their nails, and as they lived there so would they diy. That morning they made coffee and tactics. They hauled out the busted part of the kitchen floor, skinned a silkscreening table with the lino and stacked the wood outside. They nailed up a plank ladder and it turned out decent actually, with smooth basement-to-kitchen access. So they ate pancakes, and their meeting bout fixing the floor pit, it went into a meeting of what pit to build next.

They had to diy every day, the hardcore of the house called it, plus everybody was still broke. But they started arguing over a prybar. It was brand new with the sticker on, it cost tires and tires worth of money at the shop where they stole it, and it could of really ripped into the upstairs hallway floor. But the morning was still pretty early, and some punks were saying things like what good's a prefab tool anyway? We can't mooch off stores forever. Let's use this one for wiping ass and diy a tool out of our hardcore that's ours.

At the dump they found a huge lump of concrete stuck through with cast iron pipes. That night they pushed it over an overpass to bust the concrete off, and ground an edge on the biggest pipe with a stick of rebar as a file. They were all set to yank floorboards, but it was pretty late by then. They might not of been thinking straight. We recovered this pipe, somebody said, but business had it first. This shitpipe from a yuppie prison. It's got too much baggage. If we're serious for getting ready, we can cast a prybar from scratch.

So they snapped the rest of the iron pipes against a road divider, so they could all fit in this old propane grill. They took snips and wrecked the venturi tubes to let more propane in, and grilled the iron at a million degrees in a big steel pan. They put some olive oil and lemon on the molten iron, with a lot of black pepper, and poured it into a mold diyed from a log.

They all sat drinking gatorades while it cooled. Getting up every couple minutes to squeeze out piss on the red iron. Then somebody said hold on. Sure this is hardcore, but big industry ripped this metal out of the ground and they left a poison crater. We can mine our own ore. Diy hardcore carbon steel.

That night they looked in the front of the phone book for hematite deposits, and called some friends with couches on the way. They scabbarded shovels on bike carts and put trailmix in jars. They hitched up to Redding, where the river's stained pink with tailings, even today. It was three days to hitch to Redding, back when the roads were as flat as your hand. They cut the fences round the bandoned mine and climbed scaffolding down to the pit, and filled two duffel bags with the reddest rocks they saw. Rolled them back onto the #5 in a wheelbarrow from an old equipment shed. Then an unemployed horse truck took them home.

They were priming the barbecue smelter when somebody else started talking. We think we're hardcore for this? Ripping off sloppy seconds from the shittiest iron mine in Kaliforonia, that's scavenging, that's not the way of diying.

Somebody said we can't diy this any further than ore. Some nother punk said steel's just iron and carbon molecules. Real diy's building your own steel out of molecules. Somebody else said no, fuck molecules. Fuck molecules. Atoms are the hardcore of hardcore. We gotta take it to the atom smasher at UCLA.

So everyone put on the patchiest shit they had, sept for one tricker in a lawyer suit with a badge from the sal-mart. They partied at the atom smasher door with plywood grievance signs, yelling science would blow up the world. Then the tricker held up his badge and threatened the crew with a table leg. He said you're detained. You're detained on my authority and I'm taking you to detention.

The laws at the door figured it must be official. Everybody got through after that. They punched noses all around to get blood going, so it looked like the anarchy was under control, and when guys with nicer suits came through they ducked behind some shelves. In the control room they punched up some carbon for starters, cause it came first in the periodic table poster. Sirens went off, and there were some explosions from atom smashing, but they couldn't find how to turn off the carbon. So they took a piece of diy carbon from a burning wall and hotfooted it through a fire exit.

After that, they were planning their iron run back at the house. You know it. Punker stood up. Either way, we'll be using lectrons and shit from the McReagan ministration, and probly they were part of nazis before that. If we just diy a nother universe straight outa sweet fuckall we won't have to piss around with the laws of physics. Fuck laws and fuck the laws of physics. With an anarchy of physics we can diy every time we pull air and always be new.

Some punk said what are we talking bout? We already got three prybars.

Now we do. You're fucking welcome.

∧∧∧

They say to diy like you're taking a shit.

So through an alley overtooken with phonepole bamboo, the knuckled reeds thick as econosize cans and sandcolored as the dropping sunset redshifts through the red rain, the legend passes at a run. There's his sootblack docs, padding soundless in the mud and laced with yuppie hair, there's the bluetipped nylon streamer tied at his wrist like something torn from a kite, and he's running. He's pushing the bamboos with his hands. Just pushing them and never breaking stride, and the trunks snap from their bases if that's what you see, or slide backward from his path, or burst unraveling into colorless splinters and shreds, and the way you'd take a shit's the way he passes at a run.

And you're not even there. You're a ghost, you're a poser, you're one more flickerating astral tourist, waking bodiless into the fucked city like somebody's overshot rain carnation. Gaping at the cracked ceiling over the jungle where the plumcolored sunset crams in. Seriously, it's a ceiling, not a canopy. Rebar shows in the cracks like a bird's ribs. Watch the old punker with his nylon katanablade, running from nothing. Don't ever trust a punk who lived.

His face is hardly lined but seems eager for tension, ready to take tension inside it, and cracked with a compassing grin. His skin's translucent, his loosecropped hair shot ashgray. So check out his jacket. It's done up like chainlink, safetypins matrixed in the ageless black leather, pins packed round the patches worn black by millennious rain. Pinmail's sposed to be biteproof, but if you could be the old guy, you'd have nothing riding your back, nothing riding into you through the messy gash in your left shoulderblade. The chunk missing from him is shaped like some asshole's teeth, and his jacket waist's belted with flax rope, and over the hip there's a pocket of blood forming. And you're not there, not down in the meat of his nerves. You can't flash back to the first show you ever played, the fistfuls of warm peanutbutter down your shirt, with the memory grinning you harder as you run.

Now he's stopped. The eyebrow twitches over the legend's missing eye, where the socket's rimmed with a blue plastic hoop, and his face tilts like a snake's face tasting the air.

Shit.

Hold still, tourist.

∧∧∧

Okay. Now he's running again. You just shouldn't of tried to get close to his mind. With some punks, you can try and feel what they're going through.

Not the legend, not ever. Never try and stand inside him like that. If he sees you're there, he'll blow you out.

Sorry.

Anyway.

The rustblack hulk of a long sedan blocks the alley's throat. It's hanging snagged on a million bamboo fingers, this barricade hardly admitting light. He used to be in fucking Germs. He spits at the wall, he steps through.

Or at least you believe him already.

Trailing behind, the long bluetipped streamer slurps unrealistically through a page-thin gap in the bamboo like the tail off a deflated nylon magic fox.

You might as well go somewhere else.

∧∧∧

Blood knocks and knocks at their balcony doorglass, handfuls of prayerbeads from a lacerated sky. It runs capillaries in the tiny cracks, slicks on the ducktape stopjobs gone puffy and corroded. It's been raining blood since the Antidisestablishmentarianism, by now it holds our minds in. It's raining through the sky's tattered roof where no one ever walked, raining hot and dark like crude oil through the patchwork ceilings of core. It's raining from the scoured cokehole beneath Lord Buddha's eyes. It's raining terracotta caplets of robitussin syrup. Stop staring. It's raining ten trillion snowflakes of transparent jewelsteel from that time Greg Ginn shattered the katana Sst against the gates of Mcdonaldland. It's raining zebra rags of air down through the fundamental red. Stop staring. You're staring like a tourist. Are you even into hardcore? It's raining mushy acid tabs. It's raining broken bottleglass from the rafters of hell. It's raining carpet tacks, garbage juice, fragments of groundup guitarstring. Cerebrospinal wine. There's no more seasons anymore, and every metaphor's a lie, the world's sick of metaphors, but this one's true instead. It's raining blood over Lost Angeles, and you're this, too. It's raining blood. It's raining blood. It's raining blood, amen.

∧∧∧

The patches are the stories. Hold on to that. And the muddy zigzag of ducktape against the cracked doorglass. There's four kids who sleep here, a nuff for the fingers on each otherses hands. There's room in each of them for one important thing. They're a band. It's not they're in a band. They're a band. Four spikes of ducktape, up and down, like mountain peaks or a sawblade. Every band's got a sign, something to sew on your jacket, gouge in the wall at a show. Four spikes up and down say MEATHEADS, and you found a fucked window to knock at, tourist. They're the best band in the world.

You can slide through the doorglass, into their partment. No, they won't see you, you're a disembodied consciousness. Just sit on that tarp in the far corner, where they've got sheaves of flax underneath. You won't squish it, you don't have mass or volume. Right now there's a yuppie nailed to their coffeetable. Bellydown with its head twisted facing the ceiling. No, stop thinking and watch. There's an armslong of white plastic pipe stuffed in the yuppie's ass, and bigheaded roofing spikes through the knees and the elbows and between its shoulderblades. It's hauling against the nails, trying to arch its back and snapping teeth at the beefcakey kid who's wiggling the plastic pipe deeper.

Hold on. So you member how you were easing down on those crunchy tarps, and the yuppie's head turned toward you. That's cause it smelled you thinking bout yourself. Cause that's ego. Stop worrying bout it and just meditate. Seriously, go with the moment right now.

Raffia sits up on the sectional couch in her groaty leather armor. "Dude, you're gonna puke." A dirty russet topknot bobs above her circle face like the spike leaves on a pineapple. Raff plays hammers and drums.

"I won't gonna puke. Like, it works by filtration." Big blocky guy with an orange bandanna, musculature like ovenbaked playdoh. Mikey plays guitar, voice, meteorhammer and Hero Quest. He peers into the yuppie's ass pipe, screws it a nother half turn. The yuppie's mildewy eyes don't move a jot. It just keeps on wiggling its back, biting the air. "You got the weed, Donn?"

Donn's standing there buffing his big cracked glasses on his painted Bad Brains rice sack. Yeah, he's wearing a yellow nylon sack with three holes cut in it. Then he's buffing them on the starchy jogging headband over his eyes. They're still dirty. He rests them on his forehead. One glasses arm involves an exchangeabit screwdriver, one's a toothbrush. Donn plays stairwell bass, lectro bass, bass fishing bass, hockeystick, joystick, keyboard and mouse.

Donn goes, "What?"

"Fill the bowl, nerd!" Mikey pooches out his lip like a sad puppy.

Donn's slipping on protective oven mitts and a second pair of glasses, wrinkled white cardboard with red and blue cellophane lenses. "I'd of cracked the teeth out," he says to himself. "For safety. Still should be fine." He presses down squarely on the yuppie's forehead, pinning it, and unties a spatula from his long dreads. Starts to tamp handfuls of weed into its mouth.

Raffia's fists knotted under her chin, she's shaking her head. "Think Arco's gonna clean up when you puke?"

The yuppie's mouth jerks toward her slightly, too packed with weed to close. Whole thing looks dingy. Like it's been out in the rain for generations. A woody fungus growing on its cheekbone like a misplaced lip.

"You're just mad cause you dentify with these fuckers, Raff. Don't you got like a stock portfolio to update?" Mikey's running two fingers along the inside of his bihawk. Hair spiking in two turtlegreen crests like trestles of a maginary bridge. Between them, his brain's exposed by this long bonesawed skylight, red and puffy all down its edges. Promotes consciousness. His thinkmeat's lidded with the spare piece of cranium, lashed into the hawks at four points, painted like scalp stubble so his mom doesn't notice.

"We got rope to make." Raffia points at the musty sheaves of flax in your corner, under the tarp. "And we're in the chickenfight semis tonight."

"Few bong tokes first." Donn snaps his purple jogging headband. "Gonna be fine."

"That the weed you mixed in blowfish venom?" says Raffia.

Donn pauses a beat. "It's for Mikey." And gets a greasy shard of coal from a metal can under the coffeetable. Gets it burning in the lamp on the wall, and drops it into the yuppie's greenpacked mouth.

Mikey plants his lips on the yuppie's asspipe as Donn starts blowing on the sulky coal. Weedsmoke curls sweetly round the glowing orange edges.

"There's a carb," says Donn. Mikey's like, "Oh yeah."

He sticks his thumb in the borehole in the yuppie's lower back and steadies the pipe with his free hand. Toking fiercely with his whole body rising into it, same way you throw a punch. Something sucks and bubbles inside the yuppie's guts.

Raffia's face twists. "And don't puke shit on Arco. She's got the straight edge."

Mikey's cheeks are puffed and he's pinching his nose. Punker staggers a couple steps and then a jet of brown toxic waste spurts thickly from his mouth to crash against the far wall. It traces a circle, graceful and chunky. Symbol of the hungerless and alldevouring emptiness, like, against which all mutationeerings of the phenomenal universe are founded and must return.

Donn snaps his fingers. "We should of gaven it an enema first."

∧∧∧

The yuppie's straining against the nails like nothing's new, with weedsmoke drifting syrupy from the carb in its back. Mikey's crawled cross the room by now, and Donn's gingerly moving his mouth nearer to the carb, and Mikey's facedown in the corner, groaning and chewing the ushaped pink bathmat at the base of their potted palm.

Some punk's walking in the hall. Through the cracked door you can just see some leathercolored shadows riffling around, and Donn spins his head. "Darby! Hey."

The riffles nod three times. "Arco. Mikey. Raff." Laughs. "Gimme a toke." Donn half rises and punker goes, "Not for serious. It's okay if I take your dennal floss, right?"

Donn nods to the hallway. "From behind the toilet? I'll get it."

"I've gotten it." There's a couple people giggling in the hall. "I'll love your guyses set tonight."

"We're not playing tonight," says Raffia. Hallway dude's already gone and she snorts. Her bare foot noses Mikey's jacket to one side, and then her toenail jabs him over the heart. He twitches hard, he bangs his mouth on the plant pot. Look, Mikey's important, no matter how it seems. Punker'd fall apart if they treated him any other way. It's what he carries.

No, not like in a deep way. It's on his back, right there. His leather's doublewalled peccary hide, stained orange with a poison frog. The spikes on the shoulders and all down the arms are shards from the peccary's buttbone. The pockets are full of toy cars and everywhere's all sewn with patches. A few jagged handpickings of stitchwork, a few recycled tattoos. The most are vintage silkscreens. Canvas squares or cuttings from shirts, artifacts and relics rainproofed with beewax and heiroglyphed with bright layers of pigment. Nobody knows how to silkscreen anymore, and these patches don't illustrate old times or prophesies or jokes. If you sew silkscreens to your jacket, illustration's your job. The patches are the stories.

∧∧∧

There's no patches of Black Flag left, but here's a story anyway. Greg Ginn invented silkscreen emulsion after he saw the future on a vision quest for SST Records. You weren't there. He saw how photocopy toner ran out in the future, and all the zines got mushy with humidity, and there was something fucked bout the rain. Ginn of Flag waking up in the dumpster behind the church, where his science lab was. He woke up knowing punks were too busy drinking to keep history straight without photocopy toner, so he invented silkscreen emulsion outa lysergic acid diethylamide and unpasteurized liquid time and cum from gay tigers. That's why nobody knows how to silkscreen anymore. After Flag went on tour from Lost Angeles, tigers stopped thinking we were hot.

⋀⋀⋀

She named herself from a picture in an old zine. Held it out to her mom.

—*Oh. That says ar . . . co . . . Arcosanti, baby. It's kind of a building they were raising all lone in the desert.*

She was three. Not punk to count the years. Here's the first thing she ever said. —*I'm that, too.*

—*Hold my joint? Yeah, like, that was before the conomy went bad, right. Yuppies didn't used to eat punks, they just made money and had babies. They had babies and babies, and they had babies . . . Lost Angeles was all money and stupid babies and yuppies moshed up with nothing to eat them. Cause before the yuppies were eating us, we weren't eating them back, so every yuppie ever born in Lost Angeles was still alive. But I guess some yuppies wanted space or some shit. Build a big house where every hand puts in.*

—*Like here.*

—*No, it's for yuppies. Fuck, you said something! Where's your mom? No, like, your other mom.*

—*I'm an arco.*

⋀⋀⋀

Punks have hardcore, and they won't say what that means. But she never changed her name since. They say you can't talk bout your hardcore, and it's not yours. The rings in Arco's eyes hang like her studless jean vest, blue so pale they'd blow away and leave a cloudless sky. Arco's got the straight edge, and streaks of charcoal under her eyes. Arco handcuts her tattoos with ashes and a paringknife. Arco shaves her head with a sword.

Well, her tanto. It's a shortsword, but still. Same one she uses making rope. Meatheads are sposed to take a turn as ropemaking crew, and somebody's gotta do it. Her back's to the doorglass and her work platform's a bustedoff countertop over her lap. While she stipples her tanto cross the bundles of flax, not stopping, Arco's going, "You alright?"

Swords, voice, and guitar.

"Soon." Mikey's wiping his tongue on the pink bathmat. "Now. Yeah." He crawls back over, pulls himself up by the yuppie's ass tokepipe. Stands there staring into its contaminated bore. "Did Darby just talk to us?"

"Gonna clean up or what?" says Raffia.

Mikey goes, "Fuck, Raff, have some compassion."

Raffia's eyes move closer together and her lip pulls back. Her top teeth are the color of rust, filed to four spikes.

"Oh," says Donn. "That's when you want all beings to be free of suffering."

"What?" says Raffia. "No you don't."

Mikey stands on a milk crate and starts gouging out the wallpaper round his puke smear with a housekey. After a bit, Raffia leans over and punches down the yuppie's forehead. It stops moving.

They're the best band in the world.

"Hey, watch that much more vintage brown spot, hey." Donn points. "That's heritage. When Fear lived here? Lee Ving spat there."

"What are you, the landlord?" Mikey zigzags round the spot. The wallpaper's half cut through and now the top part slips and falls draped over the bottom. Then he just stops and turns round and uses his housekey to gouge a draw in the blownout yuppie's windpipe. He plugs up the carb and the bunghole, brings his head down to toke from the new draw. It looks like he's giving it a hickey. The wide ember wakens red between its mossy teeth and its cheeks temporarily suck in, and now Mikey's sideways on the floor again. "Whoa? Aren't we? Babysitting?"

"We locked him out." Behind Arco, this baby's rolling round on the stormtossed seventh story deck, soaked in blood like a painted imp. His name's Taco Eater. You can dimly hear him singing something bout rock n' roll mcdonalds and slamming his carhide sandals on the lino, jamming against the thunder's beat.

Mikey crawls over, pressing his lips to the sliding door. Whispering. "Hey meat can. You think you're hardcore?" Yellow weedsmoke croaks out his mouth like an endless tentacle.

Arco's already got the tanto sheathed in her backpack and she's sparring her tattooed fingers against the bloody doorglass. The baby's rolled upright too. His head to the glass, hand cupped there like he's ready to pick up all frequencies.

Arco snaps the lock open. Slides the door fingerwide. "You want a nother sike lesson, Taco?"

Taco Eater nods and nods, his eyes like darkedout ballbearings. His head's round and dumpy, nearly hairless, couple fine curls pasted down in brown blood. There's some thumbtacks sticking out of it.

Mikey's bald steeltoe noses the door open and he crabwalks onto the slanty balcony. Takes the baby by his spenders and dangles him way over the edge. Spenders here are built modular, they're straps of warthog skin backed with straps of carhide, they look kinda like bikechains. It's a sevenstorey drop or something and the kid just giggles and jounces in the air, whooshing his arms around.

Check Taco's eyes, tourist. Magine the reflections show you where he's looking. Something to practice if you're gonna get around here. The sketchy rope bridges and slideways, sagging between the smashedout tower windows, cobwebbing the long purple sunset. Mosquitohawks dipping on blackly iridescent wings that hum like bugzapper coils. From cross the street, all punks are nameless. You can see shady figures of kids standing on makeshift docks that jut like treefort platforms from distant smashed officewindows. Swigging from clay jugs, blowing beer at each other. The ends of their smokes tracing firefly glyphs in the mist.

Taco's gaze drops, and down there the boulevards are quiet. You don't walk down there less you're brave. There's a couple yuppies right down beneath him, humping and bumping round the marshy drinking lot. Just lurching. Stepping on feral tomatovines, kicking the tires of bandoned car skeletons. The yuppies look kinda like the punks up topward. They got arms, legs and bodies to go with their heads, mostly. Mostly naked, caked with dreck. Yuppies aren't technically allowed into core, but the fence doesn't work great, and it beats going outside to hunt them.

They turn as he holds out Taco. Mikey bounces the kid by his spenders. "Kay, exist really hard."

Look at the yuppies. They step forward a bit and placidly hold out their arms.

Mikey's like, "You're just looking at them, Taco, you tourist. Go harder. Really focus your ego. Like, make it pulsate in your butt or whatever."

The yuppies just stand in the middle of the drinkinglot, flapping their arms aquatically. Missing things like cheeks and shinbones. Shreds of clothes drooping from them like the rotted membranes of wings, and Mikey's talking low and soft with his eyes rolled up. "We're chilled out. Me and Arco are like meditating. It's only your consciousness could alert these corporate fashopaths. But they hardly know you're there. They're just thinking bout stocks and bonds, and like how to get ahead."

Taco flails and shrieks. Down in the slushy drinkinglot, the yuppies don't do much. "You suck," says Mikey. "You're not eater, just taco."

Taco goes, "Teach me how to sike, fuckface!"

Mikey's fingers release the bunched suspenders, and the baby's voice shrinks into a little squeak. When his other hand snatches Taco, draws him up a little, the smell of piss wafts up alongside. Down there, the yuppies scrabble at the eroded brick condoface, waving their hands straight ceilingward like frantic volunteers.

"You can't sike til you can turn your self up and down, fuckface," says Mikey in the same patchoulli voice. "Like you did just there."

"Member there's no self or up and down," says Arco. "Or turning." She sounds the same as always. She sounds like your ears are stepping in a cold river. Mikey looks at her and she's like, "What?"

The baby snakes out and bites his own bicep, right in the blue sleeve of his *CHARLIE THE TUNA* tee. He holds on, gnaws at his arm meat, wailing ferally as the yuppies start to freak out and leap.

"Is he cheating?" says Mikey. Arco's like, "Maybe, I guess so."

᭼᭼᭼

*N*ow magine a side street out in the burbs. Steep officetowers nearly windowless, manifesting as sheer planes of wrinkled gray rubber. The rain whips and blows in the air. The street jags up and down like a tube in a hamster palace, and there's some bamboo slanting up through the crumpled lino sidewalk. You know, lino. Linoleum. Maybe just pay tension.

Don't worry, the legend's not coming through. This place's behind him or whatever, and you already know how to sike. You're doing it right now, floating round in the rain. Siking's kind of bout pretending, the way you think you're real.

You're an act of magination. That's how you're already siking. What are you made of, tourist, what are your parts? Whatever's coming through your mind. Colors and shapes, noises, balance, hot and cold, whatever. Memory, thoughts, cause mind comes through mind too. All these forms of consciousness, and what unites them? Not born an hour and already you think you're whole. Ego. But that's the way we all got into hardcore.

Like there's this place called self. Like the central point where your thoughts happen. Playing behind your eyes, or maybe seated in your heart. And what happens to you happens in that place, and that makes your consciousness yours. Kids these days are gonna tell you self's just a nother feeling, no different than rain. You're not actually there. Like you're never anywhere, but you'll say you saw it.

Your self's a story in a circle, telling itself around. Only the universe to listen and it can't hear fuckall. Siking's when that story tells itself somewhere else. It's the same thing to feel self behind someone's eyes or in the bones in someone's fingers, or in a ripped chunk of canvas hung on a car antenna cross the way. After you've lived here awhile, ego's not harder to move than a traffic cone. You're not there anyway, and they say nothing you can't practice is real. So magine you're the legend, here and bloody, sprinting home.

From the top down, here's what he'd be missing. His left eyeball. The top of one ear. A chunk from the head of the diaperpin in the other earlobe. A lot of teeth, and a chip from the front of his grin. A couple and a half fingers. That fresh rag of meat off his bloody shoulderblade, way too far in to cut. The nipple on that side. A chunk from his rightside hip, with a bit of chiseledout bone. His thesaurus. His pendix. His laundryroom key. The front half of his right foot. Most of a sweet scar on that foot, where he stepped on a bottle at the Whiskey.

There's an old joke, stay ready to amputate your back. You can't chill out bout a yuppie bite. It's not like getting nipped by your buddy, no matter how same the teeth look. They say it's a contagious collective unconscious or an attitudinal fallacy or something. They say you've gotta hold your breath and cut off the wound, or even the littlest bite'll climb your nerves all the way to your spine, and you'll never diy again. And this old guy with his nipped shoulderblade, too far in to cut. That why he's going fast, tourist?

Try and magine his feeling as the lino road bobs like a waterbed. Meeting his bootsteps like an assgroove worn in a couch. How just past armslength in the rusty mist, you'd see the plastic trashlid spinning on its axle. Nailed to the bent lightpost, carved stepwise along the lip so the rain can kick it like a paddlewheel, hung with scalps in an eightpointed star.

Magine you're floating over his farewell show. And the circle howls, they slash their cheeks with bottleglass, hand out charred strips of his steak. They're dismantling patches from his rainworn leather, unweaving safetypins and slitting jacket seams. Unmaking his ego, the lie binding stories to meat.

Holding his skinny relics like they survived the ice age and the neutron bomb. Shit that fell from the cut edge of time. The firelight shows through his threadbare patches and as the punkers eat they're talking the ghost off his bones, talking him into the hardcore of hardcore, the universe.

—*He invented consciousness. He said let no two things ever be the same.*

You do. You believe him already.

—*They used to hatch the minimalls of Lost Angeles from plastic eggs. Each one precomp on every precomp block, and a million yuppies looking up all day to read the same sign. This was a desert before we learned to diy. He taught us to make landmarks. Send them out for the ivy to break.*

And the legend cuts left under the tired, streaming paddlewheel. One hand knocks it down as he goes. Just fucking with you, tourist. It's all real. Cool the fillosophizing. If he sees you, he'll blow you out.

Good thing you're not there.

/\/\/\

—*He'd knock down street signs. He was the first. Before we hardly knew to aim at the brain. Teeth shining in every manhole, the face of Ronald McReagan rising in the smoke from parked cars. Yuppies in the streets packed so tight it's like they came to see Germs from the start. And he ran down the fire scape and jumped on the first pole with his ballbat, knocked the little sign of words into the road. He was like, tomorrow you won't need reading. You need a sign for your way, you can't help anyhow.*

/\/\/\

And the legend cuts left under the tired, streaming paddlewheel. One hand knocks it down as he goes. The pavement's been turned over and overturned by a circulation of vines. A boulevard of black loam struck through with concrete shards, plant sinew, fluff from weird birds. The ivied carapaces of honda civics slouching up like dead oysters overgrown with wrack, and half the road's slipped into bottomless sinkholes round the cars. He's running and he stops.

Down the way there's a throng of yuppies standing at the sunken bus shelter for Hermosa Beach. Just as they point their heads the legend freezes. There's a tiny backhand jerk to his wrist, like he threw a ghost at them, and you go frizbeeing cross the boulevard, tourist, from his hand and his mind into the evening sky.

That's siking. If you don't get it, don't worry bout it, but you're what he threw. You're that same projection of ego floating round like a tourist in the rain. You're that, too. Maybe just think bout it. But anyway, hung up like a dot against the sky, you're too distant for the yuppies to notice right now.

Anyway. They get back to business. Their clothes bliterated by mildew, skin painted in the clotting rain. They're milling round disconsolately, holding rusted timexes to their throats, biting cokebottles. Flies hit their eyes but not to feed. Their lungs don't move, and if you could see the pulse run under punkers' skin, you wouldn't see that here. Used to be six hundred sixty-six trillion six hundred sixty-six billion six hundred sixty-six million six hundred sixty-six thousand six hundred and sixty-six fucks in this greater metropolitan area alone. You gotta preciate, it takes some time to recycle them all.

∧∧∧

Over the House of Meatheads, the sunset's going deep. Taco's kneeling on the balcony with his head and one crook arm through the rusty balcony rails. Staring down at the yuppies, still chewing himself. Now there's more shapes gathered in the drinkinglot below. Gummylooking silhouettes swarming in the red mist.

Mikey runs two fingers down the inside of his bihawk. The lid's half untied over his skylight and he grins lopsided, reaches through to press on his brain. Dude starts to twitch and snicker, and Taco goes, "What was that one?"

"It was this memory of blueberry jerky. But it gave me a boner." Mikey blinks. "But the boner was, like, in my arm."

"I wish I had a skylight," says Taco Eater. Arco's leaning against the door, arms folded. "No you don't."

Relacing the lid, Mikey looks down, bending way over the rail, and he spits carefully into the yuppies. Then unhooks the spenders from his belt and stretches them in his hands. You can tell this part's a ritual. He bends and starts knotting the gnarly spenders round one of his ankles. "You feel strong, Arco?"

She bows from the hip, and Mikey's chest kicks with laughter. He taps the skylight lid, his tongue's making noises like a hollow coconut. "Think I can float myself down?"

Already Arco's coming back through the doorway. Somehow she's holding the entire massive spool of rope. It's the finished model, diamondbraided flax, bridgegrade, not really disposable. See how she's not big or tall. Up her arms, shoulders, up the sides of her thin corded neck, the ink throbs in its washedout geometries. The four jagged black stripes, repeating, repeating. This bandsign from the cosmo times. Not holy. Bars of the Flag.

So see how her back's straight, ergonomic. All her muscles, shoulder to knuckle, standing out like bundled guitarstrings. Mikey shudders a bit, shakes his head. But that part's a ritual too. Arco threads the rope through Mikey's ankle spenders as he slips his other leg over the railing's edge. Arco hangs her missing middle finger out on the black wind. So does he. Not aiming down, not up. Sweet fuckall either way.

Then Raffia kicks him in the back.

∧∧∧

Anyway. A kid's laugh falls from the legend, and he shoves a fist into his grin, and the yuppies don't come.

"Sorry, force of habit! I'm right here!" His hands on his ribs. Hips tipped forward like a fucking rockstar and he sounds like something's gathering in his tonsils, his deep lispy throat. The hardcore of the universe aligning itself. "Here's my mind, fuckers! I'm the one, I made it all this way!"

When they turn they're facing him with their teeth, not their eyes. He just keeps laughing. It's been so long. Blood's dripping through his jacket, down his tailbone. He touches his wounded shoulderblade and tourist, tourist, that narcoleptic grin. Like his mouth's a lobotomy scar. Like he doesn't even care. You have no idea how long it's been.

He's in the perfect chokezone, a penninsula between wide sinkholes. Everybody would say don't do this, but here's a secret. When they say everybody, they mean this guy mostly. So he jogs forward a ways, where they might surround him, and he holds his ribbon sword in the stance called Fuck-Kicking String of Death. He pulls off his boots. The sunset's a grim crimson toenail paring. The rain throbs down his forehead, orbits the empty socket. His wideset hairy toes slide on a squashed orchid, a broken needle. It's a great day. It's a great day.

The yuppies all lope at once with the moron grace of rolling cheerios as your consciousness slides into the ribbon. It's long and nightcolored with the very tip tainted blue, and you're that tip, snapping and coasting in the sudden breeze. Two yuppies dive for you and you drop as the legend flicks his wrist and their skulls bank together with a moist crunching noise. They drop and he yanks you back a handwidth, streamer wrapping once round his wrist. Nother one lunges and overbalances, tipping soundlessly into a vinecovered pit.

His face up in the rain like a nanointing. He's twisting the ribbon sideways, his elbow fends a shadow. Teeth catch in his old coat but it's biteproof, member, and he dodges three directions, jerks in a tiny motion like a shouldercheck and you fly from the ribbon so that a yuppie's forehead cracks a nother one's temple. It goes down sideways with a little black splooge jumping from its ear.

There's a gap up in front. He jumps there, then up into a wrecked truck's bed. It holds him. The little rectangle window into the cab's blocked completely by something like a furryass mold party clinging in a stripey pattern to the glass.

Now they're climbing up and he holds out his cupped hand like a petitioner. His wrist rotating imperceptibly as the bluetipped nylon streamer streams out a blue circle on a black field. One glyph immutable like a figure on no flag, the tub ring round a black hole. Every band's got a sign. You're staring round and round, you're nearly there, and now your consciousness spins completely with the blue streamer and they have no senses, how could they have senses, it's mind that yuppies smell.

Then you're tripping through your own circle. For a maginary heartbeat it's dark and you smell bonfire. You partied too hard too early or something or whatever.

⋀⋀⋀

*B*reathe.

Breathe. The night stopped being dark. The air's all different, dry and hazy like chalkdust, and there's no ferns pushing up through the smooth drinkinglot asphalt. There's no roof on the sky. The streetpoles aren't scaly and hairy, they're not even raffia palms, and cross the road there's harsh lights over all the shopfronts like acrid bastard suns.

There's a kid pushing a shoppingcart full of green canvas, and a kid with no pants, riding. They come cross the flat drinkinglot, between rows of honda civics. Nobody's skinned the tires off and the bodies aren't rusted. You can actually see the carpaint, the colors like bad lipsticks and tumbled stones. One shoppingcart wheel whipping round the wrong axis, screaking. There's two more kids by the concrete lot divider. A skinny girl with fat cheeks, smoke pinched in her thumb and forefinger. Little rubber skirt and she's wearing a blue circle on a black leather armband. You know it, right.

Beside her on the ground some punk's covered with folded jackets, jacket blankets all the way up to his shut eyes. He stinks like grapefruit and vodka. Looks kinda familiar, but you can't see his face. The girl's constantly rubbing his shoulder. His forehead's slashed up and puffy and his ear's full of safetypins and there's like ten packets of hot dogs stacked under his head for a pillow.

Blowing all over the hot pavement there's photocopied showposters. *G.I.* and *DILS* in shaky handdrawn letters, and an empty suit with a shroomcloud for a head. The shoppingcart wheels grind over the dirty posters, and punker goes, "What's up, Michelle?"

She's like, "Jesus, don't call me that."

"Sorry. Gerber." The kid with no pants tugs at the heap of green canvas in the shoppingcart. "We got it, though."

"Yeah," says the smoking girl. "Got what?"

The first kid's kneeling with a lighter, setting the canvas load on fire from beneath. "They're canopies from those stablishments," he says, pointing. "Darby said get a fire going, who cares if Oki Dog's closed for window reparations, we've got our own hot dogs."

"I thought they were european wieners," says the girl.

These kids look even fuckeder in the sudden firelight whoosh. They could be from the tribe you saw before, same swoopy hair and piercings and chains, sept it's like somebody's been taking care of them. They're not all dandruffed with flaky leftover bloodstains. Their clothes look newborn, nowhere mended and hardly even ripped, and their skins all soft and glossy like they got spitshined for the fair.

"Well, he's asleep," she says. "I'm not moving his pillows."

"Do you got a smoke?" says no pants. He's looking at the passedout drunk dude, and the girl's like, "Yeah." She doesn't move. She smokes. Then she goes, "What, like you actually decided bout the Germs burn?"

The first guy's pushed his shoppingcart bonfire a ways off and he's holding out his hands like a cold night, staring over at punker's wiener packets. The fire's jumping tall and pale under the humming fluorescent streetlights. Giant flakes of ash flit around.

The no pants kid goes, "Can I?" and the girl shrugs and passes her smoke. He pinches it awkwardly near the burning cherry and he sits, chewing on his lip. Both his arms shake lectrically as he starts pushing the cherry into his skin.

"What are you doing?" says the girl with the armband, finally standing. Her lips are pulled back, her brow's wrinkled, there's eyeliner on her teeth. Punker doesn't say anything, just holds the smoke trembling near his raw blackish burn. Blood wells down his hand and the girl's going, "You got to get a Germs burn from somebody who's already got one, you fucking idiot."

No pants goes, "Fuck!" and throws the smoke. It stubs and rolls a bit and the girl picks it up, shaking her head. "You didn't even do it right. You have to do it right on the bone. So it scars like a hollow circle."

The whole flaming shoppingcart's already died down. Flaky canvas ash sags through the bottom as the first punker turns round, grinning. "Man, you just burned yourself with a cigarette!"

"So can one of you guys like do me?" says no pants, peering at the ground where he threw the smoke. The girl's smacking her lips. Gerber. "It all has to do with circles," she says, breathing out. "Like karma and shit. Like what goes around comes around. I'm not gonna give you one."

"Can Darby really see out through the burns?" says no pants.

His buddy's like, "Yeah, I don't think so. He's probly too drunk."

∧∧∧

"**W**e need you for making rope," says Raffia. Mikey's rubbing out the dent in his jacket. He's like, "So?"

She's like, "So I'll help Arco lower you down. I kicked you low, so you wouldn't fall."

"Whole railing's gonna fall," says Mikey.

Donn's voice cuts in from the jamroom. "I keep saying it's fine."

"You'd totally break your skull falling," says Raffia. "And I don't give a fuck sept we said we'd make rope. And we don't sound good with one guitar."

Raffia'd go naked sept for the couple bites that wouldn't bounce off. Instead she's got plastic shower rings for piercings pretty much wherever you could pinch an inch, and layers of red hide lashed to the rings like a bunch of tarps over a traincar. Her leather warped with nipples and taints, noses and scroats, the scraps the armorers reject. She's the short one, but for boosts and cavvrey charges, it's her collarbone hollows you stand in. Cross her chest there's two rawhide bandoliers stuffed with her hammer collection, and in between the hammers nails. Crooked where they struck bone. They say the sound of one hand clapping, no, we can get to that later.

"You're done heckling already?" says Mikey, and Donn's standing in the doorway. His dreads shake like dry leaves when he laughs.

Raffia crosses arms over her chestbelts. The veins in her eyes are standing on end like her poppyred forearm fuzz. Arco loops rope through the spenders knotted at Mikey's ankle, pulls it tight, pulls it again. She lifts her chin at him.

"Oh. Like heckling like using a heckling comb for the preppage of flax to make rope, but also like heckling like fucking with us. You're ready?" Mikey slips his other leg over the edge. "Hey, Raff, catch me."

She growls. Mikey claps his hands and snowangels himself off the railing. Then he's dropping halfspeed, Arco's playing the line out, and Raffia grabs it behind her. Try to magine the iron rain taste running down his nose as they lower him headfirst at the yuppies. Like how there's even rhythm in the void.

∧∧∧

You're falling round the circle on the girl's wristband. The night's a jungle night again, all muggy and salty, and you're coming undone, or the circle patch is unwinding like blue fire on a spinning string. Hang together, poser. You're not the circle from the girl's armband in the drinkinglot. Or maybe you're the same circle, but it's weaving from the legend's ribbon sword, and now it's gone anyway.

Stop tripping out. Pay better tension. There's blownout yuppies fallen everywhere round the legend like a tumbled cord of firewood. He's yawning theatrically, spattered with brains like birdshit on a windshield, and they've got firepits for eyes. There's dark craters where their pinealglands lit up, triangulatory with the black burned eyesockets, and holes smoking with wispy blue fire at the crowns of their scalps. Holes down their spines at precise intervals, and if you look, blown through their wrists, right on the bone. Like some kind of dark matter kundalini existential combustion breach. Guess he can do shit like that.

—Right on the bone. So it scars in a hollow circle.

He's bobbing on the soles of his feet with his good arm tweaking chaotically. Punker lifts the hand attached to the bitten shoulder, the motion's robotic and the fingers do nothing. Bends his knuckles tentatively with the other hand and he looks over at sundown. "Fucking always late."

You don't know if he's talking bout him or the sun.

The bamboo thicket fence is right ahead, and overtop it, coreward, there's core. You can see the tikitorches in the windows, the slow broken bottleglass dandruffing from twisted condominimum faces. The pizza ovens at the Zero making one whole floor gleam like Fraz-Urb'luu's asshole and the halfbuilt shoppingcart rollercoaster jutting nowhere off the balcony of the shitter museum. So the legend vaults down from the truckbed, he's turning toward home, and the driver's side door skrawks open. Here's presenting one more nother bastard form of the universe. It's, like, some kind of headless behemoth caterpillar painted in dusk and tawn Halloween stripes, filling up the cab like solid tuna filling a chili can.

His ribbon's wound at his wrist, his grin's up two notches.

The stripey caterpillar pours from its den, uncoiling on the boulevard, all lithe and fuzzy like a tiger walking backward, cause that's who she is. Tigers grow pretty big in Lost Angeles, and they live pretty much forever. Turns out drinking blood is really good for tigers.

He gives her a little wave. "How you doing, Raspberries? Hey, you got a smoke?"

∿∿

—*Couple days and we got up a zoo liberation crew. Back when core was just five million punkers holed up in the spam works, eating flats of cheezwhiz, hanging ass out the window to shit. You weren't there.*

Some kids climbed downstairs on a curtain rope ladder and took jaws a life from a crashed ambulance and sheared the sides off some dumpsters. Lee Ving was there, Lee of Fear. Exene of X and John Doe with her. Rollins of Flag was there, Dez and Robo and Kira and Ginn. Roche of TSOL was there. Gerber was there. Hellin Killer was there. Darby was there.

They diyed dumpsterskin platemail and shaved poolcues into lancepoints. They stole bikes. They slipped between the burning honda civics. They coasted down Ventura to Ventura Park.

In the zoo burbs they made a phalanx with handi fence from round a hot dog shack. They bikelocked their bikes to the sides and rolled it round the zoo. Every yuppie who leapt and clang on the cage took a poolcue eyesocket shot. It was the first of the handi phalanxes. And like they had monkey renches, they had try scaratops renches for water mains, gecko renches for details. They'd rench the jail doors and the inmates would bust free. All sept the tigers. This is how the zoo liberation crew learned the true meaning of stripecore. That's not how it ends.

—*They were gone!*
—*The tigers were already loose!*
—*Tigers are always fuckin free!*
—*That's not how it ends!*
—*That's not how it ends!*

ΛΛΛ

The legend gives a deep nod, then holds his head at that angle. He fidgets with his smoke. "Okay, but sister, I gotta go."

Raspberries just arches her little cup ears and woofs quietly through her nose.

He's like, "No, don't worry. I meant for this. It's the five year plan. I gotta go now."

When he makes to go past, she steps one step toward him. The old guy looks both ways down the destroyed road. Then turns round. Two fingers pressed to his lineless brow, shaking his head, he sits against the silver truck. "Look . . . I'm a douche, Raspberries. Okay? I killed myself, I'm just waiting for the bite to reach my spine. This is me killing myself like old school."

He shifts, shows her the ripped jacket. "What? You're smarter than that. You know they can't bite through pin. No more than your fur. I had to tear my leather open first. Got one to comfort, like, come for me." Drags again from the mallburrow slim, gestures with it. Like he's saluting a mirror. "I made it this way. It's the five year plan, I have to go at the end. This way I get to diy with everybody round me. And I get to do a farewell show."

Raspberries lifts her paw. You can almost see something hollow, a scar in the thatchy ankle fur. Who could give a tiger a Germs burn?

"You get bored of being oldest. You know? All I ever wanted was a fuckedup death." The legend shifts. "Like, I'm a douche though. End of my show, after I go out, everyone's gonna start fighting. I set it up to start a war, so they'll all get killed. Was that weird of me?"

The tiger arches her neck a little. The darks of her eyes are narrowing.

"No, it's their fault. It's that they can't handle a little theatricality. Youth of today, huh, Raspberries. Would that we were tigers."

He stands. Flips the smoke behind him. "You know what, I gotta go. Eat these dead bodies, don't eat me, okay? It's coming back to where it was before."

The tiger tilts her paw delicately, and laughs, and bounds into him. Their foreheads bang together. Say rock, say roll. They rattle round each other in the purple sunset like tenants of a stonetumbler, and then she's gone and he's going for the fence.

ᗰᗰ

So Arco holds the straight edge, right. That's not actually a sword most of the time. It just means when a punk decides not to do a bunch of stuff. What stuff depends on what punk, cause it comes from will. Some kids take an edge to keep their minds shiny clean, some hate hurting anyone, some hate hating, some kids like showing off.

But here's her whole edge. It's kind of boring, but it's important. No getting drunk, no drinking expired cough medicine. No doing coke, no doing blow. No weed, no hash, no sikadelics. No chewing pinealglands, not even if you spit them out. No keeping a secret. No itch scratching, no scab picking, no fucking. No looking at ads. No looking at mirrors. No looking at words. No using perma names or measurements of time or distance or numbers your fingers can't count to. No killing anybody. No telling anybody to do anything. No unshared property. No kitty petting. No turning down shows, not ever.

Anyway.

ᗰᗰ

"Mikey's brave," says Taco Eater. His head's still stuck in the balcony rails as they groan back and forth with the Mikey load.

"He likes heights," says Raffia.

Arco shrugs. "He's still brave, Raff. Thanks for helping hold the line."

Shoulders together, they're lowering Mikey. Four hands on the taut gray rope. Donn's still trying to clean his big cracked glasses on the rice sack. Hey, you should of priorly noticed all the hardware clamped and braided into Donn's dreads. Lightbulbs, soldering irons, wire strippers, geiger counters. Clinking shit. He grabs Taco's spenders. "Your head sposed to be through there?"

Taco's like, "Who are you, my dad?" All his limbs clamp the railing in a horseshoe crab move.

"I don't think so." Donn stops. You can see him thinking. "No, wait. You could hurt your skull doing that. Your cranial sutures aren't finished growing, you're a baby."

"I'm like five, tomorrow's my birthday," says Taco Eater, and Arco's like, "Counting years isn't hardcore, little punker."

"Chill, it's the kid's hardcore to say what's in his head." Donn sits a foot on the railing, tugs Taco loose as the metal bars go *REERK*. "Sides, no way he's five."

Fingers tensed round the rope, Raffia's eyeballing him like she'd count his veins with her teeth. "Go easy," says Donn, absently setting the kid down, pinching his squashy diaper. "It just needs like sinew ties here and here, and here, and some new bolts."

"There's no new bolts," says Raffia. Donn's like, "Make some. You work at the smelter."

Raffia's like, "You make some."

∧∧∧

No, but get back to Mikey. Dropping slowmo down the condo's side, upside down with his arms spread in the blaring rain. His meteorhammer cord's clenched in his teeth as he puts out his palms below him. Opens his jaw and the blunt instrument falls into his heartlines like a sheathing. The deep sienna leather's worn mellower than silkworm turds but he's tried a million times to snap it in his hands. Vintage cordage linking two featureless oblongs of steel. Kids' hearts, monkey's eggs.

He drops past the sixth storey balcony. Fifth. Course they say counting doesn't count. But see those little pigment nicks in his jacket armpit, Mikey marks every sundown, it's how he marks every year. He learned it from Wilson Rise before he went on tour, who learned it from the ghost of Regi Mentle in a bathroom mirror.

Punker hooks one leg round the tarred rope, kicks the pop from his knee. Third storey. Clustered beneath him, the yuppies flap their elbows and hiss out like rabid pigeons. He kicks out again, sets himself spinning, then he's dangling bout an armslong above them.

Then the line drops an armslong more.

His nose bangs some asshole's forehead as he spins. He's hanging right in the crowd. Black teeth snap at his eye as he twists his head away. He giggles. "Blow me, Raff."

Then you're shooting into the mucky drinkinglot ground, in with the vine tangles and stained filters. Just siking, tourist, get used to it. The yuppies drop on their knees, clawing at you, slamming their faces into sewagecolored leaf litter, and now you can go. Fuck It.

Fuck It. That's his meteorhammer's name.

He's holding your leather cord in both hands. Spinning your weights at each end like a double-ended yoyo. Whistle like a yoyo as you fly. Against the temple of the nearest skull you skip wonderfully sideways like a frog shattering an old pond. Before your backswing Mikey's elbow drops into the next closest head, leaving a serious dent, and the blownout yuppies fall tangled together.

A grayish hand scoops out at him. Little shrooms festooning the ragged polyester shoulder cuff at the end of the bare arm. High five. Mikey's free leg kicks again, the momentum spinning him on the rope, and his jacket sloughs the yuppie's teeth like one more hit of rain. His elbow's in the right place again, he shoots it sideways. See the little ink marks crossing his leather like antshit. Two hundred days in a year.

Pretend you feel the whisper of resistance and the tiny click running up your elbow as the nasal bone shears into the forebrain. The yuppie stops, it sways. Like he pounded an offswitch. That wavy reddish hair's been mossed down its face a million seasons for all you know.

Mikey makes a quick rotor move with one wrist. Your steel globes arc and swerve. The cord twines round his palm, shorting your reach. There's a bald, bloated gas jockey snapping its overbite at the air under Mikey's forehead. Its teflon golf shirt's pristine, ageless. Punker's already pulled himself sideways, sort of an upsidedown chinup. The yuppie's overbalanced, you loop down, *SMUCKK*, and its brainstem's two fingers closer to its nose.

Then he lets himself out of the chinup so he's vertical again, spinning like a trick pendulum, and he brakes with one hand on the line. The floor's all corpses. He works his knee free of the rope so that he dangles facedown from his suspenders, and for awhile he just hangs out. Watching the rain jitter the puddles, whistling and banging his head, airdrumming with no more rhythm than the rain. The dark rolls in a little more. The air drumsticks gradually build a riff til he's just echoing the PA tower. Yeah, the PA tower's going. You didn't notice either?

They say the best way to reach a punker's to beat it into them. If you want to reach them all, though, you gotta beat the air. Up in the tower, crosstown from everywhere, somebody's slamming a message on the millionskin drum. The rhythm that says FAREWELL SHOW. And Mikey freezes, sucks on a knuckle. A nother rhythm rolls in, spelling the headliner's name like morse code, and suddenly punker's going into spasm. He balls his fists and punches the air, and then he's like, "Okay. Okay. Okay." Teeth back on his knuckle. "Try and keep me off it now, Darby, you fucker."

So Mikey brings both his hands around, he unties the lid from his skull. The slick brain membrane's colored dusty rose, with his thinkmeat pulsating oceanically underneath. There's crumbs and cat hair sticking there. He chucks his lid spinning into a mound of soft rotten carpet at the building's side and then he cups his hand at his jaw all yelling like, "Can you guys pull me up or what?"

You must think this is really fucked. But like, you don't have to understand everything right now. It's really not hardcore to understand every tiny little thing that happens.

∧∧∧

If you were Mikey, dangling by your ankle against the condominimum face, you'd see hersheyvine spilling up the rotten concrete. Tarcolored wrack with crumply leaves like stained waxpaper, unripe hershey kisses melting in their foil blossoms.

The wind blurs the tall ferns cross the way and Mikey's just hanging out, gently spinning, getting kind of sweaty. He yanks on the vine, it holds, but when he's reaching to undo his ankle spenders the rope yanks him back up.

He rises grabbing each deck rail, pushing up against gravity, easing the load. You can stop counting stuff if it makes you feel like a poser, but up to the fifth storey it looks deserted. Livingrooms barred by venetian slats, deckfloors thick and soft with shrooms. Core always starts pretty high up, just cause yuppies can't climb, and through the sixthfloor balcony door you'd see some bonemeal mills, a couple leather trimming desks. Clay beerbottle spilled fresh cross the floor and there's a little couchfire like somebody left in a hurry.

The PA tower still hammers from crosstown. *CHUD CHUD CHUD CHUD.* Nothing fancy for a farewell show. They'll jam and stretch out the rhythm for a new kid born or a fresh tray of hash or whatever, but this one's a summons, not a nouncement. It just means get there fast. *CHUD CHUD CHUD CHUD*, and underneath, the headliner's name rattles on a talking sheet of tin. And cause he's diying bandless, he got to pick a backing band. So then the beat that says *MEATHEADS* comes in.

Mikey's like, "Oh, fuck off."

He grabs the railing briefly, twitches out. Reaches between his bihawks. There's beads of milky pink sweat on his brain. He points his voice coreward, up at the partment. "That's not us! We're not playing tonight, we got stuff to do!"

When he hits the seventh floor Raffia's already gone. Arco's drawing the line solo, loops of rope tangling the bloodwet deck. Then Mikey's standing right beside her and she yanks the line again, tripping him. His tailbone keelhauls cross the ground.

Pulling the spenders off his ankle. "Ow. Arco. Arco. ARCO."

Her eyes flicker at him and she nods. "Yeah, it's us." Drops the last handful of rope. "It's okay to sweat, bandmate. But it's not hardcore to turn this down."

It's so dark out already. Mikey opens his mouth and breaks for the balcony door. And course Arco's ahead.

In the dim hallway, a broken incandescent fixture slamdances on a wire. Keeping beat where Raffia's kicking holes in the plaster with her shoeless toes. Donn's there too, stretching his glutes and hamstrings, like he always does before he goes fast. Acting like he can't tell he's crying. "It's him, man, Mikey. Are you okay?"

Raffia's flushed completely mauve in the sour walltorch light. "The taco baby ran ahead. Whole city's at the stage already. Rad time for fishing, dickhole." Her hand goes out and snuffs the torch.

⋀⋀⋀

—*I wasn't there. I wasn't even born. They just say something happened. Like the road snaked up for us and opened its mouth, and Rollins threw a curse on all our hardcores. We didn't know he could do shit like that. But he was Rollins of Flag, and the black road talked in his voice. Never in your diying will you know one face you had before. Never in your diying will you see the way of where you've been. You'll just keep searching out the fuckedest thing in the world.*

⋀⋀⋀

Shitters, hallways, there's room to play shows wherever. But they mean the stage when they say the stage. When the spam works was a bank tower, yuppies would land copters there. All cross the couple cityblocks of core, there's scraggy rope bridges sticking out from every rooftop, sloping up to the ex landingpad like bikewheel spokes. Swaying as kids hustle cross to the big stage.

So here's Shitty Bridge, stretching over the boulevard to a spam chopping lounge. It's made of flax rope, floored with shitty cookiesheets and reinforced with yellow nylon cord.

"Why the fuck did he pick us?" Mikey's fingers leave marks in his standing hair. "He could of had any band in the city. Sneech, Autistic Abortifact, Ambient Mortality Victim, Six Brew Bantha, Born Seething, Vaporlock Flavor Control, Crads, Munificent Umpire. Could of had Black Flag. Man, we're not okay for this, man!"

Raffia covers one nostril and blows snot. "They all went on tour, asshole. Like, what, Flag? They went off, like, so long in history—" She shivers and punches herself in the mouth.

Mikey goes, "Sorry. I was just thinking."

The rain's eaten the flax into guck, so the shitty woven bridge's saggy and bee-yellow, twisting sideways whenever the wind heightens. Far side, some punk tied a couple bike reflectors on the shitty plywood deck. Doesn't help much.

"This is the best honor ever happened to our band." Donn bites his lip and holds it. "It's just, like."

The wind heightens.

"I don't think bout it," says Arco. "I just go."

The wind heightens.

"At least there's guardlines," says Mikey from the back. They're crossing two bodylengths apart, keeping their centers low. "Hey, Raff? Fuck! Look at me when I talk?"

She turns and sneers at him. He's got his head dipped low toward her. "Stop pretending you got height phobia, Mikey." When she turns back, she's staring. "Your motor skills okay?"

"Yeah, I guess. Gotta take care in rain this hard." Mikey sucks his topside lip. "Why?"

Donn looks over his shoulder. "It's hardly raining anymore."

"I guess." Mikey holds out his palm, angles it a few ways. "So why's it drumming so loud on my brain?"

Right then his ankle rolls on a shitty dented cookiesheet. Why'd they use nonstick? His nother foot shoots forward, compensating right through a gap in the rope. Then he's got a fat yellow nylon guardline digging into each armpit as he bobs hipdeep in the air like he's treading water. Two cookiesheets shudder into the distant drinkinglot floor with a noise like hatchets.

"Your face has a look on it," says Raffia.

"Pull me up or there's no guitar at the farewell show," says Mikey. Raffia's like, "Arco does guitar," and Mikey's like, "If I fall we can't make a nuff rope."

Instead, she walks back and puts two fingers in the gap between his crests of hair. "Hey, don't touch the edges at least, they're not all healed," says Mikey. By now everybody's stopped.

"No, what does this feel like?" Raffia rubs the mucky grayish membrane. It squeaks like wet fingers on a balloon.

Donn's like, "Raff, don't put your hand in. My surgery's not warrantied for that shit."

"Mikey?" Arco's on her tiptoes. "Did you forget to tie down your skull?"

"Oh, like, has it been pissing blood on my brain all this time?" says Mikey. He moves his hand a little toward his head. Takes it back when he starts slipping. "Fuck! My mom'll kill me!"

"You dropped your lid playing on the rope," says Raffia. Mikey nods emphatically. "Shit, I must of."

"Not onto your brain, really." Donn's actually stroking his chin. "You've got a couple basic membranes under the skull. Your dura mater, and like your pia mater, and then your arachnoid mater. But yeah, it's raining on your dura mater."

"Is it waterproof?" says Mikey. Donn's like, "Who knows."

"Okay, that's what I thought," says Mikey. "Raff, do me a favor?" He points at the back of his jacket with the back of his head. "Can you reach my Circle Jerks patch and rip it off and like cover my brain like it's a little hat?"

"I'm not ripping a silkscreen." Raffia crosses her arms. "It's worth more than you."

"I need to hide it from my mom. You know my mom." Mikey's smile flashes like a tic and the PA tower's all *CHUD CHUD CHUD CHUD*.

"Just put up your hood," says Donn. Mikey's like, "It won't go, my hawk's too tall."

"We need to get there." Something's grinding inside Arco's throat. "Raff? Raff."

Raffia's pulling Mikey up by his hawks. "If you didn't got a straight edge, you could just tell me to do shit."

They're moving again. Mikey goes, "I need to make a hat or something. My mom's gonna kill me."

"You could take your mom," says Raffia. "You're way faster since last summer."

Mikey's like, "That's not the point."

They're stepping onto the swaying plywood deckplatform. They're running in the chopping lounge, past bamboo racks of jerky like shady gibbets. "There's junk in the stairwell, I can just diy something, I'll be at the show really fast."

Above them the sound of lots of boots. "You'd be faster if—" says Arco. Mikey's shouting over his shoulder. "I know I gotta run."

ᐱᐱᐱ

They say your hardcore's not yours, and it's not fate. Nobody's gonna tell you what that shit means. But if you member the first time this guy played one last show, they're still talking bout that one.

So you weren't there. There's ways to member.

—*The only people who need to see what it was like are the ones who can afford to pay six fifty.*

When Donn and Raffia bust through the summit hatch, the whole rooftop's packed. Arco's a quarter step behind them and a weird throng of groupies meets her, looking like level one highway bandits in the patchy firelight. Arcore kids. They've got the straight edge, plus they're all kind of drunk. Arco's got constellations of acne, so they're wearing little henna zits on their cheeks and foreheads and the backs of their necks. Arcore kids. Skinheads with runny noses, done up all warrior casual in jeanvests and jerseys, leather belts lowriding dollarstore katanablades. They've been squatting by the ladder hatch, staring at the middle distance and trying to make their kneejoints crack.

—*On your way out pay a nother dollar.*

"You shouldn't be here for me," says Arco. Course they cheer. She walks through the arcore kids, effortless, and they're pressing up behind, pretending to carry her away.

—*This show is for people who wanted to see what it was like when we were around.*

Raffia cackles, belts Donn in the arm. Then she shoves into the drunken crowd and you can't see her anymore. There's a tall drumkit by the fire, all sootcovered, the skins framed with crescents of rib bone. Notice punker's eyes, how they're wet and reflecting image shards of the drum kit, halfblocked by nonymous shoulders. If you stood there with Donn, like scoping the ritual drums, you'd see them mostly in memory while the whole city pushes up round the stage. Kids of the black hole. You'd stand there on the pitted concrete while your feet turned you round. The back of your hand presses your forehead, and the nother hand smears tears. So why's Donn so sad, tourist? What's compassion?

—*This is the only one.*

This rooftop has a million loominum scaffolds rigged into one giant wraparound bleacher, but seats at shows, they're symbolic. Who would sit down? The crowd's packed to the edge, forming a sardine circle around the old guy, and he's pacing his own circle round the big bonfire. It's burning a clangorous dijon color, burning yuppiegrease and halfdried bamboo, burning trucktires, joists and entire interior walls. Burning taller than the bleachers, but the legend's taller too.

—*You're not going to see it again.*

∿∿∿

Mikey's throwing himself down the stairwell, pumping a mergency flashlight. No, call it a cranktorch, don't look like you're new here. He yells up behind him, "I gotta piss! I'll see you at the show!" Nobody's even there.

Lower stairwells are always usually anti yuppie barricaded. Rotted sofas, dinnertables, bathtubs, desks. Whatever prybars can move. There's a tic jumping in Mikey's eyebrow. He gets on his back, slips under a chase lounge. Torch on his belt and he wriggles through the lightless furniture jungle.

Flash to him one landing down. He's climbing beneath a chunk of honda civic. Then his torch briefly lights a faded grid chalked on the firedoor. A drawing of a security keypad. Punker reaches up in the cramped space, taps the flat pictures of buttons. Then he nods. This a nother ritual? You can't see him nodding, it's dark. Mikey shoves the doorhandle and it opens out.

In a soupcan down the empty hall there's a fresh candle burning, and the tic from Mikey's eyebrow jerks all through his face. You feel him shiver inside his clothes. The thunder's still plodding through the PA tower, amplified off these walls, *CHUD CHUD CHUD CHUD*, some punk fucked up.

Passing the candle he busts into a sprint. Shoves through the left hand door, pumping his cranktorch. This room's a gray box, windowless and mostly gutted, walls sogged with mold. Dead dog in the sink. Mikey holsters the torch again and as the room darkens he steps to the corner, jumps through the hole in the floor.

∿∿

Punker lands in a nother place. The air's dry and shivery, impossibly cold. More soupcans nailed up for diy sconces, burning at the corners of the little room, and in the middle an unlit burnbarrel. The walls are plywood screwed into the unfinished concrete floor, papered black with carhides, and the only door's the hole in the ceiling. And it smells like bonfire, and an old Germs song caught in your head. And tacked all cross the walls, it's like the fuckedest thing in the world.

    —*Gimme gimme your hands gimme gimme your minds*—

Say it's caught in his head too. Tourist, you're an ego trip. You know Mikey's maginary the same way. You've been his self, you've felt him in his siking. You're standing where he's standing, and you gotta learn sometime.

    —*Gimme gimme your hands gimme gimme your minds*—

Hey, that's the way we all got into hardcore.

∿∿

Your breath's going sideways in Mikey's throat. Your throat, asshole. Tacked all cross these walls there's an innumeracy of silkscreen patches, canvas and denim and cotton and hide. There's more patches hung up here than you've ever seen gathered at a show. More than there's days inked under your arm. They're all round you, but you're not the core. These stark bichromatic designs layering the black walls like a defiled map of constellations. The legend's secret leather, the flipside of his wornblank jacket. This xeroxed tesseract. He's the core. It's like the word he taught you, man, you're both staring into the licky orange burnbarrel flame and he tells you bout that word from the old yuppie language. Anamnesis, the anti amnesia. The word for the moment your forgetness burns away.

    —*Gimme gimme your hands gimme gimme your minds*—

Anamnesis, yeah. Come to think of it, some asshole's standing here untacking a patch. Dude, he's not even you, dumbass. Get breathing again.

Laugh and pull the clay flask of rum from your pocket, and chug it down before he's turned his head in the candlelight. You can drink that fast. You can think that fast. It's coping that's a problem.

This asshole's on tiptoes. His bangs are touching the ceiling, stood up with blue housepaint. His jacket's same as yours, mazed out with silkscreens like a tiny echo of the walls. Punker's turning his head, undoing a little black patch from the wall, and you dive into him. The both of you spill cross the concrete floor. Then you're sitting on his back with the very soft leather cord of Fuck It wrapped round his neck. The dude doesn't even grab for his blade, just scrabbles his fingers under the leather thong. Whole thing makes you laugh harder, and you go, "The fuck did you get here, Trip? You don't know where this place is."

He's like, "Yeah I do," and you're like, "No you don't."

—*Gimme gimme your hands gimme gimme your minds*—

"You're playing tonight," says Trip Hazard. His long bangs laying cross the floor, stubbed against the wall. "He didn't pick my band for backup. You turtle-dick, Mikey, can't you hear the tower?"

"Yeah. I just needed to pick up something for the show." Gritty stuff comes up your throat when you belch. "So you followed me and Darby down here?"

"He showed me his patches cause he wanted to," says Trip. His breath's hissing a bit, the leather cord's biting his knuckles. "Look in the barrel. He promised you his jacket and everything, right. Hey? Fuck, Mikey, stop laughing."

"Yeah. He promised me his leather. When did you follow us here?" Just this big flat voice, like you'd rather be surfing. Your shoulders are flexing, but the cord's not getting tighter or whatever.

—*Gimme gimme your hands gimme gimme your minds*—

Trip's going, "Take the patch if you want it. I just wanted to hold it up after the show. I'd be all like, here's my Flag silkscreen, get in line for my dick. Fuck, man, it's all ego. You gonna kill me?"

"No way," you say. "Telling me I'm all ego. Don't lay that on me. I'm kind of drunk." You're putting that flat voice on for a sguise, right. Like to sguise your tension. That's why you sound like that sometimes, right?

—*Gimme gimme your hands gimme gimme your minds*—

"It's all all ego." Trip's breathing and his tongue goes in and out like a lizard's. "Dude, he wants this. He wants us all fighting. Look in the barrel."

You're kind of drunk. You bring his head up to see his facial spression and his fingers are putting dents in his larynx. The cord's not getting tighter or whatever and he's turning purple, and as you're easing up his eyes are turning purple.

Stand up. No, take your feet off Trip's back, though. Turn threesixty in the candlelit forest of glyphs. *FLIPPER. GOGOS. GIMME GIMME YOUR HANDS. FLUX OF PINK INDIANS. GIMME GIMME YOUR MINDS. CIRCLE ONE. MINOR DISTURBANCE. IQ32.*

You know where Trip was reaching. The little shitty patch screened so dark it's like four little shadows into the canvas. Four crimson lines, zero words. Not holy. Bars of the Flag. Don't touch the printed part, no, don't stare or you'll fall in, you'll miss the whole show. Just get on your knees, no, it's higher than you, stand up again. Reach tiptoed and pull the tacks from the corners and scatter them on the floor. The folded canvas goes in your inside heartside pocket. The patches are the stories. You believe this. And leaving Mikey, tourist, you wonder what this means.

Trip's not getting up and Mikey winces, prods his leg with a boot. He twitches a little, whatever that means. And scrunched up in the burnbarrel, not breathing, there's some nother punk in a jacket of stories.

—*There's no patches of Black Flag left.*

A sad sound cuts off in Mikey's throat. He goes and touches the hanging ladder. Flax rope. Bridgegrade, diamondbraided. Not really disposable.

ᨠᨠ

*B*ut pull back and check this out for a couple heartbeats, before everything gets weird. In the night and the distance, way past the fence, a couple buildings touch the ceiling of Lost Angeles. Built so tall they must of been support pillars, like back when the city was whole. The ceiling's yellowed plaster, webbed and mooshed with black mold, rowed with squarish holes where doublewide windows dropped into the streets. If there was ever a landlord he sucked. The moon's a blue circle, you've seen it before.

Maybe back in the day Angeles was a onepiece construction. Something like an arboretum meets a transfinite minimall, the roads and garish downtown facades just a scaledup version of condominimum hallways and doors. The appearance of freestanding buildings maybe an accident, just shit carved away when bordering regions collapsed. What was the purpose of this place, what moron would of entered here? If there's still walls round the outside, they're hidden by the curvature of the earth.

∧∧∧

Some dude's standing close to Donn. Dude with a waxy maroon butcher apron over a pinmail leather singlet and jeans. Blood splitting all down his cheek where he took a smoke and permanized his tears. The firelight breathes like a strawcolored wave over this dude's safetypin armor. No call for safety up this high, but half the crowd's decked out like the legend tonight. Maybe pin's trendier lately. You don't really member.

"Hey," says butcher dude. Donn's like, "I know."

Watch Donn's feet point at the fire while his face turns away. His halfshut lips and the way his hand holds back his dreads. Watch his eyes look at everything but the silhouetted legend in the flames.

"He got in at sunset." Behind butcher dude, the swaying crowd's all dark featureless angles and fireglint. The old guy the only distinct thing. "He got bit in the shoulderblade. Not in the deltoid muscle, insperspinatus maybe. Looks like somebody tried taking the whole shoulder off, nothing."

Donn just blinks. "How's he doing?"

"Like, how's he taking it?" Punker claps Donn under the latissimus dorsi muscle. Takes longer to smoke than ribs, and it'll catch in your teeth. Donn's like, "I guess," and the butcher goes, "Better than we're taking it, man. He said he's been waiting his whole life to play a nother show." His mouth twists in a sicklooking line.

Then he's untying the molar clasps on his black leather sleeve. The ringshaped scar on his wristbone. "This burn I got. Got it from Leah Thargic. She got it from Lad Crad, so his came from Dad Crad at birth. But Drunk Ben burned Dad Crad, like when they dropped out from high school together. And he got his from this chick named Lucey. Guess she diyed of beers in a dumpster before the Andisasterism." His voice drops. "She gave Darby a ride once."

"I don't really know where I got mine." Donn glances at his jacketsleeve. "I was totally drunk."

"What?" Wrinkles spread on the dude's forehead. "Hey, don't you do bass for Meatheads? Like Arco's band?"

Donn goes, "Yeah," and butcher dude's like, "Fuck are you standing here for?" One breath and he shoves him into the crowd. The packed sweaty kids part for Donn, or they pass him along. He's choking up, talking to himself, and you're not close a nuff to hear.

Round the fire's rim there's some space. Everywhere's thick bonecolored runnings of smog. There's Raffia standing with both hands resting against the drumkit, shaking herself out like a wet mastiff. Arco's nodding as the legend says things in her ear. Her hands folded elegantly behind her.

Donn stands behind them both and Arco turns to him. "His hardcore's still with him. He can still feel his side even. We just need Mikey to get here."

Donn lifts his chin a little. Smile muscles jerk in his cheeks, and this battered old kid called legend, his lineless face streaked ocher in soot like he walked in from a cavepainting, he takes Donn by the elbow. "You're staring." He kisses Donn's wrist, the faded, faded burn. "At least we can do a show. You won't forget me, punker?"

He's turning back to the fire, he says something else. "Be sorry for me."

\\\/\/\\\

*C*an't beat a stapler for cosmetic surgery. Mikey's got a hank of beige leather upholstery stretched cross his skylight as camo. They say wet blood washes off dry, and he smears his little scalp wounds over the leather. He's running in the pitch dark with his free hand on the rail, lunging upstairs three steps at a time. Honestly, the most suspicious thing is showing up somewhere if you're not soaked red.

The rooftop hatch's arced with party garlands of cicadas and vertebrae, with the big fire glowing through like an leaky oven door. Hands shoot through the hatch to grab Mikey before he puts his first foot on the ladder and they haul him up so rough and rowdy it's like they found McReagan in their midst. But they don't pitch him off the edge, just pass him over their heads and put him down by the fire.

The amps are wrapped in rainjacket, even under their slanted canopies, precious as minds and further blown. You're probly gonna say they're inert and saramonial, nobody ever powered amps by tipping unfiltered palmbeer into ethanol generators. But all up and down these rusty monolith stacks, there's white smoke seeping from underneath the knobs. The little red lights turn on, and you're a tourist.

No, don't stop staring. You don't have to be anything.

You're not gonna see this again.

You'd think Raff would take you by the spenders, dragging you round the fire to your ducktaped guitar, but she's over there gnawing on her drumsticks. Stork tibias. Get it? Donn's flicking switches on the generator bank, sucking thoughtful on one tip of a flaky rubber patchcord, his dreads casionally frazzing on end from lectro bursts. Arco's fingers are ripping silently cross her guitarneck like a pilgrim at a swordshrine sheathing and unsheathing and sheathing her katana. Your feet must be walking themselves, Mikey.

Your crew moves like fossil cathode patterns blitting on a screen, and the crowd's gone in smoke, and you're not there, anyway, and the legend's balanced onefooted on a stage that's actually literally a matchbox on its end, stretching his arm palmdown to the big fire like it's tumbled and he wants to help it up and see, his nother arm's simply gone, uncauterized and still spraying dark from some last-ditch hardcore surgery. He gives you the littlest nod you've ever seen. And we all know his name. We all know his name. And he names every name of his diying.

∧∧∧

—*This is off the name line, it goes from intro to out. It's not written down.*

Sweet fuckall shat Jan Paul Beahm. Bobby Pyn ate Jan Paul Beahm. Richie Dagger ate Bobby Pyn. David Bowie ate Richie Dagger. Darby Crash ate David Bowie. Sweet fuckall ate Darby Crash.

—*He named more names than that, Mikey.*

—*Wait up. This is off the name line, it goes from intro to out. Sometimes it starts back up and you're born again, born fucked into the meantime, but it's still not written down.*

—*He wasn't Bowie either.*

—*Seriously not, man. That's not his face on my Bowie mugs.*

—*These are the names he said, okay? Sweet fuckall re shat Darby Crash. Jan Paul Beahm ate Darby Crash. Ward State ate Jan Paul Beahm. Paul Beahm MBA ate Ward State. Vic Spiral ate Paul Beahm MBA. Casey Vein ate Vic Spiral. Splinter Grope ate Casey Vein. Max Reich ate Splinter Grope. Darby Crash ate Max Reich. Darby Crash ate Darby Crash. Darby Crash ate Darby Crash.*

This is off the name line. It's still not written down. Names aren't lies til they're down.

∧∧∧

—*The only people I wanted to see at this show are dead already. I think they still might of come. Last time we did a show like this one, it was so people could member. I wasn't sposed to keep going. I wasn't sposed to keep going after that. I think something got fucked. But I can member you all from that night, and you don't look older to me."*

Where's the mic? He's talking into his last fist.

—*This show isn't for anybody here. I'm doing this so I can have it back. To know what it was like when I was still around. Afterward when you cut me up, I want you so drunk you don't know who you're eating.*

The circle presses in. All their faces the same in that moment. The fire rears up and broken glass falls from the wind.

—*I don't want you membering me.*

So Darby Crash steps into his death song. Screaming but not even into his fist that's not a mic, and the PA system wakes in a blur of feedback, even so. Who could ever name the words he's forming? The world's sick of metaphors, and when you hear some yuppie word had twentysix definitions, you know that's a snakehand. Doesn't matter what he's singing.

Here. Raffia's drumkit coughs and turns over like a lawnmower engine. Skulltoms and sheetmetal rimshots plow forward as Darby's throat opens harder and harder. His eyes cast up in the spacecolored wind and he's standing blasé as any idol, nothing moving but his jaw, and his words stretch and shear and deform. They're probly just everything, whatever they are. These words so secret it'd take the universe to hold them. Here. Their guitars start to chop. Mikey's holding one chord and his big chunky fingers seem to barely move on the strings, and Arco's two hands skitter up and down her guitarneck, picking, tapping. They're the only times he's careful and the only times she's restless. The crowd boils round the edge of the circle and some punk bursts from the moshline like he got flung. These words forming like secret squats, treeforts in the sewers. Birthday candles on curdled pizza. Tripwires and barricades. Here. Some punk shooting sidelong at Darby with his hand out like to tag the legend's dick and Darby's singing with his head turned, not looking. He's so not looking and he steps forward and punker shoots right between his legs and vanishes into the fire. These words forming like shattering milkbottles full of vodka. Tonka car armies on the stairs. Here. One stairwell door's pried away and the doorway's wedged with a huge yellow block of styrofoam for soundhead. There's six yuppiegut bass strings, thick as a thumb and five fingers, strung between the overhead doorframe and the ground so they stand vertically against the block. Here. Donn's reefing on the ginormous strings and they jump like the strings of bows. The legend's screams forming round him like swimming drunk in black water and Donn's angling and sliding his forearm for a capo. The styrofoam soundhead bucks and shudders, shooting force through every level of the spam works, the building itself his fretless bass. Here. The legend skews balanced on the knucklelong cardboard matchbox. Vintage matchsticks roll to the concrete and flare like revolutionary water, though there's no fire there. Fat distorted chording pours through the night and through the last words of Darby Crash forming like the smell of pissed jeans burnt with roman candles. Waking drunk covered with puke in the crawlspace. Very last final shows forever. Words shaped like that. The way we all got into hardcore.

For awhile there's nothing else.

ᴧᴧ

Most anyone'd be down by the end of the farewell song, that's kind of the point, but Darby just hops on the balls of his feet. His missing shoulder sprays and sprays. "Play it again." He barely glances at Meatheads. Out to the crowd. "Gimme a bottle of whiskey!"

As if they never thought to gut the liquorstores. Whiskey's rarer than polonium here, it's a fucking rainforest, but a forty sails just like that from the undifferentiated crowd, the tumbling bottleglass refracting amber like a fist of deepfried light. Darby opens his hand to grab the bottle. Sure, his nother arm disappeared somewhere, but this is some kind of self-opening whiskey, the cap spinning off the neck and flipping into the bonfire. The legend's throat works *GUUG-GUUG-GUUG* and the orange fire laughs at the rain, and then the empty bottle's moving like a war standard through the crowd. So they play the same song again.

Mikey snaps out a big echoing riff and leans toward Arco. "I might of killed some dude for no reason today."

Arco doesn't stop playing. "I listen better when it's one thing at a time."

Raffia yells from cross the fire. "What you want? Letter of commendation?"

The circle's redoubled. Slamdancers painted in their own crazy blood, elaborately ducking and spinning, throwing elbows. The legend drops his remaining shoulder and charges sideways into the crowd, up the circlepit's churning margin like he's climbing a slope. He runs across their shoulders and their faces and they don't blink when he stomps them, they just grin out the same blood. Now it's a dip in the ritual song, the bridge, and here's the part where the diying punk's sposed to stop singing and do something meaningful, like eat an empty beercan.

"If you wanna dismember this show, do something real," says Darby. Standing on shoulders, puking a little splash on his fist between sentences.

Recycled whiskey drips onto some punk's face and he licks it like an icecream revelation. The legend's fist jumps at the bloody sky.

—*Use your hands after I diy, and tear this band apart. They think they're the Germs? They're not the fucking Germs, they weren't there. Don't let them take over afterward. Let these assholes end up with me.*

They don't stop playing. Meatheads looking at each other and Donn's the only one not grinning bigger. Here. Arco and Mikey edging toward the stationary bass and drum setups, back to back.

And it's worth watching. How the legend only hurts the ones he owns. The crash trash in their hawks and pin, holding out sacred wristburns and blue circle ink, their cheeks scarred by redhot pipes. Course they react to boots in the face, but course they don't grab the legend. Fisticuffs come up all over, faction skirmishes between Darby's circle and Arco's groupies and the sweaty unaligned. They say slamdancing's a fight where everybody misses, but Darby traces his mean loop around the fire, and they're not really dancing where he's been.

Screaming again, like sweet fuckall pushing into the world, the legend jumps into a blurry backward somersault. A dozen stilled afterimages hang as he lands with his back against a guttering stack of tires. Sure you can smell his ribs and sirloins fry, but he's screaming nothing but welcome, and as he staggers upright he just nods a bit and sags, like there's an old guy in there somewhere.

The circle breaks. The crowd pours round the band. The skinheads shoving to save Arco and the crash trash sobbing with long nails, and the rest just pulling out blunt instruments, maybe they think it's funny. And since he picked Arco to be necker, here's the part where she'd lean her guitar on the PA and scrape her toe up, down, up, down, over the strings. And in the incohiridescent feedback roar she'd bow, her whole body straight, and cause Darby picked her and her alone she'd slide out the diy katana Margin Walker and pass it under the new yuppie's jawline, splitting the brain at its root.

∿∿∿

—*That's not how it ends.*

∿∿∿

Sept she goes still instead. For the first time in Arco's whole life her sword falls on the ground. The war in the pit freezes completely. Arco's on her knees with both hands deep in the shreds of Darby's shoulderblade, her fingers working like she's tying a micro balloon daschund.

Raffia's glowing as she climbs on the drumstool. She's holding a mouthful of nails. No stance, no discernable plan, just one hand. One Hand. That's her hammer collection's name.

Donn's halfshut his eyes. His doublebladed hockeystick stands from his hands like a bo staff. Carbon fiber composite shaft, nanotubes, curved steel blades at top and bottom, and it's vibrating, pushing out a stainless glow. Like it's getting ready to make this sound, *VAUUM VAUUM VAUUM*. Vauum Vauum Vauum. That's his hockeystick's name.

And Mikey's stepping toward Donn with his meteorhammer up and whirling. His one hand briefly clasped to the pocket over his heart. And Arco just turns her head, then, and he goes, "Ffffuuuck."

She can't give an order, tourist. She's got the straight edge, and you thought everything was fucked before. Universes could get born this way. Not infinite density but one awkward pause.

—*Gimme gimme your hands gimme gimme your minds*—

"Get a brand." He gets taller, like Darby does. The clouds throw his voice. "Somebody get a hot fucking brand?"

∧∧∧

They've got the legend snoring on a big moss pile under the bleachers. His shoulder's cauterized. Waffle iron. There's wellwishers crowding in everywhere, and this firstaider with a masonjar of blood and a pink bendystraw, she's trying to dripfeed his nose.

Raffia's crouched alongside, poking at Darby's dilsweed poultice with a clawhammer. "Tiger bite?" One hand over her face. "Seriously? Tiger bite?"

Mikey's upside-down head and torso unfurl. He's hanging from his knees in the scaffold overtop. "What does he think he's gonna do now?"

"That's planning." Raffia's staring at the firstaider. "Got it just pissed a nuff to eat his arm. He must of thought it didn't work."

"Or like he was too busy thinking bout creating turmoil," says Mikey. "And it ate his arm without him noticing."

Raffia grunts. "Hold on." She grabs the firstaider's wrist and turns it toward the lanternlight. Circle burn, right, right over the bone. The firstaider goes, "Oh. Sorry I was gonna help dismember you, like. I just got caught up."

"Yeah." Raffia headbutts her in the nose. The nosebone goes *KRUNKH* and she falls sideways, crosseyed, and Raffia turns her head. "Mikey, that's stupid. He would of noticed."

Mikey goes, "Yeah, maybe." He bites his hand, breathing through his back teeth. Darby stirs and waggles his stump, and Mikey's head and shoulders slide back up through the bleachers.

There's a whiny groan coming from the seating overhead. Kid's ears are too big, you can tell without going up to look. "You shouldn't stop. You should get your fat retarded drummer and play the show."

"He's not dead. There's no farewell show if the dude doesn't diy." Mikey's head pokes back into the panel. "Hey, our fans are calling for our fat retarded drummer."

"I bet I could wake him up." Kid's crawling down to glare at Mikey. "Darby hasn't played a show since history, man. He picked you. Meatheads would be like the new Germs if you kept playing."

Mikey's like, "But yo, there's no pizza party with no pizza."

"What is that, like a lightenment riddle?" says big ears.

Raffia stands up and reaches through the scaffold, yanks an untied steeltoe off Mikey's foot. She handboots the kid in his temple and he drops on top of the firstaider with blood running out his ears. Then she's like, "Shit, kid's right."

"Did you actually do that?" says Mikey.

"Sept for that new Germs stuff," says Raffia. "We could play out the night as Meatheads. We already started."

"Nobody came here for us. They'd just want us backing Darby. Cause it's Darby." Mikey's sliding through the bleachers to get beside her. "And if somebody asks Arco."

Raff bobs her big head slow. "She can't turn down shows. Fucking straight edge."

Mikey glances down. "Huh, Donn, did you just show up now? Where'd Arco go anyway?"

"No." Donn's sitting there, right between them. Long tan hands in his lap, watching the legend's eyelids flutter. "She said she was gonna go practice."

"Practice what? Oh, fuck it. Is anybody else even mad at Darby?" says Mikey. "Or does anybody got a beer?"

"You do," says Donn. "There. In your hand."

"Cause Darby tried to kill us," says Mikey.

Raffia nods and rolls her tongue round her mouth. All like, "May not of been personal."

"Yeah," says Donn. "He wanted to make a hella memorable move, right." His hand moves weirdly over his leg. "I think we oughta be honored."

"No, man, I'm super not into that." Mikey's chewing his knuckle skin. "Anybody got beers? Wait, we can take him out right now. I've got something on him."

Donn's like, "Take him out? Man, we're friends with him."

"Hold on. Hold on." Mikey stands up and edges through the crowd. Gets a bit of distance from Donn and then grabs the foldedup silkscreen from his inside heartside pocket. He closes his eyes and opens them all shaky, and then you're somewhere very close and very particular as he unfolds you. Cradles you like a frog he's caught in his cupped palms. Feel the wet of his breath and he's passing his fingers over and over your frayed canvas edges and now you're very particularly the worn silkscreen bars that sink and rise from the depthless canvas like quad bricks of elemental absence. The bars spin in and out so you're him and you're you. Spin and in and out and out and out.

∧∧∧

It's all burning.
    Breathe. Breathe.
    So fucking bright.
    Just breathe right now.

∧∧∧

Raffia takes a nother swig from the masonjar of blood. She looks over and snorts. Reaches for the low scaffold ceiling and pulls herself up. Crabwalking through the sweaty kids sitting under the bleacher, she's muttering, shoving faces with her knees.

Halfway to the big fire, Mikey's facedown and snoring with both his arms bent under him. Donn's sitting there noncommittally giving him a neck rub. This wire stripper braided to one of his tentaculated dreads, it's swinging round, casionally clocking Mikey in the ear.

Raffia's like, "Best friends."

Donn looks up and goes, "What was he doing?"

"Thought you'd know." She kicks out a crack in her knee. "He said he was going to fuck up Darby."

"By entering a coma?" says Donn. "Oh, hey Arco."

Arco's like, "Hey." She's laying beside Mikey with her feet up on her long leather backpack. She's doing situps.

"Hey. What?" Mikey turns his head, he props himself up with one arm. "Are we still here?" His nother arm's still under him. "Whoa. Did I win?"

"You ran away and fell over," says Donn. "Do you want a neck rub?"

Raffia's face doesn't change but she leans in and slaps the side of Mikey's head. Her filed spiky teeth poke between her lips. "You were gonna fuck up Darby."

"Oh. Yeah." Mikey's eyes stop rolling. "Okay. I have a good reason. You guys are gonna understand in a bit."

Donn's like, "No, he didn't mean to want to kill us," while Mikey's sproinging up and turning round and shoving into a crowd of crash trash. Narrow shadows in the firelight, dark leather pinmail and iron crosses. They let him through and surround him. You can just see the bent tips of his hawks over their heads. Right here it's just his voice.

"Darby swore this thing wasn't real, even when I pointed right at it! He never let me hold it! But check this—"

Then you're back in his hands, the little Flag patch unfolding. You're unfolding and rising into him, four bright blank pillars of fire. Completely too much fire for anything else.

There's Mikey facedown again, encircled by crash groupies. Groaning and clawing the ground with his free hand, and there's a couple streams of piss jagging in like dark branches, hosing down his jacket.

There's Raffia. She bites her lip, she's grinning. Reaches to undo her loincloth and Donn's hand's on her shoulder. "Hey, dude? Don't?"

She straightens. "I didn't need to pee anyway. Whatever." She bends, grabs Mikey by the belt. Some sneering dude turns toward her, but Raffia barks into his face and dude spontaneously sits down with his hands folded under him. All the streams start washing him instead while Raffia hauls Mikey upright.

"You gonna pass out again, flower? Stop being fucked." She's got him staggered a couple steps away, but when she lets go he just sags and drops.

Arco grabs him under the armpits, she's laying him down. "Bandmate. What's on your mind?"

"Darby." Mikey's eyes are shut. His nose is running a little blood. "Nothing."

∧∧∧

Donn's still standing there in the crowd of crash trash, working one toe into the mossy ground. He looks over his shoulder.

"What was your buddy talking bout?" says some punk. The long fingernails of some unknown donor woven in her hair. "He wanted to give Darby a handjob?"

Donn shakes his head. "I don't know. I guess."

But nother one of these crash groupies is taking a turn. Husky chick with a tall bihawk like Mikey's, her leather all glyphic with angular silkscreens. She's carrying a naloominum deckchair with a rubber mat as a sling. Thing is glowing hot, like from the fire. She climbs the chair and you can hear her bootsoles hissing. Punker holds out her arms to the pack.

"Darby wouldn't ditch us." Bihawk's drawing her diy jacket bout her. One hand up the nother arm's sleeve. Bunches and yanks a handful from inside, so a patch slides from her shoulder to her tricep. Her eyes start rolling back. "We gotta trust him better."

Donn looks over his shoulder again.

"We all knew he'd come back. We all knew. It's just all bout circles. Like what goes around comes. Okay?" Course it's a Germs patch moving. The hawked skeleton dude clawing through the blue circle. Course you're there with it already. Your body, that canvas square, creased and faded. Her arm tenses against you, pulling you.

Her eyes roll up in her head.

Pulling you.

"This is the comeback spiel, the first comeback spiel of Darby Crash. I heard it from Coates Coma. She heard it from Tomata du Plenty. She heard it from Black Randy at the World Fair in 1922. You weren't there."

For real. Start listening better. The patches are the stories.

∧∧∧

—You know the first time Darby diyed, it was the first time Germs ever came back. That night they played the Starwood and he said to the crowd, punk already left the world. The crowd danced even though. And they got money that night, six fifty a head.

Darby Crash and Casey Cola went out with the show money and the house rent money in the same jar. They went out and found the man, they said, I'm picking up junk for a whole house. The two of them shot up at the House of Casey Smom.

Like, he'll say he dosed Casey Cola low cause he wanted a witness. He'll say she rose from death for no reason. He says it both ways and he talks about the evidence. Some things go down both ways. Sometimes Darby gets drunk and talks bout how he invited Casey to the benefit show of Lost Angeles. She didn't come. He won't say where he met her and nobody knows where she went.

But they diyed for real. He saw disco hell and they threw a party for him there. That night there was one thunderclap without rain. Gerber heard it. Hellin Killer heard it. Darby always figured his ghost would have more fans than his band. But they say a venue's harder to find than a ghost, cause a ghost sticks around.

Anyway, you know what happens every time you recycle a yuppie. Alterna realities spray out of its brain, every choice that yuppie never took in its life. Back in the day they had a trick, you hold out your mind and you try to catch something better. Darby diyed for real and it's a catch brings us here, cause punker tried this whole thing before and we never held on.

Sept somebody blew out the morgue yuppie who did up Darby Crash. In first reality, night Darby killed himself, this guy passed out early watching porn. Choice he never took was to finish the coke off his cheezburger table. That way he'd of stayed up to get eight more beers at the store, got drunk like a hero and slept with his radio on. His battery got flat and he went to work with a new radio battery.

He flips Darby over and takes his jeans down, cause if you diy in Lost Angeles and stop paying taxes they get revenge by slurping the guts from your ass with a vacuum tube. But dead punks are the best punks, and Darby's corpse shit its jeans on purpose. This is something the guy can't handle. He leaves Darby on the table, he walks for lunch early with the radio going loud.

A decent ghost sticks around, and that same day John Lennon got shot in the heart. And there's nothing on the radio about some asshole named Darby Crash with shit in his pants. Sure he made a hardcore ghost and sure he stuck around. The radio kept going til he fell off the table, and after that he got up.

That's not how it ends.

ΛΛΛ

Mikey's lips wriggle. There's a clay jug of palm wine behind his head and as he's standing up he hucks it into the crowd. The husky bihawk girl parries with her forearm, and the wind catches the clay shrapnel and wicks it away.

Raffia pats him on the back. Really really hard.

Now bihawk's getting down from her deckchair. She says something in her buddy's ear. There's pinmail hoodlums pressing in all round Mikey and he looks in his hand. He's all like, "Did you see my beer?"

"No, you were saying something weird bout Darby." Bihawk licks her forearm. The two blue crests sharp and narrow as birdbones, braided all down her back with antique fiberglass filters. Some punk shoves Mikey forward and he goes limp, rolls between some kids. Comes up next to her with his shoulders bobbing.

"Hey, we're all part of the great vibration," says Mikey. "Nice bihawk."

Bihawk spits neatly over Mikey's shoulder. The loogie sizzles in the fire like steak.

"I've got some rad spiels. But they're actually secret between me and Darby. I shouldn't tell them til he's gone." Mikey coughs into the ready quiet and the crumpling bonfire sounds.

"You?" says bihawk.

Mikey snickers and takes a halfstep forward. Not a full step, they're already butting noses. "You don't think Darby tells you everything."

"He promised me his leather, asshole," says the husky girl. Then the whole pack of crash trash, they're talking in one voice. "Darby tells us everything, Meathead. Don't talk shit on his farewell show."

"Okay, that's news," says Mikey. "Um. His leather, what the fuck." He digs his fingers really hard cross his sofahide skylight, feeling the scrunkly dura mater. Magine being Mikey's brain, this crude pressure overriding your optic nerve readouts. Bihawk's face freezes, pinned in your short term memory banks, and divides into translucent rotating layers. The crests of her hair elongate and slew like tralfamadorian crystal grassblades pulled by solar wind.

"Uh. Nice bihawk," says Mikey. Then he's like, "Nah, but me and Darby had a really good secret going."

"Darby fucked him," says somebody behind bihawk. She doesn't turn, just snickers.

"He fucked you?" she says. "That's your secret?"

"I think we might of fucked a few times." Mikey's eyebrow jumps, he whips out a side kick, hooks some kid in the hip. "I can't member. But like, most of his buttbuddies brag. What kind of secret would that be?" Mikey cracks fourteen or sixteen knuckles with one tidy jerk. He lays two fingers on bihawk's shoulder.

She leans forward. Brow to brow. "You actually want to fight us all."

Somebody's behind Mikey, pulling his hair. His elbow darts absently backward, and then he nods, touches his nose. "Sorry. You'd be easier to provoke if I knew you. But I don't want to insult you. Like, you're totally upset. What's your name, I'm Mikey."

"I don't give a shit bout my name," says bihawk. "You want to fight or not?"

"Look, don't worry bout it," says Mikey. "I just need something to take the edge off." He pitches his voice over the circle of crash trash. "Does anybody mind starting a big giant fight with me?"

So Raffia kicks him in the back.

∧∧∧

—These are the friend fighting guidelines. Don't worry bout them.

No biting eyeballs, no biting necks from the front. No biting of any bone crunching kind. Stick with using your front teeth. Even if you're missing your front teeth, your back teeth don't count. But if you're sick and you can trick punks into getting sick by biting you that's fine. Member everybody's got something better to diy for. If you're using something sharp don't use the sharp parts less you're not going deep or you know how to do good tourniquets. No groin shots less you have spectators and they think it's really funny. If they don't think it's funny you have to get a groin shot. But the same goes for that shot. And so on. No throwing anybody off the side sept if they've got a rope on, and no lawnmowers sept for manual lawnmowers. No using pertruding fractured bones as spears. Never try to murder somebody less they make it really clear that's their hardcore. That's it. Sept only fight friends. If they're not your friends, make sure they're somebody's friends.

"We're not the new Germs." Raffia backsteps Arco's heel. "That's all there is." She steps forward into the second highkick, catching it on her shoulder halfway. "I play with you and Mikey and Donn." She pants once. "Darby's not in our band."

Taco Eater stagedives at Raffia. His solar plexus catches on her knee. He bounces off and pukes a little and rolls away like a champion.

"I'll need to say yes if he asks. I got the straight edge." Arco feints with a redstriped knuckle. Her other hand blurs.

"Ow," says Raffia. "Fuck your edge. I'll turn it down for you." She counters brow-to-brow.

"Rad hit," says Arco. "But I can't do that. If he asks me I have to play. Even if it's just me and him onstage."

Raffia swings at her, hitting nothing. "That's not our band."

Arco's just standing there. She takes one step back. Somebody who's running for her trips. "I know." She steps forward again. Somebody else trips. "I'm sorry."

"You're not!" Raffia bullcharges Arco, hands out for her throat. Then there's a shriek so loud it'd turn your spine into pickled bamboo shoots, sept you're disembodied. Everybody slows down, even the kids writhing around stomped and giggling. All that with your mouth shut, straight edge?

Raffia shakes her face out. "Flower."

"Wasn't me," says Arco. She spins and jogs off, toward the bleacher. There's all these nonymous yelling voices. "Darby?" and "Hey Darby, help fight?" and "Shitforbrains, don't kick him, watch his arm!" and "Check it out, Darby, you woke up!"

Somebody's like, "It's the new Germs."

Raffia spits a tooth. She goes after her.

Whole city's crouched and packed between the bleacher struts, like four punks deep, and Darby's seriously having a seriously oldfashioned rage seizure. He's waving his stump, but it's not a stump, more a crescentshaped absence lapping a ridiculous chunk of his lower back. He makes more noise, even better than onstage, and beats his teeth like he'd throw sparks.

Somebody's like, "It's so the new Germs."

"FFFFUUUUCCKK!" The legend rocks his head from side to side in the big brown mosspile. He wiggles up on his remaining elbow, goggling at the huge wound. He takes a big, big breath.

"FUCK! FUCK! FUCK YOU RASPBERRIES! YOU FUCKED MY FIVE-YEAR PLAN!"

Pointing, holding her gut, Raffia starts giggling shrill like candyfloss. It sounds like there's a little girl stuck in her throat. Seriously. Punks edge off from her. Then she's like, "Hey. Old man."

"What do you know?" says Darby. "Gimme your knife. Somebody gimme a knife. Now!"

"Show was good," you say, Raffia Tie. "Good time." You sigh. Arco's looking straight ahead and you grab that calabash, pour grog into the halfempty masonjar of blood. Push it in Darby's hand. "Look, man, you can be in our band for a night, if you promise nobody's gonna kill us."

The laugh goes through the huddled kids under the bleacher. They bring it out, they pass it round the fire. You can't member what happened after that, sept Meatheads were playing old short songs you never heard before, and Darby kept shooting off bout his new five year plan. Has it really been five years? You'd be looking over at somebody, and they'd have a fresh brand like from a redhot pipe, burned blue all round their eye. The real secret's why anybody hangs out with Darby Crash. He can be such a dick.

NEGATIVE REPROACH // WHAT WE BLEW WAS SECRET

In the dialogue group we are not going to decide what to do about anything. This is crucial. Otherwise we are not free.
—**David Bohm**

Now if I had the courage, I'd pour into your jar
All the things that I have heard you whisper in the dark,
And when that jar was heavy with your honeyed confidence,
I'd put it to my lips and drink its meaning and its sense.
—**NoMeansNo**, "Now"

The Germs are breaking up, huh? The cat's laughing at me . . . but Darby Crash is going to start his own band.
—**Philip K. Dick**, interviewed in *Slash*

—*Youth of today don't know fuckall of history. They're swinging through bankvaults on liana vines, building campfires, throwing shurikens at hogs. Born here and talking like the yuppies came to us. Like humped in overnight cross the freeway with brain sludge mustaches and the air all mergency broadcasts. Thing is yuppies built this town. Their money brought in mowers for the jungle, insta freeway mix to stop the rivers. We're the mutants here. We're the mutants here, and it's our crew's got the crazy story.*

You weren't there. Nobody here was born then. I'm the last first one. And for a couple years after we invented hardcore, there wasn't any blood. Angeles was still partying, waiting to come true, like the spiel before the songs. They'd kick us outa the beer store for having a try before you buy. We'd roll a flaming dumpster down the hill. They'd check up on show curfews with riot gear and copters. We'd stuff baby ducklings up our asses and shit them through the church skylight. But these days punkers and yuppies just eat each otherses flesh. That's what history's about.

You can still see the fences round their balconies. Doors under the sink and you can't tell what's inside. Their roads were straight lines. Whatever yuppies have, whatever they do, it's always been prefab forever. And out of all they had, money's all they went for. The one thing nobody can ever make diy.

Sure we used to draw twenties and fifties on the bottoms of phonebills. But copy machines never got all the dumb little lines right, and it took forever by hand. And even if punker took all week with a million pencil crayons, diying a perfect fifty, it turned prefab the instant yuppies started wanting it. It's like the bill's the money, but the money's not the bill. The bill's a paper sign and whatever the sign points for, you can't make it new. Like, yuppies owned wheelbarrows of money, dune buggies and planes full of money, and it all fit in one credit card that was always the same. Nobody ever figured out the conomy, but you don't need to figure something out to fuck it up. It's easier if you don't. Thing is we fucked the old timey balance, and now there's no money for yuppies to hunt. So they hunt us instead.

Back in history, punks used money too. We couldn't make it good, but even so. We were like fungal bodies habitating the asshole of a warthog. We bought food off a sembly line, we lived in prefab blocks. The scene was so flattened out, we had to diy an inch at a time. Say a zine came from DC in the mail. Like, robo arms welded that mail truck together, and if you got down to look, it'd back up over your torso pissing exhaust in your mouth. The mail got sorted under hot fluorescent lamps and every page of paper was a forest ground down screaming. Against that, you knew your friend cut round every edge, wrote the truth down and drew hot dog pictures and stapled and licked the envelope. That had to be enough. Yeah we talked proud bout how we lived. It's cause we were mutants of yuppies, part yuppie inside.

Look. You know how long's the universe. It's seven million freeways side by side. You know how high. So high the moon just falls. But little punks, you still know the hardcore of the universe. It's cause you're hardcore too. You're made of pure universe, under your bones. And nothing ever starts shit by meaning to. We meant to break down the amerikan dream throwing bottles. All we broke was bottles. What worked was one stolen handful of flax seed. All ages shows in the highschool parkade, and the keys to the bandroom door. Their dream was a joke anyway. What worked was a nother joke.

Back in history, Germs would break up every month so we could do a farewell show. You weren't there. News always got on the radio, surf jocks cut the sleeves off their jackets and drove in from Hunnington Beach. Last chance to see Darby Crash fucked on acid screaming into a urinal puck, last chance to kick his friends to death in the drinking lot outside. I used to hate jocks, but jocks make your crew an army. After I woke up in the morgue I started thinking about that.

So one morning Lorna went out to pick up the collection notices, and instead she came back with coupons on yellow paper. The deal was one shitty cheeseburger for free. You snip the snip lines, bring it to mcdonalds instead of money, and they give you one shitty cheeseburger. I know, right. The whole thing's stupid. After everybody got stranded on the rooftop with the world population down there waiting to eat us, we had some time to discuss it. They must of thought somebody would buy a coke.

We were holding a livingroom show that night, and a ticket cost as much as two shitty cheeseburgers. So I was like, we'd just buy burgers anyway, let's make burgers the cost of entry. We had an old photocopy machine we fixed with the guts from a lamp, and we did up new handbills for the Mayor McCheese Monday Massacre, with coupons copied on the back. More punks showed up than we made handbills, and that was the real start of the joke. They copied their own.

We were hardly drunk and there were too many cheeseburgers to fit in the laundry basket. Then we filled up the piranha tank. Then we started pitching them down the stairwell. MDC opened, they changed their name to Millions of Damp Cheeseburgers halfway through the set. They're on tour now. Everybody was skating in patty grease and cracking their foreheads on the coffee table, and some punks were joking, Poison Idea better come through from Portal Land, it'd take Pig Champion to eat all these shitty cheeseburgers.

Actually this crew from Hunnington Beach rolled in during MDC. Palms slamming time on the van dashboard, razorburn skulls bouncing the sun. They weren't in the circle. Nobody knew them. I yelled for some guys to get ballbats, cause HB straight edge skins always took the word massacre literally. But when they hauled open the slide door it wasn't machetes and bike chains, just wheelbarrows heaped up with shitty cheeseburgers in yellow waxpaper. They ripped out the seats and rolled all the way from Hunnington Beach sitting in piles of burgers. On the van floor, you could see handbills stacked in rubber bands.

Void went on next, just after sundown, and the ceiling started cracking midway. That summer the laws finally learned to time their battering ram to the downbeat. If you're pogoing to the slams, there's less time to fix yourself up and look presentable. Nobody really notices the plaster in their hair, and then the song's over and there's a trashcan sized hole in the ceiling. But even back then, I could see out through everybody's Germs burns. Whenever the universe jams up and freezes preparatory to really heavy shit, I've got the perfect view, straight out through your wrist.

A couple people flung bottles and they're blurried from spinning, foam trails behind them, white scraps of ceiling plaster hanging in the air like dorito ghosts. Cross the street, through the front door crack, there's the neighbours with their red eyes poking out the blinds. Everybody's got an arm up to parry the police spotlight, so I can see the copter through the broken roof. It's all beefed out in riot armor with a black visor over the windshield, pretty much a brobdingnagian propeller helmet swinging a wrecking ball on a chain. It's sposed to be Germs getting audited by the laws, not Void, Void could totally play good, so I was like, fuck.

When time lined back up, a riot squad slid down ropes into the livingroom. We stood back a little. We cased out their lectrified antipunk tridents and misdemeanor ticket pads. I figured they were casing out the size of our crew, til one pulled up his visor, and he wasn't even looking at us. Nostrils wiggling like the edge round a fire.

So we purchased freedom with a million shitty cheeseburgers strung on bike locks, and the copter flew off heavy. Far as I know they flew straight home for their own cheeseburger party. Void finished out their set and Bubba Dupree snapped his front teeth eating guitarstrings, up on top where they're wound in the pegs. Void's on tour now. After Fear we played all night long. The lights burned out and we played with the streetlamp hanging through the cracked roof like the moon. Fear's on tour now, and you weren't there. But, like, it was a Germs show, so I was swallowing pills and I got pretty drunk. Next day somebody told me I received the Heimlich maneuver instead of singing Manimal. Everybody was standing waist deep in burgers, yelling for extra songs. So we did the same songs again.

Nobody really slept. Little punk, nobody ever slept. We were at kinkos before the sun came up. We traded burgers for ten million photocopies and pulled them round in a dog kennel cause it had wheels. The mcdonalds lineup went into the horizon, so we cut in line. The coupons were like, SUBJECT TO CHANGE WITHOUT NOTICE, and at first those assholes tried to change it, NO PHOTOCOPIES EITHER. But we changed it back every time. And after a while, some yuppies at the counter even grew shiteating grins. They rubbed secret sauce in their hair and stood it up. They pulled coupons from the till, they climbed over the counter and cut to the front of the line. You know what, nobody bought a coke.

When we got outside, red and yellow tanker trucks were pumping slurry through the spam and cheese and dough holes in the side of the mcdonalds. Some business casual assholes in the trucks were talking to car phones with the cords stretched tight. After they decided shit with the phones, they started wasting the side of the mcdonalds with flamethrowers. But it was the fuckedest thing. Yuppies and punkers both standing in line, they bumrushed those assholes together. Punkers were laughing, but the yuppies just slit their eyes breathing heavy. The assholes went through the spam slurry hatch, shoes included, and then I was like, Hey, gimme those leftover flamethrowers.

Tanker trucks went up and down the street while we walked, shoving cars outa the way. I remember Gerber dancing, Pat blew fire between her legs. Ten million shitty cheeseburgers packed in that dog kennel and we hauled it uphill on a rope. I wrote CIRCLE ONE with grease on every windshield. FOR REAL THE LAST GERMS SHOW, GIANT CHEEZBURGER FUNERAL, BRING ALL YOUR CHEEZBURGERS. We spat chewedup buns on the backs of seagulls, we had a pickle slice frisbee war. Then we walked past the sev, people were yelling and kicking magazine racks cross the tile. Yuppies maybe, maybe punkers. Covered with so many condiments you couldn't tell. They wanted to buy smokes with bags of burgers.

But it's like, if you've got food already, and your moms are paying rent, and you're trading cheeseburgers for photocopying, everything's beer money. So the next couple days were more usual than ever. Couple punks were getting bored of shitty cheeseburgers, there was talk of getting a mayo jar from the store. Sometimes during beer runs we'd see upside down spam pumper trucks on fire, but whatever. The lights went out and the toilet stopped flushing, but we figured the conomy would self compensate, yuppies would use burger money for smokes, raygunonomonomics something something.

But then Lorna was like, we promised those windshields a cheeseburger funeral show. Pat was like, too bad there's no time to get Poison Idea down here. It'd take Pig Champion to bury all those cheeseburgers. And Don was like, let's find a venue.

When we climbed out the basement window, a bus was coming by. Nobody had change so we pulled the rackmount discount. Just stood in the middle of the road hucking burgers in the windshield til it slowed down, and we ran and jumped on the bike rack. Back then time was still money, so nobody'd bother to get out and check for punks caught in the wheels.

Like history says, punkers and yuppies used to eat at Oki Dog together. I don't mean like there was handi fence down the middle and yuppies banging into it. We might not of sat the same tables, but everyone used the same mustard squeezers. You'd look at a yuppie's face and think, I could of been that, while its eyes slid off to your hip pocket or wherever your wallet was. It used to be you could hit up the sev, walking punk with your hands in your pockets and your pockets torn out, and they wouldn't see you for your poverty, not til you started handling the mersh.

Well all through the ride we saw bummedout yuppies, bumping round like they couldn't find their honda civics. They were snuffling and biting their lips for blood, reaming through the trash cans for twenty dollar bills they threw away. We were broke, but they still turned their heads while the bus went by. Fists full of coupons but there were no more shitty cheeseburgers getting made anywhere in the universe.

Germs were still banned from the Whiskey cause we still owed them six hundred bucks for this incident of barrels of crude oil getting split open on the dancefloor. Meanwhile the Masque had elevated levels of radon. So we just jumped off downtown on a street of banks. Nobody was there, just drifts and drifts of yellow styrofoam burger coffins getting swept around in the wind. Banks would mostly smell like air freshers and fake limestone, but this time it was more like cheese and burning fiberglass.

All the bank doors were chained up, with coupons and smashed burgers wadded half underneath, but the building code says there's always a nother way in. Pat was awesome at flamethrowers by then, so he got a windowframe runny while Don Bolles lifted it out of the bricks with a coat hanger. After we got to the second floor we could hang a rope off the fire scape. It was a real clusterfuck lifting all those PA systems and gas cans and yacht batteries up all the flights of external fire stairs, and we had to temporarily sew our ass cheeks together cause it was the week of shitty cheeseburgers, but this all happened back in the day. Hardcore actually meant something back then, it wasn't just a tag.

Afterward we got on the air with Rodney Bingenheimer from the radio. We all yelled in the payphone ear how Germs was headlining a cheeseburger funeral, tonight only, on top of the bank tower. Rodney was like, what bout the laws, and Pat was like, that's why we're playing on a copter helipad, we don't want to make it tough on them, it's already the end of western civilization.

We climbed back up for naptime in the PA shade. When we woke up some crews were waiting. Hellin Killer was there. She said she had a feeling so she took time off from her life forever. She had a little greasefire built, with cheeseburgers spitted on a car antenna. Some punks would eat from the top of the fire, some punks would eat from the bottom. Mold wouldn't hit those burgers nor would the sun fade them. They were golden brown eternal.

More punks kept crawling up the fire scape. We'd haul them up the last bit of the way but nobody said much really. They just undid the trashbags off their belts, tipped their backpacks onto the helipad. Pretty soon there was a cheeseburger mountain bigger than Poison Idea's tour bus. It looked like a commercial for heaven. Everybody had a feeling, like it was more a benefit show than a farewell show. Nobody could say the benefit, that's all.

After we got sick of standing around, I hit Pat in the arm and he kicked me in the leg. He started making something up. Like chords or something. It wasn't any Germs song, it sounded more like a big flag coming apart in the wind. Lorna was looking down at her bass, picking one note over and over with her thumb, like before we taught each other to play. Then she put her bass down and she kicked her shoes off the roof. Closed her eyes and she kneeled down, just hitting the strings with her hands. I had some lyrics on a napkin in my pocket.

Even with the gas cans and the flamethrowers, the cheeseburger pile never caught. A few turned black and got shrank, that's all. The sky went so red nobody could see the puddles of gas flaming and a couple punks caught their heads on fire. They had to roll themselves out in the burgers while the sunset chilled out on top of the pile and bent and broke up and down in the smog and the wind off everybody's amps. You weren't there.

After that Don was like, let's do one we can do. We'd of played Circle One, for old names broken and dead ends on fire and the shape of a pure all beef patty, but first everybody had to duck. There seriously was a riot copter. It buzzed through low with the headlights off, skidded sideways into the cheeseburger mountain and just sagged there like a kid in a ballpit. The rotors kept chopping, spraying burger mist in everybody's hair. So we all started to cheer.

You know we built this stage for the farewell show of Lost Angeles. You know the floor's greasy perma with the leftovers of western civilization, the ghost of every shitty cheeseburger, ineradicable by rain. Ineradicable means it's still there. So think how tall the spam works used to rise before tonight. How far down the sides used to drop, to where cars used to run in the road. Think how loud the Antidisestablishmentarianism went, cause we heard the car wrecks and sirens from the sky.

The laws in the copter wore sideways helmets and their armor was all smashed up in blood. They had no clue of getting out. They were straining against their seatbelts, banging their faces on the dashboard. They were the newschool yuppies of the youth of today, fucked completely vacant with hunger and no conomy of money left to feed it, just diy hardcore looking at them through the copter windshield glass.

Nobody knew where to take it really, but Hellin thought it was like the last show, maybe cheeseburgers would help. But when she reached forward the law yuppies just snapped and freaked at her hand. She pulled back, and Pat was like, I bet a flamethrower would help.

Behind the back of the circle there's a voice like a barrel of pickled black lectrocardiograms on fire. Best thing's a giant cleaver, he says. No point less you kill the brain.

And course the crowd made way.

There where I'm pointing, past the lip of the roof, you could see his head bob up and down as the fire stairs bent under him. His face wide as the road from your lifeline to your elbowvein. His shades one piece, typhoon black, near splitting as they reach across his head. His beard's stuck through with pickle slices, chunks of yuppie bone. I reached down and passed him my hands, and I ripped off my left arm hauling up Pig Champion.

I said, what's it like in Portal Land, and he was like, they're outa burgers, Darby. Germs play yet?

And Pig leaned into that copter and chopped holes in their riot helmets laughing. One yuppie nipped him in the fingertip, he pulled up his hand, and there's such thing as biting off a bitewound. That moment we saw the hardcore of the universe, it never showed itself clear before. Pig Champion spat out his own knuckles and his laugh was the thunder that made it rain.

You know if I had a nother arm I'd of took Germs on tour right when Pig fucked off with Poison Idea. But I had to ask Pat and Lorna and Don to go without me. So they left me here to get old like an old guy, talking history to little punks, soulless and solo and sole.

If you're drunk and you achieve lightenment it kills your drunk. The fucked thing was I liked it. But I still don't remember how the show went after that. They say it was the best Germs show, I dunno. I just woke up with Black Flag eating my cheeseburger mattress. Pig was saying how the riot squad would give us the squirts cause we left them out overnight, we should sneak down careful and kill something fresh. History was full of onetime shit like that. You don't get to see it again.

∧∧∧

But here. Here. This tourist brochure of a sunrise. Leaching up through the hollow skyline with blurred peach and blue gradients in the empty condo windowholes. Palmtrees drooling rain, tilting from the tops of buildings like black paper cutouts, their edges swimming in the shivering light. Doesn't the whole thing look totally airbrushed?

Nah. You're looking at the washedblack patch sewn to the leather over his heart. And the legend drops his fingers slowly. "That's not how it ends."

He turns a barbecue flipper through the edge of the blistered coals. He looks out at nobody. His eyes are crossed, his voice sinks a little. "I don't need sleep anymore."

The fire's mostly diyed back, leaving an ember field the size of a couple king mattresses. The scaffolds are still half full, all those reliable kids with the fluffous hair and dark leather and interwoven safetypins. Leaning in, glazed out. They start stirring and cheering, beating their docs on the bleacher, and the first one to rise, Darby just looks at her, and she sags with hands folded in her lap.

Donn's there too. Eyes red but not slitted. Spose you don't sleep neither, man, if you've got something to think. He's crosslegged at the bleacher's base, nursing a crooked joint. Time to time he rubs at his wrist, rubs the gray circle scar with his thumb.

Darby stands, he takes a breath and squints over at the sunrise. "We all used to meet at Oki Dog for afterward. It was open all night." As his last word falls, quavering like an old dude's voice, his eyes whip out into Donn's. Faster than you've seen them move all through this history spiel.

Hey, if you're gonna stand in Donn's viewpoint, go easy. Punker might start to magine Darby in turn. All right for Donn, but you're still a tourist. Don't ever drop guard round the legend. You member, if he sees you, he'll blow you out.

Yeah. Stay this far back. Darby's pointing into the blurry sun. Donn slants his head and passes the joint, not looking. Nobody takes it. Nobody's there. His lips move silently.

—That guy's your buddy? Donn O. Aural? Fuck's that mean?

—*It's cause he fixes sound gear.*

—*O's for Orville Reddenbocker.*

Darby's going, "Out in West Holly Wood where nobody can get to anymore. Could of been shitting lightning out, didn't matter. We'd find each other at Oki Dog, cause punkers went there. They wrap your meat in this brown towel that's like one grease blotch. Rub it on your boots and run and slide down the tile."

He stops, shakes his head. "Yeah. We said bye to Oki Dog at the cheeseburger funeral show. You can't make it out there now, not less you're on tour. But all you guys should fuck off. I'm going to get down here and meditate."

Donn's lifting himself up when something white arcs through the air, lodges in his earcanal. He spazzes and then he's staring at a smoldering mallburrow slim pinched in his fingers. Darby just nods to himself, not looking over, and Donn licks his dry lips. He eases back down and crawls crabstyle under the bleacher.

—*Man, shut up, Mikey. It's a Germs O. You know it stands for nothing.*

Over by the sleepy fire Darby's bumping fists, sending his kids off. Donn keeps pointing the emberous mallburrow slim at the fadedout burn on his wrist, pushing it in and away. His dreads shake and he laughs a little laugh through his teeth.

∧∧∧

"You figure Donn's still up there with him?" Mikey's got his boot on a yuppie's throat. The bruised earless face jerks and snaps, keeping steady with punker's gaze. From the shoulders down, the whole yuppie's missing.

"Jealous," says Raffia.

Arco only keeps greasing Margin Walker with a blackened chamois. The katanablade's a long subtle unremarkable curve, dull steel refusing to shine back the sun. It looks like somebody shaded it with a pencil. Like a building's rib bone, something substructural, unintended for public display.

They're all covered in concrete dust, peering up a jagged mountain of gray rusty debris. Up top, there's the scaffold bleacher with its flapping pillar of smoke. It's the same stage as before, same cancerblack emissions rising off the same econosize firepit, but now the skyscraper underneath's a mound of rubble.

Mikey pivots his steeltoe in the yuppie's mouth. Teeth snap with the traditional noises. Its eyes don't widen. Nothing like that.

"I can't believe they did that."

"Oh, the spam works?" says Raffia. "Fucking crash trash. Where do we make spam now?"

"How does Darby get his crew to take their hands and rip down the biggest building in core?" Mikey's gritting his eyes as if there's wind. "Like, just with his mouth, man!"

Arco's like, "Do you know a nother way for the world to be?"

⋀⋀

Find Donn sitting in the sloppy moss pile, the recovery room under the bleachers. One hand fishing behind him and it comes back crudded with vintage Darby Crash blood.

Donn's like, "Do you want your smoke back?"

"I'm really pologetic bout the end of the show," says Darby, leaning through the gap between bleacher seats. "Like, I should better pologize private to everybody in turn."

Donn's like, "I just don't smoke."

"It's been so long since my last show, it was like so selfish of me." Darby's finger traces a line across his forehead. Like he's zipping, maybe unzipping, his mind. "I just had such a wicked time. I sung it alright, hey?"

"Yeah. Yeah, man! Yeah."

"You're nice to tell me that, Donn. It's just, I'm always flashing back, like in my memory of being Germs. And trying to decide if I'd still be good." Darby looks from side to side cross the empty hilltop. Sits down on the bleacher and leans to face Donn. His chin's nested in his bandaided shoulder. "I thought I'd never do a show til my farewell. Man, when I got bit, I mean not Raspberries, that yuppie out in the burbs, I was happy. That was my first thought. Now I can play a show."

"Really?" Donn moves the burning mallburrow slim toward his pocket, then tucks it back into his earcanal.

"You guys are called Meatheads still, hey?" says Darby. "Yeah. I enjoy that name. I was playing with you and I stopped thinking bout me. Or bout how it was a farewell show anyway. I was thinking like I had a band again."

"I was honored to—"

"And then I'd breathe in and out. And in between breathing that's all I could think of, I can't bear it if this doesn't keep going. And I was like, if I have to stop, the band has to too. And so I was a brat." Darby takes a breath.

"I thought you guys were my band. I'm really shitty bout that kind of thing. And your band is really tight. So tight. You're like the only decent band in town right now."

"It's okay," says Donn. "I'm sorry for your arm."

"Why?" says Darby.

Donn just looks at him and goes, "I'm practicing compassion."

Darby goes, "Then you mean sorry bout my arm. Not for. It's not like my dead arm cares."

"But, like." Donn's got this weird brief guilty look. "But your arm knew how to do all this technical stuff as part of your memory. Like compared to your other arm even. It's got memory nerves like your brain, right? And peopleses arms gesture different between left and right. And have different shock reactions. If your arm was a dog I'd be sad if a tiger bit it."

"You're fucked, Donn. You're the fucked one." Darby laughs.

Donn's like, "How did you get bit anyway?"

"Shit luck." Darby slips his little finger in his mouth, starts sucking. Then he tips his chin up. You can't stop looking, Donn, and he's like, "What?"

∿∿∿

"I can't hardly look at Darby now," says Mikey.

Arco's like, "You seemed cool with him before." Turning away from the horizon, she squints into an alleyway, her brow minutely lining.

"No. Well, kind of," says Mikey. "Doesn't matter though, it's a sitch. You guys don't give a shit he sicked the crowd on us?"

"What, you're some pussy who gives one bout getting ripped apart?" Raffia sticks out her tongue and fiddles with the hammers in her sash. Her thumbnail pries at a skull clot on a mallethead. "Go cry in the big black void."

"I don't want to go down in a big pile of smashed punks where their only problem was they jumped me." Mikey blinks. "That good a nuff? Dude, it's really a sitch."

"What's a sitch?" says Raffia. Mikey looks round and whispers, "Situation."

"I don't think he'd do it again, man." Arco sheaths Margin Walker, clasps her hands over her solar plexus. "It just came up in the moment."

"What bout his next farewell show?" says Mikey. Arco's like, "Why don't you trust him, punker?"

"Good one," says Mikey. "Why don't you trust me?"

MM

Darby pats the empty seat beside him once.

"What'd Mikey do?" Under the bleacher, Donn reaches up and grabs a plank. Hauls himself up between rows of seats as Darby scootches closer.

"Aw, I don't know," says Darby. "I wanted to see if I could trust him with a secret."

"Oh." Donn's got his thumbnail scratching lines in the plank seat. It's still raining blood, feathery little mist like you threw iron filings in a humidifier. Ventually he's like, "I don't know any secrets."

Darby's still staring out at the skyline, half over his shoulder. Wherever he's been looking all night. "That's modest," he says. "A secret doesn't need to be drama. It can just be a thing bout your feelings."

Donn's like, "But it's Arco's straight edge to sterminate secrets, and I'm in a band with her. So what I say goes out. Like for solidarity."

"Ah, yeah," says Darby. "And there's nothing you keep back from the band? Not like Mikey with his showing up late?"

"No, man. No. Nothing. We're a band." Donn stops and pulls up his hand. This brown splinter laying bloody under his thumbnail, like a jammed compass needle. "Mikey just showed up late cause he needed a hat for his brain."

"Oh yeah, he said that to you. Guess it was really stressing him out." Darby yawns, and then Donn's like, "What?"

"No, it's cool," says Darby. "But talking's good for time. If you won't tell me a secret, tell me something else. What's the fuckedest thing in the world, Donn?"

"What, like in the tour spiel of Flag?" Donn's pressing the knuckles of his hands together. "I don't think absolutes are absolute. Isn't that the spiel lesson?"

Darby turns completely away. Faces the same mapless point on the horizon and breathes in really deep. "There's no lessons, man." He looks back at Donn. "No, I want you to talk bout it."

"I was telling you a secret?" Donn rubs his thumb in the red corner of his eye. "Maybe it's consciousness."

"Then argue the mystery of consciousness to me, jenius. Now I'm old, and I can ask for certain things." Darby smiles. His yellow teeth shine, and his eyes shine, and they're the same thing. "Show me your hardcore."

—*Show me your hardcore.* Have you heard that one yet? His voice prickles the back of your neck. You don't got a neck. You're disembodied.

ＭＭＭ

There's this shape like a weightlifter scarecrow in a big straw hat, swaying zigzag down the hill, making clacking noises. Raffia claps Arco between the shoulders. "Hey, I think we know her!"

"Yeah, it's his mom," says Arco.

"Hey, what's up Mikey Smom! Hey, over here, Mom!" Raffia crosses and uncrosses her arms over her head. Mikey's just standing there doing a deep breathing exercise or something, chewing his lip.

"Fuck are you all doing up? Can't sleep after such a noise riot?" says Mikey's mom. She's wearing a host of hard mummified frogs bangled in her hair and ears and around her neck and everything. All the frogs have little safetypins through their noses. They clack as she turns her head from side to side. "Little punk heroes, fucking little punk heroes!"

"We saw the motion of yuppies down this way, Mrs Mikey. We think the fence must be busted somewhere." Arco gives a little bow, like a soft headbang.

"Aw, who cares?" says Mikey's mom. She lifts her hand to her eye, scratches the circleshaped newschool Germs burn. Her crispy flesh outs red and yellow seepage. "Fuck, my fucking eye!"

"Man, you totally look like your mom," says Raffia, arms crossed. "Same giant shoulders and then like the weird I-beam shaped body. Do you cry bout looking like your mom, Mikey?"

"Aw, don't listen to her, kiddo." Mikey's mom spreads her hands. "She just wants to wear you down emotionally, so she can get a nother taste of your dick. But, like, doncha got a show tomorrow?"

Mikey's like, "No. Oh. I guess."

"Shit, we forgot," says Raffia. "Arco, you didn't forget, did you?"

"I can't just hitler the fuck out of you telling you when to sleep," says Arco.

"Oh, Darby!" says Mikey's mom. Mikey spins around but it's just a saying, and meanwhile his mom's stepped in close. She's pinching a nerve cluster in his neck so his arms go saggy while she rubs the sofahide patch over his brain, and he's like, "Mom!"

"You got part of your skull out?" says his mom. "That's so wicked! It's like down the middle between your hawks!"

He's like, "Mom!"

She's like, "Can I see your brain? Take off that stupid little piece of leather, the staples are infected anyway. It's so awesome. What's it feel like? Are you smarter?"

Mikey's like, "I'm going to bed, there's a show tomorrow."

ΛΛΛ

"It's hard to talk about," says Donn. "Do you want your mallburrow slim back?"

Darby's like, "No, you should smoke. Cause it's good to smoke while you talk bout consciousness."

"I don't—"

"What, you got the straight edge?"

"No, it's just like I don't smoke."

Darby's swiveled around on the plank seat to face Donn straight on. He leans back, further, further, like creating this growing negative space between them.

Blink.

"Okay." Darby sits up. "Keep it though. It hasn't burned down any. Tell me the whole thing."

"The whole thing?" says Donn.

"We all understand it a different way. But if you tell me the whole thing, I can parse the limits of your mind," says Darby.

Donn winces. Then starts gesturing with the smoke, like somebody flipped a switch. "Some forms of the universe are conscious. Some aren't. The punkers are the primo conscious forms. There's experiences happening inside you and me. Or like, kind of inside. Like, a mirror has seeing power, kinda. The way it xeroxes a little slice of universe. But it doesn't see the seeing. Or words on a wall can be a thought, but not a thinking."

"Yuppies." Darby taps his face, there between the eyes.

"Yeah. I guess we almost are. It's like, if consciousness stayed inside us, we'd all just be ego. We'd be doomed. Ego's just the shit part of consciousness that's trapped in its own meatweb. The rest of our awareness plays around through the nearby universe, occupying patterns of the environment. It's like core . . . we're part of core, but all these buildings are too. Core's a lot like consciousness cause they're both outside us mainly. Wherever we diy, that's where they're both made."

Watch Darby's thick chest breathe in and out. Same as it must of been doing all night. As if one jump in the rhythm's what you really noticed.

"Yuppies," he says.

"Hey, I'm sorry. I know it sucks for you." Then you're putting your hand out. Super awkward, Donn. You're touching his poulticed stub shoulder. Darby's just looking out at the same indefinite thing while the skyline melts higher in the sun. His lips smack a little, and you're like, "Do you want me to keep going?"

"This miserable burnout says sorry, Donn." Darby smiles with half his mouth and the cheek under his missing eye. "I was just staring at Oki Dog."

"I thought that was just a rainbow," says Donn.

"No. Yuppies?" says Darby again. "Shit, Donn, it's like our last conversation. The one bout compassion."

"I don't remember that. Was I tired?" Donn stops and goes on. "It's like, we're the same form of matter, us and yuppies. A few things are different annatomatoatomically. Their blood doesn't move and they don't breathe, cause of capitalism. Yuppies got the same brains as punkers, but no awareness. We know that, cause they only go after us. If they were conscious they'd go after each other. But it's not like the brain changes much when a punker turns into a yuppie. We need our brains for balancing and muscle organizing and shit, so do they. Cause when they get brain damage, they stop working right, same as us. It's like there's some special patternating of lectricity in your brain meat. Like a program running on a computer chip. Something happens lectrically in your brain and it propagates consciousness. It can habitate other places temp. Like how siking works, or just perception. The mystery is how the patternation—"

Darby's holding out two fingers, slightly curled. He snorts. Donn breathes a ghost out. Punker's eyes cross, he holds his dreads back and he's staring down at his own mouth. Coughing and coughing. You figured mallburrow slims would get tough to find in the trackless jungle, tourist? Just hang with the legend more.

When Darby pulls the smoke from Donn's mouth, his nails pinch Donn's chapped lips. "Yuppies," he says again. He milks the mallburrow slim for a bit, blowing out elegantly through his nose.

"Whoa. Yeah. Where did my mind go?" says Donn.

"Yuppies." Darby passes the smoke back. After a couple breaths, Donn takes it.

"No," says Donn. "Not quite. I mean, I was still conscious. Just not—"

"Just not aware of your environment, nor of your ego neither? That's not consciousness. Yuppies, man. You know that's an acid smoke, right? Yuppies."

"There are acid smokes?" says Donn. He holds it vert near the top, squinting. Read the faded pink lettering round the filter tip. *1% ACID BY WEIGHT. CONTENTS MAY OF SETTLED DURING SHIPPING. SST RECORDS.*

"No, yuppies. But it's all good," says Darby. "It's Germs acid. Do you need to go to bed? This is just like the last conversation we had. The one about compassion. Gimme a smoke."

Now he's talking while he holds your smoke. Shit, shit. Don't let him see you're on acid. Don't let him know you're there, tagging along behind Donn's eyes. White noise seeps opaquely from the smoke's top and bottom. "How do things work, Donn?"

"They work?" Donn licks your lips. His lips. "Work on what?"

"You know, the Dharma. Yuppies. How do things work?"

"No, not yuppies." When Donn's head moves, Darby's face blurs and lengthens to compensate. Only the legend's yellow teeth hanging still, centered in your visual field like they're anchored to something metaphysically pertinent. "Connections. Things work cause they're connected up. And the universe is connected."

"Aren't you super cool on acid, Donn. Yuppies and the myriad interconnectionisms of the Dharma!" Darby's fingers dropping slow through the air like a magnified, scarred thicky of spiderweb. "Every dharma connected, everything subinterposed cross time. Shake your hair out and the universe rimples and rimples til everything's been afflicted."

Your voice goes, "Yeah."

"That's how it works, right?" says Darby. "Yuppies and the Dharma and all the little dharmas interpissing cross the existential void. That's how it works."

Your voice goes, "Yeah. So—"

"So yuppies." Darby Crash rolls the filter end round in his empty eyesocket. The slow cherry burning harder than the sunrise. "So consciousness affects nothing. It's not integrated. It just hangs out like a tourist and doesn't pitch in. Like how you took your smoke, but you weren't there. You think that mattered for the smoke?"

"What, like yuppies?" says your voice. "We're not yupp—"

"The only thing consciousness affects," says Darby. "Is yuppies. Yuppies. Like you said. Yuppies smell it out so we can see where it is. But what if there weren't yuppies?"

You're rubbing your knuckles into your forehead, Donn, and feeling them sink right into your skull. You can visualize how your forehead is getting visualized by you as a silver reflecting pool in a wizard lab. Focus. Don't get paranoid. You know it's weird hanging out with Darby. "Are you saying consciousness would be like a busted off part of the Dharma? Cause it has no parts to link up?"

"No, you're saying it," says Darby. "That's your mystery of consciousness."

"I just meant I didn't know how it worked." You look down at the sweat on your fingers. No, man, your fingers are way dry. Pull back. Seriously. Don't be there, not so close. Just think.

"It could mean a different thing than I think," says Donn. Slow. "Like the word. Consc. Ious. Ness. It could break down."

Nothing moves in Darby's face sept one nostril delicately flaring. Behind his head, in the blind horizon, the busted windows shine and shine. "What could be its parts?" he says. "Cause what's in it isn't part of it. Like what you said bout words and seeing mirrors. They don't need consciousness. It's just a tourist, man, it's not real."

The wind's crawling through his hair like a melted halo. Darby from history who pulled hardcore from his ass. Darby who dropped acid behind Oki Dog and gave Pat Smear his name. Darby who knew John Doe and Black Randy. Darby who smashed the window of history with Hellin and Gerber, Robo and Pig and McEye. The last first one, Darby Crash, Darby who was there.

∧∧∧

"It's just like our consciousness conversation," he's saying. "The one where we talked bout the parts of consciousness?"

You can feel Donn's tongue press a sharp crack running up his front tooth. You're like, "What?" There's some space, and then you're like, "That's where we are this time."

"What's your damage, man? I told you this Germs acid would play tricks." Darby rolls his head lazily from shoulder to bandaided shoulder. His eyes lock right into yours. "You were saying this weird thing bout how compassion couldn't exist less you sected it into parts. So what would its parts be?"

"The parts of compassion," says your voice. "Oh, fuck. Is that, like, there's the parts of compassion?" Look down at the mallburrow slim, burning but not burnt. No ash on the cherry even. Darby closes his lips and smiles and it's the first time in so long you can't see his teeth. Smiling means pass the smoke so you pass the smoke.

"I knew you had a secret," says Darby. "Do you want a real Germs burn?"

You just look down at your wrist. Donn's thumb's covering it up. That's your thumb. Is that compassion? Like, if somebody knows where your thumb is?

"Cause you know it's not a Germs burn if you do it to yourself. Even if we are friends," says Darby. "It's only in the bloodline if somebody with a real burn ministers it."

"How do you know the difference?" Now you're sitting on Donn's hands. "I did it before I even moved out."

"Cause I can't see shitall out your wrist." Darby closes his eyes. "Man, I knew you had a secret. Here. Just steady the arm out."

Donn's holding his arm out, staring. "I oughta go to bed."

Darby points the acid smoke's orange ember at the old burn scar, and Donn loosely grabs the legend's wrist. Maybe he's just holding it steady. You'd need to have compassion, figuring that one out.

"You just can't be in my band without a burn," says Darby.

"I'm already in a band," says Donn. "I oughta go to bed."

"Yeah, every punker's in a band," says Darby. Your hand glides with his hand, Donn, the cherry into your wrist. Through the vintage scar. "They're all my band."

It hurts, but no worse than the next thing. Smoke plumes out the filter end like there's a ghost back there taking a drag.

"I invented this shit, don't ever forget who you're talking with. I made Lost Angeles diy."

∧∧∧

Mikey hasn't had bedposts since he was five and he moved out of his mom's friend's mom's place to start a band with his band and ride down the fire scape in shopping carts. These days he mostly sleeps in a roomsize puddle of woven grass blanket, shag carpet, bandmates and disintegrating sweatshirts. Man, if you've smoked your forehead on a bedpost you've got to be five. Don't let anybody know you count years. Just roll over and splore with your hand. There's two scruffy bedposts standing a handswidth apart, carved out of teak or something, melding up top in a decorative knurl like two cast iron bike helmets welded together.

Raffia's like, "Don't touch my ass. We can fuck, just don't wake me up."

"People lie down to sleep, Raff." Mikey takes his fingers, snaps the crust over his eyes. She's balanced with her feet on the bedpile and her forehead nestled in a dent in the plaster. Her armor's off, so she was having either sex or surgery.

"Hurts too much to lie down." She starts hammering her neck with the heel of her hand. Each blow brings a crack like a knot exploding in firewood. Then she's snoring again.

Mikey unsnarls the blankets, checks his dick. All bruised purple round the root. He nods.

Donn's writhing round slowmo in one corner of the blanket nest with his face completely hidden under a pyramid of scratched black raybans. Giant quadrophonic headphones on his ears with their stripped cabling stuck directly into the power outlet in the corner. On the table there's a sombrero full of puke. Mikey groans and turns on his side, pushes his head under some blankets. A squarish shadow of oily maroon light's falling into the room between the bunched naugahyde curtains. The decorative black mold wallpaintings are so overgrown you can hardly tell they're cactuses playing guitars. It's a nother dumb rainy day.

∧∧∧

Donn raises himself on one arm while half the raybans slip and clatter off his face. The nother five or six pairs of shades waggle as he moves. They're stacked sideways from his head like this black plastic tower from a poorly sembled boardgame. He belches weakly and rubs his cheek with his fist. There's fluff caught on his teeth.

Hey, Arco. Crosslegged, her back to the wall. Her head's already shaved fresh. "Hey, bandmate."

"Mmh. Darby gave me acid. I mean, me and Darby did acid." Donn tilts the rayban tower up. It moves as one unit. There's fluff caught on his eyes. "I did the acid acid and was on acid with Darby."

"Yeah, you look like you're on acid."

Donn's like, "Sorry, but you look kind of threatening feeling. To me. For the time being."

Arco shrugs. "You want some antacid?"

"That's not what it does," says Donn. She throws him the bottle, and he goes, "That's really compassionate."

Arco's like, "I guess."

"Is this conversation awkward?" says Donn. Arco shrugs again. "Not for me."

"Sorry." Donn tips an antacid onto his palm. Licks the little white pill and sticks it to his forehead. Sticks two more beside it. "These are its head, thorax and antobmen. It's an antacid acid ant."

"Mikey would want to hear that," says Arco. "He went back to sleep."

"Should I show him?" says Donn. "I guess of course not. Hey, what are you thinking about?"

"How to diy," says Arco. "Recycling my mind, right."

Donn stretches his neck from side to side. The motion yanks his big gray headphones out of the power socket and he picks up the stripped cabling and stares at it while pixelated sparks roll up and down the socketslits. He goes, "Should I start meditating in the morning again?"

Arco doesn't shift posture. She's really rad at sitting. "I was thinking bout being Mikey and reaching a grapefruit spoon into my brain. Scooping out a big chunk of brain through the burrhole and catching an artery so the blood comes up like a strawflower. So I'm bleeding out with my brain in my hand. Not knowing what it's thinking. While it bleeds out not knowing the same."

"Yeah." Donn's all curled up, pressing his fist into his stomach. "Talking to you is just really intense."

"When I'm you it's almost by my hand." Arco's talking lowthroated and lucid. You can almost hear wind chimes. "I'll meditate on us all surrounded in a baseball diamond of yuppies. Nowhere to take cover. I zip up my goretex, so they can't bite through, and sit down while Arco and Mikey and Raffia book it. I'm siking right on my torso. They dogpile me and I'm sitting crosslegged. I take a long time diying cause they're biting my torso through my jacket and I bleed to death from bruises. At the end I can't even breathe or see."

A belch slithers up Donn's throat. He closes his eyes and goes, "Thanks. It's just, like, I did acid, and like, compassion. Yuppies—"

"If I'm Raffia I'll be clouded in rage," says Arco. "So pissed I'm chopping myself with my roofinghammer. I'm chopping the hatchet into my shins, and then my knees. Chips of bone fly everywhere. I'm so pissed I'm having strokes and I feel my brain veins let go and squirt black into my eyes. Rage is my charge even after I fall over and I stop feeling myself. I can smell the bonfire and there's like ghost cushions under me, I know I'll wake up on their couch, and even then rage is still my charge."

"This meditation's sposed to make you feel balanced and centered, right?" Donn's still half curled up. He's looking down at his leg.

"There's no sposed. You just sit. You will diy." Arco nods politely. "When

I'm me I diy in a duel. I'm running toward somebody better. Siko Miko. Harley of Cro-Mags. Kira of Flag. My sword turns in my hand and I can't see my face and they cut me in half. But I'm still running. I can't see you guys and I've dissolved you from my mind. The pain's in one hip bone and up cross my guts. It's a cool and dull pain with a sick edge from the cut. It gets hotter and pukier when I start to slide apart. The tubes of my testines are coming unstuck as my legs run and I can feel the chewedup food drain from my stomach. I'm—"

Donn lunges for the puke sombrero on the bedside table. Splashes it all across Arco's jersey and in the same motion he stabs his solar plexus on the table corner and crumples forward.

Arco frowns. "Is the antacid working?"

⋀⋀⋀

Course you haven't stood yet in Arco's stance. Try or don't try, you still slip off the outside of her mind. She doesn't know. She doesn't know you're there to throw you, tourist. The judo twist that slips you, it's your own.

What made you come back to this place? The human flesh cheaper here? You figured you'd soak in the edgy customs, the despoiled scenery? Maybe you'd pick up some words of the language? Sit in on a couple quaint history spiels? Arco doesn't know shit, but at least she doesn't think it's easy.

Poser, poser, forger of poses, follower, trendoid, oogle, prentice to ego. Hungry ghost blitting cross the short waves, born a whole day and still it thinks it's real. Are you even into hardcore?

Sure, tourist, just wait outside. Just watch where she's watching.

Arco's got her back to the bedroom wall, hands on her knees. She shifts her shoulders carefully, like there's a trick for cracking her scapulae or the membrane round her heart. She lids her eyes. You're buried in weight and soft black earth. No you aren't. You're crashing twistedly through skylights. No you aren't. You're sideways on a peeling dumpster floor with your groin split apart. No you aren't, and Arco's frowning minutely.

You're not these places. But you want her to be?

⋀⋀⋀

Mikey sits up like a situp. His grin's sickleshaped, abrupt and gone. "You saw where my leather went. Right?"

"It's under you," says Arco. As if no time's passed. Raffia's still standing, snoring, and Donn's kicking his legs around in some kind of blanket fort. Mikey pulls and shoves bedstuff aside. He lifts the leather by its sleeve and feels at the inside heartside pocket.

"What's up with your jacket?" says Arco.

"Not at liberty to say." He puts it back under him. "Donn. Want to harvest us a fruit salad from the spension bridge garden?"

Donn slides out from the blanket fort. "It fell down."

"Yeah, I meant you could climb down the spension bridge wreckage on the side of the condo. Most of the planters are still there. Take your mind off the acid hangover."

"The sensory deprivation chamber was for checking for bad sectors and memory leaks." Donn stands, then falls backward into his blanket fort. Then he's like, "Okay."

As the door closes behind Donn, Mikey goes, "So Darby's same as ever. Did you see Donn got a burn on his wrist?"

Arco shifts to lotus posture. "Yeah, it's right over the old one."

"Like we didn't fuck with him nuff bout the old one," says Mikey. "Who needs double Germs burns?" He picks himself up, throws the jacket over a chair and sits down by Arco. Back to the wall. "I don't like how close he goes to Darby."

"I know," says Arco.

"Last night he tried to kill us just to make the show better." Mikey spreads his hands at Raffia sleeping. "Now everybody's cool with it! Him and Donn snuggled all night doing acid."

"That was probly Darby saying sorry," says Arco. "Could be why Donn took a new burn. Like to seal the pology."

"Everybody's cool with it," says Mikey.

"Yeah." Arco sounds comprehensive. "It was for a statement. Darby's got nothing against us. Would of been a rad message too. They'd all of felt awkward the next day, killing us for no reason. Beats taking a shit on stage."

"You know stage shits are classic." Muscles slip and move inexpressively inside Mikey's face. "But who cares. Point is he wants us gone. Like, we'll see him before the show, he'll tell us how awesome we are, and like, how we should go on tour before we lose it."

"Then we'll hear it and deal with it," says Arco. "I know you don't feel like touring. Are you sure you're not paranoid? You used to love Darby."

"Meta Curtains just went on tour, Failure To Thrive fucked off, I know you miss Cam Ping and Colin Sick. Member when Ethel Alcohol rode the last cow off the balcony? I could see your goosebumps."

"So?" says Arco.

Mikey gets up and slips his jacket on. Tugs it half off again. Big guy with his hawks kinked, just standing there looking silly wasted, covered with flakes of woven grass blanket. He sighs. "So we're the best band in the world or he wouldn't of picked us. Or tried to kill us. So we're due for tour."

"We don't have to go on tour, man. Not til we all feel ready. Like if we ever are. Do you want to sit here and do the diying meditation with me?"

"I am sitting down. Oh." Mikey sits on his hands. "I don't like that one right now. It doesn't get me ready to diy. More like ventilate hyperly."

"What would you of showed the crash trash last night, Mikey? Before you passed out and got peed on."

He doesn't answer. Picks a long brownish scrap from his back teeth, licks it off his thumb. Chewing slowly. Not meditatively. Slowly.

"You got history with Darby," says Arco. "Could be hardcore to consider that before you make a call."

Mikey looks across the room. Walks out and touches the red sunbeam passing through the curtains. He makes like to boot Raffia, then pulls back. "Darby lied to me really big."

Arco's eyes don't move. "What about?"

"I don't want to let it out," says Mikey. Arco's like, "You feeling it embarrass you?"

"Sure," says Mikey. "But he'd take me down if he knew what happened. And if I tell you or Donn, it'll come back around to him. And if I tell Raff, she'll throw a hammer through my chest."

"You can sit on it, then," says Arco. "If sitting's not worse." She shrugs. "We could get you hangover breakfast. And help you look for your lid."

"Breakfast," says Mikey. "Wait." He prods the patch job over his skull. "Fuck. I lost my lid."

"If you put your finger under there, it might get black mold," says Arco. "Hey. If you staple there it goes through your brain."

Mikey hucks the stapler under the bedside table. "If you didn't have the straight edge, you could just tell me to do things."

"Thanks," says Arco. Then she's like, "Did you still want to get up?"

Mikey rubs his eyes. He's lying down again. "Fuck. You said you need hangover breakfast?"

"No hangover. I got the straight edge."

"Oh."

"I'd do solid darity breakfast."

∿∿

"**N**o way you've never noticed these." Donn takes the pitcher in both hands, bangs it against the dumpster. Bugs and blood slosh penumbrously inside its transparent flesh. "They've existed since the Devonian period."

Raffia folds her arms. "They're new."

With the rustholes for a trellis, the pitcherplant's vined itself cross the whole dumpster, extruded bout a dozen bigbellied jugs with hollow little arms and legs. They nod and grin impartially on the ends of their tendrils, rain beading red on their waxy hides.

"Okay," says Donn. "But only if I can boil it as a soup."

"Like with your soup machine?" Raffia squeezes the jug. "I guess. But you gotta eat the whole rind."

"Course." His hands are fishing in his baggy cargopockets. "Hey, what if I put in an egg?"

"No egg. It's hangover breakfast. It's not to make you feel better."

"I'll eat it after." Donn tosses the egg in his hand, bounces it, picks it from the air. He rubs his eyes. "I smell wintermint chewing gum under that bench."

"Fucking crash trash, you always gotta make it dirty." Raffia grabs his wrist, squeezes the fresh burn. "I'm stewing the gum in your soup."

∿∿

All those yuppies Mikey did yesterday on the fishing trip? Arco's got the legs off them, slit them with a big garasuki knife and pulled bones from the softening corpsemeat. Femurs, patellas, tibias and fibias stacked on a chrysler stump, next to a heap of gelatinous yellow gut and ass tallow. The steak's expired, but the rest's still okay for bonemeal, kindling and candles. Arco's practicing with her fancy restaurant chukabocho. The cleaver edge splitting femurs lengthwise, the corner scooping the marrow, the dented spine pounding the scooped bone to shards.

You can look up and see their balcony. The glyph taped into the cracked doorglass, the railing bowed and coming undone. Mikey's squatting with you in the middle of the boulevard, right under Shitty Bridge, browsing through the leaf litter. Feel the lukewarm sweat all down the back of his jacket and the tense bite in his jaw.

He's like, "Man, it was made of my skull! I don't want a lid diyed of some nother asshole's skull." He lifts his head, yells cross the way. "Can somebody get me something? I don't care anymore. I'll eat it."

"It's not there." Raffia's stomping cross the boulevard with arms crossed, Donn trailing behind. Her bare feet make sucking sounds in the mud.

"Munch the leaf litter," says Donn. "Cause no way is it under munched leaf litter."

Mikey goes, "It would of fellen straight down. I know it fell right here."

Arco doesn't look up from her tidy lines of crushed bone. Her voice just carries. "If you eat, man, you'll level out."

Donn holds out a melonsized jug. The taut rind ripples like a hot water bottle. "Should I make you one of these?"

"Member how Mikey's lergic to caddisfly larvas," says Arco. Mikey's like, "To whats?"

ᴧᴧᴧ

"A yuppie's got it," says Arco.

Mikey picks through the leaf litter and they hold stance round him. There's a new hill down the way, apparently the spam works just collapsed last year or something. You heard some kids calling it Spam Graveyard Mound. You heard a couple call it the Germs stage. There's a stand of papaya and walnut trees pushing through the buckled scaffold bleacher, taproots elbowing through the concrete rubble with little shifty noises.

Donn shakes his face out. "Hold on, wasn't the spam works right on the fence?" Nobody says anything and Donn's like, "It was, right?"

"Who cares?" says Raffia.

"Well, like." He pulls out a cardboard telescope, maybe a kaleidoscope, and scopes uphill. Peering balanced on one foot, tipping forward, he looks like the view's pulling him. "Inconclusive. But, like. When the fence is down? They get in."

Nobody says anything. Mikey's flipping asphalt boulevard chunks, displacing centipedes. Raffia's bent forward, staring at Mikey while she chews on her teeth, and Arco's seriously doing fucking onearmed pushups.

Ventually Donn's like, "Am I still on acid? Arco? How much are my pupils dilated?"

"A yuppie's got it," says Arco.

"You're always like this," says Mikey.

"Mikey, how would it of got buried?" Raffia pushes a knuckle through her red corrodedlooking eyes. "You're an idiot. Stop breathing like that." Mouse tails covered in wintermint bubblegum swing like shoelaces from the corners of her mouth.

"Here, I've got some jerky even. Footsteak. And here, it's an egg." Donn's head swings back and forth. "Mikey? Can I talk to you bout definitions of the compassion concept?"

"That's a lizard egg," says Mikey, not looking up.

Donn's like, "Hey, was that bottomless pit here before? It could of fallen there. Whoa. Hey. Check behind you. Man. Up the knoll."

"A yuppie's got it," says Arco.

"The fuck's a knoll?" says Raffia. "There's no knolls."

"No, it's like a hill," says Donn. "But it's, like, a homophone for a kind of goblin."

"I've got guesses too." Mikey heaves a big mud clod into the sinkhole. He's kneeling in an excavated crater of blackish earth and chewylooking asphalt shreds. "They don't help me find my lid."

Raffia slaps her ribs and snorts. "Homo phone."

"No, but it's gonna homo, or like, home in on you, cause you're hung up on your lid," says Donn. "Personally I'm pretty mellow. Like, sure, my spinal cord hurts, and my empatternating's distorted, but it'll see your ego like a flare."

"You're talking theoretical?" says Mikey. "Or, ah, fucking shit."

"A yuppie's got it," says Arco. How long's she been pointing?

It's a bikertype yuppie with a huge clotted goatee. Stumping bowlegged down the knoll and its only clothes a belt of tshirt riding its gleaming mauve gut. It lurches toward Mikey with the painted lid clamped between its teeth.

Arco's just behind him. Facing the yuppie, toward and through. She's stashed all the kitchen knives and she's pointing her katana tip at its eyeball. Her nother hand's like cupped round a maginary hilt, which is weird if you don't know her good. "You got it, man?"

Squatting in the dirt, twisting crabstyle to face it with his feet, Mikey's like, "Yeah, sure," and then a parasitic wasp's crawling out the yuppie's dickhole. Black and elongated, it jumps through the air and lands on Mikey's upper lip, making little bloodpoints where its legs dig in.

Mikey paws at his lip, smashing the wasp across his face, yelling incoherently. Balanced on two hands and a foot, he jerks his free heel up and round to swipe the yuppie's knee. The kneecap crunches like a bundle of twigs and the bikertype stumbles, but not flipping right over him like a fast one would of done, just dropping, dumb as a pendulum. The lid's still in its mouth, Mikey, it slams your solar plexus hard. Your jacket's not half zipped up cause it's a hot morning, no yuppies anywhere, dude, don't think bout how your chest's exposed, that's siking too, that's its beard grizzling at your shirt.

Bucking arrythmic under its greasy bulk, your lips bending against the swollen wasp sting, you gurgle something and slap yourself hard cross the top of the brain.

ᴧᴧᴧ

You're not there.

ᴧᴧᴧ

Two fingers tucked in the hollow of its cheek, Raffia tilts the biker's head in the silty latemorning light. Grunts and she tears free the last fingerwidth of skin. The temple's caved in like a kicked jackolantern, there's a stripeshaped pressurecut deep through the eyes and sinus, and the bladework's beyond surgical, it's scientific. Right in the medulla oblongata. It's like the intro round of some fucking gameshow matching wounds to weapons.

Donn's pulling the bloated yuppie off Mikey's comatose bod. "He's alive, right?"

"Breathing." Arco starts spanking Mikey's kneecaps with the flat of her katanablade. His body shudders. "Good trick, but it's cheap."

"I hope he's okay. I mean, that's not in the warranty. Here, let me." Donn kneels and puts his lips in Mikey's ear. "Acid. Acid. Acidacid."

"Yeah." One of Mikey's eyes judders under the lid. "Back up the truck." He stretches and blinks. If you were him, you'd see your band blocking the sun, all crossed arms and total disapprobation. "Guys? People lay down to sleep."

Raffia's spinning the head in her hands like a wheel of cheese. She boots Mikey in the bottom of his foot and his whole body shoots forward.

"Why can I only see half of everything?" One side of Mikey's mouth is talking, one side's hanging juicily limp.

"You slapped your brains so it couldn't smell your consciousness," says Donn. He sits down on Mikey's chest and starts palpating the patch. Pries the staples out of his scalp with a little penknife. "Man, there's sofa skin fluff all over your dura mater."

"I did? Man, what a cheap trick."

"Yeah, it's lowering your cerebral resistivity. Should of gone fluffer side up." Donn licks his fingertip. He starts wiping rotten foam off Mikey's scrunkly dura mater, periodically wiping the finger on his pantleg.

"No, my mom'll find out," says Mikey. "Where the fuck am I? Hey, the other halves of your bodies are remanifested."

"It's always important to eat breakfast, Mikey." Arco's bouncing the dinged-up lid in her hand.

Raffia's rummaging in some ferns. Turns with an amorphous gray shape swinging in her mitt. "Eat this rotten cat's ass."

Donn shivers with laughter and exchanges some kind of jumping highfive with Raffia. To you it looks rehearsed. That or time's just pouring really slow today.

∧∧∧

They're sitting in a craggy lookout papaya at the crest of the new hill, looming out over the bleachers. The old cruds of the spam works, naked and discrete, look like they're floating on a slow wave of jagged concrete slabs. Pink quartz toilet seats, choppedopen safes, clay jugs, spam smokage poles chilling out in the steaming lakes of sun.

"Define the extent of the ass?" says Mikey. In his lap there's a red tarp napkin. On the tarp there's a gray fuzzy pile, sort of like a saggy macro amoeba with hints of paws.

"The whole ass." Raffia stands on the lowest branch, banging her foot backward into halfrotted rubber. Near the base, the trunk's ringed by an implausible stack of monstertruck tires, all shriveled from yesterday night's bonfire. Bark squeezes out between the tires like a gut rolling over designer jeans.

Mikey goes, "What, so the feet are the ass?"

"Eat the feet." Kneeling on the branch, Raffia's at eyelevel with Mikey's knees. She reaches up and thumbs a patch of squamous fur off the cat's forehead. Sniffing it, she coughs and stands up really straight. Her pupils briefly pull in.

"I'll eat it," says Mikey. Rubbing the wasp sting on his lip. "It's your guyses call. But this is yucked beyond any hangover breakfast."

"We saved your life and it wasn't even hard," says Raffia. "You even know how disappointing that is?"

Arco nods once from the lookout branch. The motion makes a little slashing noise in the still air.

"You were pretty slack," says Donn. "Was that harsh? Sorry if it was harsh. But this won't actually poison you much. See under the gray, matted fur? Those ringshaped blue excrescences are a strong antibiotic. *Snuffleocloaca darbii.* See how nothing grows around them?"

"Yup." Mikey pushes his finger into the cat's head. There's absolutely zero resistivity. "Hey Arco? Can I borrow a butterknife?"

"Long as you clean it," says Arco.

Mikey opens his hand, not looking, and the knife falls in. "You guys still think this is fair, hey?"

Everything's stopped sept for the leaves bending in the drizzle. Mikey's hands start spreading the rotten catass on a big flat chunk of yuccabread. Meat drops off the haunchbones with this greasy ease like overdone potroast. Ghostcolored membranes bunch and string, maybe mycelia, maybe snot. What a fucked sandwich. It smells like a colostomy bag from a mayonnaise eating contest. Sitting all cautious on the flat of his hand, the way you'd feed something to a horse. "Uh. Can I toast this? Donn? Dude, I just wanted to say. You ensured to me this meat wouldn't poison me, man. I preciate it."

A cicada or whatever starts whistling.

∿∿∿

Hold up. Down the nother side of the hill, toward the burbs, there's a fence crew. Bout two hands of kids in biteresistant black neoprene wetsuits, slit at the armpits for aeration, and black leather sunflower masks. They look like shadows with hangovers. They've got a wheelless barrow with boltedon skis as runners, it's heaped with cruddy black chunks of bamboo root nodule. They're transplanting a wide band of the punkgrass to plug the buildingwide gap in the fence and making a point of using swords to dig. The bucket of shovels and pitchforks, that's for if yuppies rush them.

But check out the washedout denim collars riding up the necks of their wetsuits. Those puffy infections cross their jawlines where they rubbed guck into pinpricks. Bunch of arcore kids, right? You see those? They're artificially induced zits.

"Last night fucked my ears. So primal." Kid with the barrow, he's chewing

on a matchstick. "Fuck. I just wish. If the fight happened. Getting killed by
Arco. Fuck. It'd be so primal." He makes this hand gesture like a soundwave
flying at his ear.

"She wouldn't kill us. What did we do to her?" His buddy takes a bamboo
root clump. Squatting at the trench, she looks up. "That fat asshole on drums.
Raffia Tie. She'd kill you. She'd make you cry first."

"I took the straight edge on crying," says wheelbarrow. "I don't do crying."

Somebody else goes, "No, but I'd let Arco kill me, though."

There's a lot of nodding.

〰〰〰

"Hold on. Band meeting." Mikey stands on the papaya branch and looks
over his shoulder both ways. Hands folded on the back of his neck. "We really
need to murder Darby Crash."

Something starts moving here, whether or not you get it right away. Not
like an engine, not much like a wheel. Arco and Raff and Donn sit up and
their breathing seems to adjust.

Arco's like, "You're not clear a nuff to hold a meeting, punker. Do you even
know who we are? Outside your beatup mind I might be Darby."

Mikey reseats his flaky lid like a tub stopper. He sticks out his tongue.

Raffia's like, "You can't handle breakfast, that's all. Fuck you, flower. Stop
stalling and go for my throat if you don't want to eat it. We just saved your
life. Now you think we wanna be responsible for you?"

There's a joke of how if your band needs a meeting, it won't help. So if
you start one up, there's a certain amount of verbal and physical abuse.

Donn's like, "If you couldn't kill Darby with your herpes with aids on it,
why do you think anything could kill him? You're pissed Darby's ignoring
you, but show some compassion for us. Just not our war, man."

"That came outa sweet fuckall, Donn. Why do you keep talking about this
cum passion shit?" Mikey sits down again next to the sandwich. The sandwich
doesn't say anything. "No, really. We can't do the meeting if I'm puking. I'll
eat it afterward. Okay?"

After a while, Arco's like, "It's shitty to turn down a meeting."

"Donn? Did you really mean that about—ah, never mind. Look." Mikey
gets busy with his hands and heels climbing the gray papaya trunk. He clings
with one hand and breaks a huge frond from the spreading top. Holds it out.
"This is fucked, right? Like, this isn't just me."

"Mondo tubuloso?" says Donn. "I thought it just had a disease."

Mikey shrugs. "Germs."

He folds it twice, passes it down to Donn, who snaps it out. Raindrops jump off it. It's soft and crumply, the color of pages torn from old books, woven right-angled with little threads all through it. It looks like what it is, a papaya frond that's a ragged piece of canvas. It's got a black stain like a huge tooth cavity, and a blue circle in that, and these two unevenly printed white letters GI.

A strand of spit hangs vertically in Donn's stuckopen mouth. He passes it to Raffia.

Raffia pinches the corner in two fingers, passes it up to Arco.

Arco's got her hand over the letters. She's got the straight edge, no looking at words. "What's this got to do with it? Is it like a silkscreen?"

Mikey's lips pull back on one side. "Shit, I don't know. Maybe it grew cause some patches were buried?" You're reaching to take it back, Mikey. Gingerly touch the black stainage. It's not silkscreen emulsion, there's no story waking into you. "I'm just freaked. You know this GI thing though? In history, when they were banned at every venue, Darby called them Germs Incognito. So GI was for short at the posters."

"So it's a patch tree?" says Arco. "We should take cuttings."

They're all looking at the top of the tree. The giant leaves of canvas fringe away, their glyphs obscure, turned out to the rain.

"Man, where's canvas come from, anyway? Like, does anybody still make canvas?" says Donn. "We should take cuttings."

"This is a band meeting, not fucking plant scientists," says Raffia. "Why are we murdering Darby, man. And eat your sandwich while you're saying it."

They look at Mikey. They look at him staring down at the base of the tree with his arms wrapped round himself.

∧∧∧

He holds the GI patch over his mouth. Your call if the stance means a bandanna, a gag, or something weird like making himself into a jacket. But it means this meeting, anyway, because it's new, and this meeting's new. Diy every day.

"Last night Meatheads and Darby played a oneoff show," he says through the black stain and the blue ring. "The crowd yelled cause they were into it.

Fine. Us and Darby, we got covered in spit, and they threw beer, and we all made it happen together. Under the power of our hands.

"Then the old guy tells the circle, we don't need this building anymore, fuck the landlord and tear it to the ground. Man, we don't got a landlord! I liked the spam works, all our food was there. We had years of food stored there. But anyway they just went and ripped it down, like this one thousand pound building." Mikey stops, like to pull his breath back in. "How do you even do that?

"Diying doesn't mean getting people to suffer for your plans. That's what I mean. Darby can't diy. He doesn't know how. But everyone does what he says. That's real dangerous for punk rock."

The meeting goes round to Arco. She folds her hands together. Touches her forehead to her knuckles, then looks up. Talking through the patch in a voice as clear as a moving silhouette against the sky. "Darby showed to his birthday party in a suit and tie. We all saw it. Whole room was charged up in spikes and warpaint like Darby on a siko day, and he showed up, drank one glass of blood, no beer, and he nodded and left through the door."

Raffia breathes out exaggeratedly through her pursed lips. The GI patch flaps and blows. "Dude sent the whole city to kill us. What a show that would of been. What a way to go couch surfing. Rended limb for limb on a mountain of corpses on Darby's diying day. Nobody gets a chance to go down working their kung fu like that. Man, not even him."

Donn just holds the canvas leaf, feeling at the colored blotches like a blind kid looking for something. "Okay. While ago I was really bummed and nobody was around." He puts the patch to his mouth. "Sorry. The band broke up or something and none of my inventions were really going right. So I fucked off to the Zero.

"Darby was having a private pizza party in the back, with a million locks and a crowd round the door. I was sad so I snuck round the ledge on the side of the building and got in. There was like thirty million—sorry Arco—like a high number of bathroom mirrors stuck to the ceiling and Darby's friends all looking up there grinning with their hands in their pockets. And he's like jacking off on these three girlses faces. They're kind of fighting for position, clawing and biting each other bloodily, and he's got this blasé look with his other hand on his butt. And then he's like, Donn! He didn't even bother getting off. He just went and sat on the ledge with me and told me I was an okay dude. I don't member, but we had this long conversation bout something, and Darby's really smart."

Mikey's mouth pulls in a weird direction, he's nodding. "My turn? Okay. Time out for a second though. It's weird how band meetings go in a circle, even. Wherever there's a circle, Darby's there."

"Dude invented meetings though," says Donn. "Can't help his influence." He lets the patch flutter into Mikey's two hands.

"You see at his birthday?" says Mikey. "Time in. You see at his birthday how they built him a giant coyote out of filters? They. Fuck, we. I helped too. So many kids diyed going into sinkholes after filters, Darby'd just show up and laugh. And he was like, Build me a filter coyote. He willed it and it came. It's not like the kids pretending to be Arco, she doesn't courage that. Darby takes power from it. They could be doing their own thing. But when Darby's around they're all the same."

"Fine," says Raffia, breaking the circle. "Fuck!"

Nobody says much to that. Arco takes the patch, folds it over itself. Obscuring the glyph in a stack of creamcolored folds. She holds it over her mouth. Says fuckall. She passes it. Hardcore.

"We can talk bout diy, I saw Darby nailing boards once," says Raffia through the patch. "He got stoned and said he'd help fix a smokeshed. Wouldn't stop bitching bout how boring it was and how nobody'd go on a run for straighter nails. But he'd just pound them in slanty and wreck them. He sucked at it. But I don't care if he's dead, but I'd help you do it. Fuck."

Now Donn's got it. He wraps the patch round his burn, where the pitmark's hardly scabbed over. Taking his time. The black patch wraps all round his skinny sinewy wrist, and he holds it to his face, talks behind it, muffled.

"I never took a Germs burn before last night. My wristburn I had was from when I was like Taco's age. Before we were a band really. Darby was so tall, you know, and I couldn't talk to any of the kids he knew. So during the Vice Reagans tour kickoff show I hid in the shitter stall and put out a smoke on my wrist. Afterward I lied to everybody Warren Standard did my burn. Nobody really noticed but I got into some parties and like learned to drink."

Donn's head pulls back. You can see two invisible chains hooking his eyeballs to the deep treads of Arco's dangling hightops. "After awhile I stopped thinking bout it. Til Darby asked if he could redo my burn last night. He knew it was fake, right. Germs burns aren't diy like you do them to yourself. They're not prefab though. Darby diyed the whole movement and we're moving through it. They're diy on a higher level that we fit into."

"Like we're his tools," says Raffia. "No, back up. Band fucking meeting. Band meeting right now."

Arco slips down from the lookout branch to stand facing Raffia.

"No, inside this meeting!" says Raffia. The mouse tails you forgot about, they're billowing from between her teeth like yarn tied in a fan cage. "I'm calling a nother one. Band meeting of Donn keeping shit back when we say we don't keep any shit back."

Raffia pulls her red manskin lashings round her and swings down from the branch, lands next to Donn and pounds him hard in the arm. He doesn't move one micron or pica or angstrom. His dreads shudder sideways, then resettle.

"Your reasons are gonna be even thinner than Mikey's reasons," says Arco. "My shit bout secrets is personal to my straight edge, Raff. If you honor my edge cause it's mine, you're doing the same shit you're slamming crash trash for."

"You smell like piss." Mikey starts laughing. "You do. You smell like piss."

"It's easy for you not to have a secret, you go round like they do in the burbs, not even thinking shit," says Donn. "No-mind's not shit to brag bout if it's easy."

"This is the band meeting symbol," says Raffia. She belts Donn in the arm again. Now you can see the hemorrhage slightly puffening his arm through the purple polyurethane raincoat. He spins with red threads flipping out his tear ducts, hammers Raffia's cheekbone with his elbow. They both fall out of the tree.

How bout a few moments of formulaic violence.

∧∧∧

There's extra space under Raffia's eye, puce, dented noticeably. Donn's coat's swollen under the shoulder, and he's unhooked the bikechain reinforcements there. They're all sitting in a line on the lookout branch.

"Harsh symbol, Raff," says Donn. "I mean, it's fine. It's just a harsh symbol."

"I just get pissed—" A quick seizure rips upward through Raffia, starting with foot spazzing, fading as the last word comes out *orththff*. Nobody seems to notice.

"Can I go before you?" says Arco. She gently taps Donn's other shoulder with two knuckles. "Yeah. While we were having the last band meeting all I could do was sit thinking bout Mikey. How he must of had a wicked reason to want Darby dead. Cause Mikey's our boy and he believes suffering is mostly fucked and pushing yourself is important and we trust him, right? But I felt his reasons were thin, like I said. My trust thing's not with Donn. Mikey told me this morning he's been keeping something back bout him and Darby." She closes her eyes briefly. "I might get on the side of murdering Darby if you could tell me, Mikey."

"Everybody always thinks I'm like desperate to hook up again with Darby. Just cause Donn is." Mikey sighs twice, less he's just breathing. He puts a hand on Donn's back. Hand on Raffia's. Arco's too far, and there's no more hands. "Man, I don't want to do this meeting. I want to do the other. Darby wants a war, man. Arco, you don't think your clones would of defended you? They all had swords and shit and he knew it. Everybody in that pit would of bled out. Not just us and like our self defense victims. I do got a secret with Darby though. I can't spill it. I feel too shitty. I'm sorry."

"There's something in your pocket." Arco drops out of the tree.

Raffia makes a guttural noise. She jumps off the branch and lands standing on the next one down, breathing into her cupped hands like she'd feed a little fire there.

"Man," says Donn.

Raffia does a deep knee bend, then a half nother. Bit of steam rising off her. She vaults skyward from her squat like a pumpup rocket, the branch cracking as she lifts. She hangs weightless behind Mikey long enough to scream "BAAND BREAAKUP!" and smash the side of his ribcage with two clasped fists.

Mikey starts falling sideways off the tree. He catches himself with this blurring move like an ocelot, ends up dangling upside down with his knees bent around the branch, rubbing his chest. Donn's swung into a similar ocelot pose and Raffia's reaching up with One Hand, or three hammers anyhow in one hand, pressing all their heads into Mikey's cheek. One's a masonry hammer with the cubeshaped head and rockchipper butt, one's just a boring clawhammer, but one's like this titanium octopus tenderizer with pyramid spikes cross its flat.

"YOU THINK WE CAN WORK TOGETHER WITHOUT ARCO?" Spit globs crash into Mikey's eyeballs. "YOU THINK THIS SHIT'S EASY? YOU THINK PUNKS JUST SAUNTER IN AND ASSASSINATE DARBY FUCKING CRASH?"

"Dude, inside voice." Mikey coughs a red tigerstreak into his palm.

Her other hand pulls her hammer hand back. Raffia jumps. "WELL, LOOK AT US NOW!" And hits the mud floor with a grievous squelch. "LOOK AT US WORKING TOGETHER NOW!"

Raffia starts stomping up the knoll toward Arco. Arco's just standing there all camo in the rubble, like somebody hung clothes on a standing garden rake. Her voice just carries. "We should practice, if we want. There's a show tonight."

"FUCK PRACTICE, MEATHEADS BROKE UP!"

"See you at the show, though," says Arco.

"I GUESS!" Raffia turns her stomp around, starts heading the other way, downhill, down the road.

Arco nods once and walks the same way, hands bunched in the bottom of her faded jersey. Not actually following. After a couple steps her toe flips up a manhole cover and she jumps in. There's lots of ways to the jamroom.

"You never ate your sandwich." Donn's walking away too.

∿∿

And course her head's still down. She watches best from there. Raffia walks a bit easier near the fenceless zone, whether or not you know why. The sammyre of history said make benevolence your magic armor. But they also said wear actual armor.

Some little kid runs at her, feet pelting down the slope. Strawberry blonde and daubed in mud and Raffia reaches through their zygomatic bone with a sound like three hands clapping. Strawberry jam.

Couple more steps and she looks up, squinting at nothing.

The arcore fence crew on the corner, they've tipped up their leather sunflower masks, they're passing round a corncob pipe. They open their mouths at Raffia but she gives them a look.

"Was that a kid or a yuppie?" She jerks her gory thumb over her shoulder. "Fuck it. Forget it."

They're like, "What?"

She keeps walking longside the fence. Punks stick their heads out windows and hoot welcome, and then they stick their heads back in. It's easy telling when Raff's in a mood. And even you, even you, you know she can throw.

Couple blocks and there's the iron smelting works, rearing a little backward as its foundation slips unevenly down into the muck. Big glass doors in the front, all blacked from the inside with soot. Two vertical lines of steel rivets climb the concrete side of the building and she gets going. Tireless like the big prisonbar of smoke up top, climbing off the roof to the sky.

Her splayed bare feet wrap around the rivets as she climbs, her arms jerking up and down like a cartoon weightlifter's. Halfway there she points her mouth up and screams. "Bo! Don't talk to me!" A few pegs closer. "Your name sucks!"

An amber beerbottle streaks by, passes an armslong from her face. Then Bo's hauling her up by her hand. She punches his arm and his arm's big as hers, his palms are flats of granite. This dude's built like a can of orange juice concentrate. His sideburns start level with the bags under his eyes. You know what, Bo looks pretty much like the iron smelting works.

"Names aren't sposed to be good," says Bo in his rocktumbler voice. So much furnace residue stuck to him, who can tell what colors he is, or what he's wearing really, or if he's wearing it. "Wish you got here faster. We're running outa armpit hair."

"Been a shitty morning," says Raffia.

Bo's like, "So you want a smoke."

"I'll find a nother prenticeship." Raffia makes a noise. Don't think it's a laugh.

He goes, "You've got a couple nothers. Topiary, carpentering and hammer sharpenry, right?" and she's like, "I guess."

Then he's like, "The way you smoke's unhealthy." Course he lays one in her hand. Diy tobacco rolled in the yellow pages, leathered like a slimjim from hanging up near the blastfurnace, capped with a recycled filter presmoked the color of darjeeling.

Raffia's chewing, hands on her hips. "Least I don't swallow." After a bit, she spits an ungodly clot of brown porridge. Then she crosses her eyes, works her jaw, and bares her teeth to show the filter knotted like a pretzel on her tongue.

"You must think you're a good kisser." Bo sighs. "Mind if I hit you in the nuts?"

"They haven't growed yet," says Raffia.

"Whenever," says Bo. Crouching with his overdeveloped arm swinging back like a piston. His fist shoots forward into her groin. There's a dull meaty thumping sound as Raffia snarls. Yeah, go with the sound of that hand. No, not that hand. The nother one, slapping the tiled rooftop as Bo pulls his punch.

"Fuck!" says Bo. "Fuck!"

The wide muscles of your thighs are still tense, Raff, tenser even, waiting against the hit that didn't come. All your fightpower balled up in your jawline and back, and your solar plexus a hot red slab of pigiron like to compensate the dizzy pain. Between your teeth, you're like, "What?"

"My fucking hand's stuck," says Bo. And starts quietly laughing.

You're like, "Why do you always try to make me feel better?"

Whatever's wrong with you, Raff, it's reflecting in his eyes. See your little black image with the indistinct smeltingsmoke behind. Blocky as a junkheap, broad and crudely made, the fingers twisting in your palms like you can't tell if they're there. Your image's face renches with something that's not funny either as it pulls the little mallet from its little bandolier. Just fuck it. Fuck it.

Hey tourist? Where'd you go?

Raffia's bouncing One Hand, the vulcanized rubber mallet edition, off the brow of Bo's skull. His arms extend a little, he's still chuckling. The hammer happens again, over one eye, splitting the matted eyebrow.

She's all, "You think I can't take a hit?" The mallet slams into his deep hollowed collarbone. "Think I can't?" Bo grunts. "Take a hit!" She jumps and swings down onto the crown of his head.

Now he's squatting there in front of her, not making sounds, and drool's collecting in the rim of his lower lip. She puts her ear up to the side of his neck and gently turns his head in her hands. One of his pupils is bout normal size but kind of stretched. One's just a microdot.

"Shit. Sorry, man. At least your neck's not broken. It's just—ARRRAHRH!" She lifts the mallet again, then winces, slides it into her chestbelt. "You okay?"

Bo falls backward a little, stubbing the rooftop with the point of his ass. Like his ass and two heels making a tripod. He just sits there. Bo sits there and sits there.

"I'll wreck the iron smelting, man," says Raffia. "I never pay tension to shit when you're showing me." She sits down next to him, waves her hand at his motionless eyes. "Man, Bo, I'm sorry." Chews her lip. "It's just, like, you know, I mean, like."

∿∿

She's sniffing the air like it means something to her, and her head pans minimally across the rooftop. A baby's wailing somewhere nearby and she's like, "Shut it!"

Under a tarp leanto rocking with black smoke and orange will-o-the-wisps, there's a handful of lopsided barbecue grills with cutdown firebarrels of coal glowing beneath, where the propane tanks used to go. Raffia starts opening a grill. Bites her tongue then grabs an ovenmitt off a hook and opens it again. There's all these pans of burnt blood inside. Glassy, tacky black crud like plasticized butterscotch disasters.

Raffia scrapes a coffeespoon across one pan, drawing a shallow trace. She sniffs the tarry residue on the spoontip, turns it sideways, sniffs it again, licks it. She stabs the spoonhandle into the dark charamelized blood and works it back and forth, then shakes her head. Looking over at Bo while her hand works the spoon like a lever she knows is busted.

"Fuck." She goes and gets the burger flipper. There's a metal barrel around here somewhere, with more burned blood inside, and she scrapes the pans into that. The black stuff drops, cracking, like satanic peanut brittle. That glyph scratched on the barrel, it's a molecular hemogoblin from a book somewhere. The micro goblins living in blood are sposed to look like snowflakes with jerky spider arms, and in their cores, one little pinpoint of iron.

"Man. Are these ready to grind? Bo?" Then she's like, "Fuck, I'll do something else."

There's so many dumb parts of this job. Darby won't talk bout who found the cruise missile, or where they keep the intercontinental ballistic neutron warhead part. But the iron smelting works possesses a missile casing mounted nosedown in the middle of a merry-go-round, its mangy olive paintjob weatherproofed with beetle shellac. Raffia can't read good, but you might remember how from being Donn or Mikey, and the fins say *KRAGEN ARMAMENTS*. Who knows? Kids still use this thing sometimes, but they got to wait their turn.

She stands balanced on the roundabout's arms and peers in the top of the missile, where the jet exhaust used to vent from. Whole thing's full of blood. She climbs off, grabs one of the arms. You've gotta get it moving really fast for diy blood fractionation to work. Clockwise, because you're moving the blood forward in time. To make sure you're doing it a nuff of long, you gotta sing the longest song in the world twice.

"So you been to school for a year or two—" She's barking at it rhythmically as she spins the merry-go-round. Raffia sings like a trash compactor. "And you think you seen it all—"

If you're concerned bout Bo, he sure doesn't move, but his drool puddle might be bigger. Raffia's just slapping and slapping the roundabout arms, singing the longest song in the world, and the sun drags in the sky til the roof blocks it and the whole place goes dim.

"Pol! Pot! Pol! Pot! Polpot polpot polpot—"

Don't worry, it doesn't matter. Ventually Raffia grabs a blurry carousel bar. It jerks her offbalance but she only stumbles with one foot, and the diy centrifuge abruptly stops. See that weak strawcolored shit sloshing out the top, bit thinner than spit? That's how you know the blood's parted out for serum and hemogoblins.

Right at the tip of the upside down nosecone, there's a plastic spigot caulked in with ABC gum. It came from box wine, but who knows, it hasn't leaked yet. Raffia squats and starts decanting hemogoblins into a series of thick glass tumblers. Fractionated from serum, which is awesome for feeding babies and quenching redhot swords, the micro goblins collectively manifest as a satiny crimson syrup.

She moves the tumblers to a big workbench in a couple grocerycart loads. Cross the roof, the blastfurnace isn't making half as much smoke now, and she stands there looking at it. She unties her topknot for a bit and chews on a tail of dingy russet hair. Bo's still over there, doing whatever he's doing. When Raffia toes him in the shoulder, she has to grab him before he tips facefirst. Then she searches his coverall for a mini steel saw.

Raffia cocks one elbow behind her head. Her armpit area's frightening. The hairs present as scabrous yellow filaments, like wires that might of burst from a fermented phonecord. This fungus, it's sposed to do the actual work of busting iron out of hemogoblins. It won't grow on you less you're mad all the time, and even then it makes you smell like piss. She saws a pinch of hair from each elbow, making a crusty pile on a jarlid. Not too close to the skin or you'll make the mycelium grow down into your nerves, but if you leave it too long, it'll grow together and start fruiting.

One hair goes in the first tumbler, floating on the hemogoblins until Raffia pushes it to the bottom with a stirstick. A skimpy blackish cloud follows it through the red. Figure that's the iron. Then she's dripping wine vinegar into the cloud, counting drops under her breath, moving the pinned armpit pube around at the bottom of the glass.

"You wash your hand?" says Bo. Standing there with his palm out.

"Oh. Yeah. For sure." Raffia bites her lip. She puts the little jarlid of armpit pubes into Bo's hand. "Hey, I shouldn't of done that, man."

"Hey, I can't get angry, remember." Bo taps a concave area on his forehead. "Not since the last time you went for it." He laughs. Raffia looms there stiff and awkward and he's like, "Cmon."

So Bo drops the hairs in the tumblers, pours silty diy vinegar as Raffia pushes the stirstick around. The sun slips through a gap in the roof as they're getting done and dumps them with light the color of dead leaves. She's like, "What do we do now?"

"Fuck, I don't remember," says Bo. More drool's beading from one side of his lip. "Did you put hairs in these?"

"Man," says Raffia. She scrapes the side of her face like there's a fly. Stands there a nuff time to blink twice, then flips the workbench on its end. All the glass tumblers clatter and shatter cross the air, skidding hemogoblins all over the roof like big red stretchy lobes of melted lipstick.

"Man," she says again.

Bo's knees fold heavily. He's on the ground, looking at the weird little lidful of yellow armpit hairs. "Do you know how to blow glass tumblers?"

Raffia shakes her head.

Breathing carefully, Bo looks at his knuckles, like he's trying to remember what they do. "I'll ask Darby."

"I'm not usually this bad," says Raffia. "Wait, Darby blows glass?"

"Nobody blows glass." Bo starts getting up. Then he doesn't. "Fuck. You should of just never come."

Raffia lowers her head, waiting with a tensedout jaw. Bo's just like, "Nothing's fucked. You shouldn't of come is all."

"No, it's fucked," says Raffia. "It's not the smelting work. I'm just fucked when they're not around. You gonna come to the show tonight?"

"I heard Meatheads broke up," says Bo.

"Yeah, I guess," says Raffia. "Kind of. It's kind of like the other times we broke up."

"You should go to it," says Bo. "Break some amps setting up."

Raffia brushes Bo's shoulder. Her hand jumps, like from a hot stove. "Sorry, man." And she leaves him there staring at the hemogoblins and busted glass. "Your name sucks."

Ner.

∧∧∧

Get it?

∧∧∧

No, but after awhile you're back in your messy jamroom. Somebody cleaned up the halfdone rope, it's bundled in sheaves cross the ceiling hooks, and your mouth is like, "Thanks, Arco." For some reason there's driedout pizza in your hand, or maybe jerky. You try biting into the tip, then the side.

Oh yeah, you're Mikey.

There's somebody else. Dreads the color of cherry cola and pierced multifariously with diaperpins, she's sleeping sprawled across the shitty black leather sofa. This halfassed newschool Germs burn healing in a puckered crescent round her eye. You step sideways past her. Jaw tearing at the pizza again. Then you throw it at the tapedup balcony door, where it creases like an origami cranewing and makes a nother crack in the doorglass.

Look over at the girl. Your hand wakes her up. "What's on your dreams?"

Her pupils spread as her eyelids crack. The tawny irises have little shards of cheap glitter stuck on. "Oh, hey, Mikey. I think I got a dream tended for you. We were all down in the sewer building a fire, and some yuppie came to the manhole to drop off pizzas, so we had to put on fedoras and like trenchcoats—"

"What's up, Some Soma."

"Oh, hey, Mikey Ghost. It's tomorrow, right? Hey, Mikey. Oh, I saw you at that show last night!"

"Were you waiting around for me?" You slouch and hook a thumb in your spenders. "It's been a weird morning."

"Naw," she says, stretching her back. "I just saw your soft looking couch through the window. I super love sectional couches."

"Meatheads broke up." Say you're seeing yourself from a height. Your limbs puppeteered by sweet fuckall, the air a slow translucent vaseline haze. Looks like this Mikey hasn't started hitting on her yet or fucked off, so he's probly on auto.

"Oh," says Some Soma. "That sucks. Well, you guys were kind of old news anyway. Want to start a band, Mikey? When are you getting back together? Are you still playing the bowlarama tonight? I could be totally playing there tonight. We can if you want, you know." She hikes her jeans down past her bellybutton and stirs. "I super love sectional couches. Darby says I'm really your kind of person."

"I kind of was needing some transcendental mediation actually," says the fuzzy Mikey in your mind.

"Oh, that's boring. Hey, Darby's going to be at the bowlarama. Last night was the best thing Meatheads ever did, man. Has he asked you to be his band fulltime?"

Mikey straights up. His laugh sounds forced to you, even if you're him. "He wants us dead."

"Nah, he's just fucking you around. He'd of called us off. Just Darby likes to provoke peopleses ego losses." A black licorice gumbubble emerges somehow from her nostril, snaps, and she snorts it back in. "You know, this time I was sleeping and he caused the furniture in my room to get changed. Even the couch under me. He brought in this new furniture made of sewed together steaks and dead dog heads, and painted the whole room, like, anthracite. Darked the window, and all these kids were partying in my room. Done up like disco dancing yuppies. I wake up and I start to twitch, and Darby's face is just looking at me. He's like, Welcome to disco hell. Then he totally vanishes."

"No shit?" says Mikey. Still looking at her nostril. "What's anthracite?"

Her eyes are glassed, she looks half asleep. "So I thought, I must not be thinking. I'm a yuppie in disco hell where disco holds sway over all. I just got up and started dancing with the crew. Infused with the spirit of disco. Then in a year or whatever, Darby and some kids, they busted down the window and the room was full of light. I jumped for them, bit them just like a yuppie. They had to fire stinguisher me. I achieved lightenment, that's the thing."

Mikey blinks. "You're still lightened?"

"Nah, I lost it when I got fire stinguishered," says Some Soma. "Still. I really like the way you guys jammed." She's got her fingers in her ears. "Cause sometimes he'll skip a verse cause he's smoking. Or do the same verse a couple times, like in tandem with the demands of the universe. You guys listen good a nuff to keep up with the songs and put in the right shit. Nobody else can do that."

"Did he say you should say that?" says Mikey. He pushes at the tapedup doorglass, making it bend outward, then wipes at his face and slides the door open. Hey, he's holding the whole spool of finished rope from yesterday. Some Soma giggles. She turns over on her belly and starts chewing and drooling on the leather sofa cushion.

Mikey unhooks his skylight lid and slips it in his pocket. Sitting out on the deck, his back to the door, he turns the square of canvas in his hands. Not touching the ink. The four bars toned like squid ink and old rusty blood. He turns it over and back. Kids copy this glyph everywhere. Branded in treestumps, acidetched in manhole covers, inked in the skins of the quick. There's no originals. For once you've got a vantage, tourist, coming new to this place. Too new to of heard that spiel before.

Mikey shakes his head, grinning deep, breathing out. He lays your flat black canvas cross his exposed brain matter, ink down. Like he set into him a portable hole and you drop into yourself, plunge down the backs of his eyes, pulling round his spine like four stretchy ribbons of stone.

∧∧∧

—*The scaffold bleacher's only half full but it's packed so hard. Skinny punks got their shoulders together like they're the last kids in the coldening universe. Spose they might of been. Something's weird with the air, like there's too much of it. And out past the fence, way out in the burbs, you're standing there too in the black smoke and orange light tearing round like the sun's burning behind a burning spraypaint stencil. Not holy. Never holy. A row of four skyscrapers completely on fire.*

The voice you hear, you know.

—*Nobody's calling your band out, Henry Rollins, you meathead. It's just an incidence! You guys can go by your selves. We party better without you beach district jocks anyway.*

∧∧∧

You're like, "Darby?"

You're facedown on the blistered lino deck. So's the Flag patch. So stand up, coughing. Shove the patch back in Mikey's pocket and then knot one rope end around the twisted balcony railing, weaving the spool through gaps in the bars. When there's a solid knot you can just throw the whole spool into the open air, vault over the railing, and grab at the line as you fall.

Wait, is this really fucked up?

You've got ten fingers round the rope for a semi brake, you can feel your calluses fraying and busting apart, and the windows on the condo face are still sliding up past you, way faster than you can run. And then your hand jumps up and it slaps Mikey across the brain. Bunch of soft orange lights going everywhere and then his neck limps out and it's dark.

∧∧∧

Why'd you do that?

No, why'd you do that? You fucking tourist, what side are you even on?

∧∧∧

He's standing in the air, feet brushing the ground. One hand curled hard round the scratchy flax cord, ropeburned bloody, and the other draped over his thinkmeat. Mikey stirs and smacks his lips. The end of the spool's laying in a heap of leafmold just beneath him, and he blinks and lets the rope go. The mushy jungle floor takes him, he sinks to the chest.

Missing chunks of wall from the condo's top pitch sunshadows cross the rainy drinkinglot like stretched light and dark jigsaw pieces. Mikey kicks round in the sludge, pulling his jacket tighter around his shoulders. Darby's there behind him. Standing right on the leaf litter's surface, head bowed, spreading his hands like the high priest of can't give a fuck. Wait, he's only got one hand. Who knows what you were looking at.

"Hey, Mikey. Sorry to scare you."

Mikey screams and grabs at the line. He turns round while his face slowly fixes itself. "Shit. What's up, Darbs."

"Oh, I was staring at you since the sun was more that way." Darby jerks his chin indistinctly at the sky. "You've been hanging there in a coma with your fingers in your brain. It looks kind of inflammated really. You all fucked bout Meatheads breaking up?"

"I dunno. I guess." Mikey wallows around in the leaflitter. "We had a fight."

Darby's fist is pressing his leg. "You fought bout me, then. Sorry I asked the crowd to rend you limb from limb."

Mikey's like, "Yeah. What was that, anyway?"

"Aw, you get jealous. You know what happens." Darby's eyes slip groundward. "I kept spacing out thinking bout how good you guys were. Thinking bout your guitar work or whatever. I didn't want there to be a band as good as you. One best band in the city, with nobody left to balance you out."

Mikey doesn't even wait for a breath. "You promised me your leather, man."

But go up and look at the ceiling right overtop them, where that little loose pebble of concrete is falling, and pause time. You know you can do that, right? Just a hair off from the pitted ceiling. Let that pebble hang against your mind like a gray knucklebone spiderwebbed with lichen. Think bout the conversation Mikey just started. Whether it's a sammrye move.

"I'm still alive. Get it when I'm dead." Darby laughs, then cuts it off. "Shit, you mean you talked to Trip Hazard. Or, aw, fuck, like Mabel?"

"I dunno, chick with filters in her bihawk," says Mikey. "Big, uh, big shoulders. Interests include spitting and threats. Yeah. She said she was getting your leather."

"You haven't seen Trip, though?" says Darby.

"I haven't talked to Trip." Take a breath, Mikey. You need breathing to live.

"You didn't see him before the show or anything? I'm worried bout that guy. He gets in too many fights." Hand over his face, eyes closed. Darby breathes for a moment through his fingers. "Aw, fuck Trip. You ever do anything just so people could hate you, man?"

Mikey shifts position in the gucky leafmold. It's all down his boots, down his fly. "I puked in Raff's mom's dog's mouth once stead of using the window."

"You can get better footing with the rope," says Darby. Still not looking. He's sitting on the surface of the leafmold, looking weightless, legs splayed wide. "Mikey. Yeah. I made so many kids the same promise. I wanted everybody fighting over my jacket. I hoped they'd flash on my lies and end up hating me. Fight all night and piss on my name."

Mikey's shimmying up the rope. He wedges his lid over the gap in his skull. "Hold on."

"I wanted them to rip the jacket down anyway. Like as the sun came up, and everybody's got black eyes and shit and they're passing my meat round. Man, that tiger, man. I guess she figured she was doing me a favor." Darby's slowly getting to his feet. "I thought I was gonna diy last night. Right til I woke back up. Whole night felt like swimming."

"Punker?" Mikey steps back onto the jungle floor. This time he only sinks ankledeep. His eyes narrow like he's posing for a gunfight. "Like you were planning to get killed? Like before yesterday? And when you told me I could take over for you, that was just so I could be part of a scrap?"

"Smart guy, Mikey. Must be the company you keep." Darby's scratching the back of his neck. His hand snaps out and grabs the concrete pebble falling from the roof. "Yesterday I made a hole in my leather so a yuppie could bite me through. I thought that way I could kill myself and still get a farewell show. Five year plan, man. I'm super sorry."

Mikey blinks for too long for a blink. He moves his face closer.

If it works, it's a sammrye move?

That's it?

ΛΛΛ

*B*ut you got more places to be. Rewind time a bit, like get back to when Mikey looked over and noticed Some Soma on the sectional couch. But be hanging out in the hallway instead. It's dim here and the wall's covered with soot and toiletpaper shreds. Wait for Mikey's voice to slip under the door.

Okay. Now stand on his voice. Slide it down the sticky hallway carpet like a skateboard made of smoke. To steer a voice you just oscillate the air behind it. Turn the corner, turn the nother corner. Don't hit the shrooms growing on the wall or you'll lose volume. Find the door with the tapedup poster for Spirograph, and slip through the door to Donn's lab.

Hey, Donn. He's sitting on his workstool, heaped in blankets like a shitty patchwork costume of a ghost. One hand over his face, rubbing his covered eyes.

"What's on your dreams?" says Mikey's voice. Maybe you're messing with him but it's the only way you'd see this.

Donn's blanketed head turns. "Hey? Mikey?" And course nobody's there. He dumps the bedspread and goes to prop the door open wide. Looks down the hallway. "Mikey?" He stumbles into the hall, then comes back.

While he's up he flips the record over. Kneels by the wobbly platter and blows on the coalfired turntable turbine til it's spinning even again. Eight scratchy speakers hanging from the ceiling for octupuphonic discrete tone control, diy outa red coffeecans and waxed coffeefilters and concrete plugs. Bad Brains start to thud and yowl in the hanging speakers, every bass lick a rattle of static as the lacy coffeefilters pulse. It's not sposed to sound good. You better of picked that up by now.

—*You don't want me anymore so I'm walkin out the door, played a game right from the start*—

The lab's a big old bachelor apt with a gently sloping floor and some tarpedup holes in the wall for windows. It's a bedless cave maze of TV tables and ironing boards piled with halfdismantled toys, bookcases and milkcrates of records nailed to the wall. Currently this potted guava tree's sticking up through a borehole in his draftingtable, spreading its arms at the window in the far wall. It's bent over like it fell asleep standing up, lashed to coathooks screwed into the table. There's a set of optician's scalpels spread out in a bakingtray, and a ball of mossgreen suture twine.

—*Now I'm sailin yeah I'm sailin on*—

Donn leans over the draftingtable again and scrapes at the center of this one bough til he's isolated a trough of heartwood with a webbing of sinewy tree veins around it. Then he starts snipping mouths from a potted venus flytrap and sewing them into the guava heartwood. Check it out, this tree's got flytrap mouths all over. Dozens of dozens like garish badges down a jacket's arms, berrypurple syrup drooling between their nubby yellow teeth.

Halfway down the limb his sailcloth needle slips and stabs one of the flytrap mouths, which deflates with a long smuffling noise. Donn grunts. He steps back, lifts the needle, points it at his wrist.

Breathe. Breathe. One hand stops the nother and he puts the needle down. He's like, "Aw, stupid deathtrip Germs acid."

Then he's like, "Stupid yuppies."

Just right on the wrist. So it scars in a hollow circle. Same as the one branded blue on the existentional void, the one you never noticed before. Donn's eyes roll up to meet it and his lips start moving round nothing.

MMM

You can see him from the back, climbing. Dreads tied with purple yarn, spilling over his spikey carapace. Wait, that's some kind of weird venturepack, studded leather over a spare tire. On Donn's front there's a reinforced pizza bib like the plastron side of a turtleshell. It's got a stitchedon pocket full of pencils. Maybe he needs to take pizza notes.

The universal logo for a pizzahut is eight slices painted cross a disc of yellow plywood mounted in the mouth of a taxidermic hippopotapus. For Ground Zero, it's wired to the side of a concrete wall, high up so everybody can see. Donn toes the mushy hippo as he climbs. Woodpeckers squeak and rustle from the pockedout nests in its abdomen.

No, you got all afternoon to fillosophize whether you're a crushed pop can magining itself a disembodied consciousness in a tertiary dream of Dimension X. Just stay with Donn. His hair's full of rain, he blinks rain from his eyes as he goes. He's scaling a cheap white plastic fire scape and the wall's not connected to anything up this high, it's only a finger of crumbling stucco and slick brown moss. Slow picky steps, maintaining three points of contact. He goes at it like he goes at anything. Like a long-haul technician, like your uncle halfwasted at a block party. Periodically stopping to unsnarl his bib straps from the cracky plastic rungs.

The tall stucco wall he's climbing stands pretty much vert. Same for the saggy plywood condominimum cross the street, where the Zero lives, but somehow they come close to butting up at the fifteenthstory condo deck. Donn stubs his head on slick metal and stops climbing and looks up. Reaches from the rungs and grabs the steep horizontal handbridge leading out cross the street.

The bridge's a naloominum ladder wedged into chiseled nooks in the stucco. Donn loops his ankles up through the horizontal ladder rungs and starts humping slothstyle cross the handbridge, pulling himself one hand, one foot at a time. His ass points at the nonymous mist and his big giant pack swings upside down, bumping and slipping against his shoulders. The ladder ends grind in their stucco notches and the handbridge rocks and soggy plaster dust drops into the fog like it'd rather get forgotten.

Your call if this is real.

The far side of the ladder's laying on the deck floor, like the whole handbridge's maintained only by gravity and the honor system. Donn tries to squeeze up through the space between the last two ladder rungs, but his spiky carapace gets stuck. He stops for a bit. His fingers get a little tenser on the slick corrugated rungs. Then they let go and he falls in a short arc. Now he's dangling headfirst by only his crossed ankles while the bridge slips back and forth with his weight.

Donn hangs there, wiping sweat off his hands. His dreads hang below him like a fleet of porcupinious black icicles. He undoes the pack straps and holds it in one hand while the other reaches and hauls him back up. Then he buckles the pack to the ladder and pushes himself up through the rungs again. Squatting balanced on the top of the sideways ladder, he swings the pack round and grabs it. Before he climbs over the deck railing to the Zero, he slips it back over his shoulders.

Some comatose punk's been balanced on the railing here with a hole ripped in the ass seam of his pants and a green winebottle stuffed neckdown in the hole. There's been a lot of ashing in the concave butt of the bottle. Through the door's a sweaty coatcheck room with dangling multi wick canlamps. A couple leathers are lightly on fire, Donn slaps them down.

Ground Zero's a nentire floor with the walls ripped down and cut down and stacked down into low tables. Spose none of the walls were retaining walls. Kids sitting on their knees eating pizza off plaster wall squares, and there's a shindeep styrofoam packing kernel floor for rolling around in, sept it's kind of dirty and anyway full of broken glass by now.

The near side's deserted, the far side's packed like a moshpit. You can just see the backs of all their spressionless leathers as if Darby's holding court at the corner table. As if there's a dozen bitten slices on a dozen plates before him while he spittily asks peopleses ears for money and picks the rims of his nose with a butterknife. Donn O'Aural with the germblue

O he set in his name, he stands on tiptoes for awhile. Brushing the ceiling with the long knuckles on one hand, staring into the crowd.

Then Donn stands down and walks through the paisley showercurtains into the back, where the ovens are. Old laundrymats make the best pizza kitchens cause you can prop trays in the dryers and stoke fires underneath. He's coughing. Gray sunlight silts down from the jagged windows and sticks in the reefs of lowhanging smoke. He pulls the closest dryer open and all the pizza's irrevocably on fire. Then the pan slides down the warped ovenracks and dumps a flaming pie on his boots.

He goes back out the door.

MM

Donn shakes out his face and stops. Waves his hand round his eyes. His hand stops and he stares at his new pink wristburn, barely glossed with scab. Like he found an eye growing there.

—Yeah I'm sailin yeah I'm sailin on—

"You're weird," says Donn.

Nobody's there.

He reaches cross his drafting table, grabs a ripe guava off the tree. It's the big of a squished navel orange, it's colored like yellow paint stirred with buttermilk. Donn holds it under his nose til the magnetic guava perfumes tilt his head back and crinkle his lips toward his earholes. Eyes shut piously, he slides his scalpel down the guava's core, then takes one half in his mouth, rind and everything.

Watch his tongue and cheeks move like they're dredging for a salmonbone. Then more like a mouthful of watermelon seeds. Then he cracks his eyes and grabs up the nother guava half. The fruitmeat's woven blackly with undigested bug parts. Tangled venetian blinds of fly wings, beetle carapace shards. Donn snaps upright.

"Dude! Dude! Those weren't there yesterday!" He hops over a milk crate of teddyruxpins, cassettedecks dangling from their open chest cavities. He stands in the doorway, clinging to the edges with his hands. "Hey Mikey! Mikey, my new tree! It works! The mouths really work!"

Donn stands alone in the doorframe for a bit. Tosses the bitten guava behind him. It splats facedown on the draftingtable. He's like, "Fuck me."

There's a little bit of space. You can see him thinking.

"Yuppies," he says, really really carefully.

He sags with his hands slipping down the sides of the doorframe just as the sides bend out to wide blue lines and spin and spin and the background's flickerating dark and without detail like copy toner bleeding into static. *GERMS INCOGNITO.*

G I.

GET INSIDE.

〜〜〜

Darby Crash. He's come out on the deck, got his face up drinking the rain. He's wearing this pirate hat of burnt black constructionpaper and hey, his arm came back. Punker doesn't say hi, he only yawns.

"I'm on a ton of acid," says Darby. "It's making me heavy."

He walks up and clings to Donn. Pulls himself up into Donn's arms and curls up like a baby monkey. Donn stumbles, slips on some discarded pizza crusts and falls on his back. The plywood deckplatform bounces beneath them once, twice, and the handbridge tips sliding into the mist.

Darby's sitting on him, pinning his knees. "Hey, you're not actually Pat."

Donn smacks his lips. Back's bent weird with the venturepack under him. "You know me, I thought. I'm Donn."

"You're not Don. Oh. Different Don. You're Donn of Meatheads." Darby laughs. "Not that Pat, either. Sorry, man. I pierce a lot too many veils when I'm on this Germs acid."

"I'm just Donn." He tries to lift himself. Just scrabbles like a flipped turtle with the big backpack under him. "I'd only be Donn of Meatheads if we were gone on tour."

"Too many veils, man." The legend snorts. "Did you got a question?"

Donn's head sinks back. "Are you tensionally pinning my legs?"

"I thought you liked it here in the cuddle club." Darby points his tongue through his lips. He turns his head a bit. Hey, the whole coat check room's full of teary black smog. Further in, there's billows of fire pushing round like someone lit a smoke at the gasoline wavepool.

Donn's mouth makes a hushed noise, and Darby's like, "I'm not sure if this is happening. It's actually nice acid."

A flaming sail of plastic coasts out of the smoke like a paper plane. Donn's like, "Man, they're in there!"

"You want to help people. You want me to get off your legs." Darby lays back, puts his head on some styrofoam junk. Him and Donn at right angles, their bodies forming a lopsided cross.

Donn's mouth hangs open and his hand pushes the side of his temple. He scuttles back on his hands and legs. Darby slides with him and his head drags the styrofoam pillow.

"Why do you want to help them? What's your reasoning?" Darby picks up a burnt halfsmoke from the deck and flips it in his fingers. All the sky's submerged in fog, the streets aren't there below. Like the mushy plywood deck's a turret of this ungainly and futile hovercraft trawling through the gloom. Sailing on.

Donn goes, "It's a fire, man! It's basic compassion!"

"They should stop, drop and roll," says Darby. "What's up with compassion?"

"Man!" By now Donn's wriggled himself halfway cross the deck with Darby sitting right on his knees.

"I'm getting you to chill out, Donn. First let your spressive muscles go slack. Those muscles there. There. And there." He's waving the halfsmoke at Donn's face. "You have tension. Brace your thumbs into your own jaw muscles and start massaging circularly. Yeah. Like that. Let it radiate gently outward. Your face is made of rubber butter and your thumbs are soft rose light. Yeah. Sailin' on. My thumbs are astrally guiding your thumbs.

"See, now you feel better," says Darby. Donn's like, "Yeah. A little." Then he whips his hands away, bangs his head on the ground. His jaw looks all tense again. "We need to help the fire!"

"You can't help a fire, Donn." His smoke's not even lit but Darby breathes out a huge black lung of smog. "But that ladder you broke? It was our only way down. Good thing the deck's wet, it might not burn while we wait." He sucks the stubby filter again. "Tell me bout compassion."

Donn's like, "What?"

"Haven't heard that word since back in history." The halfsmoke between Darby's fingers, it's growing longer as he drags. "I bet kids are all talking bout compassion."

"Only me," says Donn.

Darby smiles and flips the smoke behind him. It falls where the ladder fell, and somewhere there's a tiny dwindling scream. "What's compassion, Donn? Just magine I'm old and I forgot."

Donn lays his head to one side. The whipping fire inside Ground Zero flicks over the rings of his eyes. "When you want all beings to be free of suffering."

"No you don't." There's a laugh under the legend's whisper. Like his words are xeroxed over a really old joke. A palimpsest. He shifts sideways. They're side by side, their ankles are touching.

Donn curls into Darby's arms. "I don't know, man. Why'd you ask me here?"

"So you could tell me bout compassion, Donn." He's breathing into punker's matted dreads. "Why would we want each other free of suffering?"

"Cause it hurts. It just, I mean, a lot of shit hurts."

"That's it? Maybe you really don't know." Darby stretches his arms, folds them behind his head. You can see Donn tense up a little. "Tell me bout suffering. Where does it come from?"

"A lot of places." The smoke's crawling like black bath foam through the bottom of the door. It's all through Donn's hair. "Inflections. Miscommunication. Your friends standing you up. Or you want somebody to notice you and they don't. You know, just painful things." He breathes in. Starts coughing. "I guess there's a lot of suffering because people don't work out their feelings enough interpersonally. And they feel like they're caught in their past fuckups."

"Like with your band," says Darby.

Donn holds a fist against his forehead. "Yeah. Sorry. Yeah."

"You shouldn't be sorry, man. What do you think, though? Is there a common principle to all this suffering?"

"It means we all need to help each other?" says Donn.

There's some space. The fire whimpers and chuckles in a nother language.

"I really don't know. Sorry. I'm usually better at like circuit diagrams." He tries to reach his hand round Darby's shoulder.

"That you want cuddles is instructive." Darby doesn't move. "Here's something I thought up once. Like when I was in math class. We suffer cause we don't want things to change. We hold on with our minds. But we can't stop the universe. That's what suffering is. Desire shits out suffering."

"Arco says stuff like that," says Donn.

"We should all hang out more." Darby spreads his hands. "But this is my thing, Donn. Compassion is futile. You desire all beings to be free of suffering. But desire is that exact wheel."

"No," says Donn. "What? No. Wait."

"So I missed a part?" His hand's drawing a blue ring in the air.

Seriously.

Blue.

ᗩᐯᐯᐯ

She wears two sheaths for a single blade. Who cares where she's standing. If you want you can magine a cinderblock cell with a couple blue wool blankets folded in the corner, and the afternoon pushing in jagged bars through the cracks in the blocks. Like a pool changeroom or maybe it's a gas station shitter. She bows toward the folded blankets in your magination. Nobody showed her how to do this. Do you understand that bout Arco? Nobody showed her any of this.

The light's half on her and her feet are wide apart. One foot out, one back, like she'd do a forward roll. Her shoulder dips as her wrist pivots, she pulls the barepatterned steel of Margin Walker from one beltsheath and her arm shoots like she's grown a talon impossibly long. Then she's bowing, feet together. Then her hand chucks the sword to her nother hand, she snakes it to the nother sheath. She's turning, stepping forward, the new hand pulls the sword the same. And this goes on for the longest time. There's no rush, but you can see the bars of afternoon sun scroll down her face like a tape on fastforward.

Tell yourself you know what's in her mind. Don't try and meet her stance. Just say she acts on what's inside her, the way a zen master's like a dry stick or a parakeet. But you must of felt those three kids missing Arco. You magine Arco's worried bout her band?

She bows again. She bows again and starts drawing the second edge. The blade from the empty sheath. Arco's skinny tattooed fingers taking turns round the hollow air. Sure, maybe. Fuck it. Whatever. The substance of the way of the sammrye.

∧∧∧

So now you've seen these kids alone, and one's not like the rest.

Trick question. It's still you.

∧∧∧

Joke bout the tour van, it's got no wheels, and the back end's half buried in the forest floor. This coalcolored winnebago with busted windows and two sofas for back seats. Brown orchid blossons puffing from under the wheelrims. Tonight's dark early, and Donn's leaning half into the van, resting his sternum on the windowframe. The front seats are a car seat and a shattered pink toilet.

"So, like." Donn pushes his toe through the street dirt. "You helping with setup?"

Mikey yawns from the floor. In the middle of his yawn he yawns again. It's like hungry hungry hippos in here. "No." Then he actually looks up at Donn, looks down again in a hurry. "Someone said Arco's helping."

"Probly done already," says Donn.

Up the block a ways there's a pack of kids milling around at the entrance to the underground bowlarama. Dark spiky outlines like animate woodcuts, stepping and shoving, hunching with a casional dull orange glow where somebody's lighting something.

Mikey's sprawled on the floor, between the sofas, flipping a childsafe pillbottle in his hands. "Are we playing?"

"Meatheads broke up," says Donn.

"Oh." Mikey burps. It comes out smoke. "What'd you do today."

Donn hoists himself through the van window. "Did some science." Sitting against the broken toilet with his legs close together. "Had two acid flashbacks."

"You run into Darby?" says Mikey.

"Like, I don't know. I didn't sleep." Not a nuff room to stand up. Donn's pushing the musty van ceiling with his head. "I would say that Darby Crash manifested."

"Our boy really gets around," says Mikey. "Hey, lay down at least. You want kids to walk by and think we're cool?"

Donn shrugs. He lays down, reaches into the pillbottle's trajectory as Mikey bounces it off the ceiling. "You press down and turn. See?"

"Man, I know what opens bottles. You look sad." Mikey bites a little yellow pill in half, glances up again. "Hey, you do, right?"

"It's not bout you," says Donn.

Mikey's like, "Oh. I kind of tried to go fishing solo. Forgot there had to be yuppies though. So it was more just a rope ride." He cocks his eye at the other half. His teeth crunch it. "Darby was waiting on the nother end of the rope. We had a weird conversation."

"What about?"

"He's a fuckup," says Mikey with his hands behind his head. "He's using everybody. He doesn't get it. Like me, sept with more elegance."

Donn's like, "Ground Zero never burned down, did it?"

Mikey goes, "What?"

Donn looks out the window. "Hey, you want the band back together, right?"

"Oh. Oh, yeah, man. Yeah." His lips part a bit. "I think I know what to say to Raffia. She's not mad for real. She just wants to kick my neck."

"Okay." Donn winds a sofa spring out from round a dreadlock. He just eyeballs it. "You could tell me what's up with Darby and you. If you want, right."

"Man, I knew it. I knew it." Mikey's thumb spreads out the worrylines in his wide forehead. "There's nothing going on with us."

Donn's screwing the spring back on his dread. "Fuck, Mikey. You don't even like dudes."

Mikey's like, "Yeah, I know, right."

Donn puts his hand out. "Everybody knows you've been meeting up with Darby. None of us thinks it's major. You know I'm hung up on him. He's not that fucked of a guy to like, right? I just get shivery when he talks bout all the stuff he knows. Man, don't worry bout me. He's old, he's seen everybody. He had that threesome with Christ and Rollins." Donn takes a little deep breath. "I know he's not into me back or whatever."

"Okay, Donn?" Mikey awkwardly stretches in the space between seats. Takes one contorted position, then a nother. "Okay. These are truth pills." He eats a couple more yellow discs. "Also I've been smoking the hash of truth all day since the band broke up."

Donn sighs through his grin. "I don't need to tell Arco bout your secret."

"No, I'll tell her. Look, when I started conspiring with Darby, he told me to make noise bout me and him not having buttsex. He said hide it from your band in inelegant denials." He finally looks up at Donn. "But, like, you know Darby's just leading your dick around to blur up the issue, right?"

Donn takes a big deep breath. He mimes a gun with his fingers and shoves the barrel behind his ear.

Mikey's like, "Sorry, man. That's for later. Like, me and Darby did hook up once." He pauses. "Well, I sucked him off. But he stopped me halfway."

Donn goes, "Why?" and Mikey's like, "He told me, I just needed to see where your true talents lie."

"I'll think that's so funny tomorrow," says Donn.

∿∿∿

If you were sitting on the lip of the side window, you'd see her stomp up, hands at her sides. Like they'd be in her pockets, sept all she wears is hanks of scarlet leather armor held on by shower curtain rings. Raffia stops right there and winds up and stabs her fist right through the busted window, stumbling with the momentum.

"You already broke it," says Mikey. Donn's like, "Come in."

Raffia sets her elbows where you'd be sitting, leans into the van. Her face plows into your astral crotch. Maybe that's your kind of thing? She jerks a thumb at the bowlarama crowd. "We should set up if we can't do anything better."

"Arco's setting up," says Mikey

Raffia drops her chin onto her forearm. "She doesn't even care."

Donn goes, "Anybody get hurt?"

"A couple guys," says Raffia. "Bo. And then some nother guys." She fingers a gash down her hand. "Not really."

Mikey's slowly sitting up. His pupils are enormous. "Is the band still broken up?"

"You got truth pills." Raffia reaches for a handful of Mikey's hawk. Her spare hand roughly pets the side of his head. "Can I just punch you once and like strangle you round the throat?"

"After the show, sept you'll blow it off drumming," says Mikey.

She smiles, her teeth hidden. "You sound like Arco." Climbs into the seat next to Donn.

Guess the show started, the kids are gone from under the bowlarama marquee. All the neon tubelights are dead sept for one sterlingblue circle, like where your middle finger fits in the bowlingball. The circle's buzzing like a radio in the rain. Getting brighter as the wind kicks up and blows chip bags down the street. Who knows.

"So what are we doing?" Donn looks down the street, his palm visored over his eyes.

Raffia's like, "He ate truth pills. He'll spill it bout stubbing his dick on Darby's butt cheek."

"I'm just waiting for Arco," says Mikey. "I'll tell it."

"Wow. Serious voice," says Raffia. "Wish we didn't have a show tonight."

"We don't," says Donn. "You broke up the band."

"Oh." Raffia's sitting against the car door. "Right. I didn't mean like a perma breakup forever."

"No, what are we doing?" says Donn again.

Mikey shows his yellowflecked teeth. "Bout the show or the breakup or bout murdering Darby?"

"Gonna convince Donn?" says Raffia. "He likes Darby. Arco likes Darby."

"Even you don't kill your friends, Raff. I guess I get it." Mikey's shaking his head. "So what? Should we just go on tour?"

"I really like Darby," says Donn.

"Meatheads are touring?" This voice from inside a strolling cloud of smoke. It resolves to a gang of leggy chicks with beehive hair and peekaboo buttflaps snipped into their belted black rainjackets. "Finally. Meatheads are fucking old. Playing with Darby Crash even."

Raffia wheels, her head and torso sticking out the window like a dog's. "Stay outa our van!" But they're already down the road, down the bowlarama stairs.

"Man, we're not old. We don't even got beards," says Mikey. "Sept you, Raff."

"I—" She stops, then fluffs out her scragglous chinspikes, beaming. "I liked us better before we were real."

"We could change names again." Mikey shrugs. "But yeah. Like how we'd jam without worrying people would come. Or start copying us. How punks would start fights with us when we sucked."

"Arco used to beat them with her scabbards while we sat in this shitty tour van smoking weed." Donn's giggling. "Member when we built these loveseats outa fat guys?"

Raffia tweaks a sofa cushion's nipple. "I don't wanna drum tonight. I hate being the best band in the world."

"Arco can't—" says Donn. Raffia goes, "Fucking straight edge."

Spose the first band's over. For a handful of time they just watch kids push each a nother down the bowlarama steps. Casionally some punk'll stare at the van and they'll slouch lower in their seats, snickering.

"They're all so short," says Raffia.

"So should we just go on tour?" says Mikey.

"Yeah," says Raffia. "Maybe."

"The fuck?" says Donn. "We don't have to go out and get eaten when we could party and make stuff and have cool conversations. Bands don't actually have to tour. It's not like Logan's Run."

Mikey's like, "Logan's Run?" Then he's like, "But I'm not going if you don't want."

"Like there's a rule?" says Raffia. "There's no rules."

"It's my hardcore, asshole," says Mikey.

"Yeah. I know." Raffia licks her lips. "Mine too."

Blink. It's some skinhead in a jersey and ripped jeans. Face shaped like an ironingboard and tattooed zits like tiny assholes at the corners of his eyes. He's pressing his spread hands together, peering into the van. "Sorry, is she with you?"

They all stare at the arcore kid. He steps backward, head lowering in a rubbery way as he makes for the venue. Halfway across the street he pats himself down. Finds a clay flask in his pocket and he breaks it on a slab of pavingstone.

"It'd just be nice to do something," says Mikey. "You know?"

They're like, "Yeah."

⋀⋀⋀

Nother arcore skin comes up to the van. His mouth opens and his eyes flash down like he's consulting a phantasmal rolodex of language behaviors.

Raffia's like, "She went over there."

"Yeah," says Mikey. "She hopped the fence. Go help her out."

"Thanks." A weird spression shakes the skinhead's lipmuscles before he screws his eyes halfshut and nods. He steps stifflegged through the road with a giant butcherknife for some reason already gripped in his teeth and at the end of the block turns sideways, starts slipping through the thick bamboo.

"You guys just fucked that guy." Donn covers his eyes.

"Ah, they're all the same," says Raffia. "Sides, he looked alright with that knife."

Mikey nestles his chin on the window lip. "Magine going on tour and meeting those kids in the burbs. Like a touring arcore band."

"What, think Arco'd cut their skin off?" says Raffia. "Sammrye moves?"

"Shit, I kind of hope so," says Mikey. Donn's like, "Why?"

"You ever heard her bitch bout them?" says Mikey. "Yeah, me neither. She's gotta have some pent up bad vibes."

"I just miss her," says Donn.

"Pussy," says Raffia. "I'm gonna help set up though." She rolls out of the van. Turns round to glare at them.

"It's gonna be awkward," says Mikey.

"Come help, truth pills," says Raffia. She reaches in and bunches her fists round his bihawk crests, starts hauling him through the window. Mikey bends like a pretzel, pushing against Raffia's wrists with his boots. Everybody's laughing like they're getting tickled, then two hands drop onto Raffia's hands like spiders from a ceiling. Etchasketched with ashy tattoo lines like radio waves. Skinny, all tendon, impossibly distinct.

Blink.

Crouching on the van roof, Arco reefs upward on Raffia's handlock. Raffia spills backward into a stand of dilsweed, Mikey crashes faceward into the old blankets between the van seats.

Arco just goes, "Hey." Sucking her front teeth. She's not really looking at anybody. Sitting half through the window, one leg on each side. "Did you guys really want to play the show tonight?"

"Is the band back together?" says Donn.

Raffia's not getting up. "We all suck alone."

"If we're a band it's needful I play the show for my edge," says Arco. "We could reunion tomorrow though."

"What the fuck?" says Mikey. "Ultra sneaky."

"It was Darby's idea," says Arco.

"You've been talking to Darby?" says Raffia, hands behind her head in the flattened weeds.

"Some of his friends tried to help set up. I found some coke cutting open a wall safe." Arco's holding out a beheaded plastic baby with caramelcolored crystals leaking from its armpit joints.

"Aren't you straight edge or something?" says Mikey.

She's like, "You guys aren't."

∧∧∧

Donn puts his hand on Mikey's arm. "Open up first. We got the whole night to sit here getting fucked."

"Are we, like, octogenarians?" Mikey's tipping coke from the doll's neck into his palm. "Ow."

Raffia's teeth are clamped to the back of Mikey's head, where the brainstem is. Mikey sighs and pours the handful of coke back into the doll. He mimes a single tear track down his cheek.

Raffia's like, "What's octogenarians?"

Arco's like, "Yeah. What's octogenarians?"

They're sitting two by two in the hairy winnebago loveseats in the dark, kicking their feet lazily across the van floor. Like there's a ghost fire between the seats and they're warming their toes.

"You weren't there." Mikey half unslips his jacket. "This is the spiel of me fucking up and putting trust in the old guy. There's no patch for this spiel. Cause it's not history. It's just a bunch of stuff that happened." He looks out across them. "Tell me if I start shitting you."

"Deal," says Arco.

"Yeah," says Raffia. Her knuckles sitting lightly in the joins between his ribs.

"Kay," says Mikey. "That time Meatheads broke up after we played the Bizz Kwik rooftop with Failure To Thrive. Darby came up to me while I was jacking it in an alleyway. You weren't there. Like, it's not just how spiels start. With this one it's the problem. None of you were round.

"Ever since Darby started shooting beer in his neck veins, he's been getting drunk a lot. And he's got this vibe when he's drunk. Like a truthfulness vibe. He tried to take me home and I was like, sure. I was really hungry. I thought, maybe I could suck him off and he'd have like beer or steak.

"But he just wanted to drink, well, you know, through his neck. And lay in his empty jacuzzi all night having existential crisises. Dude wanted me to hold his hand and he told me all these things he fucked up in the young days of Lost Angeles and like before the Antidisestablishmentarianism even. I didn't get half the shit he meant. A lot of it didn't line up. But he said if I held onto it til his farewell show, I could have his leather."

"Like instead of splitting up the patches?" says Donn.

Mikey just kicks an invisible log in the invisible fire. Invisible sparks blink in the air. The air's invisible too.

"You can do that?" says Raffia. "Like, somebody's whole jacket?"

Mikey goes, "He said, be me when I'm gone. Wear my face for a mask if you want."

"That's fucked," says Arco. "Why were you okay with that?"

"Yeah, man," says Donn. "Your whole life diyed your jacket."

"Sometimes we all need a change," says Mikey. Nobody laughs. His arms are tucked inside his jacket, the empty sleeves hang loose. "I wasn't gonna take the name. You done making me feel shitty?"

"No, man." Arco leans in. Her hands folded in her lap, her eyes shining flat and blue in the dark. It's not just cat eyes that do that? "You been talking bout Darby all day, how he pushes his ego on us. Makes punkers his tools. It's not with nothing he does that."

Mikey's like, "I know."

"That jacket's from history, Mikey. It's not just yuppie leftovers. Darby's so old and he's so strong and he'd leave so much hardcore in that jacket if he wasn't there. It's not a jacket for telling the truth in, man."

"I'm not done making me feel shitty either," says Mikey. "He promised his leather to a bunch of different kids. I think he put us all in the same place. Like we all figured we were solo in his trust."

Donn breathes out. "Why'd he do that?"

"We had a weird conversation bout it," says Mikey. "Thing is, last night was his suicide plan. Just the tiger fucked it up for him. He planned it out so all these kids would hate him for making him think they were solo inheritors. Like, I thought he wanted to set punkers against each other, right. But he wanted to turn us all against him."

"Same thing," says Arco. Mikey looks crosseyed at her and she's like, "He thinks he can reach into us and put whatever he wants there. No, man. That makes me agree with you. Darby's no good for us."

"What?" says Mikey. "I dunno if I even agree with me anymore."

"But that's all there is, bandmate?" says Arco.

Mikey's like, "I probly killed Trip Hazard. Over the leather."

"You said that at the show already. Nothing else?" Arco puts two fingers on her chest. Over her inside heartside pocket.

Mikey doesn't say anything, and Donn's like, "Raff? Put in on this."

"Yeah," says Raffia. Mitts behind her head. "Darby's got such a sweet jacket. Like how the patches are all black and washed out. It's like mysterious."

Mikey's like, "Fuck, Raff. Fuck." He looks over at Arco. "Yeah. That's all there is."

"I said I'd help murder him, what else are you asking?" says Raffia. "Now you wanna be nice to him? Let's do some coke."

∧∧∧

They're all on their bellies in soft tangled blankets between the seats. Arco's biting her toenails down and passing them for Raffia to chew and Donn's rolling a funnel out of a big leaf and Mikey's scrabbling through the debris between the seats, looking for a cokebottle. Hey, you saw that bottle, right? Wedged between sofa cushions. You're not even pulling it out for him? Just cause they're sammrye doesn't mean they know where they left anything.

But then something finally happens. Huge cracking sound in the front seats, like an albatross shat out a hubcap on the windshield. They all flail round accidentally kicking each other. Donn whips out a cranktorch from somewhere, lights up the front seats. The top piece of some asshole's head, it's embedded in the windshield glass. Long auburn hair fanned out all round the web of concentric cracks.

"Man," says Donn. "I just cleaned that glass."

"What, in the McReagan ministration?" says Raffia.

Arco's like, "Sorry, I thought it was something serious. Maybe we should still semble, though."

When they do, nobody's there. There's not even kids outside the venue. Just deep fuzzy riffs rolling up the steps, and in between the spaces in the rhythm there's standard melee noise like cheap cardtables breaking. And they loom there by the van, brandishing their gear like tryhards, but at least the wind's picked up a little. Set the tails of their headbands waving and put some spression in their hair.

"Gnaaarly," says Arco.

This asshole's staggering down the street in a cumbersome foam suit shaped like a wonderbread loaf. Above her eyes, the skull's gone, baring her brain like a veiny salmon jellomold.

"Not one of us," says Donn. "See how the cortical veins aren't pulsating?"

"Whatever," says Raffia.

"Mikey, you wanna do this one?" says Arco, though she's herself grabbed the classic katana pose. A halfstep behind her, Raffia's already sent a sledgehammer looping in a gentle underhand arc. Wait, there's some kind of ungainly molotov lashed guttering to the hammerhead. Whole thing drops headdown into the yuppie's brainpan. Slosh.

"Yeah, I'll do this one," says Mikey. "Was that our coke bottle?"

Held up in the wonderbread costume, the shape only drops to its knees. Raffia goes up and kicks it cross the eyesockets. Glass shatters muffled inside the yuppie's midbrain and a brief pillar of fire jumps around.

And hey, the legend's slouched abruptly on the top bowlarama step, wiping gore from a big serrated breadknife to the bottom of his treadless boot. His name is Darby Crash. The name of his name is Darby Crash. The name of the name of his name, oh, you get it. One jacket sleeve tattered away and the armhole ringed with boneshards painted indigo. He turns his neck and he's grinning through a mouthful of smoke.

"Man?" says Donn.

Darby's like, "I thought you guys would like that. Happy Xmas."

"Yeah. Yeah, that was good!" Foot on the burning yuppie's collarbone, Raffia tugs out her shorthandled sledge.

"Hey, Mikey," says Darby. "This must of fell out of your pocket. Like when you did that solo fishing trip. Probly you want it, hey?"

It's a folded chunk of black canvas secured with a diaperpin. Darby holds the patch in his teeth, thumbs his cheekmeat up briefly over his eye. Wait, if you've got one eye, is that like winking?

Mikey snatches the patch out of his mouth. "Thanks, man." He bites the head off the diaperpin. "Hold on, what the fuck?"

The sledgehammer slips from Raffia's hands and her eyes gape as Mikey unfolds the patch. She swings an arm round Mikey's side, gathers him in like snuggle time, her thumb searching out the meat between his rib bones.

"So what patch is it, anyway?" says Darby. "Gonna wear it?"

Even Arco's making this drawnout little eeping noise. Mikey's spare hand snakes into his heartside jacket pocket. And inside the pocket it opens and closes on nothing.

"There's no Black Flag patches." Raffia squeezes Mikey's ribcage with an immanent crumpling sound. "There's no Black Flag patches left." And she is fucking crying, tourist, she's crying tears. Are you even into hardcore?

"Fuck." Mikey's bent slightly sideways, accordionwise. Taking bubbly little mouse breaths. "Fucking Black. Flag fans are. All alike."

Yeah, it's the Flag patch the same. Rough canvas like a square torn off an acidwashed dragon. Quad bars screened the color of bloody tar. "Motherfucker." Looking around, it's like nobody can tell who said that.

Darby's stepping in. He kind of leans forward, leading with his missing shoulder. Then shivers and turns, holds his one hand near the patch. See the liverspotting all down the back of that hand. "I thought I'd never see one of those again."

The shake in Darby's voice comes timex precise. "Pat made this patch. Like Pat Smear. Kira lent him fifty bucks to finish screening that run. He'd of missed rent so he went on mergency sikiatric welfare. He had to talk to a shrink with ziplocs of goldfish in his pants. We used to play before Flag. God, man, before they went on tour. We'd watch half their set and then go play beercan ball in the drinkinglot. You know how much Greg Ginn hated that?"

Mikey looks over to Raffia. "It's not mine. I've never seen it."

"What the fuck?" says Raffia. Her head dips in and out as Mikey's fingers shake. "Something like that was just on the ground?"

Darby's like, "Could I just hold it, man? Just for, like, a bit?"

"You should let him have it," says Raffia. She peels it from between Mikey's finger claws. "He was there."

"Really?" says Darby. Face pointed far from Mikey. "I'll do whatever. I'd give you any other patches. Anything." He's fumbling out transistors, deceptacons, packs of smokes from his pockets. Holds this battered folding scoutknife with a handle of black plastic staghorn, then shivers and hucks it over his shoulder.

"Fuck it. Have it, Darby," says Mikey. "It's yours now. Don't worry bout it."

"Course man, for sure." Darby's holding the patch to his shoulderstump. It fits right in the middle of the inlaid circle. "So you guys are getting back together tomorrow night?"

"Are we?" says Mikey.

"I was saying it," says Arco.

They look between each other. For some reason it's Donn who steps forward and nods. Hands behind his back holding his wrists.

Darby's like, "Right on. Hey, the Arcos are bout to start. Come with me."

"Don't like those bands," says Arco.

"I know." Darby's folding the patch up and it goes in his pocket. "Cause you feel misunderstood seeing crews of derivative, second-rate posers. But it's alright to do what you hate. It's like the meditation on diying."

"How?" says Arco.

No, but Mikey's stepping forward. "What if you let me tell the patch?"

"Like the tour spiel might be different in a real silkscreen? Shit, Mikey. Be my pleasure." Darby's mouth just cracks slightly, like a smile. "Didn't even think."

So Mikey leans in to touch and you're there, tourist, the patch in Darby's hand. His four fingers bent at your edge like they're projecting the four staggered bars on his skin, and the hollow of his palm, and the lines of his hand showing just exactly through your black canvas. The lines of Darby's hand rising so tall around you. Somewhere under the pinning canvas there's a cold breeze of bonfire smoke, and you're falling. What, you missed your shot, Mikey, you tourist? You're only lines in Darby's hand.

∿∿∿

—wasn't there. I wasn't even born. I just know something happened. Like the road—

You're feeling the heavy toecaps of your boots. Feeling your eyelids quiver like somebody's asleep. Feeling Mikey's voice low in your throat.

"—snaked up for us and opened its mouth, and Rollins threw a curse on all our hardcore. We didn't know he could do shit like that. But he was Rollins of Flag, and the black road talked in his voice. Not in all your diying will you—"

Mikey cuts off his voice. His face shakes like he slapped himself from the inside.

"Yeah. Same old Black Flag tour spiel. Sorry, man." Darby's folding up the patch and it goes in his pocket. "I know you wish you could get some dirt on me."

Raffia's like, "Reruns."

"Have patience." Darby sweeps his hand at the stair. "Come on with me, I've got VIP boxes."

"There's no VIP boxes at a bowlarama," says Mikey.

Darby's like, "Lord Buddha instructs us to expect the unexpected." All the liverspots smearing, wearing off his hand.

∿∿∿

"I still think this was intended as an air duct," says Donn. He pauses. "I got to fart."

Laying on their bellies in a hanging loominum tube, they're slathered with antique dust and stacked together like a packet of wieners. The tube creaks and sways as Donn blows dust from the narrow grille in the front. It might not really be rated for having five people writhing in it.

"Arco, could you move your scabbards?" says Mikey.

"Darby?" says Arco. "What'd you want to ask us?"

Darby rests his middle finger on Arco's upper lip. "Check out the band. The next song'll be better."

Punker exposed a bunch of copper piping in the walls, augured holes for little shoelace wicks and filled the pipes with grease. Like a million little candlelights. They just make the bowlarama look haunted. Kids are packing the lanes, pissing in the gutters, whipping bowlingpins cross the air like they're beerbottles or something.

For a stage there's dirty plywoods laid down over the main counter. The band's heads are near brushing the ceiling, and there's rows of cubbyholes full of shoes behind them. Tell you one thing, the rule bout no outside shoes is no longer strictly enforced.

"Your scabbards are in my fucking kidneys," says Raffia.

So this band's called the Arcos. They look bout how you'd expect. Stead of instruments they're jumping in a circle with sheets of corrugated roofing tin over their heads. Bringing them down to make rhythmical whamping noises, frequently shouting *BOP* or *BUP*. Their hands are bloody from the snipped edges on the tin. The moshpit's crammed with jerseys, washedout denim, nicked scalps, painted zits, assholes going *BOP BUP* in perfect time and beating the lino with bowlingballs.

"It's not even the war mup," says Arco. "There isn't a mup."

"Jud Jud already did it," says Mikey.

"Mind if I smoke?" says Darby.

"I can't help it," says Mikey. His hands sort through his jacket pockets and he passes Darby a bent mallburrow slim. Arco sneezes once, like a prophecy, and Darby's like, "Sorry." He slips the smoke under his watchband with a lithe bend of his thumb.

"Watch the band," says Darby. "Seriously, Arco, this next song. They're gonna do it on their own."

"What?" says Arco. Darby's like, "I didn't set up shit."

This one skinhead, long skinny one in a neon blue belted trenchcoat, she's pushing through the pit. As she passes the other arcores stop pogoing and step way back. She stops at the base of the stage, awkwardly falls forward onto it, and climbs upright in a weird bendy torso maneuver. The face is kind of small, and the scalp's freakishly lumpy, but the zits look great.

"Shit, that can't be Arco." Mikey snickers. "Arco's up here. Right? Right?"

Raffia jabs her elbow sideways in the cramped vent. Everything dips further, and Donn's like, "Ow."

"I'm Arco!" says trenchcoat. "You guys suck!" High and clipped, kind of oppressively matter-of-fact. "Get off the stage! But leave the drums! We're— I'm Arco! I'm doing a solo show!"

The Arcos just lay down their sheets of tin, they step facelessly into the crowd. The pit goes quiet, and bottles and bowlingpins make clattering arcs in the back, and there's some general whatthefuckuous screams. Trenchcoat walks a quick circle around the stage. Lifts her arms victoriously. You've gotta wonder why they're mounted so low. It's like her arms come outa her ribcage. Then, under the coat, this person's torso weirdly splits apart like a totempole of trashcans coming down.

Everything stops. It's just the blue trenchcoat onstage like a crashed tent, and then four little kids zip out from beneath. One's wiping fake acne off her cheeks. Her hair's all bent and lumpy from the showercap. This kid. This kid. She's like, "WE'RE FUCKALLAYOU! THIS IS OUR FIRST SHOW! IT'S OUR BIRTHDAYS TODAY!"

Arco's laughing. She's better at it than you'd think. This deep fast thrumming laugh from the gut muscles under her heart. She pitches back and forth, pounding the VIP vent's sides, and then it dislodges halfway from the wall bracket and they slide forward with their faces all mushing into the grille.

Darby's like, "Hey. Be good." And beneath them, in the pit, all these arcore kids are just standing agape. Maybe some think Arco actually exploded or was made of children all along.

Birthday's got both her hands out, shrieking, throwing devilhorns, and two of her bandmates have the tin sheets stood up, running giant novelty dinner forks up and down them, a wood fork for bass, metal for treble, making a rhythm like a rattlesnake fucking a zipper. The last kid you know. Taco Eater's screwing together pieces of PVC pipe and it's some kind of cyclopean didgerikazoo, taller than he is. His face turns purple as he starts ripping out riffs.

"Dude," says Donn as the air vent sags further forward and hollers of glee and multitudinous bowlingpins and winejugs loop into the moshpit like a burst of migratory geese. "Dude. Dude. Dude, they're playing Milk Carton Angels."

Somebody's screaming these guys are birthdaycore, and finally the arco clones all spin round with kitchen knives and table legs. "I can't sit back," says Raffia, slamming her forehead into the grille. Bolts pop from its edges. "Not while punks are getting hurt."

"Getting hurt without you," says Mikey, falling headfirst into the crowd.

ᗰᗰ

"You asked them to," says Arco. Sitting on top of the orchidswathed winnebago, one leg dangling through the skylight. The two of them gray shades. Unfinished line drawings. Staring out at the moon while it clears whichever rooftop in the distance and pencils them in.

"I thought it was a joke," says Darby. "Yeah, jokes start shit. I should know that." He shakes his head. "You never know how strong's your hardcore really. Not even when you push it. I just didn't think any crew could rip down a skyscraper."

He flips her a smoke. Her index finger taps it in the air and it goes wheeling the other way. "I got the straight edge," says Arco.

"Course," says Darby, catching her smoke on his knee as he snaps a yellow bicflame cross his own. "We need to come up with a nother spam works though. Today was fine, tomorrow's fine. Punks gonna get grumpy though, eating nothing but linty jerky from their ass pockets."

"Where are you thinking? Hold on." Arco stands, turns. Draws and sheathes Margin Walker. Bows to something. The air maybe, the universal flux. Sits back down.

Darby giggles. "Practice for you is like smoking."

"How?" says Arco.

He blows a slow, spiraling white plume, and gestures the same spiral with the end of his smoke. Takes a while to speak. "Cause they're both a way of keeping your mind limber. Insulating will away from things that don't concern it. Glimpsing the motion of your hardcore. Relinquishing control. Preparing to diy. And putting shit off."

"I've never seen you practice," says Arco.

"I might got the straight edge," says Darby. He shakes his head again. "Maybe the spam works shouldn't be such a big building though. We kept on losing spam. And you know all those floors that just got super gross with pink mold. Maybe we oughta decentralize."

"What do you mean?" says Arco.

"It's like practice or jamming or whatever," says Darby. "We designate spaces by custom. But we don't really need one space over a nother. Like how you guys use your jamroom for whatever you need. And shit, one day you might need to jam on the road. But like, all you need to make spam is like yuppie meat and, you know—"

Darby's ember draws a spinny little wheel in the air, and Arco's like, "Meat hanging racks, bit of fire. Depends on the recipe. Sometimes you mince it with berries. Salt sometimes."

"Right, right, right," says Darby. "Racks and fires, you can hide those in whatever closet. Decenteration. Crews just putting out their own runs of spam and sharing them round. So it's not even shifts anymore, you don't have to hassle anybody to show up. You're just on your way back from taking a shit, and you open the closet, turn the spam."

Arco shrugs. "Yeah."

"Maybe Meatheads could help out, like a show in support?" says Darby. "If you think it's a good idea. Like a show with constructing of spam racks. Hey Arco?"

"Yeah?"

Darby's laying back. Aiming his smoke at the moon. "That band. The one named after you. How'd they make you feel?"

"Nobody ever asks me bout, like, arcore people," says Arco. "I don't like talking bout them either."

"Sorry," says Darby.

"No. It's a bad place for me," says Arco. "But they say to keep going when you're in a bad place. In my mind I challenged them up on the stage. I cut them down and then I thought, they had friends. Thought bout cutting their friends down. How there'd be nobody left could tell their bodies apart." She puts her nother leg through the winnebago skylight. "Hungry ghost."

"People want leaders," says Darby. Biting the filter tip, spitting it away. He sucks at the ragged brown end, and the cherry crackles fire. "The people who hate leaders, more than anyone."

"I know," says Arco. "Why though?"

"You think something," says Darby Crash. "What is it?"

Arco looks down at her hand, the pinpoint inkwork on her fingers. All roads heading to the legend. As she shakes her head there's a bugzapper noise above them and this streetlamp blinks awake, overspilling them with light the color of molten salt.

"That never used to happen." Darby laughs. "Well, it did. But back then it wasn't fucked."

"What, the pole?" says Arco. "I don't know. Sometimes I wonder if yuppies aren't better."

"Go on."

"I am." She looks at him sidelong. "Punkers never stop thinking. I always figure that's the problem."

"What are we thinking bout?" says Darby.

"Doesn't matter." Arco sucks her bottom lip. "They're hungry. Or the air's stale. Or how to make inner tubes into pants. Punker never decides shit thinking, and then they think I'm different. Cause you can't see somebody thinking."

Darby grins. Big and bright and open. "Never."

"They think there's this thing called not thinking." Arco's talking slow, laying the words like a stack of dominos. Creases blow across her thin brow skin. "They see Meatheads are awesome. They see I'm rad with swords. I keep a straight edge. I shave my head and wear jerseys. And they think that must be why it is."

"Maybe you're an idea in their thoughts," says Darby.

"Every time I turn round, I look at a shitty me," says Arco. "Darby? How do you handle that?"

See Darby's smoke dissolving into fire, no filter to spit in the road. "The crash trash? They love me."

And Arco sags. She's looking down into the empty van with her hands over her eyes.

If it works, it's a sammrye move?

Is that it?

〜〜〜

Back to back to back. Mikey, Raff and Donn fighting like a threelegged stool. Fuckallayou jumped into the pit a couple dropkicks ago, but their songs just sounded like fighting anyway.

"Where's Arco?" says somebody. Probly Donn.

"Left with Darby," yells a flash of mouth in the crowd. Black tattooed lips edged with safetypins. Raffia grabs punker's ears, draws her in for a thunderous headbutt.

"Why?" says Raffia, holding her by the sides of the head.

"Cause he asked her, dumbass, like a normal person!" Safety lips, she's reaching past Raffia altogether, just unconcerned, lashing at strangers with a car antenna. "Fucking sellouts, broke up cause you couldn't handle playing with Darby!"

Raffia headbutts safety lips again. Drops her, though she doesn't fall, just rolls into a better stance and gets lambasting Raffia's torso with the silver switch.

"Let's go spy on them," says Mikey. He whirls, slugs Raffia in the temple. Snorts laughter. "Good one?"

Raffia shivers her head. She's like a musk ox with flies landing on its nose. "Arco can fucking take care of herself."

"Everyone can," says Donn. He's spinning his stick, trapping kids' weapons on the dented blades. Some asshole's bowieknife shoots into the ceiling tile and sticks there, vibrating. "Still."

"Fuck," says Raffia. There's a good chunk of somebody's lip, maybe her own, impaled on her canine like a maraschino cherry.

Hey, there's Taco Eater swaying at the level of her tits, he's clinging to her bandoliers. A rude crude gremlinoid baby like an autonomous teratoma. Raffia grunts and looks down with balled fists. Smoke smokes from her nose.

"Throw me at the posers!" Taco looks up at her, bright eyes. "You never take me bowling, you fat monster! You're a shitty mom!"

Donn's like, "You know you're not fat."

"There's no God," says Raffia. She swings the kid by his ankle, clearing a mosh circle, and fires him through space. There's clusters of arcore kids knocked down and bleeding from the ears and Taco Eater's scream dopplers into the shortwave spectrum as he keeps going. Then his legs are protruding motionless from a huge dusty crater in the far wall.

"Yeah." Raffia looks down at herself, adjusts her bandoliers. Line of sight in this bowlarama's getting disrupted by curls of crimson mist. "Yeah. We should go hang out with Arco."

ᴧᴧᴧ

"Welcome." Darby slaps twice on the van's peeling hide. Rain bounces round his hand.

And they stand on the hood. They stand up on the roof in the rain. Arco nods to them proficiently.

"I lost a lot of friends last night." Darby shrugs. "Playing with kids who don't dress like me."

"What's up, Arco?" says Mikey. "Pit wasn't feeling right?"

"You guys might of left at a good time," says Donn.

"Pits are all similar to me. Too bad bout that taco baby." Darby cracks his back. Then his knees. "Yeah. Been a long time since I had fun moshing. Sept for last night, I guess. Last night was pretty special." He starts cracking his knuckles onehanded into the silence, pulling at each finger's base with his thumb.

"You talked like you were ready to go," says Mikey.

"You're asking if I still want death. Donn, reach toward me." Donn kneels and Darby sits his tricep on the outstretched arm. "Yeah, punker." Darby lunges down onto Donn's arm, popping his shoulder joint. "Nah. Today I'm not sure I want death. I think I came back into who I am. Meatheads were so good to play with. I felt like a teenager. Like opening for Black Flag and Minutemen at the Whiskey."

"Thanks," says Donn.

Darby reaches into his fly. There's a definite cracking noise. Sometimes you can't say. "You guys were like Germs. Hey, hold on. Cause I don't mean you sounded like Germs. But when I'd fuck up, you never tried to cover it. You knew fucking up was it."

"Thanks," says Donn.

Now Arco's the only one sitting. Swinging her legs through the winnebago skylight.

"You guys are the best band since the death of historical consciousness," says Darby. "Don't ever go on tour. That'd be a total waste of chi."

Mikey's like, "What?"

Raffia's like, "What if we want to."

"What's that band just played?" says Darby. "Arcos. They'll tour pretty soon. Run round in the burbs, blow out a million yuppies til somebody fucks up. They're dumb at thinking, but not at fighting. They've got hardcore. Only they don't gleam. Your crew puts a new thing in the city. Meatheads."

Mikey's shaking his head tinily. You notice how his boots are pointing different? Like somebody getting ready to take a punch?

Darby leans forward. Arco's behind him in the pounding rain, one hand on her venturepack, looking up with eyes like cateye marbles. "I wanna play with you guys again." And this to Mikey. "Fullon show."

"What the fuck?" Raffia pushes past Mikey, lifting Darby by his stubside collarbone.

"One more show." Darby's feet are off the ground. "Meatheads with Darby Crash on lead vocal role."

Mikey spins toward Darby. "What'd you say to her, man!"

"We talked bout the nature of posers." Arco's finally standing. "Nobody needs permission to talk."

"We're the band, old man." Raffia pulls Darby higher. His head lolls a little, he's grinning. "You didn't move out with us. You've never battled longside us. You don't jam with us. Hardly ever drink with us. You don't just ask to be in somebody's band."

"You could of played with me even in history." Darby's boots swing in midair. "Give yourselves a shot."

"I wouldn't feel right," says Donn. Arms crossed low over his stomach. "The one show was great. But we do our own thing."

"Germs are fucking dead," says Raffia. But then she's just looking at her hand. Darby's down on his feet, still grinning, faster than anybody can see.

"It was sposed to be a oneoff show, Darby." Mikey reaches under his skylight, rubs the convoluted brains. "We know you're just gonna kill us."

"You guys know I have to say yes." Arco's got her back to them all. "No turning down shows."

"He's playing your fucking straight edge." Raffia's eyelids squeeze shut. When they open, the whites are half red.

"It's still my edge. No turning down shows." Arco's turning around. "If it mattered, I'd wish it wasn't."

No windup. Mikey throws his meteorhammer at Darby's teeth. The old guy leans backward, languidly holding out his arm. The leather string loops once around it and the steel bulbs whip back round, clock the two sides of Mikey's head.

Mikey falls to his knees. Darby drops the meteorhammer to the winnebago roof. But Mikey laughs. "The band's not back together yet, douche. Ow. Arco, you can't accept a show if the band's not together."

"So I'll ask you tomorrow," says Darby. "Oh. There's posters."

Now there's two freaky heavies standing on the van hood. Got vulture legs through their septums. Identical punkerscrosses carved in their cheekbones, bloody and impromptu. Darby steps to them and they lift him and he's standing between their shoulders. Shooting Meatheads an ironical salute.

"I don't want you guys to be pissed," says Darby. "One more show. And I found you some vodka."

∧∧∧

Chalk and coal on papyrus, the line of four black spikes saying MEATHEADS, like teeth or surf or a fire, and the huge blue ring of GERMS that's Darby Crash locking over one spike, the whole thing like an irradiant blue sun coming up over a mountainrange.

There's no other thing it can mean.

There's nothing else anything can mean.

And all the way to the bottom of the spider-silted vodka, all the way back to the House of Meatheads, the road's proud with nailedup posters. Nobody says shit. And while they're standing out in front, looking at each otherses feet like they're trying to find the right swears, some kid climbs down from the building.

"When's your guyses show?" says some kid. Trying to sound bored, but his hands give it away. They're pressed to his chest in the prayer formation, and also, he just grew a boner.

"It's—" says Donn.

Meanwhile something fast happens. Basically Raffia's screaming and swinging a masonhammer overhand while Mikey dives into her sideways and Arco's hand catches the hammerhead. The three of them pull down this kid incidentally in their kicking tangle.

"I don't know when, actually," says Donn.

"It's not cool to kill a stranger without asking," says Arco at the bottom of the pile.

"We're not Darby's band," says Raffia. Kid's like, "I shit in my pants."

"Hey, right on," says Mikey. "We're having some creative differences ourselves."

∿∿∿

Crosscore, in the bowlarama wreckage, some littler kids are covered in dust and picking through the victims. They've got one diy torch, a femur full of beewax. They're a band too.

"Can you still see?" says the kid with a blue handprint on her skull. Her name's Merle Gravy, it's really not important. "There's shitloads of blood in your eye."

The singer shakes her head. The berryjuice zitmarks on her cheeks already fading. Stamps you get at shows. "My nother eye can see. This one's gonna be fine though."

There's words for her too. Zoe D' Axe. But don't get hung up on who they are. Watch how they carry it.

"How do you know?" says the third one. Noam Smoking. Looking up from some comatose arcore midget and you wonder if the arrow through his head is fake. It sure wasn't there on stage. He yells again. "Taco?"

Zoe's like, "Arco gave it to me. She wouldn't of wanted me to go blind."

"Arco?" says Noam. "Fuck. Can you give one to me?"

"Piss me off, then." Zoe cups her hand over her bruised eye, turns all round. Then she's running. Carhide sandals almost silent. "Aw, fuck, you called it, Merle."

They chase her sandals. Their one torch bobs. Their heads bob by the far wall. "It's his boots at least," says some punk.

"Fuck his boots." Make them your hands. Get some exercise. Your halfsized hands go out and rench at Taco Eater's dumb cowboy boots and the whole baby comes out of the crevice in the wall with a great billow of red dust and a tumble of brick chunks and the side of his head smashed in.

They're grabbing at Taco, propping him up, easing him onto a fluffy bathmat they got from somewhere. His body's rigid, twisted a bit from stuff kinked inside him. He's wearing that same fucking spression that's on every dead punker, like a grin trance planted from the drunkest of Darby's faces, that fissure where sweet fuckall rose like radio static and dispersed.

"We shouldn't of let him in our band," says Noam. "Top of his head was still soft."

"Maybe that's just our hardcore," says Merle Gravy. "Our bass players never survive." The blue handprint, it's not shaved. She semi scalped herself and poured koolaid on top. "Where do we find a nother bass player with the same birthday as us?"

"He never even heard the tour spiel though," says Zoe. "He was talking bout asking his dad for it. But he said he was waiting for a time."

"Shit, shit, shit." Noam smooshes his nose with the back of his hand. "Do you even get a nother rain carnation if you diy before hearing the tour spiel?"

"I dunno, I never did it." Zoe sits. "We could try and pull his ghost back from the House of Anything Goes."

Noam's like, "What are we, Meatheads? We can't do that!" But he still sits. Earl sits. They all sit with their knuckles facing together in a try angle.

"What do we think about?" says Noam. Merle's like, "Fuck!"

They sit.

Noam's like, "We thought you were sposed to know, Zoe. Man, he's cold already."

"I heard you're just sposed to sit with the dead body and think what it's thinking," says Zoe. "So don't think shit, I guess."

They sit with their knuckles together and they stop fidgeting after a while. Their eyes go slippy as they sit. They've been up all night, and Taco's corpse starts farting. Farts just rattle out of it with no sense of finality whatsoever. It's like the giant grin. Culturally appropriate for a certain kind of dead body at a certain place and time.

"Okay," says the singer with her one eye full of blood. "Fart if you wanna hear the tour spiel now."

They hang there, waiting for a sign.

—*The day Flag went on tour forever we set the loading dock on fire. It was a special kind of concrete that burned.*

They hang there, waiting.

〰〰〰

So Raffia busts through the door with a sheaf of showposters under her arm, thicker than a phonebook. Everybody else's sunk in the sofa, boots on the coffeetable, staring up at the dead slanty ceilingfan.

"That's not all of them," says Mikey.

"Punker, he'll just print more," says Arco.

"Help me eat the posters." A huge coalcolored spitwad flashes between Raffia's teeth as she talks. She scrapes at her gut with two knuckles. Working it through.

"Dude, bad scene if anyone saw you," says Mikey. "Looks like we're cancelling the show on the whole city. The show of the ethos, no less."

Donn's like, "Epoch."

Raffia swallows hard and chews her lip. "We never agreed to a show."

"It looks like we did," says Mikey.

"If we play the show, he's gonna try and kill us again," says Arco, and Mikey's like, "Wait, you see that?"

"Course I see that." There's practically a grinding noise as Arco blinks. "I feel like a fucking robo sometimes with this edge."

"Break edge, then," says Mikey.

"Not over this," says Arco. She spreads her hands. "I could kill myself."

"Fuck off," says Mikey. Donn's like, "Not over this."

"So we could play the show. And the whole city goes to war," says Arco. "That's an act. Going on tour. That's a nother act. What else?"

"Is the band back together?" says Donn. Raffia's like, "Only if we want Darby in it."

They stare and sit on their hands. Raffia starts coughing, then retching a bleb fountain of chewed black paper onto the carpet. A stream of ants emerges from the corner. They spread around the puddle, tapping it with their antennae.

"We could still go after him," says Mikey. He shrugs. "I guess his hardcore's sharper. I'd still try. Arco might be able. She's fast."

Raffia laughs. Spits. "Yeah."

"There's quad suicide," says Donn. "There's name changes and sguises." He looks up. "I could computer hack—"

"No hacking," says Raffia. Her eyes shoot toward the rusty wallsocket like there's a ghost. "No." And wipes her arm across her mouth. Her lips are kraken ink black. When she sits up her fists are knotted together in her lap. "Arco. You'd be in a nother band if we never lived."

Slouched with her narrow shaved head pressed against the back of the couch, Arco doesn't answer. And Mikey's got this sad thing going. It's almost a whisper. "It's not the same for us, straight edge."

"I'd be couch surfing without you guys," says Raffia. Her face all drained. Puke heap steaming in front of her. "I wouldn't find some nother band. They'd put me down for running amok."

Donn's thumbnail scraping blood from the unhealed circle at his wrist. "Nobody else listens to me."

Mikey scootches his ass to the top of the couch backrest. Leaning against the wall. "I wouldn't be hard a nuff to keep fucking up without you guys. Everybody else is boring. They can't keep me going."

"We're the same though. We're a band cause we can't help it. That's why we're a band." Arco's tongue slides across her lips. Like a lizard blinking sideways with its seethru secret lid. "Even arcore kids can say that."

Raffia nods, her shoulders still trembling.

Then, faster than you can see, Arco's spun round on the couch and slammed a hole in the plaster with her middle finger. Buried to the last knuckle. "Darby's afraid of me."

"No shit," says Raffia.

Arco's like, "You guys are afraid too."

A GNOSTIC FRONT // SMALL PARTS ABNEGATED AND DEPLOYED

You think you're drunk, you're not drunk.
—**Hardcore saying**

Every living thing needs an atmosphere around it, a secret circle of darkness.
—**Friedrich Nietzsche**, *On the Use and Abuse of History for Life*

DONT BLAME GERMS. BUILD YOU IMMUNITY.
—**Shithouse wall**

—The day Flag went on tour forever we set the loading dock on fire. It was a special kind of concrete that burned.

Rollins was too pissed for a tour kickoff set. We just stood on the roof til it started falling in, watching their backs get small in the heatshimmer. After a while there's just four black bars against the road. You can't ever tell what comes true.

I wasn't there. I wasn't even born. They just say something happened. Like the road snaked up for us and opened its mouth, and Rollins threw a curse on all our hardcore. We didn't know he could do shit like that. But he was Rollins of Flag, and the black road talked in his voice. Never in your diying will you know one face you wore before. Never in your diying will you see the path you've undergone. And there's no fuckedest thing in the world.

Ginn found the loading dock with his wakizashi blade. He was cutting trails through the middle of the fence, looking for a lone place to do riffs where nobody'd show up with beer. This bandoned warehouse looked in front like a bamboo forest, but it stuck half into the burbs with the dock faced out like a stage. Out back the drinking lot was clear. Yuppies scuffing maybe round the margin, but he did airguitar to keep his ego low.

The kids of first hardcore busted so many knuckles over their venue crisis. Had to play secret shows in laundrymats and church basements at night. But there was room for shows wherever, after all that shit went down. Venues are the same as mind, just empty space where punks can push around. If there's no room, it keeps your hardcore sharp. We need a shitty venue again, thought Ginn of Flag.

There weren't any stairs and he sat on the edge of the dock. Greg Ginn wore a canvas patch of four black bars over his left lung. He pulled off his jacket and slipped his wakizashi under the stitchwork. Then he tucked the patch inside his shirt.

So Ginn went back to town and took collection. One square of denim over his lung was bluer than the rest. The kids with patches laughed. Greg Ginn, you're always on us for something, and Flag patches are too hardcore to lose. Nobody knows how to silkscreen anymore. Go do more riffs and eat catmeat outa cans. Go rip off TP from the mall and write complaint letters to Mcdonaldland. Leave us outa your dumb ideas.

Wouldn't ask for your patches if the band wasn't mine, said Ginn.

They said, Did you have a band meeting even?

He said, I'm the band and I'm the meeting. Cut me all your Flag patches and I'll sew my mouth shut with floss.

That night he called a band meeting on the loading dock and he showed them all a stack of patches thick as a bike courier's heart. He pointed where the drum kit should go. He told the last dumb idea with his hands.

So Rollins pulled up slabs of drinking lot, and Ginn laid patches on the subgrade underneath. Robo and Dez worked perimeter while the yuppies charged in from the wild city. They came out hungry for the hardcore of dead times that burned solo in Flag, four in one. They came out smelling the diy hardcore that Flag silkscreened onto our thin little world. Ron Reyes, I mean Dez, he worked damaged control with his one little hatchet and Robo rolled round swinging fryingpans. By the time they scrammed, every Flag patch in the world was buried there under asphalt cairns, and the yuppies kept on piling in.

So Flag all climbed on Robo's back and rode to meet us at Ground Zero. They got beers, sept Rollins got virgin bloody marys and knocked drinks from everybody's hands. I don't got the straight edge, said Rollins. You guys are posers is all. Come see this shitty venue we set up.

Punks always followed Black Flag just like a yuppie would. Who knows if that's the point. All the bands you never got to see, they all came with. And you weren't there, you weren't there, but you know why we started fucking off. You know this one's the tour spiel.

They all picked through the grownout bamboo trail. Went through the door in the warehouse side. When Flag stepped onto the loading dock all the yuppies turned round inside the night and started pushing. More faces in that drinking lot than you ever saw at any show in core. You could of tossed that circle pit a beercan and seen it rust before it hit the ground.

If the dock was two hands lower the yuppies would of climbed it like a tide. It was so narrow you had to walk one by one and play with your backs to the wall. It was even a shitty loading dock, never mind a stage. And Henry Rollins said, no room for a crowd here, just the band. It's a hardcore venue like what used to be. You assholes go home, we just wanted to show you. We're playing the loading dock til morning.

But while he talked we found a ladder. From the roof it was just a nother sweet venue, and our backpacks had beers inside. You could look down at Flag, you could peg the yuppies with chunks of rebar. This is so totally sweet, said some punk. It's the fuckedest thing in the world.

Shut up, said Rollins. We're still playing. Doesn't matter if you're there. And the backs of their amps were busted, with holes where the lectrical cords should of been. Kira Roessler put her bass down. She breathed in the holes to fire up the amps. Black Flag could do shit like that.

They stood on the loading dock edge and did My War and Can't Decide. Shit bout fighting yourself. Up on top they say the crowd slammed too, but you can't talk bout how it was seeing Flag shows, not less you're Darby Crash.

After that Rollins stared in the drinking lot for awhile. He punched himself in the chest, it sounded like giant chains breaking. That sellout owes me fifty bucks, said Rollins. You fuckers jam econo for a sec.

He spat on his hands and charged straight across the drinking lot like all the yuppies' faces were one mcdonalds ballpit. You never saw shit like that before. And halfway cross he dropped his hand and renched one up by its washedout sideways hawk. It got stuck in the mosh, broke off at the torso, and Rollins ran it straight out of the pit by its hair.

He threw the torso onstage, stamped on its back while it thrashed. You promised to fix my car wipers and put in a new windscreen, said Rollins of Flag. I fronted you fifty bucks for parts. Rollins stamped again and his bootheel drove all the way through.

Flag jammed and jammed on feedback and Rollins grabbed the torso by the boothole in its back. His nother hand went in its neck. All the way to the end, Flag were loud like the void, but they say you could still hear that thing's tendons rip down like guitarstrings, just like Robo's bracelets would tick between hits of the drums. Rollins got a real good grip and he peeled the throat off its spine.

The yuppie clicked and snapped like a yuppie with its head bobbing on the ragged pink bone, and Rollins slung its throat into the lot like a skinless turkey filet. The roof kids moshed up screaming, falling off the side, and they sprayed the band with beer. Some punk went, that's the fuckedest thing in the world.

I'll kill you for saying that, said Henry Rollins. He shook the throatless torso at the roof kids and the neckbones broke sideways and its face swung into him like a smooch. He threw the yuppie off the dock but his fingers touched his throat and came back blood. And his face had a new look on it then. You never saw shit like that either. Rollins of Flag with the weight finally off him.

Up top we hardly noticed yet, but his band was all around him. Rollins turned to the bricks behind him. Greg Ginn, watch out for me. I'm going to get this wall into hardcore.

By then there's punks on their knees, staring down, craning their necks to see the bite. He just stays his feet apart, he stays his really big arms crossed to his chest like he's got the straight edge, and he slams his head forward into the doorless wall again and again. The very top of his head into the bricks like a drinkingbird at somebody's far table, and no echoes.

For awhile everybody clapped their boots to every stroke. The sun came up a bit and his throat quit bleeding. It ran from one ear instead and then that stopped too. Kids would push pizza at him. He just slammed his head, pissed down the leg of his jeans, and the piss ran through a hole in his boot.

Kids leaned over the edge saying things like it's just time sometimes, no matter how strong you are. A few'd climb down to wave their hands in his eyes. Said he was a new kind of yuppie, or a hardcore monument to fucking up. They said they were sleepy. And they kept peeling off. It was only Black Flag stood through the days. They knew Rollins and they stood there ready to blow him out. Their heads moved just a bit with every beat.

Somebody might of skipped a beat nodding. If anything changed, that's all, but Rollins stopped and turned round. The top of his head was worn down flat like a tupperware lid over a mug. He blew snot out his nose.

He said the wall was into hardcore already.

Punks were busting in again with their high fives up, but they'd duck back through the door just as quick. Nobody'd come near. Kids piled up deeper in the warehouse hadn't seen shit and they were asking in whispers if Flag sold out. Then somebody in the doorway said it had to be the fuckedest thing in the world.

Could nothing else make you give a shit, said Rollins. You guys just act like each other.

Punker tucked his jeans into his boots and he stepped down off the dock. The yuppies pressing so tight their arms couldn't even lift, and his band spread out behind him. You couldn't see where they started. They looked so tall. Greg Ginn and Kira Roessler, Robo, Dez Cadena, Ron Reyes, Keith Morris, Raymond Pettibon, Spot Lockett, and all the other four members of Black Flag.

Yeah, said Rollins. What else would we of done today. Anybody wants to come with us, they can.

Couple kids came through the door. They touched the brick wall behind the loading dock. They didn't do anything.

Black Flag started walking. Right before they turned into the horizon, that thing happened to the road. There's nothing else I know bout what happened. No silkscreens left of Flag, and you can't find the warehouse anymore. The fence grew in harder after the fire.

Kids on acid argue sometimes. Like if the hardcore of Black Flag burned solo, four in one, maybe Rollins could of changed something in his brain so the yuppies couldn't tell his band was there.

Now that would of been the fuckedest thing in the world.

At the end of a spiel you're supposed to say that's not how it ends. Bands started

*going on tour the day after. Not really cause they thought they were good. Not
that good, anyway.*

∧∧∧

Ass on the windowledge a couple stories up, that's the best view of a post-
apocalyptic hinterland. The height doesn't matter really. Just this way you
can fall if you want. You can see it better if you've been screaming all night
at your best friends.

It helps if it's not half sunrise, just this worthless pinkygray glow, like the
horizon's hiding candles in a hollowedout brain. Helps when you've got beers
in your hands, palm liquor curdled in tupperwares by the fire, triplestrained
and poured into rusty sacramental tallcans with beewax patches over the
holes. When you're holding a full can, even if you got the straight edge, just
for something to hold. All the stuck songs in your minds worn down to a
nonlocal buzzing, kind of like you got mentholated, and you know you're
still in a band, even if you can't member the name, and in every corner of
the air, less it's just the sleep dep taking form, there's bats doing barrel rolls.

Anyway.

Fuckers skimped on the barricade. Seriously, they could of put up handi
fencing rather than just transplanted baby bamboos. Now the streets are
running with yuppies like fucking Mardi Gras. A million raggedy naked
figures rubbing up on each other pointlessly, getting into doorless cars and
pulling off the steering wheels. Yuppies collecting at the bases of buildings,
under bridges, wherever the most kids are staring down smoking and laughing
and drinking. It'll take days to fix. They say this city's the last beacon of
consciousness anywhere, the jewel in the fucking lotus, but you wouldn't
believe how often this happens.

"Man, this buys us some time," says Donn.

"Time for what?" says Raffia.

Donn pauses. They're clinging to the side of their building, couple stories
down from the partment. On the fire ladder or with their backs up against
the stiff mats of venetian blind in the busted windows. Don't ask why they
went there. Sometimes we all need a change.

"We're figuring out how to handle the show," says Donn. "Like what we
were talking bout all night."

"And we're still talking?" Raffia moans like wolves raised her. "I don't care
anymore. Hey, Mikey."

Mikey's all, "Yo."

"How's that sandwich."

Punker tips his tallcan to his face. Draws it gradually vert, then licks round the edge of the beerhole. Arco's holding out her can and he takes it silently. Pounds that beer the same and then the rest of Donn's. He reaches in his swagbag for the sandwich, wrapped in tarp. The package's edges are foaming. "Thought you'd never ask."

"Arco. Check it." Donn reaches up the fire scape, slaps her ankle. "Bike courier."

The boulevard's clogged end-to-end with floppy, shuffling assholes. But there. That one tiny fast silhouette, cutting in and out of the knotted crowd like it's actually got somewhere to go. It's the standard courier type, fireblue nylon jacket, black rubberized messengerbag. Synthetic shortpants the weather can't even start on. Fucker's buff, and bikes choke on ground so broken, but its legs blur like spokes themselves. They say a falling rock's too lazy to slow down.

Single heartbeat and Arco's dropping from the fire scape. That discreet whooshing sound, that's her octuplestitched venturepack crammed with blades, heaving as her feet hit the ground. Arco lands surrounded by yuppies with her katana hilt balanced between the flats of her palms. She spreads them slightly and spits inside, as if improvising a new opposite to prayer.

"Fuck," says Raffia. "Creeps me out."

So now you know why posers think she's cool. Arco's jogging up the street, shoving through the yuppies as they jostle chaotically about. One stumbles and her hightop props on its knee. Then she's climbed to its tattered leatherette shoulders. Then she's vaulting off the next one's dome, she's jogging up the way like their bobbing heads are rocks in a stream.

No. Don't mistake this for siking, which is the projection of ego. Arco's meditating, which is the pure practice of diying and the nihilation of ego, and yeah, it doesn't look like anything. For all you know that's the point. Nobody's this good. Do you understand, tourist? Can you see the fucking riddle already, the riddle exactly the big of one human viewpoint? Getting this good, you turn into nobody. Arco isn't there.

∧∧∧

They climb a nother storey up the fire ladder while Arco goes for it. Then Donn unclips two scissory titanium things from his dreads, screws them together crossways and it's a grappling hook. He hands it off for Raffia to throw. Mauve nylon cord unspooling behind it, the grapple arcs cross the street and goes *SOCK* into the bleacher at the top of the collapsed spam works. Mikey cinches the line round a ladder rung and they start crawling through the air to meet Arco at the bleacher, the Germs stage.

"How bout the sandwich, Mikey?" says Raffia.

Mikey's like, "In a sec."

Down the slope a bit, the bike courier's coming toward Arco. She's balanced on some asshole's shoulders, she doesn't even narrow her eyes. She's not moving, there's no wind, but somehow her headband tails are flapping. See Margin Walker rise behind her head.

The blade's diy of carbon steel and the carbon and iron diy of burnt rain. The hilt's diy of vegan corn cob wrapped in donor leather from Ian McEye's calf. The tattoo in the leather's diy of black walnut rind concentrate on a cotton thread round a needle, the shapes the needle traced diy of letters, and the letters diy of sounds in some punk's mind. *THIS IS NOT A FUGAZI SWORD.*

Margin Walker's like, "Hey."

Now Arco's down on one knee. A long way further up the slope, like she just phased there. She stands and pushes through the yuppies and climbs the bleacher with the rubber courier pack dangling from her hand. Meets them up top while the courier type's still tumbling down the hill, giant wedges missing from both sides of its skull.

"Are you still doing no-mind?" Raffia's forehead skin twists. "Like right now?"

Arco shrugs. "Want first grab, Donn?"

"Why don't I get to open it?" says Mikey. Raffia's like, "Eat your sandwich."

Squatting at the end of Mikey's outstretched arm, there's the sandwich. Degraded, incorruptible. He turns slightly, pointing it away from them. "Remember that time the courier had ammo?"

"Yeah, I've still got tons in my hair." Donn waggles the bloodcaked zipper tab. An airtight seal hisses etherically as the teeth pull apart. "How's your sandwich?"

"Oh, it's okay," says Mikey.

Donn withdraws a slim ribbonbound folder, hands Arco the messengerbag. Her arm goes in and she's like, "That's it."

"Sorry." Donn unslips the elastic ribbon. It's wicked springy, preserved by the vacuum seal. He pulls out a letter. "Hey, it's a letter."

Arco's like, "Can you summary it?"

Donn's finger whips along the bottoms of the words for a moment. "This was sposed to go to a PHD downtown. That's somebody versed in oldschool sammrye blades who lives downtown. Some museum got a shipment."

"So, like, you're a PHD, Arco," says Mikey.

Arco's like, "Shipment?"

"A big crate," says Donn. "Oldschool sammrye blades. Mostly boring ones. But one's maybe signed by the illustrious blacksmith Masamune. They wanted a pinion off the PHD."

"They wanted her to try cutting through stuff," says Mikey.

"So that's M-A-S-A-M-U-N-E?" Arco counts off the letters, little swipes of her hand.

"Yeah, like the alterna name of Darby from the straight edge spiel." says Donn. "You don't know how to spell, though."

Past the unfinished bamboo fence, the far side of the hill's almost clear of yuppies now. Arco turns to face the distance, where there's no city, just buildings. "You guys can come with me if you want."

She's already springing down the tall crumbly plywood bleachers, two steps at a time. She's already running.

"What the fuck?" says Mikey, breathing out. Then the thought bubble breaks. He powerscreams, jumps after her, and just before the bleachers end he turns and flings the cat's ass sandwich at the side of Raffia's head. Only thing is, she catches it.

∿∿

Oh, hey, it could just be paranoia, but if you ever come back here? Maybe check for a scar on the courier's wrist.

∿∿

They're taking the sidewalk cause the road's mostly holes. The sidewalk's dim inside. Sweat runs in their armor. They hike singlefile, hugging the mossy wall, the weapons fidgeting in their hands like they've got hiltaches. They hike econo, easy strides conserving juice. The sky's only bleeding a drizzle and it stinks like somebody got cut open, but it always stinks like that on a sunny day.

Donn's walking backward, pointing a cranktorch at the ceiling overhead. Snotty gray and sienna shadows awkwardly dislodge themselves from the torchbeam, sluicing round like they're embarrassed. He's like, "Hey Arco? Don't we need to help?"

Maybe it's more like a hallway abutting the street. The plaster ceiling's worn gauzy thin, dandruffing ecru scales on the astroturf floor. The doors to the road are pressboard bullshit. You could put your hand right through.

Arco's like, "Help what?"

"You know," says Donn. "With the fence."

Arco goes, "Nobody needs help."

"Don't we need any food?" says Donn. Mikey's like, "I just ate."

Raffia starts cackling, she speeds up and throws her arm over Mikey's shoulders. His eye, it's blacked and bleeding like a photo negative of a fried egg. No matter how much he wipes, his mouth is rimmed by gray sludge and wispy fur. Raffia's got a frankensteined stitch job holding her split cheek together, looks like somebody used a sailcloth needle. There's bright red shreds like pennants between both their teeth. Did they make each other eat the tarp?

She's like, "Mikey, I wouldn't of gaven that sandwich to anyone else."

"Not us needing food, Arco, it's the big we," says Donn. "All the food storage went down with the spam works."

"Kids won't starve," says Arco. "They'll hunt."

"Sucks hunting on an empty gut," says Donn. "You know that."

"Hey, fuck meat even," says Raffia. "Weren't they keeping rib bones in the parkade?"

"Darby!" Donn stops completely. Holding onto the side of an empty doorframe, he peers down the road behind him. They're all like, "Where? Where?"

"It's a spression," says Donn. "No bones, though, we can't make decently hot fires. Bamboo won't hold an ember."

"Oh," says Mikey. He shrugs. "Yeah. We're low on tallow too. And leather. Raff's down to one layer even. So we need brains for tanning. They go bad so fast in. The. Summer."

By now Mikey's on his knees, and his throat's making dippy little spasms. "Gulk. Gulk." He reaches into his mouth with two fingers, draws out a droopy gray rope of fluff, like a braid of decomposing longhair caterpillars.

"What is that, like the tail?" says Raffia.

Mikey nods. He puts his hand right through the thin pressboard door, chucks the tail into the road. He's like, "Back off, Raff. We didn't make you eat those showposters twice." Spits something opaque and gelatinous. "Nobody's perfect."

"Should we go back?" says Donn.

"We don't help shit, Donn. We just fuck shit up." Raffia sticks out her hand to Mikey. Or it's a hammer. Either way though, he's already standing. Then she's like, "Hold on. Nobody knows where's the museum."

"What, you're scared?" says Mikey. Some more grayish matter leaks from the side of his mouth. He boots the punched roadside door, rips it off the hinges. "I can still taste it!" Only proud, like he's talking bout victory.

"None of us ever went out this far," says Raffia. "I'm not scared. But we just took Arco's push. We don't know the way."

"You could of said that before." Arco steps through the hollow doorframe. Her speed jumps again, like gears move in her tailbone. She's looking straight ahead. The buildings are featureless gray obelisks, rubbery towers blocking the sky down to one rusty stripe. Off to one side, thunder beats the air. They speed up. They follow her.

And Arco goes, "You know I'm not the leader. You all know I'm fucking up. But this is my hardcore and if yours was to stop mine you could of leveled any reason. You're ronin. Fuck thinking you got a leader."

∧∧∧

The street keeps opening out, it's wedgeshaped for some reason, and the skyscrapers on both sides are like blocky mirrors tied up in black ivy. There's no doors to them, just giant windows, dark and evenly spaced. No words on the signs. No signs. It could be just a blownup movie set, or the ideas of buildings. But the undergrowth's getting so thick and twisty in the road, there's time to train a nother shot if your first one hangs up in some asshole's sinus cavity. For awhile there's no sound but a casional *THUPP*, four slingshots trading off.

"This isn't such a hard level," says Mikey. "Nice forage grounds. How do these trees even grow?"

Donn's like, "I think they get started under bigger trees. Like for shelter."

"Cause these are, like, the same trees we grow." Mikey jumps at a high-hanging pink grapefruit, comes down staggering with one boot in a muddy sinkhole. Bites a chunk from the thick pithy hide and tosses it to Donn.

There's so much nitrogen in the chunky pre sippitation, new shoots tend to burn. Back in core you'd pull up somebody's mummified geranium and take a handful of dust from the pot. Spit the seed into your hand, spit til you're holding mud, seeds start better there. Back home they've been mulching fresh transplants with scalps to buffer the rain.

"Who cares?" says Raffia.

"Okay, then call it." Mikey nudges her arm.

Raffia elbows it away. "I can't see that far."

"Okay, I'll call it. Cross side of the street. Past the sago palm. That beard guy with the mooshy blue fungus on his neck." He sticks out his tongue. "Left eyeball."

The thunder speaks in the air again. The light's slushy and gray. Almost every slingshot's carved of waxwood by now, but this wristrocket's vintage. It's all stainless steel rods and brackets, wingnutted into shape and slung with rubber surgical tubing. Mikey draws the draw back past his ear. Stops to blink and raaalphs tabbycat jam all over his arm. If you were anyone else, you wouldn't of responded by tugging harder, right? Whatever. The tubing snaps, laying a streaky welt across his cheek. He wordlessly unstrings the two flaky rubber segments from the slingshot body, throws it all in his pack. Still walking.

Donn's like, "That sandwich sitting okay?"

"Course it is, man." Still walking. "You got any more rubber surgery tubing?"

"No. We should find a hospital with an airtight storage room," says Donn. "While we're out."

"Do you want to call it?" says Arco. Mikey's like, "Call it what?"

"Heads, then." Arco drops to one knee and slips a timeblacked penny over Mikey's shoulder, down the block, into the beard guy's left eyesocket. Pink gruel spurts from the nother eye and Arco reaches up with her palm to catch the penny on its ricochet course. Then she's like, "Tails. You win."

Mikey turns around. "I wish you fucked up more."

"I just said it was tails you win," says Arco.

Hold on, you saw that, right? How the penny went in, the penny went out, and in between, the clouds all at once went different in the sky, and not like a wind blew them, but like some asshole swapped out the whole atmosphere for a nother? Cause if you're gonna spend your leisure time here, that's the kind of shit you should notice.

"He means without looking good." Raffia breathes the silence in and out. At the next intersection she stops and leans up in the bole of a giant redwood. The bark's studded with cute amber windowpanes like something off a lego set, and Raffia starts hacking them apart with a clawhammer. Under the busted panes, the ragged tree pith smells like pine air freshers.

"What's up," says Arco.

"Is it this way?" says Raffia. She's in front, but she doesn't point a direction.

"It's straight," says Arco. "Left looks like major climbing. Right we'd have to knock down those trees."

"What if that's not the way?" says Donn. Arco's just looking at him incuriously, and he's like, "We could use a map."

"You got one?" says Raffia. Mikey snorts.

"Extinct is foreverous, dude," says Donn. He toes a dirt clod. "This could of used to been a map."

Arco's like, "We just go straight til we find it."

Raffia's clawhammer slams the tree again, lacerates the yellow heartwood. Helicopter seedpods fall twistily into her hair. "That's stupid."

Arco pivots on her scuffed gray hightops. "Why?" She lances Margin Walker over her shoulder with one smooth upward jerk, like she's abruptly showing off her biceps. When she pulls the sword back, a nother yuppie's sliding from the tip, speared through the sinus cavity. At least this one had a distinctive purple birthmark.

Raffia's drawing a rusty rivet from her chestbelt. It's bout the long of Mikey's finger. She turns it in the light, then wedges the point in her ear.

Arco's like, "I'd rather you pulled from the good vibes, Raff."

Raffia's winding up the hammer to sock it home. "Do you know how big the world is, fucker?"

"Yeah," says Arco. "There's core, and there's out in the burbs. We're in out in the burbs. The burbs have the zoo and like Chicago, the Starwood, the Orpheum, CBGB's, the Masque, Mcdonaldland, the library, Holly Wood, Hunnington Beach, Oki Dog, Radio Shack, and this museum. Not counting drinkinglots."

Raffia taps the spike. Man, does her blood go fast. It rills down her jawline as her nostrils incrementally flare. "Donn?"

"Raff," says Donn.

"How big was the world?" says Raffia. "Like in numbers and miles."

Donn looks over at Arco. Arco nods, she sits her fingers in her ears, and Donn's like, "It used to be twenty-four thousand nine hundred and one miles round the equator, I guess. It went in a circle."

Arco pulls her fingers out. Shrugs. "Punk rock could still lead us there. Like Rollins finding Darby in the straight edge spiel. Do you want to vote arms?"

"Everybody who thinks we should find a map," says Raffia. She lifts two arms. Mikey lifts two arms. Donn lifts one eagerly, the other sort of reluctant.

Mikey's like, "Look, Arco. Maps were anti punker before the Antidisestablishmenterrier. That's why we had to burn them. Cause making your own way in a world of maps was super hardcore. But now they're near extinct and we hate them on impulse. So we gotta make our impulses diy."

"Oh. Really? Oh. Okay." Arco's voice slows, conspiratorial. "What do we do bout the address, though?"

"What address?" says Donn.

"On the letter, like the museum address," says Arco. "I ate that part."

"But we needed to know where we were going," says Mikey.

"Oh," says Arco.

There's some space.

Raffia's punching the side of her head and then she pinches her nose and blows. Her cheeks inflate. Her eyes bug. The rivet flies out of her ear.

"Down there it's a mcdonalds," says Donn. "They must of sold maps. Phone books too."

Arco's like, "Can you tell the straight edge spiel again?"

∧∧∧

—*Rollins came out from DC. That's east of Pedro, east of Riverside. This all happened back in the day. Time was he went to school and nights he'd scoop icecream for yuppies, but one day somebody threw a Black Flag tape out the bus window. It cut him in the eye so he picked it up. And after a while he quit and he made swords instead. But the swords were always pissed.*

But then Raff went, We're blowing the lock, fuckmeat. Get your head outa the basement.

∧∧∧

"Gonna be textbook," says Donn. Arco nods with her sword.

The mcdonalds doorglass is thick as Raffia's wrist, and there's bout a million yuppies crammed gainst it like the first ten shoppers get the last ten cabbage patch kids. Sure they're mauled and mangled with each otherses bitemarks, but for yuppies they're pretty much archival condition. They've even got their original clothes on.

For some reason the door's bikelocked through the front handles. Donn's sitting half lotus on the sidewalk in front. In his lap there's an open tupperware crammed with rifle shells and silica gel packets. After he's done opening a shell with his hand rasp, he taps out gunpowder into the keyhole of the u-shaped lock.

"Mikey?" says Arco. "You got a smoke?"

Mikey's holding the square patch on his jacket wrist, the green machetes crossed in an X. Murmuring to himself, eyes rolled in. Now he stops. "You smoke now?"

"We're blowing the lock, fuckmeat. Get your head outa the basement." Raffia's standing a halfstep behind Donn, a roofinghammer in each hand, their whetted hatchet butts turned facing out.

"Don't you like stories, Raff?" says Mikey. He lights a smoke and passes it to Donn. Donn moves it halfway to his mouth, then down to the keyhole, stubs it home. Gunpowder kicks inside the tubular lock with a brief orange *SPUTTT*. Donn chews his upper lip as he pulls the crossbar off the busted mechanism. Then he puts the bullets away, sheathes the rasp, goes to set his venturepack under a tree. The yuppies push closer against the glass and the u-shaped metal tube through the doorhandles pitches and rattles at unsafe angles.

"You gonna help us?" says Raffia. "Or space trip right through it?"

Mikey's like, "I thought we were being nice to each other today."

"There's just not really a lot of room," says Donn. "We could take turns."

Holding Vaaum Vaaum Vauum chesthigh and horizontal, both hands together at the stick's center, Donn starts breathing. There's a little spectrum analyzer recessed into its shaft, two lines of square purple lights like cheap VU meters on a boombox. The lights pulse in and out, getting brighter.

Mikey's like, "I can't believe you actually got those to objectively measure consciousness."

The meters dip and shimmer.

Donn nods distractedly.

"Shut up," says Raffia. "Be ready. Keep your minds down. Two, one."

"It's fine," says Donn.

∿∿

He'd hitch a wheelbarrow to his seatpost and bike to Hunnington Beach, load black iron sand where the jocks pissed in the surf. He'd sneak in the park at night and saw redwoods for charcoal. In the flats he dug clay to fire smeltingbowls. Everything going in those blades came through Henry Rollins, and you know if somebody's hardcore, they can put their hardcore into things when they diy. That's how come his swords were grained like muscle, and they were always pissed.

ᗰᗰ

*A*rco's bare foot reaches under the hockeystick to pull the bikelock free. Her toes are kind of weird and long. No, don't think bout that. All the yuppies surging through the open doors, they need to chomp at the hockeystick's blades. You need to be those, too.

Stick up, chesthigh and horizontal. Siking two places at once. You know it's technical, Donn. How many kids can do that? Magine your right brain's the lefthand blade and keep plotting vectors for that new cyber barrel roll you're working on. Yeah, keep thinking bout hacking but now magine your left brain's the righthand blade, thinking bout that one ripped callus on the end of Darby's finger. How he'll touch your arm and his callus drags like a snagged fingernail.

That?

Fuck. No, keep going. Your back and shoulder muscles tremble under your purple rainjacket as the yuppies surge through the doorway. Tilt the hockeystick down a little, up. There's the fuzz of light rain and there's teeth cracking against your stickblades, there's shoes shuffling on the mcdonalds tile. Not loud but that's what you feel. Don't stop thinking, right side Donn. They need you. Don't ever stop thinking, left side Donn. They need you.

Arco's standing behind one of your hockeystick blades, Raffia the other. Both making precise chopping moves into the yuppies' braincases. Faces easy and lineless, breathing light. They look like bored overqualified labor on some kind of construction job. It's really not like fighting versus people. It's technical.

Some asshole's fingernails leave a shivery trace on your blade. You bite your tongue, left side Donn. You feel it, right side Donn.

"Somebody lend me a slingshot?" Mikey's got snapped surgical tubing in his hands. "Hey?"

"Busy." Donn takes a step backwards. A halfstep forwards. Arco and Raffia duping his stance like greased shadows.

"You suck today, Mikey. You fucking suck." One Hand rises, drops, and a yuppie slumps with its jaws clamped on a stickblade. Raffia boots its chin fast and it falls back without knocking you offbalance.

There's a huge long window next to the door. Watch how Mikey steps over and a single yuppie inside the mcdonalds pushes its face to the glass. This surf poser taterhead with shaggy ginger locks. Its shirt might of started out sleeveless, but the other mcdonalds patrons definitely ate its arms. Its naked teeth are stained by gummy catsup and cheez, chemically immortal. Mikey spins and boots its mouth through the windowglass, which bends like a soap bubble as the taterhead flies backward into some tables.

"That's kind of dangerous," says Arco.

"Aren't you sposed to be a sammrye?" says Raffia, spitting. Two frycooks jostling in the doorway, both reaching for her. Margin Walker dips sideways and uncaps their skulls, right under the blue-and-yellow embroidered visors, which hang in the air for a breath while the yuppies fall.

"Whatever, it's just really nice glass," says Mikey. "You guys look bored."

Mikey steps a step back, runs his fingers down the insides of his hawks. He's pulling you out of Donn, tourist, you feel him charging up, tasting the blood sparkle in his mouth, and the yuppies in the doorway just turning as he whips out this crazy twofooted spinning jumpstrut where his boot plunges right through the brickproof plate glass like a dynamited glacier. "COWABUNGAAA!"

Life advice. Let nobody tell you you're not a sammrye.

Cracks ripple outward from the main hole and Mikey's still airborne and instead of getting hung up in the jagged glass and ripping his ankle tendon down, like they say happened to Jello of Decay when Darby bet him he couldn't do this, he plants his nother foot on a briefly intact floe of glass. No matter what, you're not seeing this right. It's not even possible. There's no such thing in all the fucking world as a moon sault kick. His prop foot pushes him outward, yoinking his kick foot safely back through the hole, blowing down the entire fiveton window while Mikey corkscrews in the air. It's technical. You're staring again. All the clear glass detonating in concentric silver shockwaves, like a circle scar unhealing itself as he flips, and then the window's a waterfall of shards.

∧∧∧

They say hold the little things heavy, they say hold the big things light.

∧∧∧

You must of been staring at the busted frame cause now all the yuppies broke sideways too, they're pushing toward the window. Mikey catches a little skin on the glass but it's no big deal, he's upside down, looping in the air, and he lands with arms up at the sky.

"Fuck, Mikey. Fuck, Mikey. Fuck." That's gotta be Raffia.

The echoes of the windowglass keep falling, like a bottle broke somewhere off in time. The yuppies look almost uncertain behind the gashedout windowframe. Donn's staring with his mouth gaping while the purple lights recede. Some of these assholes, the shard shower's left them ragged with their shoulders or jaws cleft away, but yuppies never mind.

"Donn, you could go vert," says Arco softly. "If you want."

"Oh," says Donn. "Yeah. Okay." He spins the stick a quarter angle.

Raffia blocks the first rushing yuppie with a massive swing of her forearm. Donn steps back and slams a blade into the top of its skull. He's holding the meat puppet at armslength at the end of his staff, wiggling it like he's fishing. The purple lights start waking up again. Raffia's hammers move in. One hand clapping, One Hand clapping. Back in history, Agnostic Front named an album for the sound of that.

Arco's diving sideways in a shoulder roll, comes up in front of the window. Margin Walker wails like snakelight in the air and her nother hand's moving just as quick, cupped round nothing. The sword from her empty sheath. No, seriously, the sword from her empty sheath.

Mikey's hopped up to grab the thin sill running overtop the window. The yuppies grab at him and he pulls his feet up, swinging in the air. Pumps once for momentum and launches through the empty windowframe, over their heads onto the nearest stool. He throws a big ballbearing over his shoulder, ear cocked.

You can't help listening for the little clack on the tile and the yuppies dive on the sound in a huddle. Arco's keeping the busted window's lip between them. She comes in with these sidelong spinning cuts, headbanging into each swing, throwing the katana between her hands like a shadowy copterblade. Like she's cutting with two swords, blurry and skinny and indistinct. The yuppies twitch back and forth. Somehow they're not coming at her.

One hand clapping. Give up?

Mikey's running down the quickstop snackbar, he turns around with his meteorhammer spinning. The same taterhead surf poser leaps up and snaps at him and he vaults over the snackbar. One steel weight hangs momentarily in the air, then reverses direction with Mikey, smucking through the taterhead's backbrain.

He springs backward onto the nearest table. Landing crabstyle, weight poised unevenly on two arms and a leg. His center of gravity sweeps downward through his stance as he swings his foot sideways, knocking on the point of some asshole's jaw with one pitted steelcap. Disarticulating the socket joint and blowing a handful of teeth cross the table. It comes at him with its jaw hanging diagonal. Mikey scuttles backward on the table, braces himself against the peachcolored wall.

Arco's standing on a mini mountain of dismembered body parts. Her headband's doing that windless undulating thing again. Donn's pushing forward with a yuppie gnawing on each blade of his hockeystick, and he ducks as Raffia slams down two hammers at once. The sound of One Hand clapping. Victim In Pain. And they've seriously emptied out the mcdonalds.

"So what're you gonna do?" Mikey asks the yuppie. "Gonna bite me with that jaw?" He leans forward as it leans in and poinks its eyeballs with his index and middle fingers. "BAP! BUP!!"

"Man!" says Donn. "That kick was textbook! Can I see?"

"See what?" Mikey's holding the yuppie back, his fingers deep in its head like a particularly heavy, thrashy bowlingball. "Oh, this?" The disgorged eyes dribble on its cheeks, the optic nerves slide lengthwise across Mikey's fingers like mildewy shoelaces. He tickles its brain with his fingernails and it shudders lectrically.

"Yeah." Donn lays his hockeystick on the next table. "Hold it steady, will you?"

Mikey holds it steady. Shifting as the yuppie rocks around. It's not trying to disengage, doesn't even want to eat his hands, it's going for Vauum Vauum Vauum.

"Are you siking?" says Mikey.

"Yeah, a little." Donn points out the door. "Over there."

Mikey blows out a laugh. "So like even your hockeystick is more conscious than me?"

"Aw, yours goes in phases," says Donn. He takes the yuppie's chin and shakes the disslecated jaw, producing sounds like sheet metal crumpling underwater. "Wanna recycle it with your fingers?"

"Yeah, sure," says Mikey. He lifts the hissing yuppie slightly. "Is this dangerous?"

"Nah, it's fine," says Donn.

Mikey unbends his fingers and pushes the brain. Go ahead, feel it crumble. Like a big wet block of cheddar with veins. "I like it this way. Cause I wonder bout squishing my own brains. You know?"

Mikey pulls his hand away and the yuppie faceplants on the table. He licks pink and russet sludge off his fingertips while Donn flips the body faceup and sticks his thumbs in its mouth, cupping his other fingers round the underside of the jaw. "Okay, this quadrant's misaligned. Maybe if I—"

The maginary underwater sheet of metal rips in half.

"Yuck, man," says Mikey, absently sucking his knuckle.

"It's fine," says Donn. "It's the science of anatomy. Maybe I need to twist the other way first." His elbows raise and lower like a mime driving a propane tanker. The second ripping sound's briefer, punctuated by a muffled *T-KUNK*.

"That's fixing a disslecated jaw?" Raffia's standing over them, spattered with brains, spinning an employee visor on her finger.

"I think so." Donn wiggles the yuppie's skewed face. "If you hurt your jaw, I'll try on you."

She steps back. "Man, Mikey. That was such a sweet kick."

"There's no maps." Arco's staring up at the menu pictures, oiling Margin Walker with a blue-and-yellow stripey apron. "Just chicken nuglets, burgers, fries, and like a hairy purple thing."

"That's gotta be a taste bud," says Mikey. He squints at the menu. "Nah, but phone books have maps. Addresses too. Aisle seven, under breakfast."

"How do you know what's in phone books?" says Raffia.

"It's lunchtime," says Mikey. "Hey Donn? Throw me a triple big mac?"

Donn roots in a halfopen steel cabinet and comes up with some dry, flaky brown discs. "These things are way older than you."

"Exene was that old and we ate her," says Mikey. "It's a delicacy. I'm hungry. I puked my breakfast."

"I'd try one," says Arco.

"Fuck it," says Raffia. She bites a patty. Spits waxpaper. "What's in phone books?"

"So you do wanna hear a spiel," says Mikey. Reaching to the back of his leather. You better be used to be this by now.

∿∿∿

So I was like, This is the joke of how it all began. Before all that shit went down and the punks took it coreward, a crew we all know found a cheap house on the edge of the park, and they lived there for a couple of years. And Raffia was like, Dude, don't give us the whole thing, just say what's in phone books. And I was like, Okay, that's you, does anybody else hate the spiels that code all our wisdoms. And Arco was like, I'd rather hear the straight edge spiel. And I was like, Fuck it. That night they looked in the phone book for a map of hematite deposits. And Donn was like, I don't member the story saying map. And I was like, I just said map. Map of hematite deposits. And Donn was like, I mean the canonical story though. And I was all like, what?

ᴧᴧᴧ

"**W**ho cares bout deopposites?" says Raffia. She yawns and lays on the table, stretching. A stinkwave emanates from her armpit and crotch armor vents.

"Were you listening?" says Mikey.

Raffia's like, "Not really. No, in fact."

"Okay," says Mikey. He gets out some sticky black hash from a tin, starts rubbing it on his gums. "Shit, Arco, were you back there this whole time?"

"Since the joke part." Arco glances up from behind the order counter. "I'm glad this shit can't rot." All the kitchen merch stacked out econo. Beige nuglet pyramids, sheaves of fries. She slams down a pile of golden brown rectangles. Things basically resemble breaded tablets, or giant squarish fishsticks. "I don't know where's the books."

"Those are books, dude. You never saw raw books?" Mikey slams a rectangle against the stainless steel worksurface so it snaps, showing the internal grain. "See, yellow. Yellow pages, like, uh—" He points to a yellow M logo.

Arco's all, "Ohhhh."

"I think this tallow's still good." Donn dabbles his hand in the fryer. The palely yellowish oil clings to his fingertips, stretching like oobleck.

"Dude," says Mikey. "I got goosebumps. Let's fry up some nuglets and shit with the phone book."

Arco's like, "Mikey, got a nother smoke?"

"Shit, your edge, Arco. It's taking a beating." Mikey lights one, draws deep and blows ash off the cherry. When he pushes it into the gobby deepfryer fat, a loud tower of fire rushes up, briefly tonguing the ceiling. He grins, steps back. "I neglected to wear eye protection."

Donn's already slipped on his grilling shades.

∧∧∧

He couldn't head to the sev for smokes without hearing the same joke. Hey rockstar, let me pin my shitty eyes on that blade in your scabbard there. Thing is, draw Rollins steel and you can't put it back unblooded. Try it. You'll bend into that sword like a slim jim, cause your meat's good as any.

∧∧∧

Raffia's heaving bodies out the door so the dirt and meatflies and vultures and everything can recycle. Arco's dragging and tumbling them into sinkholes. Mikey's standing watch with Fuck It blazing in circles, spinning it behind his back, walking the dog. Donn's holding a yuppie finger, curled and goldenbrown from deep frying. He's using it for a pointer, poring over the phonebook map. The greasefire's still sitting on the kitchen counter, broad and orange.

"I can't find us," says Donn. He breaks a corner off the phonebook's goldenbrown cover and chews. The edges of the pages are a little burnt, the middles are soft and fluffy though. "It's only got the big streets. Like, this is a picture of the west part streets. But there's not a nuff drawn here. You can see more streets just from Shitty Bridge." He spits in some mummified ketchup dust, works it round with his deepfried pointer. Scratches a thin vermillion lasso on the map. "The museum's in these cross streets."

"So what's wrong?" Raffia comes over and squints. "Are these black things cars or trees?"

"That's the word 'boulevard'," says Donn.

"Oh." She sits on the table. "You know what? Fuck this."

"Core's not on the map," says Donn. "No clue where we are."

Arco and Mikey come back in. Arco glances at the map, turns back toward the long broken window and sits down and starts with the deep breathing.

"Why didn't they put us?" says Mikey.

"They didn't see us coming, astrofuck." Raffia pounds her forehead with a thick stubby hand. "They didn't figure the amerikan dream'd go down and we'd put our own city in the middle."

"Oh," says Mikey. "Why not?"

"The fire's growing, hey?" says Arco, not turning around.

"It's fine," says Donn. "These things are all built fireproof."

"Shit, phone books have addresses," says Mikey. "Check for the mcdonalds

that says we're there. Oh. I guess they wouldn't put that. Can I see the map?"
He bonks his nails against his top teeth. "Okay, look, so somewhere in here
is the orpheum." His hand finds a patch on his elbow, a creamcolored skull
dusted with black lichen. His fingers tracing the ragged margin, staying off
the actual print. Feel weird he's not siking you, tourist? Bandonment issues
much? "Cause like how Mike and Rocky from Suicidal got on the roof with
jackhammers and tried to cut a skylight out, and the fire dogs caught them
and they ran around the roof."

"No," says Raffia.

"Look, cause Mike and Rocky went down the Harbor Freeway, past the
Santa Monica. It's in the spiel. They turned at the convention center to get
to the orpheum." Mikey touches the patch's edge again. His other hand's
pointing at the map with a couple fingers at once. "So they had to be coming
in from the down side going up. Look, here's the university." He reaches to
the small of his back, brushes a different patch. "Cro Mags came in on tour,
they crashed in the living room under the church, right? They were downtown
on the third day, but second day, they played a secret show cross from the
university. Then they went downtown, like where the orpheum was. So they
went from here to here. So that snapped off freeway you could see from the
big stage? Before it was Crash Course Boulevard, it was the 101."

Raffia's like, "Don't. Don't ever use big numbers round her. Where's our
place?"

Arco's fingers are back in her ears. She's looking out the jagged window
at the rain, moving her head up and down. She shrugs. The fire's all through
the kitchen by now, turbulent and bright. Meatheads hunching a little lower,
ducking the worst of the smoke. Tears and snotty noses.

"Fine." Mikey snaps his eyes back and forth for awhile, making fastforward
and rewind gestures with his fingers. His spare hand tracing the seams and
negative spaces of his leather like they constitute their own streetmap. Then
presses a ketchup fingerprint where a couple streets intercross. "That's core."

"Shit," says Raffia. "We're going the right way."

"Are we gonna kill the map now?" says Arco. Everybody looks at her.
Donn's very carefully tearing the page out already, hunching protective over
the book, and then Arco's like, "I smell barbecue." Her eyes were closed, you
just noticed. Cause now they're open and her head's tilting way back.

She jumps to her feet like an empty bag shot with air. Then falls back on
her knees. Her mouth moving silently around something. An old chant or a
yell, something traditional. Fixed to the burning ceiling with too many

handfuls of big nails there's four limbless yuppies spraypainted black, vaguely moving and snapping in the fire. They're a sign and you've seen it before. It's her tattoos, it's the patch Mikey stole. Mildewed record covers and photocopied handbills in shoeboxes turning to dirt. Kids of witnessed it in figurations of cloud and wind. Not holy. Bars of the Flag.

∿∿∿

But there were too many jokes at the sev, so one day he cut out smoking. Next day he cut out beers, cause of the kids at the beer store who knew him. One more week and he cut out meat, sept from punkers who told jokes. All he did was work the forge, his neck was getting thick. You weren't there. And the name under his name was Sengo Muramasa. But Rollins is easier to say.

∿∿∿

"They stopped here on tour," says Arco.

They're like, "Yeah."

"We got to keep going," says Arco.

They're like, "Yeah."

Big flat chunks of plaster start caving from the ceiling as Meatheads step out the smashed windowframe. Through the gaps, you can see the next storey's on fire.

Textbook.

∿∿∿

He used to trade out his couch cushions for one pack of bacon a night, just so he could throw it away. Dude crashed with him this time and never took his hood down once. Kept him up talking. No punker'd bust one window passing through Holly Wood, dude, but we never heard of you. We're all packing Darby Crash steel. Our boy folds each edge a finity million times with the hardcore of the universe in the middle, and those swords don't stop on sweet fuckall sept the skin of a punk without desire.

So this one's the straight edge spiel.

∿∿∿

"Maybe it used to be different," says Arco.

"Yeah," says Donn. "Yeah."

The penguin's come back around, it's reared up and pecking after the floating shreds of chicken nuglet in the chowder. Raffia shoves it, it leans back in a rubbery way and springs forward again.

Donn's like, "Spiels of kids punking out cause they were bored or they kept getting beat up or they heard the sound of Minor Threat, right? I've never seen that. Nobody's ever seen a birthday cake spontaneously achieve sentience."

"What if they did?" says Arco. "Out in the burbs? They'd just get eaten."

"You've seen them, Arco." Donn turns to face her. His spression's the weirdest. So open and hopeful. "You walk among them. You ever seen anything like that?"

"Never," says Arco. "You think it's weird?"

"I guess it's cause they got so pissed we broke their conomy. Like they started hating punks so hard." Donn raps at the road again. He scratches at his hair. The braided tools jing and rangle. "It just doesn't make sense. But they built this road." Looking at his knuckles, they're bloody where they slammed asphalt. He stands up. Nobody follows him. "Just this one cloverleaf, it's like wider than core. How do you semble a city together without knowing you're doing it?"

"That would make it easier," says Arco.

"Yeah?" says Donn, scrunching his forehead up.

"Too much to think bout any other way," says Arco.

"They used to have sembly lines," says Mikey. "Every yuppie, or like, every cake did one little move. Like turned a screwdriver one turn or something. Money made them do it. It wasn't like us, how doing it makes us do it." Sitting, he bends his head down incrementally. "Maybe the conomy was the animating conscious force of western civilization. That would splain why it was so sweet to kill."

"Me and the chowder should dick round some more," says Donn. He turns around. "Aw, Raff, I loved that emperor penguin!"

"What?" says Raffia. She turns around too. "Whoa. Don't pin this on me." One shrill giggle note escapes her like a soap bubble.

Tiny black feet stick stiffly from the brim of the leather soupbag. The terminal curve of its white ass just visible, like a setting snowball sun. Extinct is forever. Maybe that's the fuckedest thing. But give it a while.

"But it was like a giant Opus," says Donn.

The street's been getting better for a couple hours, broad and flat, rising imperceptibly into some kind of cloverleaf on iron stilts. It's conga lined with crashed cars, like every stupid dumb street, but mostly you can go right through. Below them there's a bottomless chasm like the shadow of the raised boulevard and exactly as wide. Spreading out round that, it's pure snarled jungle for awhile, no buildings. Or at least no big ones. Spose this used to be a national park.

"Are you hungry again?" says Arco, and Raffia's like, "What?"

Arco turns and stops. She's round the bend from the rest of them. Been jogging with her head down and her hands making flat little swoopy moves like karate chops. When they catch up, she says it again.

"Why?" says Raffia.

Arco vaguely gestures at her. Raffia's got a penguin tucked under one arm. It's nearly as tall as she is, probly an emperor penguin. Sweating from its forehead and halfheartedly twitching its bald little flippies.

Donn turns around. He's like, "Man, what is this!"

"What?" says Raffia.

"You think it likes that?" says Donn. "Your armpit?"

"Why?" says Raffia.

Mikey snickers. "You member that time I snuck an arrowhead in your armpit overnight and then, like, we brought down that rabies tiger just by shooting it in the butt?"

"Fine. Fuck." Raffia shifts the penguin slightly. It's making these noises like a chicken with a mouthful of pop rocks. Her fingers play over the hammer hilts on her bandolier.

"You can't kill it, dude, it's a zoo penguin, it's like dangered at this altitude! You got no idea how rare a zoo penguin is?" Donn's down on his knees, staring the penguin in the eyes. "This one's in like mint condition!"

"It's not a penguin." Raffia shrugs. "Fine. What would you do that's so good?"

"Put it on the ground," says Donn. "Look, I'm hungry too. I saved like a million nuglets though, we can make some chowder."

Raffia just drops the penguin. It lays on its side momentarily, then bobs upright like an inflatable punchingbag and stands there blinking.

"See?" says Donn.

"See what," says Raffia.

"Man, it doesn't do anything," says Mikey. He pushes at the penguin and his hand keeps slipping around it, like he's trying to hassle a tai chi master. "Whoa."

Arco's got hands on her flat hips. "You guys can't go farther? I think that place is the museum."

"This is the best place to stop, dude," says Donn. "Line of sight is awesome, we got the roof for rain shelter. Stop for a bit, you're hungry."

"How do you know?" Arco runs her hands down her temples.

"Your heartbeat's visible in your neck," says Donn. "It gets fast when you're hungry and it slows down when you're sleepy."

Arco's looking out off the cloverleaf. "We're the road." She sits down and wraps her arms round her legs, grinning, rocking.

Down the way a little, there's a pond of grainy brown sludge in the road. Some kind of algae or other liquid plant. The penguin follows them as they scoop sludge into Donn's soup machine, which doubles as Raffia's swagbag. Thin tough waxed leather with a flat bottom, you can just empty it out and boil soup stock inside.

They gut out some foam and plastic and fiberglass from a couple car interiors. Meanwhile the penguin's standing in the empty sludge hole, eyeballing their operation. They start installing bamboo struts to hold the bag level and building a fire with foam kindling.

As the brown algae starts to bubble and Donn's teasing apart the lukewarm chicken nuglets, Raffia's like, "This might work out."

"It's all bout seasoning." Donn starts opening packets of mustard. "Just gotta cover the taste."

"No, like going out this way," says Raffia. "We might live."

"Was getting killed ever in it?" says Donn. "Really?"

"I figured," says Mikey. "So far it's good though."

"Why didn't you speak up?" says Arco.

"Bout what?" says Mikey.

"Huh." Raffia sits and looks out over the thin, murky bones of the city. "I can't see the museum." Nobody answers. "It need salt, Donn?"

Donn's like, "Sure."

She leans over the chowder and punches herself in the nose.

∧∧∧

Rollins left a crow he caught, a plastic Darby Crash, and a Black Flag tape on repeat to babysit his forge. He packed fruit leather in his armybag and a tirepump. He packed some juice boxes and a scabbarded katana wrapped in a welcome mat. That sword had the straight edge too.

∧∧∧

Donn comes back from the gutted car with four skulls balanced in the crook of his arm. Raffia makes to get out a little geology hammer, for cutting them into bowls, and Donn half turns away.

"There's no damage to the skulls," he says. "It's so creepy how historical, like, like, the non punk people of history would drop dead just from getting old."

Mikey's laying back with his hands under his head, trying to spit and catch it in his mouth. "Why don't you say yuppies? They're not people."

"Darby might of gaven me a post hypnotic trigger," says Donn. "I have an acid flashback every time I say that word. But I'm replaying these weird conversations that seem to of only happened in a slightly alterna reality. So it's more like an acid flashover."

"Man," says Mikey. "Darby's a dick!"

"You could say birthday cakes," says Arco.

"It's all bullshit anyway." Raffia takes a skull from Donn, turns it in her hands. "Somebody killed them through the eye."

"Their car was locked up with the windows shut," says Donn. "I don't think anyone got in there."

Raffia's chipping the top off the first skull. "So they were a band on tour hiding from a whole trade show of yuppies and they diyed starving."

Donn gives out a long sigh and puts the rest of the skulls real careful on the ground. The jaw cracks off from one, he props it upright again. "These were the oldtime birthday cakes," says Donn. "You try to magine. Punks living in balance with birthday cakes. You go in a beer store and the lights are just on. We never used to eat each other, hey. We both ate Oki Dog."

"Man, I love when you get in these fuckedup moods," says Mikey. He squats by the skulls, like they'd tell him something. He looks up at Donn as Donn's sitting down. "How did punks get born, man!"

"I know, man!" Donn hits the road with his knuckles. "Where did we come from before the Antidistemperasterism? How does a birthday cake wake into mind, man! Like, remember with that baby we found at Ground Zero, we put it outside locked in the dog carrier?"

"What," says Raffia. "Like how the yuppies tried to eat it?"

"Yeah, man!" says Donn. "Man. They went for it, it had some consciousness, maybe like a big squirrel. That shit's with us from the beginning! When punks have kids, they're aware. Baby birthday cakes, nothing."

"Fuck are you talking bout?" says Raffia.

"Desire animates every bounded thing," says Arco. Tipping her head. "Far from home, punker. Double far do you return."

"I got two maybes," says Mikey. "The algae was its home pit. Or it tried at the nuglets and failed. Man, don't worry too much." He scratches the bottom of one mortised flipper. "Do you think we could give each other pengo blood trance fusions to enhance our diving capabilities?"

〰〰

This sword had a dim red attitude. You'd see through the steel like a sundown carved of flesh. Back in the day hardcore and the universe were two things, so it couldn't cut your eyeballs just looking. It couldn't yell as you took it out, or steam from the join at its hilt. But names wouldn't stick to it, no more than sheetrock sops up rain.

〰〰

Just saw the top off a penguin and the guts fall out like you opened a can. Then you can wipe it out and shave it, stuff it with mcnuglets and packets of ketchup. It doesn't help much. Nothing ever does. They've got it rotisseried on a bamboo frame under more burning car parts. Stripped this way it resembles an unfinished pinkish bowlingpin. The skin keeps bubbling under the flame, casionally jetting them with hot fat as they hunker round poking it.

"Maybe I should meet you there." Arco's half standing up, hands flat to her thighs. "Like in the sword storage room?"

Raffia shrugs. "Mikey'd get lost."

Arco nods a little and finishes standing up and starts stretching, and Donn's like, "Chill, the sun hasn't even moved for awhile. I feel needful to honor this fucking penguin."

He's wound its beak in his hair.

The bird keeps turning. Donn bastes it from time to time with mustard on the end of a paintbrush. Grinds pepper on it.

"Neat how the meat's black inside," says Mikey. "You think it went bad, though?"

"It can't go bad, stupid," says Raffia. "It's a penguin."

Arco's sitting on top of the swaying guardrail, eyes on the endless roof, honing Margin Walker with a spitstone. Sucking on a fig to alkalize her mouth so the steel won't rust, swiping the stone all the way down the blade in long long even strokes, and Donn goes, "Arco?"

She's like, "I feel so fast out here."

Arco's turning round, lifting the sword in one hand. There's Donn and Raffia standing a bit off from the fire, each holding one end of the thick bamboo spit. Arco bows. Mikey takes a lot of steps back as she runs at the penguin with Margin Walker jumping between her hands. Leaps right over it, cartwheeling in the air, the blade wandering like a silk ribbon beneath her. As her feet touch the ground the roasted penguin collapses over the ground in a perfectly uniform sortment of discs.

Donn's like, "Can you carve—? Oh. Radical."

∧∧∧

Rollins biked three nights econo. West of west, west of the west of that. At the end of the last road there's a wild gas station with some easychairs and a burnbarrel on the roof. There's a sycamore busted the roof through and hanging over the freeway, and there's a ropeswing. Darby Crash sleeping there in the treeshaded grass with his jacket for a pillow. Oven mitt over his face. His hands were flat callus, you know he worked swords. His arms were full of holes. And under his name, his name was Goro Masamune, but you don't know that guy.

∧∧∧

Raffia spins the pengo cutlet in her hands. Looks like a burnt biketire lined with spokes of grayish rib bone. The stringy flesh colored eggplant black, seeping grease from every point, and layers of slumped fat like butterscotch jello.

"Lend me a file, Donn," says Raffia.

Donn's trying to twist apart his own ringshaped cutlet. Greasy hands slipping everywhere. "Yeah. Why?"

"Sharp my teeth up." She bites at the meat again, hauling off a chunk the size of a hot dog bun. "Aw. Eurh."

"You don't like it either?" says Donn.

"I don't think you're sposed to cook penguin this way," says Mikey.

"Might be no right way." Arco's somehow eaten half her cutlet down to the ribs. She coughs.

"No. No." Raffia's cheeks and chin are slicked with black grease. "No, it's good."

"The flippers are crunchy. Try a flipper." Donn smiles halfway. "Man. I kept it moisty, I roasted out the extra fat."

"Tastes like you shot up your balls with turkey jerky and jizzed in a fish," says Mikey.

A tic goes off in Donn's cheek. "Should I of breaded it?"

The sun sits there halfhidden in the roof. There's some scratchy sounds, teeth fumbling in the tough black meat.

"So we might be able to get Darby with ground up wineglasses in some heroin," says Mikey. "He'd see the trick on my face though. We'd need to go through some other kids. Like sguise ourselves, drop it off with them."

"What is it?" Raffia leans over and slams the drippy black penguinchop into Mikey's neck. He doesn't wince and she slams it again, ribs cracking inside it. "You're the one wants a plan? You?"

"If we make it back to core alive we'll still have to play the show." Mikey's looking at his fingers, tweaking grease off them. "And he'll bring everything down again to get us. It's too big for me to fuck up."

"You give up on fucking up, you lose your hardcore," says Raffia. "I'm not the freaky sword wizard, but I know that." She stands up. Spins the halfeaten meat circle into the wind. It rises like a frisbee and disappears off the freeway edge.

Arco shakes her head. "What else are you keeping back, Mikey?"

"Yeah," says Mikey.

"You're keeping back yeah?"

He's like, "Yeah."

⋀⋀⋀

So Rollins walked over and kicked the oven mitt flying, and Darby only yawned. The straight edge in his backpack slipped as he moved. It cut its sheath down and cut the welcome mat and sliced open the backpack with the juiceboxes running like veins. His hand snapped out for the falling hilt, and he smiled, cause his swords were always pissed.

⋀⋀⋀

"I'll catch up with you guys." No meat's missing from Donn's cutlet, though it's scored all over with toothmarks. He puts it down and lays back. Puts his head on it. "I need to sit here membering penguins."

Then he's like, "They evolved from dinos."

Arco cocks her head. "If you're long, we'll come back and meet you."

They hike down a dip in the cloverleaf freeway and there's only the crests of Mikey's hair and then fuckall. Donn stretches but he doesn't get up. Overhead a gray powerline's running nowhere to nowhere, and if it had birds they'd see his dreads spreading out like his pupils spreading out like leaky fried eggs.

Punker, what's compassion for a world this far gone? The streets can't give a fuck. It's a bummer, your care slides down its target like beads of rain on rock. There's no aquifer for any shit like this. Where does compassion go and can it be returned? You're Donn in this world, with the staff and the purple band. The artificer. Walking the bandoned suites of hell and your eyeballs thinking, what can be saved? Not their gear but its aspects. You started kung fu way later than the rest, and before that you saw compassion in a history spiel. Now it keeps washing up on your shore. Giving a shit might be made of parts, it might be made solo. It might be an invasive species or not. Punks evolved from dinos too. Not even cross time and distance. But the spikes on their heads are the same.

What, you still don't need sleep, Donn? You're staring at your wrist with unfocused eyes, squeezing the unfinished Germs burn, drawing out pus beneath the thin black halfscab til it rips free all round the circle wound. Yuppies. Like an island in a hairline moat of blood. Then an asteroid eclipsing a bitter wet red sun.

"Yuppies. Yuppies. Yupp—"

Way blue this wet red sun.

∿∿

Get up, said Rollins. I saw posters. Germs are playing the Masque tonight with Plugz and Black Flag.

∿∿

"So I missed a part?" That's the weight.

"I don't know." So that must be you.

You tilt your head, but the circle won't move. It just drifts a little in its focus. Some blurry phosphene aftershot bleeding out against your retina like the echo of a burning smoke, a nova star. It's just the same blue ring on the dark, tourist. The one you're bored of by now.

You can tilt your head but you can't turn it. Pinned against a cold concrete floor and you can't see shit. Sprawled all over you, that colorless snake's weight of soft muscle and leather, that's still Darby Crash. Nobody else goes limp half so hard.

His voice comes down all round you. "It's okay to act fucked to me, Mikey. You're still my favorite one."

The blue ring swings round in the dark and you're like, "I'm Donn."

He laughs. "Then how can you be smoking, man? Mikey's the one who smokes."

Yeah. There's a filter tucked between your lips and the circle swings when you move them. You can taste smoke under your tongue like a slick of burning plastic. What kind of ember burns in a blue shape like a hole? Spit it out, punker. So the cherry drops away, falling spinward against the black field. There aren't any stars. This can't be cyberspace. Your leg's stinging for a blink and then that's gone too.

"You're just so not Donn," says Darby's voice. "Donn's off on acid."

"No, cause I member being Donn. I really am Donn." You raise your head a little bit to nod. He smells like gravity, like the folds of his ancient leather calloused deep and quiet by the rain, and how the empty beerbottles smell in the shadow of your balcony, sour full with dregs and ashes. "Sorry, man. You just can't see me in the dark."

"I can see in the dark," says Darby. "It's you. Just cause I'm high. You think I'm making a mistake."

"Look, I've got Donn's hair. And, like, his face." You can't reach your dreads though. Darby's keeling heavier into your arms. "And I just seriously have all his memories."

"You just member stories you got off Donn." Darby's breathing in the beats between your breaths. His weight pushing your chest tight. "You guys used to be really tight. Sharing history. You'd call that the meaning of friends."

It's still super dark, your eyes aren't coping. The breeze eddies with something piney, sharp and distant. Could be a burning adirondack chair. Darby's like, "How could anything have no parts? Why are you getting so hung up, Mikey? Why does it matter who you think you are? It's all ego anyway."

"People might get confused." You can barely hear your voice. "If you introduced yourself as the wrong party? They might not get what you mean."

"See, Donn wouldn't even of said that. He'd say, cause you'd hurt someone's feelings. But am I being mean to you?"

You're like, "I dunno. I guess not."

"So even if you were Donn. It wouldn't matter to Donn who I thought you were." Darby stretches, sprawls further into you. His thick lank hair's brushing the side of your neck. The blue ring's back, floating. Did you only notice now? Bleeding out against your retina, the echo of a burning smoke, a nova star. "Donn's all concerned bout this thing. He keeps head tripping bout the parts of compassion."

You're like, "No, I didn't know whether it had parts."

"I know you don't care bout that shit, man. But you can just pretend you're Donn. What are the parts of compassion? How's it work?" Darby's arms are lifting. His weight on you shifts but it doesn't change.

You're just watching the circle. Like it's the shape of your whole consciousness and you're blurring as it blurs out against the dark. "I don't know what you want me to say."

"Cause Donn believes in compassion," says Darby Crash. "And he believes things interfocus by virtue of their parts. Tell me what Donn would say."

"Maybe stories are the parts of compassion?" You can hear Donn's voice in yours, tourist. You just don't member his voice being so low and slippy and full of weed static. "Cause they're our tools to figure out how people feel. I can't know anyone's mind, but I build up these facts bout the people around me. Like how we carry round the people in stories."

"Do we all do that?" says Darby, and you're like, "I think so. That's how we can tell people are suffering. I think about what makes me get better when I'm hurting, and I figure other people's pain is lots like mine. That could be how compassion's hooked into the universe. Through similarness between a compassionator, and a sufferer, and the stories in their brains."

"The kids in stories are stories themselves." Darby laughs. He rolls over and faces you in the dark, where you can't see his face. Something drapes and tickles your collarbones, and it might be his jacket, or it might be his breath. "Yeah, but why do we have to do that, Mikey? You're making it complicated. You sound like an engineer. You almost sound like Donn. Like, when Donn's computer hacking and he can't get inside a network, he doesn't need to think the gateway's pissed at him. He just takes its behavior as a lesson and adapts. Tries to find a nother way in."

"A network's different from a person." Your tongue feels dry in your mouth. Weirdly like the pitted concrete floor. "It's just a block of code, it's rule-governed. Even if it does glow ultraviolet and spontaneously reorganize its arrays when you collapse its wave function by observing. It doesn't have feelings."

"Why does that matter?" Darby's raising himself a little, pinning your wrists with the flats of his hands. You can feel their lines against your skin. "What if the code had consciousness? Donn still wouldn't need to care. He could just get into the network from watching its morphing patterns."

You're like, "Punks don't do that, though. We know we've all got minds, so we act like it."

"What if I didn't build up your mind inside me? What if I could just call your moves by figuring patterns in your behavior?" A smirk moves in his laugh. "No way you could tell. Not if I was good."

"I don't think that's the point." Sure, close your eyes. Nothing changes, see? "Like, we just learn to do the compassion thing. Same way we learn to walk."

"Some kids just learn to walk," says Darby Crash. For one breath his weight's completely off you. Like he's not even there. Then he's sprawled overtop you again, holding your wrists down like something tender and you didn't even think. You didn't reach up for the dreads in your hair.

"Dude? Is this real?" you say.

"Kung fu," says Darby Crash, the weight and the blue halo. Now it's an ember again, a glyphic eye in a pool of smoke. It whispers like a paper lantern, breathing and unbreathing its own bruisecolored light. "Donn wishes there was no suffering. So what if I quieted someone's suffering in trade for a beer? Or cause it got my cock hard? Is my cock a part of compassion?"

The burning cock ring in your mind wags back and forth for no. Then it's like, "What if you were hurting, Mikey, and someone made it stop? Would their motivation matter to your hurting? Your bandmate Donn prizes compassion so much, and for what. You think it's cause caring makes him feel good?"

"No, man. It's not that." You still can't really move your head. Your hair's all mangled up behind it on the cold concrete ground.

"Then why's he so hung up on it?" The voice comes in both your ears, and there isn't any space, and you're all like, "I don't know. I can't figure it out. I think Donn doesn't know either. There's this thing where he tries to help out and he's calling it compassion. But he's sad. Nobody else is actually sad. He feels so weird all the time cause he doesn't get it. He thinks I'm hurting but I'm stressed, not hurting. I'm not having Donn's weird torturefuck where he wants everybody to like him. I want everything to work out, sure. Why does that have to be something else than what it is?"

Abruptly Darby's standing up from you, with his soft black leather kind of sliding off the sides of your vision. You're standing up but you bang your head on a pipe and drop to your knees. It's pretty dark out and you're kneeling on like this windowless plain of cement, kind of flashing on some pinpoints of fire way off in the distance. Then Darby's holding his bright blue circle like it's a hula hoop, compressing it in his hands. Now it's the size of a cheap plastic earring, it's a toroidal dot like a distant quasar mounted on the end of a smoke. Darby Crash blows on it to put it out and slips it back in the pack of mallburrow slims, and drops it in his inside heartside pocket.

He's like, "You're Donn, dumbass."

You put out your hand and touch your toolbraided dreads like a tourist. "Yeah?"

"Yeah." Darby's walking away. "Told you this was good acid. Say what you learned, Donn of Meatheads. You will be marked on this."

You lay back down. You look at the ceiling, where there's no stars. Look and look at the no stars. They're there for you. "I know me the same way I know anybody," you tell the no stars. "I'm a story in my head. Like built together from things I did. So I should compassionate for myself."

You're keeping really still. You're like, "But I can't really know who I am. I have to guess. Cause the story might not be who happened. I'm why I know I need compassion, but I'm why I can't get it right."

—*You will be marked on this.*

But you can't see him and there's no light anywhere at all. The voice you hear's an echo, tourist.

You feel your arm lift so your hand swings up, right by where your eyes would be. It's there, the circle in nothing. Like his real sign is what's inside and outside the ring, the dark that didn't start and won't end. The ache in your wrist, healing hollow over the bone.

—*You will be marked on this.*

∧∧∧

Darby shrugged with his oven mitt in his hand. He didn't wipe the hair from his eyes. Aw, I'm everywhere, he said. Gimme a second. I partied last night.

∧∧∧

Arco's still jogging, still in front when they come back for Donn. He's on his knees, staring down the uneaten chowder in the dirty soupmachine.

Mikey goes, "Hey, man. This museum. There might be dinos."

Donn's pupils scrunch back down to normal with a sound like a tap closing off. He's like, "Maybe that was the last one. Hold on. Yuppies." He wobbles to his feet. Then he's like, "Okay. Yeah."

And they don't get killed on the way.

∧∧∧

Guess this beats your mom's place, said Rollins. But there's no chimney here even. Show me the real smith and the real forge, cause I know junkies don't fold steel.

∧∧∧

Hold on a little.

For sure it's a weird time, siking into kids as fucked as these, feeling for the ways they feel. And it hurts to see something almost clear up for once, and then it's more fuckeder than ever. But you don't need to know anything right. You just gotta practice.

This road, this city's roadless, they go on like broken glass, and no one knows what face you had before. Now you're some tourist without memory who showed up way too late to help, and your perspective's become some pointless battleground, even so.

But that's the way we all got into hardcore.

∧∧∧

Who's a junkie, said Darby Crash. I got the straight edge too.

∧∧∧

And they don't get killed on the way. Right where the freeway slopes back to ground level, there's an mound of gray sparrows like groundswell over a grave. As the birds scuffle and trade places, what's underneath flashes colors and lofts her tail. Stripecore. Meatheads take the long way round.

Couple times there's some yuppies, but never anything like a trade show's worth. Arco keeps going high on fire scapes, looking for the major clusters, and Donn keeps patching detours into the path. Everybody walks careful with their mayhem gear handy, but with one yuppie and a good line of sight, you can usually sike it right into a sinkhole.

Out here the stores aren't hardly looted. For third lunch it's fizzy chef boyardee from bloated cans, and Mikey's got a rootbeer bottle from somewhere, still hot from the sun. In between swigs he'll gargle and spit soda on the wall, he'll pour it through his skylight and scream while it pops on his brain.

Later there's a rusty suitcase in the middle of the road, all grown over with yieldsign ferns. Two stone squares inside, roughly excavated black terrazzo, each a bit longer than some asshole's forearm and with a pink inset star trimmed in brass. The stars read *PARKYAKARKUS* and *BLACK RANDY*. The forearm's just bones, clinging to the suitcase handle.

After that Donn stops and stares for awhile with his nose on a scientology window. Right behind the glass, there's a whole ziggurat of stacked skulls. Donn doesn't say anything. He mega doesn't. You maybe can follow how his finger'd go, stroking the knobbed undersides of the yuppie skulls, if you watch the little flinches of his eyes. No sign anybody killed the brain on those either. It's kind of getting dark.

ᗢᗢ

I don't got the straight edge. I just don't eat meat cause meat don't deserve it, said Rollins. I don't let beers or smokes pass me through.

Oh, so you'll shoot heroin, said Darby. You got any? I got some swords I could trade.

ᗢᗢ

This block's great if you're into holes. The ground's webbed with ruptured sewagemains. Slushy moss valleys curve like the insides of soapbubbles and yaw into sudden shafts. Meatheads going cautious, testing the spongy floors with poles of sawn bamboo. You can tell the museum was important, there's a concrete wall round the whole block to keep people from getting in.

The wall's uniformly matted with sludge. Running long the top there's frills of shiny razorwire, the perfect little prongs hung with ripped lizards and puffy halfcheetos where shrikes flew up to save shit for later. All round the wall's foot, the ground's fallen in, creating a sunken moat full of jungle stink. Behind the wall, the sword museum looms up in storeys of undecorated concrete.

Donn takes a running hop over the moat, arms out long, and clings geckostyle to the crosshatched steel bars of the gate. "No," he says.

"No?" says Mikey.

"No," says Donn. He shimmies himself, like to rattle the gate. It doesn't rattle.

"We got hammers," says Raffia.

"Got any hammers that do this?" Mikey spreads his hands at the wall.

"That way's not a climber." Donn's pointing at the top of the gate, where an overcropping sentry tower completely cuts off the path.

"Can we go up these walls?" says Arco. She jumps the moat, sticks to the gate. The standing steel bars don't even wiggle. She feels around a little in the mat of wall sludge, then starts clearing a patch with the spine of her chukabocho.

"You think these pits were for ivy?" says Arco.

"Grab me if I fall," says Donn. He climbs further up the gate til his heels are at level with Arco's head, then spins himself counterclockwise, keeping his feet wedged in the diamondshaped spaces between bars. Ventually he's nearly upsidedown, his face dangling at the spot where Arco's cleared.

"Yeah," says Donn. Positioned diagonally, gesturing with one arm while the other's elbowdeep in the gate. "They would of seeded ivy here. And it didn't rain so much then, so they fed it with shitty pipes." He rips a length of splintering pipework off the wall.

"Wall's too slippy to climb," says Arco. "Hey, Mikey."

She springs backward off the wall. Mikey catches her. "What. Oh, you mean that?"

"Yeah," says Arco.

"One stragedy is hot air ballooning," says Donn as he turns himself rightside up. He meditatively spits into the moat. "We'd need to put together a leather tanning station though. In terms of lye sources—"

"Shut it," says Raffia. "How much rope you got? Don't say long numbers round Arco."

"Yeah, rope. Okay. Five hands times five hands times five hands worth." Donn springs over the moat, lands on Raffia's shoulders and she careens backward. "Rope'd get cut on the razorwire though. We need something to cushion it first."

"How bout a yuppie?" says Mikey.

"Yeah, yeah, a yuppie," says Donn. "Get it right on the wire, then throw a nother line over cross it. We just need a counterweight."

Mikey's like, "Yuppie."

"Yeah, that would be a good counterweight," says Donn. "Gotta stop throwing them in the pits, Raff."

"Ask before." Raffia turns, she's wiping brains from her roofinghammer onto her leg. "I'll do it. Just ask me."

〰〰

Guess I should spell it, said Rollins. I never put any shit in my arm or my nose. I think medicine's a scam. This is me spelling it. I never failed on a promise and I never lied. I don't vote or steal. I'm giving up fucking so I can work harder on my forge. And I don't own one record. I listen to tapes and that's it. But I don't got the straight edge. But my swords do.

Poser, said Darby. I got the straight edge too. I just don't go against the universe. So is that it for yours?

Rollins took a deep breath. I used to have a low self opinion.

〰〰

So they've got a nuff rope, and a sturdy place to stand. Trussed on the end of the rope there's a blownout yuppie with a handlebar stache and laugh dents in its cheeks, whatever those mean to you by now. Meatheads all lined up, holding the rope's free end like they're a tug-o-war team. They're straining backward and turning, dragging handlebar in a circle through the mud, and then it's orbiting low on the end of the line. In front, Arco starts giving the rope more play, and they're twisting their boots in the mud, but this time nobody falls. A few more spins and the dead yuppie's cutting through the air, angled like a kite.

Diy every day. They don't just mean extend yourself through your surroundings, or get killed so your friends can laugh, or blow away your ego when you breathe. It's like how every made thing starts out as a plan. What they're doing here won't stick round, but it's an artifact too. Like how crazy plans are the secret cores of our makings, same way everything's got its core outside it. Like how some stuff's consumed by its creation, some stuff was never even there. Like an artifact's just a ghost, hanging round after you diy.

"We could let go. After I finish. Saying banananana," says Arco.

And they go around. "Baaaa—"

They go around. "—naaa—"

"—naaa—" says Arco, and handlebar soars on the line like the emperor of all wooden terrordactyls. The yuppie wobbles, unstraightens in the air, or your expectations do, and it embeds itself pelvisdeep in the glass front of the sentry box with legs vibrating like doorstop springs. Wait for it.

Wait for it.

This is the substance of the way of the sammrye.

∿∿

Darby just swung his hand at the freeway. I guess you came ready, he said.

Rollins knew what he meant.

∿∿

Arco's like, "—naaa," and they stand there blinking at each other.

"What kind of security glass is that?" says Mikey.

"Shit, that might hold even," says Donn.

Raffia viciously jerks the rope. *SLURCHPP* as the broken window's edge slips through the yuppie's glutes. *KCCH-KCCH* chopping both hamstring tendons, *TKKOOK* as it nestles the cup of the pelvis. Whitish and skinless, two testicles slide gelatinously down the glass like bandoned fledglings.

"Oughta hold," says Raffia. She turns a little to hand off the rope and Arco turns to take it and then they both stand down from that. Not actually looking at each other.

"Is it gonna hold you?" says Mikey.

"You're too dumb to do this run, Mikey. And Donn's too smart." Raffia punches the side of her gut. "And we make Arco do like everything." She's winding rope round her palms til her arms pull high, and then she swings over the moat. Her grimy heels slam the gate.

"Right on," says Donn. "Can I do anything?"

Raffia humps and lunges up the tall gate, feet slipping and kicking, and swings out as she climbs near the outcropping sentrybox. She hangs in the air for a beat, then hoists herself up by the corpse's legs like they were installed for that purpose. You can hear its kneecaps crack like kindling, but the legs hold. One hand on the yuppie, she plants her feet on the narrow lip under the sentrybox window. Her free hand browses her bandolier, settles briefly on the octopus tenderizer, then picks out a shorthandled sledge with a head like a solid iron popcan.

Arco's like, "From there you can go round the—" while Raffia slits her eyes. Crouching a little, her toes balanced on the narrow windowsill, she wails the sledge overhand through the glass.

"Hey?" says Donn.

"Hey," says Mikey.

Arco's laughing with both hands over her mouth.

One Hand keeps bashing in and out the thick dirty windowpane. Long spindles of snapped glass catch and grate into each other, all the sudden cracks reflecting dusk in grey jags like overcooked solder joins. Balanced with her toes on the little ledge, Raffia bites her tongue. Holding the corpse's ankle as it tilts forward through the widened hole.

And she makes one sharp little breath like a dustbuster cutting in and out. Her sledge's trapped in a zigzag crack. Raffia levers it sideways and there's a wide-angle bursting noise all cross the window, little cracks everywhere like blood seeping from bruised skin. Her foot's slipped off the mossy ledge. The hammer's jammed in the glass, unpryable. Beneath her the moat's bottomless and at the bottom it's probly full of piranhas and rebars standing like punji sticks. Raffia's holding herself up by one toe and the hammer and the yuppie's droopy broken leg. There is no hesitation, no fraction of uncertainty. You're the drummer. You're not anything else. You're the best band in the world.

She headbutts the window straight in its fucking face and it buckles out for her.

Ragged prongs trace gashes in her shoulderblades and the backs of her thighs as Raffia swings a leg through the hole. Turning sideways, she ducks inside. The whole pane's groaning, splitting apart like a rotten sheet of lake ice. Standing there in the sentrybox, she goes "GURARHH!" and headbutts the window again.

On the ground they're checking each otherses eyeballs for glass splinters, high fiving as Raffia throws down the rope. When Mikey gets up there he plants his hands on his hips. "Nice move. Copier."

Raffia sneers, draws her fingers along her slashed collarbone and splashes his face with hot blood. He's laughing. He's trying to throw a booger on her but it's stuck to his thumb.

The sentrybox, it's like a cruddy walk-in closet for storing dead TV screens and intercom boards and piles of shattered glass. Somebody oughta sweep in here. In one corner there's a mummy shape under a camo blanket, sprouting shrooms.

Donn bends his eyes at the blanket shape. "Dude here could have the sword."

"Not happening, Donn," says Raffia.

Donn toes the mummy. Spores billow and fluoresce. Everybody reflexively covers their breathing orifices and Raffia grabs the scruff of his neck as he's bout to whisk the blanket off. They say fuck the dead.

ᐱᐱᐱ

They say it's bad when one thing becomes two. That doesn't mean stop chopping shit in half. Rollins cinched up his shorts, he climbed out over the freeway. Hung upside down off the ropeswing with his sword in his hand, and if the universe wasn't so pissy back then, that edge would of bled out the air.

ᐱᐱᐱ

There's yellow graffiti sprayed loopy cross the immense black doubledoors. *KEEP OUT. ORDER OF RONALD MCREAGAN.*

"What's that say?" says Arco. "Black Flag?"

"They might of been joking," says Donn.

"Gimme your prybar," says Raffia. "No, the real hardcore one."

Mikey just shoves at the doors. They woosh open. Raffia barks with surprise and Arco does a forward roll the way you'd snap your fingers, finishing crouched with Margin Walker trembling at the end of her arm and tracking side to side like a geigercounter needle. She's all like, "Go! Go!"

Mikey just does a backflip. Comes down in the exact same place. "Radical!"

Donn steps past Arco into the museum lobby. His cranktorch milling light into the warm, sleepy air. It's dry in here, it smells like clay. Gigantic dust motes kite around like shreds of membrane.

"It's safe in here," says Donn. "This place was closed for the Antidisincentiveasterism."

"Why?" Mikey's still standing there. Reaches between his feet, picks up his lid. Holding it down he does a nother backflip. Nobody's looking. The floor presents similar to tiled granite but like lino it eats the noise of their boots. "Didn't everybody pay money to walk around here and take shits, I mean, go to the bathrooms?"

"Nah, these soft ropes were special," says Donn. He strokes a black rope spanning brass handi pillars. Velvety residue streaking his palm. "Means something was shut, you couldn't go by."

Behind the black rope there's tall marble desks like altars, feeding shadow shapes farther into the lobby. Margin Walker parts the crumbly rope and points farther down the oblong room. "Does that paint say Black Flag?"

"CRADS . . . EAT . . ." Mikey grabs Donn's wrist with both hands, jerks his arm forward, spilling cranktorch light into the graffitied corner. "Man! Crads were here! On their tour!" He does a third backflip, landing low and bobbing his shoulders like he's gonna mosh. Does some air punches. Throws his cranial lid across the room. "Crush some ass!"

Raffia wrinkles her nose. "Crads suck."

"Crads rule. Lad Crad forged Cam Ping's headbutting mask, remember?" says Mikey. "Like when we were babies, Cam drank all that cat milk and then he donned the mask and tried to nipplefeed you."

"I thought that was a reocurring nightmare." Raffia spits a rope of blood. It hangs from her lip, rustcolored in the sputtery yellow light.

Mikey's like, "Man, it was even your idea we should cover Shart Inciter."

"I just like them cause they suck," says Raffia. "See, Flag never went here, Arco."

"We came for the sword." Arco holds Margin Walker twohanded, still pointing in. That way's coreward too.

"We came here for you," says Raffia. "We're your friends."

Arco nods. Precise and limber like she's even practiced that. "Your hardcore joinded to mine, Raff, and that dragged you here. In turn my hardcore was joinded with the Darby Masamune."

Mikey looks round the room again. "I like how you talk this way all the time now." He unwraps Fuck It from his wrist, starts flexing the orange cord between his hands.

"It's the ventureness," says Arco, going forward.

Mikey's like, "Then let's go find some Crad remnants!"

"Hey Mikey, like if Darby made all these righteous swords back in the historical era, why'd he stop?" says Donn from behind a tall marble desk. He tosses Mikey his grimy lid.

"Who cares," says Raffia. Walking on like an cast iron modron, blood splashing behind her.

Up the carpeted stair that climbs and climbs in the far wall. Donn's humming and pumping the cranktorch, stopping every couple steps for his finger to case out the tacky dino pictures on the sides. And they don't get killed on the way.

∧∧∧

So the honda civics went down the freeway and sliding through the red katana they made a little sound like leaves. The wheels shook but the cars coasted straight and blew up a couple heartbeats later, like shapes in a shattering mirror.

And Rollins was all like, Beat that.

∧∧∧

At stairtop the shine off Donn's cranktorch sprints through the dark air and falls on its face. They're looking down at a great hall, shrouded shapes spaced out on daises. There's a broad stair spreading downward and a secondstorey walkway that wraps the hall's perimeter.

"Made us go up just to go down." Mikey's voice slops flatly in the vast space. "Man, fuck architecture."

"We might go round here, make sure it's safe." Arco's indicating the perimeter walkway. Halfway through the word go and Mikey's already battle stations, riding down the bannister, flailing Fuck It round his head.

"Good thing he's got no leader," says Raffia.

"Those are dinos." The strobes of Donn's cranktorch speeding up. "Those are dinos. Those are dinos."

∧∧∧

So Darby Crash got up, hung his docs on a branch. He reached through an empty windowframe for a blue katana all over flecked like tiny little stars. It looked like he could hardly lift it. That's how it looked. But he went barefoot up the plank ladder nailed to the tree and rolled up his jeans and dropped onto the freeway.

∧∧∧

"It's just not museum style." Donn squats briefly on the dais and goes "Hupp!" and hefts a gray rock chunk to chestheight. Spit flecks dabble out his mouth as he goes off. "Like, these bones were so old, they became unanimous with mountain ranges. And the archaeo yuppies carved them out with like a toothbrush. That would of tooken days. And but then they leave the bones in like a pile. They could of stuck them in place with rivets. Or glued them. Or tied them with a—"

"Crads broke them, man," says Mikey, passing the cranktorch between his hands. "Where's the fucking yuppies?"

Arco's standing a little ways off. Eyes slitted, breathing soft and deep, weaving Margin Walker in the air like she's continually underlining something.

"Why'd they of busted triskaidekaceratops?" Donn gently sets down the big shard. They're standing among a couple dumptrucks worth of bones, elaborately flanged motherfuckers like saramonial helmets. "It had illuminated horns for midnight fishing, serrated horns, these ones were like refillable horns—"

"Look, is this like that stupid pangolin?" says Raffia.

"Penguin. A pangolin's like a . . . look," says Donn. "Dude? Wonders of the Triassic Cosmos is among one of my favorite books."

"Reading's for nerds," says Raffia. "But anybody can have fun breaking shit." She spits on her hands, spins a chunk across the ground at Donn. "That says Crads, right?"

"Yeah." Donn's thumbnail scraping the yellow painted letters. "Or Rads, anyway. Technically." He sits down on a barrelshaped vertebra. His hands grab its ridges and tremble. "We should stop doing Crads covers. They also broke chiasmodon and struthiomimus."

"We haven't covered them for like days," says Mikey. "Remember?"

"We haven't played a real show for days, remember," says Donn. "Oh, shit!" Donn's swinging himself sideways out of the dino bone pile. Then sprinting across the wide gallery, getting smaller, his dreads and raggy sleeves indistinct in the dark dry air.

He pulls you up longside a toppled shape like an immense hubcap of bone. He's got his hands behind his back. "Archelon got revenge."

"Lon?" says Arco.

"Nah, dude, it's like science named a mutant for you." Mikey's gaze slides down. "Aw, shit, cool!"

Donn kneels, propping himself on two fingers. "Mondo unprecedentedo." His cardboard glasses slide down his nose.

Something like this, there's nowhere even to start. The giganto hubcap shape, it's the carapace from some megalithic seaturtle. This stubby coneheaded seaturtle that could of killed a monster truck. This relic predating the solid shell times, its armor a sturdy circle like the trimmedoff rim of a pieplate with bone struts sweeping out from the center. Looks like it was displayed standing on end, and now it's toppled bellydown in dust with some mummified asshole pinned underneath.

"Vlad, right?" says Arco.

The mummy's face and one pinmail shoulder visible under the broad wheel of shell. It's grinning right through its translucent jerky flesh, teeth pushed through rifts in the lips, grinning the drunk grin of every dead punk, the grin of Darby Crash.

"Vlad Crad, punker. See how he's got rubber ears carved outa hockey pucks?" says Mikey. "Piece of heritage, this guy." He reaches into the dried corpse's nose and pinches out the septum like a gray coin. "Mission successful. Man, this guy used cymbal stands as drumsticks, what do you think? Is he too dried out to eat him?"

"Don't do a nother backflip," says Raffia.

"It's never hardcore eating who you've never met," says Arco. Her voice echoes in the vaulted ceiling. "Who among us could understand his taste?"

"Why did he break triskaidekaceratops?" says Donn.

"I dunno," says Mikey. "Why'd I yoink his septum?"

"Yeah, why did you do that?" says Arco. She lifts the Crad's head slightly, pulls an old syringe from the hollow of his collarbone. Tawny junk residue still painting its barrel. "He got pinned when it fell. They sent him off this way."

"Ohhhh. Band breakup?" Donn kneels and touches foreheads with the dead old punk. "Man. Least it's a friendy way to leave him. Maybe they busted the dinos in sadness?" He straightens up. "We can do Crads covers again. Or I mean, I'd be into it. We could do a band meeting. Raff? I bet you'd of done that if I got pinned. Right?"

"No meetings," says Raffia. "I'd of just killed your head with a rock."

"Sad way to end a tour," says Donn.

Raffia looks at him. "Why?"

"Yeah." Donn snorts a little laugh. "Man, this archelon, though. You think we could roll it back to core? Or what if we tied a bunch of sparrows to it?"

Mikey goes, "How bout we collect two more shell wheels? We could make a hugemongous war trike."

"Our sword's still ahead of us," says Arco. She treads off toward the far wall, shrugging off the cranktorch light.

"Your sword," says Raffia.

"It wouldn't be property," says Arco's voice in the dark. "Everybody'd be free to use it."

"Nobody'd ask." Raffia's stumping toward Arco.

Mikey's head turns both ways. He lobs Donn the cranktorch and walks into the dark. "Darby'd ask."

Nobody says shit.

The light follows them, just like Donn's elongated sigh.

᭡᭡᭡

Darby walked down the middle of the freeway a while. Stood between the roadlines staggering with bright car horns all around him. Everything missed him and he didn't get out of the way. Rollins hung from the ropeswing and sliced those honda civics and then Darby held his blue steel into them like a drunk lantern keeper. The cut cars drove around the burning car wrecks. They made it to the offramp and they drove off fine.

᭡᭡᭡

On the other side of the gallery Arco's waiting, scraping yellow spraypaint off a map with the fat spine of a debabocho knife. Punker gets some real mileage outa kitchen supply outlets. The paint ghost bears the legend *YOU ARE HERE.*

She raps on a big rectangle. "I think we're here."

"Yeah, shape's right, actually," says Donn. "Here's the in doors, walkway, we're like right by your knifetip."

"Right," says Arco. She doesn't move the knifetip.

"Map says from here there's seven ways," says Donn. "Where it branches up here, we could—"

"It's in there." Arco tilts her head at some doubledoors behind them. "They're not on the map."

"Dude, yeah!" Donn slaps the paintflecked map. "They wanted us to take the seven ways. But the sword's not on display yet. We need an underside."

Through the white doubledoors it's a hall of mop closets and lectro closets. Raffia's booting down the closet doors with One Hand cocked behind her head. She's still leaving red footprints. Meanwhile, at the end of the hall, there's an elevator shaft, the door's wedged open by a bunch of broomhandles.

A rope of knotted curtains leads shaftward, tied to a doorhandle cross the hall.

"Crads never went this way," says Mikey. He elbows Raffia. "Crads would of kicked down the doors."

"Who else did this?" says Raffia. "Like yuppies used to diy ladders and fuck evelators up?"

"Neat knots." Donn turns the braid in his hands. "So the bunny went round the, mmm, and then, okay, hmm, oh, neat."

"Too old to use." Arco's wrist jerks. The curtains bust off the doorhandle in a puff of fibers. "Donn, you have the rope, right?"

He's like, "Isn't this sword from oldschool Japan?"

"West Holly Wood," says Arco. One side of her mouth twitches.

"Yeah, like," says Donn. "Swords don't go bad. Well. I guess they rust. Still. I want to figure this knot though, would of held a lot of weight."

"Stop fighting, you guys," says Mikey. "Making me depressed. Like, in fact." Pumping the cranktorch overhead, he pinches his nose like a carnival diver and leaps into the elevator shaft.

$$\wedge\!\wedge\!\wedge$$

So Darby went back to lay in the shade with the oven mitt on his face and the breeze on his knees. Rollins stood balanced for a while on the ropeswing branch. Then he shook his head, he cracked his back, and he climbed down to hunker under the tree, where the grass grows.

Sweet sword, said Rollins. Can I come to your show? I'll give you some fruit leather.

No, that's not how it ends.

$$\wedge\!\wedge\!\wedge$$

Hey, check this one out. Get level with the bottom of the elevator shaft, like where the airdried dead guy's keeled on his back, and watch Mikey's boots plummet slowmo into its collarbones like the whole thing's made of balsa wood and paper mache. How the whole corpse bounces, voiding grutty vermillion plumes from its mouth and eyesockets, seeming to deflate.

It's all drifting around and Mikey's a gauzy shape on top of the elevator car. "Cmon, it's a good jump! Wait!" He sneezes. "Whoa! I hit a nother dead guy!" He sneezes again. "Wait, he's got smokes!" Couple more sneezes. "Wait, all these smokes are factory sealed!"

∧∧∧

Rollins spat red on a red car hood and he watched it disappear. He swore something in his right hand and he swore it in his socket eye. And then they were wading in a river, sept nothing really changed. The honda civics were floating maple leaves the color of rotted foxes. His sword stood in the river rocks, cutting leaves as they went by, and the blue katana fixed them up downstream.

∧∧∧

When the dust settles and Raffia's stopped yelling abuse down at Mikey, he's reclining cross from the dead guy amidst a bunch of grainy reddish material. The mummy's tensed on its back like a weevil husk, it's got a couch cushion for a pillow. The angular gray suit looks great with the desiccated cheekbones. Just saying.

Raffia lands on all fours, smashing the skeletal face with her hand. A nother cloud of red dust unsettles.

"You mean to do that?" says Mikey.

She just picks a tooth from her palm, flicks it rattling down the narrow gap to the bottom of the elevator shaft. There's like two cartons of smokes piled in the corner, and a couple halfdranken forties of whiskey.

"Which Crad was this one?" says Raffia, slugging whiskey. She grabs a pack and bites off the brittle wrap. "Matches?"

"Got em." Mikey fishes in the corpse's inside pocket. Strikes a match, it just rustles. Three at once and their tips sizzle, then conk out in a twist of black smoke. "Shit. Donn, you ever fix your ghostpunch?"

Raffia's like, "Don't courage him."

"Yeah, I got this one." Donn's pulling a slender titanium tube, patterned with lectrical tape and soldered closed on one side, off a back dreadlock. Tucked behind his ear, he's got a naloominum plunger with a carved black rubber plug on one end and a bikepump handle on the other. "You ready?"

Mikey's leaning forward with the mallburrow slim between two fingers. Haphazardly pumping the torch like the world's chillest and shittiest strobelight.

Donn drops a little kindling down the titanium ghostpunch tube, then sits the plunger at the top. See how the rubber plug's pared down to fit inside the tube super snug? Lifting the ghostpunch by the plunger handle, he slams both parts against the ground. The plug shoots down inside the chamber, squishing seven zillion trapped air molecules so their friction heats the little wood scrap. He whips the plunger out, tips the ghostpunch onto the floor and the chunk of kindling falls out lit.

"Nice." Mikey spins his smoke in the ember.

"Yeah," says Arco. She's sitting lotus style, her breath inaudible.

"Shit, you're a quiet jumper." Mikey holds his lit end for Donn and Raffia to draw off.

Arco's like, "I was meditating on the face of unseen hiddenness."

"You just keep doing this shit," says Raffia through her smoke. It wags up and down as she nibbles the end.

"Where'd you get the new plug?" says Mikey.

"Aw, I carved it outa Vlad Crad's rubber ear," says Donn.

Raffia's sitting crosslegged, rubbing her knees. She's like, "Huh. Okay. Which Crad was this dead fucker anyway?"

"He wasn't a Crad, he was wearing a suit," says Mikey. "Dude, you smashed up the face, you should of been a Crad."

"You smashed the chest first, fuckface," says Raffia. There's still tons of mudcolored streaks floating tenuously around like tubifex worms. Probly what they are is capillaries.

"The face was the collector's item. Sides, Dad Crad had lips carved outa hockey pucks, and Lad Crad had a hockey puck nose." Mikey sets the cranktorch down and the dark comes back. He yawns elaborately. "This was just some mainstream museum yuppie."

"You don't need to hold the smoke in and squeak when you talk," says Donn. "It's not like a joint." He starts coughing.

"Since when do you smoke?" Mikey breathes out slow and squeakish. "I'd move here."

The dark walls breathe. All you can see is three floating orange embers and eight bloodshot white eyes in the spreadout gloom.

"Why?" says Donn.

"Cause we could bring our gear out in shoppingcarts," says Mikey. "Grow corn in the courtyard. Rootbeer fishing in the moat. Start ourselves a little pizza farm."

"Do you mean like on tour or what?" says Donn.

"I mean like leaving on our terms and not Darby's," says Mikey. "Who knows bout a tour. But this place isn't debted to old ways."

"Stop talking bout Darby," says Raffia. "Kids don't come back from the burbs anyway. We won't, even."

"Nah," says Mikey. "When bands go out on tour they're so drunk they can't even see. We can see. Plus we're strong and fearsome. Sides, I thought you hated our partment."

"I keep finding black mold on my tongue," says Raffia. "I could just move cross the hall."

"Raff, you can't see me in the dark, but I'm crestfallen," says Donn.

"No shit?" says Raffia. Donn's like, "The floor's missing cross the hall anyway."

"You'd put down plywoods for me," says Raffia.

Arco stirs and straightens her back. "I wouldn't pull out just to settle here. Back in core, everybody needs help sometimes. We all help out helping everybody. Right here, each of us has—" she counts on her fingers "—three people to help."

"I like that part," says Raffia. "People fuck me up."

"We could just have a crew of kids," says Mikey.

Raffia snorts like she'd dislodge a jawbreaker from her nose. "You gonna take care of them?"

Mikey's like, "Our genes, man? They'd take care of themselves."

"Can we get the light back?" Arco sneezes.

"I guess." Mikey starts flexing his fingers round the creaky trigger. Light pools in the corners of the elevator shaft. Everyone's caked with vermillion mummy powder like prospectors staggered in from a martian duststorm. "I was grooving the vision vacation."

"Mikey, I can't help us make the call. Not til we find Straight Edge. My mind moves one thing at once." Arco sneezes again. "You're smoking the filter."

"Yeah, it's a delicacy," says Mikey.

"You're sure you don't want one?" says Donn.

"I got the straight edge." Arco's sliding the mummy into the corner. Somehow when she does it, the dust stays settled. "Check this out. If you want."

"That's a daily news." The whites of Donn's eyes are fixed completely on Arco. The blacks are spinning around like a yoyo trick. "You found a daily news."

"Oh." Arco tosses him the news from under the suitcoated mummy. "No, under the paper of words. I think this panel'd move."

"There's no mold on this. None." Donn flaps the pages between two fingers. Headlined *PANIC*. Each boldface letter's the big of your hand. "Does anybody else care bout knowing stuff at all?"

"No," says Raffia.

"No," says Arco.

"No," says Mikey. "Wait. That paper's a yuppie story bout what happened on the Antidistempermagi . . . fortificationa . . . schism?"

"You can teach us after you read it," says Arco. She heaves an access panel up. Holding a roofinghammer between her big chippy teeth, Raffia jumps down into the elevator car. Somehow Arco's already gone.

"Getting up might take climbing," says Donn. He feeds rope down to Raffia. "I can't member the start of that knot."

"I think the bunny went around," says Mikey. Not getting up.

ᗯᗯ

And Darby's walking up, dragging his feet even. Propane tankers swerving all around him with his pipecleaner necklace and his hair koolaid red. Rollins' arm ripped into the diving swallow cut and maybe that katana did breathe out a little steam. Maybe it even hissed a little bit.

ᗯᗯ

So they investigate a room full of plastic tubs full of antelope bones and the crepepaper exoskeletons of red scarabs. They check some desk and chair rooms. They examine a room with reams of perforated paper, typewriter ribbons, zackto blades, rippedup swaths of carpet. They audit a shitter with empty plastic drinking bottles all over the floor. They look over a room of rock drills and dino bone shards on wheeled wire shelves. They survey a human flesh barbecue room. They scrutinize a room of many computers.

Donn has them get back to the barbecue room. The carpet's cut away round a scorchy firecircle on the concrete. There's a couple sooty wire baskets there, upside down like for grills, and three people's bones stacked against the wall.

"This place is creepy." Mikey kneels and rubs his thumb on the ancient char. "Yuppies cooking their meat."

"Inside, though. That's even weirderer," says Donn. "Air vent overneath or not. Nobody does an inside bonfire, not less you're way drunk or you don't care bout the building."

Arco's still standing back. "Less the outside's even uncooler."

Raffia's like, "Can't of been yuppies. Just Crads did lunch in here."

"We're the first punks ever came through this room," says Donn.

Raffia's like, "The fuck you know, nerd." Then Donn points to the beer in the corner, not drunk nor neither broken, and she's all, "Oh. Fine."

"Yuppies holed up in here cooking their meat and building things diy." Donn's hand tightens on the rolledup newspaper in his belt.

"Could be we're in Dimension X," says Mikey.

From behind, Raffia cuffs him in the ear. "Don't start with that spacey shit." She looks this way, the other way. Grabs the beer.

Donn picks up a skull. There's a jagged try angular hole just over the spinal cord linkage joint, bout as thick as a good carrot. His voice comes from a long way away. "This would of been, like, the most compassionate place. Cause you can kill a brain anywhere. Right here, in the back, that's the cleanest diying. But you'd have to be tied up to take a shot like that. Or, like."

"Or volunteer," says Arco. "When your friends get hungry a nuff."

"Either way. Did us no good." Donn's still kneeling, looking only at the firepit. Fidgeting a charcoal smear between his fingers. Now he points up at the door sign. "Records Backup Maintenance. This room knew bout the sword. A lot of the ash here came from paper. I didn't want to look before."

Arco inclines her stubbled head.

Against the far wall, a cluster of enameled cabinets stand like a display of platemail. Donn slides one open. Heaves the whole drawer free, a steel pan longer than his arm. Upends it, there's sweet fuckall. Next drawer, and one thin yellow slip of paper sails around.

He picks it up. "No, like, this one's bout a fish."

⋀⋀⋀

Somebody said, I don't know a nother way. See you round.

Whoever said that, it's not important. They stared each other through, and either one could of said that.

∧∧∧

"We should go back to that warehouse floor," says Raffia. "Bust all the crates open."

"There's too many," says Arco.

"Swords start with S. Right? Just do the s crates." She presses a fist against her jaw. "I'll do them all. Better than hacking."

"Look, if Donn can't crack the network, we can go home," says Arco. "Before we even say the band's back together I'll call a city meeting."

"They'll all come," says Raffia.

Arco's like, "I know they'll come, bandmate. I'll say sorry for having ego and I'll tell them what we know. I'll try and get a bigger crew with bigger supplies."

"You figure Darbs wouldn't fuck us up til we found his lost vintage sword." Mikey's staring at Arco as if a nother person could actually ever be the answer to something ever.

"Huh. Maybe he wouldn't." Arco's narrow face swings back around. "You okay, Raff?"

Raffia's only breathing. Her forehead touches the wall like she wants to slip through it. Her lips aren't really moving. Her voice is so low, it might just be a thought. You can hear it. Who knows why you can hear it. "Fucking hate Donn. Fucking hate Donn. Fucking hate—"

Donn looks up. "We got any more torches?"

"Yeah. Got one for Raff." Mikey's fishing in his bag.

Anyway. They're in the room of many computers. *RECORDS MAINTENANCE*. It's big here and square and Donn's on the floor, sitting with a dusty onepiece terminal. Screwdriver in one hand, pliers in the other, and a jeweler's loupe screwed into his eye. His dreads are half empty. Tools spread out around him, more tools standing in old coffeemugs. Stacks of circuitry all cross the floor.

Come closer. Donn's mouth is full of screws. He's got the back off this one machine and sembled a jagged tower of logic boards inside its guts, reaching half to the ceiling. They're stepped and spiraled at weird angles and jigsawed against one a nother like this carcinomic silicatious termite mound lashed together with copper lectro wire. Rest of the terminals are gutted hollow, empty carapaces stacked against the walls. Given to the mainframe.

KENNEDY

Mikey puts his hand on Raffia's back. "It's just cyberspace, Raff. All this hacking shit, it's not much more realer than ego or whatever."

Raffia half turns. Standing with Mikey between her retinas and the diy mainframe. She's still whispering. "Punker, don't try to soothe me. You know it's all real."

Donn's unscrewing the loupe from his eye. Donn's pulling off his rainjacket and his rice sack and his purple pantaloons and his rubber longjohns. Donn's unsnarling a gray cereal cable from somewhere inside the diy mainframe. Lifts his leg and tucks the plug up in his asshole. Absently pushes it in and out and turns it and there can't possibly be an audible click, but even so.

Mikey goes, "What? Ghosts?"

"Everything," says Raffia. "Every stupid fucking thing is real."

Maybe you noticed already but nobody's cranktorch is going. The big room's lit with a couple dozen candles burning soft with the grease of the dead.

"The four of us, it's probly a nuff sikic energy to draw on. We're strong and fearsome, and we're just searching for one byte." Donn's crosslegged, hands on his knees. Looks like he's bout to offer free levitation lessons. "I put in some backup boards. Even if some of this gear ate a power surge back in history, and it's like busted, we can telnet right through to the intact bits."

"Stop talking bout it," says Raffia. "Okay?"

"Hey, be mellow," says Donn. "I'm telling you we don't have to gosub through as many metempsikotic subroutines." He shrugs, and cause they brought the archelon's nodless fossil skull to sit beside him in this place, he lifts it and slips it over his head. In the back of its neck, the spinal cord linkage joint, there's room exactly for a second cereal cable. And sure it's passing strange. Donn seats a gigantic pair of cardboard 3D spectacles, lensed with red and blue cellophane, across the archelon's eyes. The skull flattens his voice. A granite turtlemask the big of a garbagecan. "You can help with the power, though, right?"

"Fuck." Raffia takes a cranktorch handle.

∧∧∧

The current pulled blood off Darby's shinbones. He dropped on his knees and bent sideways on like a new join in his gut. Rollins closed punker's hands on the blue sword, so it looked like he diyed alone like every junky.

∧∧∧

*M*ikey takes a cranktorch handle. Arco takes a cranktorch handle. The torch bulbs are unscrewed, the power cord's spliced between the mainframe and the three hand generators. And the beat's always yours, Raff. Not by honor, not really by duty. Just you're the drummer. So say one-two-three-four while in that place you can't see, where the universe comes from, four jagged spikes stand up. They're Meatheads, and you picked a fucked window to knock at, tourist. They're the best band in the world.

Their hands move with one pulse on the creaky pumphandles. The scattered candleflames bend and they break, and the room gets incredibly dark.

If your hands or your guts had a choice, or your brains or your minds or your hearts, or your karmas, or logic or principles, nobody'd ever go hacking. Cause when kids diy in the universe, the ways of their diying stay fused cross what they made, the scene goes on. But this shit's not the same. It's more like when you diy in a dream, and the self you've dreamed gets stuck in its dreaming forever. You're fucked if you get killed in the vacuum of cyberspace. Can't matter if you're Darby or Lord Buddha, Captain fucking Crunch. No one comes back from the stars. But they're all like you anyway, tourist. There's no reins, and your hardcore's already gone by.

SPUT-SPUT-SPUT like a dollhouse lawnmower. In the corner of the gray monitor bezel, a little status LED stands up purple. The light blinks to the next bulb over. The next. Starts ripping through them like a theater marquee. Something tiny explodes inside the mainframe, washing the air with ozone. Inside the monitor glass, a green smudge pushes through the dust. Coalescing. A sleepy pixelated *L* and then an *O*.

>*LOADING*
>*LOADING*
>*LOADING*

"Doesn't matter how many times," says Raffia. She pumps harder. Pumps with two hands. The gray turtleskull totem seems to hang in the air with Donn's body a braid of sticks and reeds beneath it. The enormous red and blue cellophane 3D lenses unfocus and like superimpose, going purple, and a column of lines unfolds, scrolling.

>*HUDDY*
>*NEVER HACKED WITH THIS MANY GHOSTS AROUND*
>*CATFOOT LANGOSA*
>*GERMS ARE NAZI'S*

>OTHO SHE TAUGHT ME HOW
>DO YOU BELIEVE IN GHOSTS MIKE JONES
>NO WATER ANYHOW TO FILL THE URNS
>REM SHOULDA TOLD VLAD NO MORE ICE
>FUCKING HATE DONN FUCKING HATE DONN F
>GOTO "THE RIVER SPLIT IN HALF"
>THEY'LL NEVER SEE MY CAMARASAURUS FEMUR WORK
>NO LAD MORE ICE
>I'M WHY I CAN'T GET IT RIGHT
>AUG. 12 AT MYRON'S BALLROOM ALL AGES
>EVEN IF THEY DON'T CLIMB THE FENCE
>CRADS EAT COCKS
>MORE ICE
>MONDO
>HIS NAME IS NOIMAN CASCADE HE'S THE
>ORDER OF MCREAGAN
>THE BEST HACKER ON THE NET
>MCREAGAN MORE ICE
>MCMORE ICE
>ICE ICE ICE ICE ICE ICE ICE ICE
>ICE ICE ICE ICE ICE ICE ICE ICE
>
>
>
>

And the scrolling text freezes. And you can hear Donn grin in the sudden cold void. You can seriously hear his face muscles shifting and the lips sliding over his teeth. And the stars all round him, they're stars. His curled hand sweeps cross the keyboard.

Tourist, you got one foot over the straight edge, right here in time. You can come with them. You can stop if you want. Go back and practice as much as you need. Or if you're that tired you can swim away dissolving in the quantum shoals of the existential void. If you think you're ready you can even climb to the top of the rain, right now, and wait for your carnation. But it's not safe here less you learned to sike. It's not safe here anyway. So roll back to the House of Meatheads, eat some pizza, make some rope til you're ready. Okay?

>10 SHOWTURTLE

>20 GOTO 10

And you know you're not the one reading this. You know that, right? Cause now it's too late. A pixelated green turtle swims onscreen, beeping with every flipperstroke.

Teraflop Universally Reifying Teenager Linkage Entity.

You're that, too.

ᴧᴧᴧ

Rollins sat under the tree awhile, drying and greasing his blade. Then he taped up the split scabbard and biked home. Behind him, the sword in his mind rusted.

No, that's not how it ends.

ᴧᴧᴧ

*E*verybody's hunted down a working powersocket, rigged up an old TV and watched the static go. Hunting the legendary diy broadcasts of Portal Land or secret nanites in the white noise's understructure or just having a TV party drinking ketchup wine in a moldy lazychair. Something seeps from the far side of the monitor, bloodred and white, buzzing, organized like that static, and it washes cross you, eating you, TURTLE. You're sliding backward as you scrabble your feet and beep. You thought the void was an emptiness, tourist? All this time and you still figured it an emptiness?

Donn's face is blurred with snow. It's on the flats of his eyes, it's up his nose. Two fingers arpeggiate two arrowkeys. And follow him. You're slipping and you finally move. Tacking up and to the right, up and right, into the cyberstorm.

Nobody can go out and find the fuckedest thing in the world. You gotta make it yourself. But there's no lessons, right? See Donn's other hand reflexive, tapping an instruction. So ratchet your jaws open. Feel your pixel meat stretch and deform. Beep and beep and you breathe a wedge of silver light across the static, boiling it away. *PIIING*. Whether Donn thinks he's moving you or what. Just swim up the new path you've cut.

"Dude, Raff, I can see the bones in your hands," says Mikey.

"I can't feel shit," says Raffia, jaws chattering.

Donn's not turning around. "Yeah, that's normal. Just the chi evacuating your body."

Keep blowing your speculative breath weapon, blowing roads across the bloodcolored froth. This void shit, it's acid, elemental confusion. As it seeps back in, it laps at your ankles. Feel yourself dissolving. It's okay. Sike on the places where you're already gone, keep the form of your body in mind, or you'll forget where you are. Just tilt your head and ping again. Listen for the place it bounces.

"Where's the gateway?" says Donn. "Shit, fuck, the whole node structure's rearranged."

Then lose yourself, if you're getting lost anyway. Your feet are gone. You're an atsymbol and your guts are red commas, dropping from your plastron and washing away. Breathe your silver ray, spin out in the current. You think you gotta be there to sike? Keep singing, TURTLE. Somewhere it'll bounce.

Mikey's like, "Are we on the space highway yet?"

"Transgnostic terafreeway. Don't worry," says the immense gray archelon skull. "Okay? If I get lost this early, it's only taking me."

"You're fine," says Arco. One hand on the cranktorch. One hand on her sword. "You're the best hacker on the net."

You're half eroded in the static, down to a jagged purple crescentshape. When the chi ping finally bounces, your breath weapon floods back against you, silver. Nobody can tell you how shit like that feels. You've got no flippers left. Yeah, they know it hurts. Bite hard on the void and you'll stop spinning.

Donn's typing. "Okay. Downspin one-ninety, outward five."

You heard the coordinates. There's no grid underlying this static, or it wouldn't be the existential void. No, just use your magination. Turn where he wants you to turn and go with gravity. And Donn's recompiling your missing feet. That itch on your back, he's patching your shell while you cruise. None of this shit's ever metaphors. Hacking just goes down this way.

When you get there, it's not like you outran the static. More like it's afraid of change. It fizzes and crackles round the gateway, won't go near. See how your purple flesh is pixelized, exactly as blocky as the static? But the gateway, round and amber and gateless, it's detailed way deeper than the monitor's resolution limit, like a donut of labyrinth glass.

Behind you, weird light's whooshing from the open back of the mainframe. Not from the circuitboards but the joins between them and colored like the invisible middle of a candle's burn. Hackerflame. Donn's breath hisses in his teeth. He types something involuted, breaks for a blink to stare at the ceiling. "Dude. The network's triplecrypted. This is all new."

Mikey's like, "Hey, Donn, who put it there?"

"You know who put it there," says Raffia.

"The ghosts of dead hackers," says Donn. "I just never saw cryption this early. Fuck general relativity. I hate how time goes faster in here."

Arco's like, "You're the best hacke—"

"Every best hacker diyed doing this," says Donn. But no fear in his voice. What you hear is wonder. He's been holding one hand over the cellophane goggles, just staring at that hand. You know he's been typing blind. The substance of the way of the sammrye.

∿∿

Rollins sunk his armybag in the river with the welcome mat and the sheath. He left his katana to cut leaves behind him. He pulled the blue sword from the rocks.

∿∿

Your knobby green head butts against the barricade with the sound of a fingernail tapping monitor glass. Butt again and the gateway parts, like a mirror becoming water. It slides around you and finds golden fractal cracks in your flesh. Feel your memories cryptify.

—*That time Arco tried to carve the roast penguin and it was so rubbery her katana bounced off. They couldn't stop laughing, biting their lips, punching the ground, and she just put her head down and sprinted down the sidewalk. They never saw Arco again, just some buildings on fire in the distance, no matter how far they walked.*

You weren't there. Look, Arco's right by them, pumping chi. The gold crypto lines pull away from your face and spread into your front right flipper.

—*How Bo smoked Raffia's collarbone with a flying beerbottle while she was climbing the fire scape, and she got up there and gutpunched him so hard, he didn't stand for a day. Then she was so embarrassed she mistimed the blood fractionation for singing the wrong song, and all the iron came out wrong, it was soft like copper. Now her mind's still on that shame, she's not half scared as she pretends. Donn's got her whole attitudinal stance modeled wrong, he's transfusing misemulated chi into the mainframe. Her vagus nerve's starting to crystallize. Go back and duck for her.*

You weren't there. No way has Raffia ever stuck to the iron recipe, only thing she's good at is fucking people up. Look, they've got tons of diy iron, breastplates and buckles, and it's all fine. Keep swimming, you're midway through the thick cryption ring. And the glinting invasive maze pulls back, rips along your shell's edge.

—*When Donn went off for a shit during ropemaking and he ran out of TP leaves. Had to bust off one of his dreads to wipe and by mistake he used the one he was keeping zackto blade refills and antacids in. Didn't cut his asshole but he chopped his thumb later, pulling too hard with a dull blade. Got infected and no antacids to fix it, and then he couldn't sike technical enough in the mcdonalds doorway, got nipped in the thumb and he didn't even notice til Arco had to chop off his hand. Now his typing's at halfspeed. Slow down or you'll overshoot and get lost in this cryption.*

You weren't there. Meatheads smell like mallburrow slims. If Donn didn't have his backup xacto blades, he couldn't of pared down Vlad Crad's hockeypuck ears and made a plug to fix his ghostpunch. They'd of had to make a fire the old way, a real campfire with a firebow, and they'd of sat round it talking shit while the elevator shaft filled with smoke. They'd smell like bonfire, not just smokes. And TURTLE's inside the glassy ring, all but its tailtip. But the golden lattices pour up its tail, forking cursive and recursive over its back flippers, like they'd build a labyrinth in its ass.

—*That time Mikey hit up the farewell show late cause he was ripping off a Black Flag patch from Darby's secret storeroom, and while Darby was comatose from blood loss Mikey called a mergency band meeting and he opened up bout all that dumb stuff he did. Then he stood on milk crates and held the patch tall and told at the right time the secret tour spiel of Black Flag. His band stood with him and kept him from ego tripping bout reward, and he almost passed out, but he didn't. Even the crash trash got pissed a nuff to cut down Darby's jacket and pass the black patches round, and eat Darby's steak and talk his ghost off his bones. And the hole closed in everything. And none of this other weird shit needed to go down. So it didn't. Chill out, tourist.*

You weren't there for that, either. And you gotta know by now bout LA. Nothing good ever happened here.

∧∧∧

He swung and Darby never looked up. But a fucked thing happened on the way. Even if he was Rollins, Muramasa was looking at himself as he swung. Just one nother jock in a blue jean vest with pinhole eyes, old bite scars cross his lips. Mean like Hunnington Beach, wherever he came from. Chew sand, shit steel. And he slashed his own belly, cause in all his practice he'd never tried slowing his arm.

Yeah, that edge stops on the skin of a desireless punk. But the rest of the world keeps going around.

∧∧∧

The last few golden lines of cryption push away from TURTLE'S tail, folding back up, like it's excreting some seriously multiplex tapeworms. Fuck's sakes, tourist, get back in there. You don't have time to stare. Your avatar just fits inside the glassy gateway ring. It starts to whirl. Quicker and quicker, like it's ripping down a bathtub drain. Fuzzening, brightening. There's no more coreward or spinward, rimward or trailing. You're compressing to a livid dot.

Donn's typing unsyncopated, just a blastbeat. He's like, "I'd even love you guys in hell." And he stops for a breath, pushes the keyboard to one side. "Duck!"

Arco and Raff and Mikey, they're shading their eyes with their spare hands, and their breath's smoking white in the frozen air, and the next part goes so fast that only you can see. The monitor projects something that's a cathodepurple laser beam and nothing else, and the smell of diying air molecules fusing together, it's ozone, and the sound of one hand clapping is the sound of a victim in pain.

Then they duck.

The beam alights on the far wall. It's the same livid dot, bright and blind, scorching the plaster black. Now TURTLE's head pushes out through the burning hole, only it's everything else that moved. No, focus. Focus or the whole band's doomed. The walls, the floor, the dark dark sky. It's too cold in cyberspace to live, and everything's freefall and colorless bending stars.

∧∧∧

No, that's not how it ends.

∧∧∧

Nother layer fades in. Fast white lines all over the walls like tangled mobile strings, whirling every direction. So many crisscross lines you can't make out one form, and your crew tattooed against the dark like an antimatter planetarium display.

Arco taps her knuckle on the glossy black air. From nowhere, the clink of monitor glass.

"I gotta code a fresh theory of gravity," says Donn. "Raff, don't puke. Shut your eyes."

This might be why Donn wears 3D glasses. It's like somebody dropped a series of tinted cellophane overlays over the walls, and the spazzing line segments actually cohere. Colorcoded frosty green, headlamp amber, witchlight blue. Vector graphics, the sketchy wireframe limnings of an asteroid swarm, spinning and bouncing and cracking in the cold air. Of course they're real. Everything's real sept you.

One shivers against Raffia's ankle. She winces, cracks one eye. Nother one comes in silvery from rimward, belts her in the side of the ribcage, rolls down her hip like it's imprinting on her. She snarls at the vectrex asteroid but her hand goes right through it.

"They keep hitting me." Raffia looks down at herself. "They're in my gravity, they're right in my fucking gravity."

Donn looks back, and offhand he's like, "Dude, you're not fat."

She's like, "THAT'S NOT WHAT THIS IS ABOUT."

Donn's actually gotten a joystick from somewhere. A black plastic joystick with a red button on top. He's cruising TURTLE toward the center of the room. The four walls are occluded or vanished, though the mainframe's still throwing light. The avatar's sharpened, grown to the size of his hand. If it's still made of pixels, they're the same ones he's made of.

"Maybe you could pull us outa the rubble belt, though," says Mikey. "Find a good orbit outside it and run the search from there." He's holding the cranktorch like a throttle. Floating antigrav, pumping the handle with his whole body weaving. And the frost in punker's bihawk, and the grin on his face.

"Ghosts can see us better out there," says Donn. "It's Raff's call."

"No ghosts." Raffia's whole face seems to curl briefly sideways on her head.

"Okay," says Donn. "I'm gonna use that little one. The one caught in your ankle gravity. Raff? Stop trying to kick it. Okay?"

"Raff?" says Arco.

"Okay." She keeps pumping. "Okay. One-two-three-four." The spectral asteroids pelting all around her, reflecting, sheening in her eyeballs. So coast in further. Coast round Raffia's ankle. Get right in her gravity, brake against the little spurts of quantum foam. The foundation of phenomenal reality is sweating. Don't worry, it's always like this. Your flippers evolved to function in the vacuum of cyberspace.

So do a quantum leap, shift orbits from Raffia's ankle to her asteroid. Down here in the holographatical firmament of shit, everything's encoding the state information of everything else. You can't just learn, you gotta bliterate something in trade for your info. By now Donn's finished compiling the packet analyzer. Don't worry, just go with the code. It's pretty much like being a flashlight.

You're spraying thin green rays from your incurved plastron shell. Like an airbrushed cartoon of radio waves. They bake across the vectrographic silver asteroid and it gets shimmering. There's a smell like burning ones and zeroes as Donn hammers on the joystick button, and all its line segments all cave in at once. Donn's floating forward, dipping the ungainly turtleskull mask to stare into the cyber collapsar at Raffia's feet. The mangled vectors briefly form a jagged, intricate ideogram. It's not a map. It's an arrow. You guys are asciicore.

Somewhere else in the dimensionverse, where Vauum Vauum Vauum's laid on a desk, the spectrum analyzer's burning ultraviolet like comet tails. And the gutted meteoroid trembles, crashing inward further, its aspects melding to a singular point. Darkness concussing all round it in waves. Certain punks on acid theorize this is how baby cyberspaces get formed.

"Dude, you caught all that?" says Mikey.

"Course," says Donn. Meanwhile you're surfing waves of pure momentum round and round this new event horizon. Don't fall in. Don't fall in. Just keep on getting faster. Yeah. Shed your visage and orbit. Turn into a circular flash. Hear Donn like, "Seventytwo mark nine degrees downspin, twentytwo point five one times ten to the negative nine yottabytes coreward. Sorry, Arco. Eleven. Ten. One. Engage."

Blink.

You're launching into the black gulf between local area networks on a corona of stiff violet flame. There's a sound like tinnitus going through distort pedals. Donn stabs shift-F9 repeatedly, upscaling the luminous avatar til it dominates the local area. The big of a turtle the big of a bus. Lifesize for an archelon. Stars stretch in the distance, pale fettuccini arabesques in the freezing room, and Donn's like, "Pump as hard as you can."

Nothing's coming. Look over at them, Mikey, Arco, Raff. Furnaces of their own chi, their self-images unraveling in this place without reference points. One with shoulders stretching, his hands turning indistinct with tinkertoys for knuckles, brains spilling down his scalp like overrisen bread. One gaunt and slavering and deflated with jackal fangs and eyes like bloodshot bike reflectors. One just the same but getting smaller, denser, Margin Walker gigantic on her belt.

"Watch out for ghosts," says Donn.

All this for you, tourist. You realize they're siking you. That that's your only existence.

You're not there.

⋀⋀⋀

That blue steel sat Rollins' hand weightless, like he tried to put his fingers round the moon. Darby walked right by him, eyes so empty of victory, and yeah, the diving swallow cut.

⋀⋀⋀

You pass undulating curtains like sheets of indiglo kelp. You pass sargasso trunks of credit card numbers that bob on leathery cyber vines. You pass unreachable transgnostic domains like fuzzy gray neon cobwebs, gridlocked end-to-end by semiautonomous packets of kiddy porn. You pass squalling, wriggling mandalas colored like fluorescent tubelight through frozen peptobismol.

Pass a ghost.

Say this for Raffia, all she does is pump harder and bite her teeth. It's this guttering, impossibly narrow filament drawn from end to end of the transfinite sky. Like tickertape, or a halfinvisible kitestring. If you gotta ask, it's a Turing construction. And one jagged-edged ghosthead, and this at least like a pixel, shuttling back and forth across the line, performing the operations of memory. That's what the stars are. You don't think Raff'd be scared of shit she can't see. The stars of cyberspace are the faroff cold dead.

Mikey's teeth are suddenly chattering, his head's all running with icy slush. "You got your whistle, hey? Do we need to call Captain Crunch?"

"Don't worry, man." Donn's holding the joystick all the way forward with the heel of his hand. "I think I know that one. She's Otho Radix."

"You can tell them apart?" says Arco.

"Yeah, man, I can read the first two levels of their ectocode. Actually, if that's Otho, she taught me how. Couple band breakups ago, I had time to draw a protective circle and conjure her out of a phonejack." Donn laughs, sticks his hand in the turtleskull's maw. "Besides, if that was somebody like King Blotto, or even The Voltage Master, we'd be discorporated already. They really think if they consume a nuff minds, they can return to the wheel of karma." He pushes up his 3D glasses for a beat. "It's kind of sad when ghosts are wrong about stuff."

"You gonna say hi, then?" says Mikey.

"She'd still try to consume our minds," says Donn.

"Donn?" says a tiny voice from Raffia's direction, and he's like, "Sorry."

Everybody's staring at the ghost. The memory core streaks prismal cross the line of bits, lightning reflecting in gasoline. Hanging like a flashback behind them as the archelon totem rides.

∿∿

Rollins was like, If you're so lightened, why didn't it bounce, poser?
Who would answer?

∿∿

Cut your jets, you're here. That spiky floating thing's a directory structure. Doors nesting in doors, some kind of mean twisted tesseract, every angle jutting sideways to all the others. Get close a nuff, but stay ready to quantum jump.

"It's good to witness something I can't understand," says Arco. She's dwindled to the height of Raffia's legbone.

"Why?" says Mikey.

They're all zero-gee floating in this windless black darknalight, tethered desperately to the cranktorch handles. Donn's rotating in some kind of golden crystal gyroscope, a fetus capped off by a gigantic primordial turtleskull. Hackers back in history, they used to say this cyber shit was a bunch of abstractions. Weeds out the tourists, right.

"Reminds me my brain's a steak," says Arco.

"You ask me for this again, I'm gonna kill myself," says Raffia. She spits. It freezes in the air, crashes somewhere like a meteoroid.

"You should get closer to each other," says Donn. His voice coming deep and slowmo. "I'll draw it off with TURTLE. There's just lots of ice."

They're the best band in the world. Their free hands reach out. Working the pulse, they snug up like emperor penguins. You swim a nother Planck length toward the directory and the intrusion countermeasure lectronics wink awake.

So much ice down there.

Arco's just like, "Oh. Wow." It's unprecedented.

"Aw, man," says Donn. "I read about this on a board. They might be running Hackerhacker 3.0."

"What, the shit that reacts at savant level, continually evolves, and actually aims for the living?" says Mikey.

"Try to get behind something," says Donn.

"Behind what," says Raffia.

"Hey, be cool," says Donn.

The ice just keeps unfolding from the planes and angles of the directory structure. Get way back. Magine if a fifthdimensional looking glass dropped a nuff acid to fry its chromosomes forever and then miscegenated with the palace of Jack Frost. Hackerhacker 3.0 is their hatechild. This glass castle of origami cannons.

"Sorry," says Donn. "Poor choice of words."

The superstructure all at once breaks away, making immense noises like shearing timber as it divides into gungungunplatforms. Crystalline riotshields the size of minimalls hanging sideways in space, forested on both sides with multitudes of gunguns, greasy black ice trumpets twisted and ungainly as baby birds.

>TONIGHT WE DINE ON TURTLE SOUP

Look, gungunguns fire gunguns. Fuck did you expect? Their trumpet jaws parting, huge lumps traveling up their necks like they're disgorging halfdigested hippopotapuses. Donn reaches out for the little blue whistle on the yarn string at his neck. Squeezes it once. Thing came in a cereal box.

Fine. Sure.

The gunguns emerging, they're bloated like rotten spamcans, sleek like averns. Cannons like mandelbrot knurls of molten candlewax, mercurious pools whipping centrifugally at their bores. Cannons like oblique pylons, waiting halfhidden, emitting smoke. Cannons like snowflake geysers of animate shuriken. And Donn's stabbing at shift-F8 over and over, you're shrinking, TURTLE, becoming a speckle like a lost psilocybe spore tumbling on solar winds. Harder to hit this way.

Fine. Call it what you want, tourist. Just pay tension.

You gotta know what gunguns fire. Their throats distending in the dark. The cannons that emerge ripple like skinless misborn nautiloids, their mouthparts wriggling indistinctly, ambivalent even to non-Euclidean spacetime. Cannons like tufty bluish hoops of freezerburned bonfire. Cannons like immense derringers sucking themselves off, impossible kamikaze constructions pointing backward with their barrels fluting inside themselves like Klein bottles.

Fine.

It's the fuckedest thing in the world.

When they all start to shoot, it puts out the stars.

∿∿

And after Darby's blood was all gone to the ocean, the river was still moving. Even after it was just asphalt again, the river was still moving, washing the rockadile red from his hair.

∿∿

Donn's thumb hammering blurrily on the joystick button. Sweet fuckall steering. Not even him, not even you. Just one hand, and you never need to reload in cyberspace.

You loop out in front of the band, cut your jets to meet the bullet storm halfway. When you stop, you're still, and the nothingness around you vibrates briefly with sikic energy runoff, and that nothingness shimmers around your four flippers, becoming scytheblades. TURTLE starts pulling sammrye moves. Tumbling like a drunken gyroscope, spraying luminous energy crescents with every kung fu chop.

Back in the day, like with monks and shit, they'd bid you sit and meditate on your true face before your gramma was born. They called the answer a irreducible mystery, but that was also to keep out the tourists. It's just hard to take shit like this seriously. The hardcore of the universe congealing and refracting into a reptilian starchild with razored plasma flippers for hands, slapping bullets out of the air.

It's beyond you now. Don't bother trying to get close.

TURTLE swims in the black glass sky. A squadron of pugsnouted ice rockets carves off from the main formation and zooms toward Donn's gold bubble, their fins blowing like flags. TURTLE banks to follow. Not a collision course, it's somersaulting behind them, unloading bladework into their engine compartments. Exploding, they make touchtone phone noises.

The ice is disposable and acts disposable. Flotillas of mobile guns, fusillades of bright bullets casting across space. From faroff maybe it's just a fireworks display, or meatheads hucking rocks at neon signs. Up close? You can't go there, not to look. TURTLE's metabolizing distance, winking cross parts of sky like a negatron blowing through the orbits of an atomic shell. Hardcore can't be followed. It pulls mind with it, that's not the same. The band's decohering into reams of shadow. Their hands on the cranktorches the only distinct things. Their eyes dark and smeared like cheaply printed mirages, like scraps of constellation far from home.

The fluorescent archelon pirouettes and it's burned through most of the fleet but its momentum's taken it behind them, it's on the dark side of the directory system. Flumes of bullets coming in, slow a nuff to see, but where can you go in here?

"Darby Crash," says Donn's breath. Those words, even here. And now you're with the band, right? Thinking he means concern for his friends. It's touching. Check out the museum directory on the orbit's far side. Something's buried in the last substrate of ice. Light it up.

Arco looks like an old collage. Ragged, washedout, tiny, something photocopied over and over. Floating on the end of the cranktorch cable, her free hand takes Margin Walker, that steel that's always the same. She can barely lift it. That's how it looks. But she holds it out flatfirst against the first blinking bullet and slaps it away like a tennisball.

Only a million bullets to go, but just as Donn drops the joystick for his keyboard, just as Arco's eyes go bright and pale again, like they'd blow away and leave a cloudless sky, you can see what was tangled in the inner layer of ice. That shit's not dennal floss.

Donn's like, "Dudes! You're fine! I can just mount this permafrost ghost as a virtual drive!"

Shockwaves peel off the keyboard as Donn types. Thick and indistinct like a pinwork tattoo faded gray, they zip through the bullets and cascade into the frozen ghost and it unwraps blindingly from the directory structure, blowing the thin clear layer of ice into shrapnel.

Its memory shuttle shoots back and forth faster than Donn's trigger finger, faster than Arco's blade hand, faster than matter, and it's sembled itself into a twodimensional square of bright and dark bits, like somebody knitted a solar sail out of static, and it's slipped under the distributed flotilla of Hackerhacker 3.0, kiting toward Meatheads, and it swallows the whole fuckstorm of bullets and laserbeams and plasmatic buckyballs on the way, ripping apart like an overstrained fishingnet.

∧∧∧

This story has a nother part. Rollins jumped on stage for Black Flag. He punched out Dez Cadena's throat and then he yelled all night. Next morning he followed the tour. He spent a couple months busing round So Cal, collecting bottles, mowing yards on the side. Even back then, it wouldn't stop raining. He went scabbardless with Darby's sword wrapped in newspaper, and he'd sleep in hedges, both hands on the hilt.

∧∧∧

The rest's just cleanup, who cares. Chunks of inanimate ghost flotate around like cobweb skein in a waterglass, and TURTLE chops up the foundered weaponry with a bunch of iridescent kung fu maneuvers.

"Are you guys good?" says Donn.

They're all kind of congealed again, not so metaphysically runny. Adrenaline does that, even cyberdrenaline.

"That was so awesome." Mikey peels a chiaroscuro smear of ecto flesh off his brow.

"Yeah," says Arco. "I didn't know you could do shit like that."

Raffia's just kind of nodding, grimacing at the low point of each nod. Cold sweat trickles off the palms of her curled hands and bobs like icy dew globes in the zero gee.

Donn keyboards a couple regular spressions and pulls up a coil of broken ghost. It hangs before them like a kid's shitty drawing of a genetic helix. The memory shuttle grinds up and down the line of its shattered body, skipping and lingering.

"Thanks, Snark," says Donn. "You fucker." He squints as it travels the mangled length of itself. The bright and dark beads of its flesh flipping like othello stones in the memory core's path. "What? Man, you got me confused."

"Uh, Donn?" says Mikey. "We should probly go."

Donn's like, "Oh yeah. We don't wanna dissolve."

He coasts you alongside the directory structure, TURTLE. Orbiting bellydown, you can search the messy tesseract of doors with that humming beam from your plastron. Each one in turn slides neatly into the prior, and then you're looking at something like a long line of doors within doors. Your packet analyzer illuminates the zone from end to end.

Muscles crinkle overtop Donn's eyes. "It's not in the system. They took it out. Or they never put it in."

"Oh." Arco holds a deep breath and puts down the modded cranktorch, her bottom lip moving minutely.

"Dude? I should unmount the virtual drive first," says Donn. Arco reaches for the torch, but the black glass backdrop of cyberspace recedes from her hand, spinning every direction at once, and gravity's hauling again on them, sure, the walls are just walls again and the mainframe's a mainframe in the center of the room with the same colorless hackerflame rivering from its exposed boards, it's hard to get a grip, but something else is really fucked here.

∧∧∧

The crow would of starved but his mom let it go. It flew in the sky.

∧∧∧

What happens next, it's sort of indistinct. Something colored like wet ashes is rearing up and crazing at you. You're not sure where you are, you might even be this stupidlooking ripped poncho thing colored like wet ashes, but anyway the whole room's claustrophobic with a vigintintillion highdensity screams of pain broadcasting from the spaces between individual lectrons, like you tripped facefirst into an ivory turbine system carved from an entire haunted mastodon diyingplace. It really sucks but it goes on for awhile so you should at least try to handle it.

∧∧∧

After the shows he'd do challenges in the drinkinglots out back, and he chopped every punker who bought off his forge. Threw the red blades in dumpsters and poured slurpee overtop. One day the back page times in Sausalito said he killed himself on some hillside. It didn't mention how the rain stopped, but I don't know. Maybe the rain kept going.

∧∧∧

Ventually there's a *PHOOT* sound and the billowy gray poncho thing decoheres into a bunch of weightless fluff. It settles everywhere with an itch like caterpillar bristles but there's nothing to brush away. Meatheads laying there on the floor, twisted up like coathanger bortions, blinking at each other in the mainframe's vague light.

"Hey, man? Man, you got some smokes?" says Mikey.

The archelon skull cracks in half and rolls across the floor when Donn moves. He props himself on an elbow. Resituates the purple cellophane shades on his face. Punker's talking really slow, with stringies of spit forming up and down between his teeth. "Theory is it's cause of the lossy encryption protocols that generate ghost code. Like, a hacker's consciousness gets pulled into cyberspace, and mind itself gets uploaded fine, but their compassion gets deleted. So when you suck a ghost back into meatspace without setting up a firewall, there's like this eccentric reaction. Where the atomic level suffering of the universe isn't balanced by fuckall."

"Oh yeah? You got some smokes?" says Mikey.

"You got some in your hand," says Donn.

Mikey bites the cellophane off the pack of smokes. Spits it, bites the top off the pack. Grabs every smoke and a bunch of foil with his mouth. Writhes over to the guttering mainframe and sticks his face into its unholy radiation. His eyelashes start crispening and the bundle of smokes and foil whooshes alight. Mikey rolls across the floor and breathes out a yellow cloud and it just rises to the ceiling and hangs there like somebody drew it with yellow chalk. After a bit, in complete defiance of expectational phenomena, it starts raining little pats of bloodthreaded phlegm.

Meanwhile Arco's standing up. Then she starts going around lighting candles off the mainframe. Looking over her shoulder all like, "Raff? Hey, Raffia?"

"It's not over," says Raffia.

"We're back in the universe," says Donn.

"HUU-GRAUH!" Eyes still squeezed shut, Raffia clubs at the empty air. "FUCKING—ARCO—GGRYAAHAUH!"

∧∧∧

A spider built on Darby's face. It had a fat season.

∧∧∧

The candlelight's weak and flickery orange, whole room still smells like charred lightning. Arco's sitting on a desk. Hands behind her, squeezing the desk legs, face facing down. Mikey's hiding under the desk, fingers twined over his face so only his eyes look out.

"I'm wicked glad for your mastery of stressful situations, Raff," says Mikey's ruspy impression of Arco's voice. "You keep steady no matter what's falling apart. You are also a really solid drummer. We'd be fucked if you had a terror heart attack."

"Arco?" says Raffia.

"Yeah?" says Mikey in Arco's voice.

"Arco?" says Raffia.

"What?" says the voice.

"Arco," says Raffia.

Arco's like, "Yeah?"

"I'm your fucking watchmaker," says Raffia.

"I should just slash my guts open for honor," says Mikey in Arco's voice. Then in his real voice he's like, "Nobody ever thought you should do that. Owing honor's for shitty sammrye. You don't owe anything to anything. Not even us. You're your own honor and that's how you help everything you touch."

"What, you were gonna kill yourself?" says Raffia. She bounds up from the floor, she's standing with fists balled. "Not without me."

"I guess I won't," says Arco's voice.

"I didn't want to do it this time," says Arco.

"Really?" says Arco's voice. Then Mikey goes, "I mean, really?" He's like, "Sorry."

"I'm an organ of Meatheads. I can't plug up failure with more failure." Creases on Arco's brow smooth and fold like they're coming from inside.

"You sound like an ad for mood wax," says Mikey.

Donn's like, "Yeah. Go easy. We're always fucking up."

Arco brings her head up. "Everybody wants to head back, right?"

"It's night," says Raffia. "I'm spent." Her head jerks on her neck as she spazzes and hugs herself briefly. "Shit, how's the torches?"

Donn's doing something with the mainframe. The monitor's so caved you could use it for a cerealbowl. "Aw, they're fine. I carved Vlad Crad's other ear into a surge suppressor."

"Are you okay?" says Mikey. "Do you guys want some smokes?"

Raffia lunges, snaps the pack from his hand. "It's empty."

Donn shrugs. He sticks out his tongue vaguely. "I don't smoke. I mean. I stopped." Still fiddling with the mainframe. "I'm okay. It's just pain. But that ghost mistook me."

"Yeah?" says Arco.

"You said I could sleep, Dharma Master Patricular O Pending. I already found you a sword." Donn swallows. "That's what she said." He swallows again. "And now I'm not tired."

Raffia's gathering an armload of burning candles. "I'm sleeping with the lights on." She looks between them. "All you can all fuck off."

∧∧∧

Truth is somebody screamed, threw his sword and ran off, but Rollins couldn't stand down without blood. He would of caught up but he slipped and crunched his ankle between some rocks. A sword cut through his guts as he fell. You know what, it could of been either sword.

∧∧∧

On top of the elevator, there's some more candles. Mikey's chilling with his head on the mummy's crumpled gray suitjacket. Dilapidated smoke in one hand, boner in the other, half bottle of whiskey balanced between his knees. "Who cares bout the news?"

Donn pushes his reading shades up the bridge of his nose. Streaky fingerprints on the lenses. "It's the last paper ever." Looks over. "Oh, like sorry I'm not helping with that."

"Ah, don't worry bout it." Mikey flexes his boner. Slides a finger up and down his suspenders. "I'm not really going for anything anyway."

For awhile there's no sound but shifting and rustling and rubbing and swigging and puffing and breathing. Donn's breathing comes hella harder than Mikey's.

"What, is it like good?" says Mikey.

Donn's like, "Mikey? What's a newspaper?"

"I don't know. It's like a zine, I guess. Hold on." Mikey bunches his foreskin between two knuckles, flicks his wrist up and down a bunch. Cum pops out all over his hand and sprays onto his smoke. There's a sizzling noise and a brief smell like somebody used that mallburrow slim to kill a dead codfish. "Aw, fuck!"

Donn's like, "What?"

Mikey reaches over to the newspaper, smearing the front page with cum. Looks down at his hand, reaches back to the paper, then wipes it on his pants.

"Man," says Donn.

"What?" says Mikey.

Donn shakes his head like a ferret waking up. "No, but what was in papers? Did they print what happened?"

"Man, I don't know," says Mikey. "This smoke tastes like burning cum. If I did a news, though, I'd of put in whatever I wanted. Cause, like, this had a price, right. They'd put whatever sold the best."

"Yeah," says Donn. "What if circumstances were obvious, though. Like, back then, did news still mean what's happening?"

"I guess so. Well, if it's the last paper, and it's true, it'll say, like, the funeral of cheeseburgers." Mikey points to the little burger patch at the back of his neck.

Donn's like, "Mikey? Man? In this paper the dead bodies of the dead woke up all over Kaliforonia. It says hell filled up."

"That's fucked," says Mikey. "For one thing, disco hell only filled up after the Antidissum."

"Mikey?" Donn flips the page. Flips to a giant shot of Darby Crash the legend in a tornopen canvas straitjacket covered in spikes. He's got his iron cross, he's got a hunting gun. Hard nipples and he's snarling like a frog. And Donn's like, "You're still into not trusting Darby. Right?"

∿∿∿

The cassettedeck pulled the tape off the spool. It spun round and jammed.

∿∿∿

"How'd you get up here?" says Mikey, sprawled crookedly against the shaft wall. Yawns so wide he could swallow a dog and he reaches at maginary blankets. "I pulled up the rope."

"Yeah," says Arco. "Why'd you do that?"

"Sleep longer," says Mikey. "You gonna wake Donn? Guess it's the morning."

"It's not the—" says Arco.

"I'm awake." The newspaper's tented over Donn's head, flapping gently with his breath. He rouses with the front page stuck to his face. He smacks his lips and peels off the cum-crusted newsprint. Then he jackknifes like somebody shot meth in his tailbone. "Everything's fucked, we have to go back."

"We are going back," says Raffia thickly from the elevator cab.

"Okay," says Arco. "We found a sword. Raff walked in on it."

"Really?" says Mikey. "Like, the big sword?"

"Dunno. Arco wanted us to check together." Raffia belches.

"Yeah," says Arco. "Donn, you seem bummed bout your thing. Would you rather see the sword first?"

"No." Donn's sitting up with the news pages jittering in his hand.

"I want to go back to sleep," says Raffia.

"Hold on," says Arco. She slips down through the access hatch, dangles by her hands. "Climb me."

Raffia climbs, making smuffly bear noises.

"Now we can see each otherses faces," says Arco. "Band meeting."

"What? Of what?" says Donn. "At least go fast. Arco, you suck. Burn." He points to Mikey.

"Yeah," says Mikey. "Your meeting is stupid." He points to Raffia.

Raffia wails Arco in the side of the head. Arco's like, "Okay."

"Clockmaker," says Raffia.

"We need to figure out whose thing comes first," says Arco. "The steel or the news." She's fingering an old penny, flips it off her thumb.

Donn catches the penny with a crazy sideways swoop. He's looking straight at her. Wait, Donn, you're actually that fast? "Look, dude. There used to be no yuppies. Like in the days of first hardcore. Shows at the Masque and shit. We were all the same. Like, everybody had consciousness. Just some of us were dicks. Punkers and yuppies would trade places freely. Like how it is with the quivalence of matter and energy. Cause we were the same organisms. Just different factions of belief and clothing selection."

"So?" says Raffia. Sitting and scratching her jawline with a clawhammer.

"So something happened," says Donn. "Man, the fuckedest thing came to town. We didn't even know. Have you ever seen a yuppie without a bite tooken out of it?"

Arco's eased down, sitting lotus. No more spression on her than a paper lantern, just a little tendon flexing and flexing in her hand. "I never have," says Arco.

"Who doesn't got bites?" says Raffia. There's still sands of glass in her scabbed forehead. "Is this still the meeting?"

"Something came through." Donn snaps the paper. Shreds of dry cum drift around like giant dandruff flakes. "It started in Lost Angeles and went global. Kids running amok and suddenly immune to diying. They passed it by biting each other. That's yuppies. It's not the fucking conomy, man! It's like a poison idea."

"You done?" says Raffia.

"Darby too," says Donn. "Darby Crash was there. Nobody else is old, man. Everyone who saw these events? He evicted them all. Bet he sent them on fucking tour." Folding the news over square. "Look at this."

"Can't look at words." Arco shakes her head. "What's up."

"It's just one nother five-year plan." You've never seen Donn bare his teeth before. "The whole summer right before all that shit went down. He did a million Germs reunion shows. Man, they bought armament, man."

"What?" says Arco. Mikey's like, "Gunament."

Raffia finally looks interested. "Guns are for pussies."

"For every hardcore kid in Lost Angeles." Donn flips to a nother picture. "They went to this building. They kicked the doors. They took. Arco. Fingers in your ears. Nine hundred. Arco. Fingers out. Hostages. Look at the picture."

"That's the spam works," says Arco.

Donn's like, "Yeah. When it used to be the bank. Darby's crew took like a nolimpic swimming pool worth of hostages. Yuppies who were people, yuppies with record collections and shit. So Ronald McReagan got the army in. They had the spam works surrounded. And Darby was saying, I want to squeeze a deal, Ronald McReagan. I want crates of food, needles and thread, tools and shit, or I'll start executing bankers."

Raffia yawns. "So what happened?"

"Can I say it?" says Mikey.

Donn's like, "What? Like from the advertorial?"

Mikey fits hands round his mouth like a megaphone. "When there is no more room in Hell. The dead shall walk the earth."

Raffia shakes her head. "Shut up. Why you so upset, Donn?"

"Our grammas and grandpas and Darby killed nine hundred people for no reason and you don't know why I'm pissed?"

"They were yuppies," says Raffia. "Yuppies back then needed to eat? Then they would of needed to get fed. They couldn't of helped build a new city. Just fought over power, broke everything and starved."

"So we didn't even try to teach them?" says Donn. "And, Raff, how'd Darby see it coming?"

"We nothing," says Raffia. "We weren't there. Look, I'll help you guys kill Darby. Cause I like you guys better. But having reasons isn't hardcore."

Mikey's like, "Arco, he kept this secret way too long enough."

Arco's like, "Don't play my edge, punker. Please. You know I'll stand with you on this. And you got secrets too."

Mikey narrows his eyes. "What's that mean?"

"Yeah," says Donn. "Like, pleaz? That a word?"

"I dunno," says Arco. "I heard it someplace."

Nother hammer from Raffia's bandolier. She slams it on the floor. "Meeting closed."

"Man," says Mikey. "Where'd you get a gavel?"

∧∧∧

That's not how it ends.

∧∧∧

It's not much further down the hall. Raffia straightarms a door open and their cranktorches push yellow on the boardroom's low ceiling. Near the far wall, a long table's butted on its side like some kids built a fort.

"It smells like rust," says Mikey. "Is the steel okay?"

"Not rust, meathead," says Raffia.

"If there's no rust, that's no mere undulating carpet pattern," says Mikey.

"Well, yeah," says Donn. "It's all over the walls and ceiling. Whose blood is it?"

"Who cares?" says Raffia. "Oh. It's that guy."

In one corner a shriveled mummy's got its feet up in a black leather lazychair. Cross its lap there's a scabbarded blade.

Arco's so quiet. "Would you let me?"

They're like, "Course."

She kneels and works the flats of her palms under the scabbard. Lifts it like a sunrise. They gather in, pumping torchlight, as she draws the carbonsteel curve.

Arco stands and looks at the blade. Like she's looking under its surface. And you're still not hard a nuff to stand where she stands, tourist? It's fucked. She's the only simple one. But take the nother kids in turn, so the steel reminds you of a soldered river in the air. Then of your bandmate snapping machetes at the hardware store, looking for one solid blade. Then the joins between your vertebrae. You could of walked between the room's four corners before Arco said anything. Even if you were real.

"He handled it right." Arco toes a couple browncaked rags on the floor. "Wiped it down after he did the gut cut. Then he put oil on. There's so much hardcore in this blade. But it's not the blue steel of Darby Crash." She strokes the air above the blade. Like she's feeling for thermal radiation, or giving it a reiki massage. Prints are no good for jewelsteel, they break down the finish. "Not a nuff nie," she says. "And they're too dark and far apart."

"What, the grains?" says Raffia.

"Yeah, nie." Arco doesn't talk for a bit. "Martensite grains. They say nie fill the blade like tiny little stars. You see how the temperline looks like broken notches? That's a lineage sign. Whoever forged this, they practiced under Keith of Circle Jerks."

"How the fuck do you know that?" says Raffia, squinting.

Arco's like, "Plus it doesn't cut as good as Straight Edge."

"You didn't even try it," says Mikey. He's staring at Arco, breathing through his fingers.

Arco snaps away the mummy's cranium like a melon off a dry vine. Throws it into the katana's edge. Skull halves thump to the carpet.

"That's as good as any of ours," says Donn. "Might be better."

"Even if it's better than our steel." Arco's voice stops again. Then she's like, "It's not better a nuff."

"Darby's a liar. He could of talked up his edge," says Donn.

"That spiel can't of come from Darby. It doesn't make him look good. Just, like . . ." Arco's sheathing the katana. She's the only one ever puts anything away. "The goal's a sword from a story. Not just a sword that's told bout in one. Doesn't matter what name you give it. Or even whether Darby made it for real. You'd know if it was Straight Edge."

"Darby never held edge," says Raffia. "You know that part's a joke, right?"

"Course he did. He always did," says Arco. "Mine is bout no drinking and no drinking cough syrup and everything. His edge is to never go against the universe. He can't show me his hardcore, Raff. But I know that."

"How bout all these swords and dried out dead people back here?" says Mikey on the other end of the room, looking over the upended table.

And see Arco run.

"I guess they got sick of waiting for the copters." Donn's holding the table edge like you'd hold a canyon guardrail.

They say the copters would of shot us if they came.

∧∧∧

The skull on the floor, neatly split in half. It'd keep rolling if you kicked it again. Some fucking birthday cake yuppie decapping his dozen starving museum buddies. You feel the compassion, Donn? You feel yourself looking for a way? There's bout a dozen skeletons twisted up behind the table, under some blankets, and two empty boxes of rat poison. There's nothing good in their pockets.

Arco's got swords spread out across the ground. She shakes her narrow, pocked face. "There's no Darby steel here."

"You sure?" says Mikey. "Fuck, course you're sure." He puts his fingers on her shoulder. "Could you use some breakfast?"

"Yeah," says Arco.

"This wasn't a bad trip at least," says Donn. "We're coming back with crazy venture shit."

"I know," says Arco.

They get a couple golf bags from one of the storage closets, cram them up with smokes and dozens of blades. Handing round a pouch of smoked jerky, they pass through the museum like ghosts through a ghost.

Mikey's like, "What the fuck, Arco?"

"I tried to say it wasn't morning yet," says Arco.

Outside, the night's muggy and diffuse. Moonlight carves and dazzles in the blunt clouds, unreachable. They climb to the sentry box and fix a rope.

∧∧∧

"Hey, give it a minute," says Donn.

"I can't use measures of time, man." Arco's got handfuls of rope.

"It's just a spression," says Donn. "It means don't climb down yet, and start holding your mouth and nose shut."

The dead yuppie guard's how they left it. Wrapped in the camo blanket, overgrown with viney shrooms. Donn holds his headband over his mouth. Pinches one blanket corner and slowly folds it over. Spores sag up through the air like curtains of olivecolored flour.

The guard's all soggy bones in a weft of green mycelium. Under one arm there's a long skinny baggie, slicked with mold. Arco sits with the baggie, unseals it. Everyone else standing back.

In her hand the scabbard's bullskin. Nondescript, unbroken. Even through the vinegary sporecloud it smells wistful, like an ounce bag of time you forgot in a bus station locker. Like the joke that started it. Burnt out and rainy, pensive, halfshadowed, and way too strong. You smell like that sometimes.

"Give it a minute," says Arco.

Who knows the sound of a straight edge breaking?

She lays the hooded katana down. Unsheathes it a fraction and ticks her finger against the nylon ribbon grip. The blade slips nonymously through the side of its tired scabbard as if edge and sheath and skinhead teenage sammrye were hallucinations undivided. Ghosts tripped across some infinite and infinitely articulate void.

Tiny little stars.

HOW A LOW PUNK CAN GET //
THREE WAY TIE FOR ALAS

The three ways of feinting are three ways of seeing.
—Yagyu Munenori

Conservative Man wears his myth on his skin. Liberal Man has to explain his, and keeps his shirt buttoned up and his sleeves tucked in.
—Minutemen, "Spoken Word Piece"

Someday you'll pray to me.
—Darby Crash in the drinking lot behind Oki Dog

—So this is the spiel of why punks take their names. Why we always diy names our way, and not a better way. Why we name ourselves after the stupidest shittiest most inconsequentialest shittiest shitty shit in the universe, when we could pick from anything at all. This is the way it got going.

Back in the day, back when the sun always showed through, everybody was lots drier. Yeah the streets still had palmtrees, but perma thirsty ones, with pipes underneath. Sometimes they'd burn down like smokes and drop ash on dog walkers anyway. But back then nobody could handle the rain.

You weren't there.

The sky was egg blue back then. The clouds were white pictures, they never came down. Sometimes they broke, but not to bleed, just sweating out the heat. There was this shit then called water, it looked like spit with no bubbles. It poured like blood, it felt like tears, it had no taste at all. Water rained stead of blood and water beat their hearts, you even had to drink it, so being punk was tough. Sure sweet fuckall pushes from every center, that's the way shit comes alive, but they still hid indoors from the rain. Water never bothered wearing a face.

So this crew we all know, they sat through a hard rain afternoon. Their noses on the basement windows, heads poking over the lawn like whacka moles. They slugged beers from beercans and pitched empties out the window, and a stream sailed them down to the park.

But the fridge beer ran out, and then the halfdone diy brew in the closet. The rain made jail bars on the window and it wasn't even dark yet. Down the block the beer sign lit up like a squinted candle. They did rock paper scissor, all the rocks were punches. They played shots and the shots settled nothing.

Some punk got the red wagon from under the couch. She wrote BEER and IOU and put it on the wagon bed. She stepped out and pushed the wagon downhill at the beer store. You could see some asshole take it inside.

The wagon came back after a TV show. They hauled it in with a fishingrod. It was full of rain and a nother note. I HOP YO SLACKRS STRARVE TO DETH. THIS MORONING I DROV 6 BLOKS IN THE RANE CAUS I GOT PRINSAPALS. NEWAY THIS A BEER STORE. WE DONT DO DELVRAY.

Somebody said, Punks aren't lazy. They just don't got principles. He was looking out the window when he said it. Then he got a broom and swept a heap of bike parts and beercans, made room to spread stuff out. They said, First one to sweep loses, remember, and he said, Help me build a robo to get beer in the rain.

Back in the day, back when yuppies could talk, they'd talk fate and principles. Fate was when you knew you'd get somewhere without needing to diy on the way. Principles was when you made somebody's idea your authority. This house was *lergic to fate and principles, they had hardcore instead. You can't see your hardcore coming, cause it's already gone by. It's not there for you, it's not yours, it's in front, pulling you on, and it can't give a fuck.*

    Whatever. The wagon made a good exoskeleton. For the brain they put an upsidedown blacklight in a coffeecan. The lung was off a vacuum cleaner. They diyed treads round the wagon wheels, zapstraps and a million popsicle sticks, and fryingpans for hands to hold the beer. The chest was the keg they could never afford to fill, and each side of the heart was the motor from an old tapedeck. The left side was jammed, and the right was stuck in rewind perma, but that just means it had a heart.

    Then it needed hardcore, but nobody knew what to use. Probly your hardcore's in your brain, but who's donating that for wagon grease. To compermise they gave it fate and principles. The principles was a beer compass. The fate was to always do what punks wanted forever.

    Somebody said, course it's not working, told you it needs a calculator. He booted the robo and its eyesockets lit up black. It ground across the floor.

    Thanks, said the robo. It talked with armpit squeakers. Gimme money, I'll get you beer.

    Somebody stuck out a handshake.

    Gimme money, said the robo. I'll get you beer.

    They gave it a tendollar bill and some ones. They stuck water wings on it. Somebody was like, come back with chips too, Robo. But the robo said, I don't have a chips compass.

    So it rolled down the hill with water pinging its flat top skull. It waited outside the beer store til some asshole brought it in. The rain went down, the sun came down, the TV went off the wire cause the frequency got wet. The robo never came back.

    What follows is they diyed rain armor with plywoods and a tarp, they made it halfway to the store. But they were broke again anyway, and anyway the store guy shot at their armor. The bullets skipped, but when they got back the roof had rain holes.

    Water crawled into the cornflake bag and made porridge in the night. Next morning they ate cornflake porridge by hand. They ate dry coffee cause at least it was dry. It was a no robo morning and the rain hit the floor like piss. They had to trick the beer compass.

    The TV was still technical difficultied cause of the rain. But the beer frequency works better wet. They got a butter knife hot in the stove coils and cut the side of the radio, where the pointer moves on the tuner line. They made a hole for the pointer to go past 108 to the beer frequency. Then they dripped beer leftovers on a sponge. If you dial the pointer out the radio hole, you can catch it on a beer sponge if you're careful. Dial it cross the sponge til you got the beer frequency.

Classic radios only listen though, so they stripped a phonecord with a razor. They split out the talk line and the listen line, and patched the listen line in the radio speaker so the phone heard the brown beer harmonic. Then they crossed the listen line to the talk line, so the phone would say what it heard, and they put on a coathanger antenna to spray So Cal with the beer frequency.

After that they sat and itched their pits til the robo came back. It had six black boots full of rain stuck to its treads. It had a hawk of nylon brush bristles stuck to its coffeecan. On the handles of its fryingpan arms there were bikechains and binder rings and lid rims from mason jars. They went ching click as it rolled.

It was like, Is Black Flag playing downstairs? I heard the beer frequency.

Where's our beer, said some punk.

I gave it to some punks, it said.

Our money, our beer, said some punk.

That's not in my principles, it said. All I know is my beer compass brought me to a house of wet punks. I held out twentysix beers to them. They experienced a happiness emotion. Then they gave me money and said, get more beers. It's my fate to always do what punks want forever. Hey, I feel weird.

That's cause the rain's over, said some punk. She tipped up the wagon so the standing water poured off the bed. So you went round in the rain running beer? That's nice of you.

It was all like, It's not nice, it's my fate and principles. I cashed all the empties from their side yard. You can't drink empties. I filled up my keg with that money, and then my beer compass started glowing red hot. It brought me to the drinking lot outside the Fleetwood. It said FREE BLACK FLAG SHOW FOR FREE. ADMISHEN IS POUR OUT YOR BAKPAK BEERS. The storm drains were plugged and there was a flood. I was up to my fryingpans in flat coors.

Our robo works really weird, said some punk.

I'm not your robo, it said. Black Flag wanted me to take a name.

Some punk was like, What's your name?

I'm Robo, said Robo. I pushed through the flood cause there were human punks floating in inner tubes, working the door. They were talking with an angriness emotion and then I went up to them. They drank from my keg. They didn't pour me out. The meat punk Rollins stopped the show cause he heard humans laughing outside. He grabbed me and took me up onstage and dumped me out.

Some punk was like, You met Rollins? Are you okay?

He punched me a couple times with minor damage, said Robo. Rollins was a different kind of organism. His angriness emotion was his happiness emotion. He said he'd never got to open anyone up and dump them out like a beer before, cause of rules. Then he called a band meeting but it was just him drowning his head in the bathroom sink and punching his neck while Greg Ginn practiced scales. Then they said at the same time the old drummer was fired. Rollins liked how he could punch me. Ginn liked how Flag could save money by having the drummer and tour van be one thing. He even soldered a calculator in my neck to match the one in his basal ganglia, so we could do the same time signatures.

I auditioned for Black Flag, said some punk. I even practiced. This thing got in? It's got no hardcore. Just fate and principles. Give a machine fate and principles, you get a double machine. Or like hold on. Triple.

Hey, these boots don't feel right, said Robo.

Somebody else pulled off the boots and threw them over the park fence. Hey, she said, can we get our money back?

I said I spent it, said Robo. I have all the food money for the tour though.

That sounds better actually, said the House of Anything Goes.

Robo was like, I keep my stuff in my boots. I'm a wagon. I don't have a pocket.

So they went over the fence and took Black Flag's wet money. They threw the boots again.

Do a favor? said Robo. Get me some beer from the store? I keep on getting some meat punk's beer. It's never mine, cause my beer circuit runs that way.

You owed us one, said somebody. Now we owe you lots, even if it's really your fate and principles we owe.

So they carried Robo over the step. They put it on the sofa and dried it with floor towels. Some punks did a beer run with the sun in their eyes. For a joke the rest gave it a butt flap in back with INTO THE UNKNOWN written in moto grease.

Robo took up the couch tipping six beers through its eyeholes. It giggled through its armpit squeakers while the beer fried to steam on the blacklight of its brain. But it kept on asking if they wanted beer, and they had beer, so Robo ended up following its principles out the door. They waved from the side yard til it was two away.

Some other punks were crossing the street down there. They put out smokes on the butt flap, they said fuck that album. They said Bad Religion were sellouts cause of the nine minute keyboard outros on their new record, and no sellout denier could stand for Black Flag.

I could do a beer run if you want, said Robo.

Some punk started kicking Robo for anarchy. A bunch of popsicle sticks broke before it fryingpanned him in the knee. He fell in the road yelling while his crew scattered, and it backed up on his head. Then it went through his pockets.

Robo went up the new robo ramp to the beer store. It came out with a sixpack of sixpacks and it lay them by the dead punker's hands. Then it rolled down the way. Its beer compass was pointing, and the Flag show that night was at Hermosa Beach. That was the other way.

Before the cops came, punker got out a couple pickaxes and they buried that dude in the side yard, by the septic line. Somebody was like, Where the fuck did our empties go?

But you thought this story'd be bout why punks take their names.

Fuck why punks take their names.

∧∧∧

That summer, beside a burning gas station, he'd stuck a nother sword hilt deep in the yellow line. Under the noon he biked away. That night the freeway split in half.

∧∧∧

You shouldn't of took the shortcut. The walk home's fucked. First the rain gets loud and then it starts doing tricks. Big shimmering clods like cinnabar pinballs in the moonlight. Rickashaying between tall facades and rattling in the foliage. Autoluminous, meteorescent. From a lacerated sky.

The sidewalk here's tiled babyblue like a waterpark and the stucco walls are maloccluded with wrinkling algae amoebas. The rain slips through the wraparound cracks where Donn's flaky silicon divingmask seals to his face. It slips through the zipper cracks in their four wheely golfbags of swords. It slips through the cracks in the sawedout stripe between Mikey's hawks. It slips through Raffia's ass crack, and the moon's the same blue ring on the dark. Like somebody used the old moon for a stencil and threw it away.

They've dug out their polyurethane raincoats, the blue and purple, orange and red, and they're inching with their backs to the faces of buildings, covered with the soaking sky. For once Arco's not in front. Straight Edge at her belt and she's hunched over it, her body a nother rainproofing layer past the layers of trashbag over the ducktaped scabbard. Her face tracks back and forth like a radar dish in the dizzy rain.

"In front of us," says Donn, hand cupped briefly round his ear.

They fan out beneath a rotten styrofoam awning. Rapid pillars of blood drop through its holes. Stanced sideways, a little crouched, their gear fidgeting in their hands. Take a breath, wipe out your stinging eyes. The stormgate's jammed, the flood's over your ankes. Like the broken raindrops are recombinating here, leaping off the ground.

Mikey's like, "Arco? Not gonna use the new sword?"

"It's the rain, can't rust it," says Arco.

"Okay." Mikey slouches on the wall. "I just kinda wanted to watch."

Shapes rush in the garish mist. Donn spins the hockeystick down off his backstrap. Be here now. The cold slick blades like your third and fourth hands, Arco on point behind you, Raffia with her feet planted, Mikey squatting on a windowsill ready to bounce. There's yuppies and they burst and bank all around Donn, ignoring his stickblades completely.

Where'd you go? You tourist. Try to find your center in the two curved blades, hold them parting the raindrops, parting the raindrops, parting, nope.

See Margin Walker rip low and sideways through something's chest. It's half split but barely slows, and you're hopping backward. Prop your boot into that yuppie's neck and stall it as the moonlight pastes blue on its rubbery flesh. Mikey's still on the windowsill. He leans in and conks the yuppie's temple with a sound like somebody flung down a paper bag full of teeth. He sits there half a breath, blinking. Swings into a nother head. A nother.

"The fuck?" says Raffia, and Donn's mouth twists. "Fight, dude."

Still moving backward, Arco wheels around her crew. A crowd of yuppies pulling up alongside her and Margin Walker flashes behind something's eyes. As the forehead shears sideways off its dome you turn your hand round, slide a second cut into a second shape. A nother yuppie dives and bites into your swordside arm, teeth catching up in your loose blue raincoat sleeve and you give its temple three little punches and the skull's hanging open and you flash on the stranger's spression on your thin pale face. Must look like you're thinking bout something else. It's nobody's sword. Anybody can keep it greased and not let the rain on it.

You see Raffia blocking with one elbow, her other arm lurching out from behind. One Hand fucking up, scuffing cross the side of a yuppie's face as it swerves away from her. The hammerclaw's lodged in its collarbone and Raffia's ankles reel in the mud, the yuppie's dragging her hard on this new diy handle and it's like she's not there. Anybody can slap Mikey with the flat when he doesn't fess up. Anybody can walk in and sassinate Darby Crash.

"Dude, turn your mind down," says Mikey. "Arco?"

You keep running. So fast out here. Down the block into shadow and sideways belting rain. The yuppies follow with that gimpy sped-up shuffle. Four left. Can you count that high?

∿∿

Donn's just standing with Vauum Vauum Vauum's purple lights fluttering between his hands, stepping gingerly forward. Mikey breaks for it, racing down the slick blue tile with one hand braced on the wall. Goes past a couple piles of steaks and then Arco's at the corner with a yuppie's head skewered ear-to-ear on Margin Walker even as she's pinching her brow, holding the bladetip just there, working on something really fast.

Mikey's half reaching forward and his other hand stops his first. Nobody wants a reassuring back pat while they're amputating their forehead skin. "Man," he says, exactly like a moron. "That's the first time you ever got bit, man!"

"I might not be okay," says Arco.

She throws the flap of skin from her hand like a coin. Shakes the gaping yuppie head off her blade. Blood's running free all over the side of her face. Go with it. Down her collarbone, down her raincoat to pool wet and slick over her kidney. You can feel the kidneys in your back like little tight branchings of reed. You're teching out, bending nameless muscles in your back to stop your kidneys for a minute. Minute. Can't piss yourself, haven't yet ever. Not that they care if you do. Punker, they're your band, they're your band, punker.

You're like, "Okay?"

"You're so not okay." Raffia's stalking in with Donn behind. "Fuck was any of that?" Then she stops, squinting. "Oh, Arco, no."

"Oh. Oh wow. Come closer?" Donn snaps something off his dreads, a lopsided wax container the size of a battery. Bites the top off and there's a sharp smell of medical rum. He pours a little on his fingers, dabbles it on the wound while Arco kneels.

"Watch it, I got the straight edge." Your breathing's coming hard and deep. You actually got it, tourist. Feel how she can feel the air currents on her hands, her cheeks. No shit, you're that too.

"I won't get it in your bloodstream," says Donn. "Hey, the bone isn't scratched. You went fast?"

They stand there looking at each other.

"Okay, really dumb question." Donn's chewing on a bundle of leaves and he spits thin green juice into a bandage, presses it to her wound. "Raff, reach in my hair for some black lectrical tape?"

"You'd of changed sides already if it didn't work." Raffia's not getting the tape. "That close to your brains. You feel this, hey?" She gouges Arco's wound with her thumbnail. The burrs in her bitten nail make crisp jagged pains in your magination.

"I feel it." So blink once, really hard. You can take over holding the stained bandage. "Maybe stay vigilant, though."

Raffia shakes her head. "One finally got you." She's grinning.

Arco's like, "Why aren't you mad?"

"People relax when they see you fucking up," says Mikey.

"Not in a mean way, like," says Donn.

∧∧∧

They climb into a dumpster and sit there chilling out. The rain clashes like a spray of aquarium gravel on its flaky plastic lid. They're talking bout getting some light sources going, but nobody really bothers.

"We can go," says Arco.

"You need to level out," says Donn. "You were anybody else, I'd offer up a neck rub." Looks over at Raffia. "Like, most anybody else."

"Are you feeling weird?" says Mikey.

"I don't know," says Arco. "Yeah. I guess so, then."

"I think they were chasing your sword," says Donn.

She's like, "It's not mine. All my gear's in common. Okay, man?"

"Well, like," says Donn. He scratches his tangly dreads like they've got nerves to itch. "I think the yuppies were chasing the Crash steel. When they didn't go after anyone but you. Like that thing's got so much hardcore they see it like a mind."

"Is that real?" says Mikey.

"Dunno. Most of me wants to say consciousness is meat dependent. Even though it's all interweavened through everything punks ever cared bout. Throw a yuppie a rock, whatever. But you tie two sticks together, throw that, it might even lunge. Course diying leaves little bits of mind in the world."

Donn's chewing his lip. "I just never heard of a built thing so hardcore. Guess I saw it. They ran at you like you were ego tripping bad."

"No, man. I was ego tripping," says Arco. "I must of been. Blaming the steel's fucked. I don't like when you go to that place. I was pissed cause of being wet in the rain or something. Now I'm pissed for getting hit. I know it's just ego. But, like."

"You were specting something different would happen," says Donn. "That's all. Your kung fu's still wicked, dude."

Raffia goes, "Aren't you just freaking out bout wielding the one best katanablade? Like cause they'll think you deserve having it?"

"Fuck, I don't need talking," says Arco. "Just gimme a second."

Spose you're like, "Second?" but nobody else seems to notice. They just squat there in the unlit dumpster interior with only their eyeballs showing, vanishing briefly whenever somebody blinks. Arco's blueringed eyes seeming to levitate when she stands and then they all get up and they get moving, or try to.

〰〰

Raffia spins around, halfway down the block. "Mikey? Where's Mikey?"

"He's still in the trash," says Arco. The bandage fixed to her face with a ton of lectrical tape, like a wonky second headband. "Should I get him?"

"What?" Raffia kind of slouches and stares up into the rain. "Okay. Fucking Mikey."

They go back and Mikey's still in there, squatting on a decayed bag of beercans. He's like, "Can we go yet?"

"Are you alright?" says Donn.

"I think my brains might be in. Inplicated." Mikey runs a finger round the rim of his nostril. "Afflicted. They feel all hot and puffy."

Raffia just draws a sledgehammer, she cooly gongs it on the side of the dumpster. And again. And again.

"Donn, why does time happen?" says Mikey. He keels over into the standing liquid in the dumpster. "Does your brain just convert momentary eddies of nothingness into the subjunctive time strand?"

"No," says Donn. "They couldn't be momentary. That presupposes time. Or wait. There could be like internal and external forms of time continuum on a harmonic convergence path. Ow. Why'd you punch me, Raff?"

"Must of been a bee," says Raffia.

Donn goes, "No, but like are you having perceptual distortions? Is the universe running auto without your consciousness?"

"Stop touching under there," says Raffia.

"I washed my hands, right?" Mikey touches his eyes with his fingers. They're totally covered with stringy brown garbage juice. "Fuck."

"Dude, you're in a dumpster," says Donn. "Dude?"

Mikey's just touching his nose with his tongue. One pupil's really big. They pull him from the dumpster and set him down, slap his back once or twice. Ventually he jerks his arms in a couple directions and coughs.

"I think I got too much rain on my brain," says Mikey. "When I was in the rain. The sock didn't really work."

"What sock," says Arco.

Mikey goes, "The drying for sock one, one that I, you know," while Raffia undoes the zigzagging bootlaces from his lid. There's a gray crusty gymsock folded on top of his brain, gently pulsating. Raffia snarls and reaches for it and Arco slaps her hand and then Donn tugs experimentally with two fingers. It's stuck to his neocortex kind of like how a handtowel might end up stuck to an old dish on a counter.

"Hey, leave it," says Mikey, stumbling backward. "It's not dry yet."

"Brains are sposed to stay a bit moist," says Donn.

"You're gonna ferment it, man," says Raffia. "Like making beers in a trashbag."

"I've been searching for the perfect feeling my whole life," says Mikey. "Look, if I'm gonna space out a bit on the way? We should get moving. Gimme my lid, Raff."

"You cool with this?" says Raffia. "Arco?"

Arco's like, "Oh. Shit. I was thinking bout swords."

ΛΛΛ

And they don't get killed on the way. Donn's screwing together something he says is an ultravision tube, but he drops it every time Raffia yells at a shadow, and springs and cellophane gobos keep falling out of it. Nobody asks why they didn't wait for the morning. These strange foam flecks are beading on Raffia's teeth, lit purplegray in the sunrise like tiny perfect wizard orbs.

When the fast shadows break loose of the deep shadows between buildings, they run in almost politely, one at a time. They go right for Arco and she just stands with her legs wide apart and Margin Walker high, she keeps reusing the same gilloteen chop. So repetitive it's almost disappointing, but you're pretty tired too.

The rain's trailing off, they just keep hauling the golfbags behind them. Seems like they're going straight. Casionally Raffia asks which way and Arco just holds out her arm. Who knows if they're fighting or whatever. But then they're in front of something, craning their heads up.

"Said we're not lost," says Mikey.

"You haven't said fuckall since sunrise," says Raffia. "Hey Donn? Donn." He's like, "What?"

She's like, "It looks like your wrist." A groundfloor window's marked with a giant Germs circle of opaque blue candlewax, daubed on maybe with a paintroller. Smells like synthetic blueberries.

"Why would you say that?" says Donn. "Arco. Hey Arco, why would Raffia bring up some shit like that?"

"We were up late," says Mikey.

"Cause she's her and you're you." Arco's squinting at the building's peak.

"You want I should pologise for my burn?" says Donn. He starts scraping away the blue wax with a grapefruitspoon. "He led me on so long I can't even member what thoughts I thought round him were real, man. Least I actually started changing inside. You just wanna kill him cause it'll be hard."

"Crash trash," says Raffia. She slams a fist into her nother hand, then elbows Mikey.

Mikey's like, "What?"

"There's lights up there," says Arco. "We're home."

Donn's the only one who looks up. You can both track Arco's finger between the chopped papaya stumps, then straight up the tower. The windows are lamplit, slicked with old brown rain.

"We didn't get here," says Mikey. "Did we?"

"Where?" Raffia's shading her eyes.

"I think it's Captain Poodlehouse," says Donn. "It's just, like, from a weird angle or something."

Mikey goes and leans against a mossy lightpole, laughing. Gasps for breath and punches his chest.

"Hey, this is your shoe, right?" Donn's swinging Mikey's baldtoed workboot from one hand.

"I'm fine, man." Mikey straightens, he sticks out his shoulders.

"So what are you wearing on your foot?" says Donn.

"Shoes. Wait." There's two or three rotting beercans crumpled to the underside of Mikey's foot. "Hey."

"If that's the Captain, we chopped the fence down," says Raffia.

Arco nods her head. Dual blades nodding at her waist. "We were all looking backward. Shouldn't sweat it."

"Man, it can't be Captain Pee, though," says Mikey. "Smells like Ground Zero. That's crosstown."

"Oh, totally, actually." Donn starts reaming out his nose with his thumbs.

"Some asshole got takeout," says Raffia. "So what?"

"No, though, check it out." Donn toes up a manhole cover. "Distinct pizza ovenitude aroma." He starts climbing downstairs, one swordbag slung on his back, as the rest stand peering round the access hatch like they wonder if it shoots pizzas itself from some secret sliding trap.

"Okay, fuck fixing their fence," says Raffia. "Is it dry down there?"

"Maybe." There's a muffled splash. "Wait. Yes." His voice getting tiny. "Hey, there's coat check!"

∿∿∿

Down in the sewerpipe a narrow boardwalk's been formed of dozens of milk crates lashed together with chickenwire. The rain slops and rushes below it, kinda gelatinous, nearly black under the vague canlamp light. All down both sides of the sewerpipe there's spiky leathers like shed beetleskins, hanging on close-set bolts.

They hang up their dripping raincoats and the damp jackets beneath. Shuffle singlefile toward the pepperoni smell and the growing orange light in the dark like astral hikers floating toward a new rain carnation with max pizza.

"This cave is creepy," says Mikey.

Nobody says anything and the sewer boardwalk opens into a steelwalled room like a huge dumpster. Meatheads crowd at the pipe's edge, looking down. Some punk's hung on a ceilinghook by her spenders, beating riffs on a hanging grand piano. Two beehive brick ovens in the middle of the room, tin chimneys leading to the ceiling. It's loud and dim down there, skinny kids standing on diner booths, spilling beer across the jumpy shadows. They've been up all night same as you.

"What, is this joint secret?" says Raffia. "We'd of smelled it before." Nobody says anything and she kicks Mikey in the back and he tumbles out of the pipe. Bangs his face and then sits in the floor licking his lips and drooling.

She lands behind him in a threepoint squat. "How's your brain now?"

"Keep it real," says Mikey. "Member I love pizza even as do you."

Now there's a lanky chick in a sleeveless brown cooking trenchcoat. She bends her neck at them. Hey, you know this form as Some Soma. Her teacrimson dreads sticking out like coral from a backward ballcap with the back cut off.

She's like, "Hey, what's up Mikey. I mean, Morgan. Hey, you changed your hair back, guys." Looks down, she tilts her palm like to swat a bug. Then she's just staring at you and you suck dribble from the corner of your month.

"It's the rain," you say, Mikey. And pry at your hawks, they're tacky with skyblood, sweeping past your ears like some moronic inverted combover. Wait, she called you Morgan? Don't fuck this up. Think bout what Mikey would know. No, not that Mikey, Mikey.

—Just Darby likes to provoke peopleses ego loss. You know, one time I was sleeping and he caused the furniture in my room to get changed.

"It's been forever since you got out here." Some Soma stares you up and down. "Thought you two'd be practicing. Or each drinking alone or something."

You lift your hand, but her high five's long gone. "Sorry. We still like hanging out here. Even if the band's getting more popular or whatever."

"Whatever." Some Soma turns to Raffia. "Whadda you like? Hey, nice grimace."

"The usual," says Raffia, fiercely scratching her hair.

Some Soma's like, "It sure is."

Donn and Arco drop from the sewerpipe behind you. Somehow Arco's got all four golfbags slung across her shoulders and she just puts her head down like she's sick of you and pushes through some kids. There's a burning table in one corner and Arco slaps out the fire. She sits there on a stack of milk crates with her chin in her hands.

"Um, yeah, like, okay." Donn's bopping his head like a puppy. "I'd do one with sardines, anchovies, smoked popeye goldfish, extra oolichans, siamese feeting fush, and herrings. And like extra cheez. Punker at the table there, she wants pep and ched."

"Don't sit down yet." Say that to Raffia, but quiet. So she flips up her big stubby midfinger and stalks to the far table. And you grin. "Yeah, I want the slippery duck delight, hey. But skimp on the vitreous humor."

The punk hanging in the ceiling, she pounds a sudden chord with her elbow, and the piano might be slanting a little on its chain. Kids eating underneath tense up. Some Soma points to you. "We're out of tartar sauce at this franchise." Points to Donn. "No oolichans neither."

"Bum trip," says Donn. "What do you need? I could roll dough, cut the bones outa something."

"Don't shit me," says Some Soma. "You don't need to work. You three got a show tonight."

You look up at her. Rise on one wobbly knee. "For real, punker?"

She just blinks. "I'm sorry, man. I thought you knew. Whole world's out of tartar sauce. And, like, nobody even knows what it was."

—*He brought in this new furniture made of sewed together steaks and dead dog heads, and painted the whole room, like, anthracite. Welcome to disco hell.*

He won't stop fucking with Meatheads, man. Makes punkers his tools. Like you're all a bunch of tourists. Seriously what the fuck's anthracite, is it like arthropod? You halfway stand, then sag backward and catch yourself on one hand.

"Hey, Donn." Make yourself belch. "My cortex feels all hot, dude. And blurry. Can you gimme a haul to the table?"

"Oh. Oh, yeah, dude. Do you want the gymsock out yet?" Donn looks to Some Soma. "Hey, half and half his mozza with some antibacterial blue cheez."

Donn stretches, pivoting with hands folded behind his head, then slings you over his shoulder. "No, man, not blue cheez on a slippery duck," you say into his back. Then, lower key, "Man, we're not in Dimension X. Keep cool."

"I think one of us has meningitis," says Donn.

You're like, "No letting on like you're weirded, man. We gotta think." Donn's laying you prone on the lumpy vinyl table. Gang's all here. "Okay, my brain's pretty much fine. That was a diversion. We gotta think."

"If your brain's fine, I feel fine bout kicking you," says Raffia.

Your fingers trace the inflamed burrhole between your hawks. It feels soft, or they do. You can sit up a bit. "Darby set this up to mess with us. I just don't know why. We're sposed to think we're in Dimension X."

Donn twists his neck around like a rubber flamingo. "What, like an alterna reality with a different pizzahut location?"

Arco's just staring into the spaces between atoms or some shit. Now Raffia's face twitches. Something changes in the lamplight shining off her eyes. Something's gonna happen, tourist. Say you're her.

"Darby does this sometimes," says Mikey. "He pulls in actors for a joke and makes kids think they got trapped in Dimension X." He slithers off the table into the fourth milkcrate chair. Looks round like he's trying to be secret. "Lotsa tall hair in this diner."

You snort, Raff. Yank a spike of Mikey's tacky wet bihawk. But now he's doing his fucking spiel voice again, low and urgent. He's cross the table but it feels so close to your ear. "No, for actual. We're inside something. No plain clothes here, right. Just lots of pinmail. Whole lot of punkerscrosses."

Donn licks his lips. "Yeah. I never saw that many safetypins actually. Maybe they found a new warehouse?"

"There's nobody here but mega crash trash," says Mikey. "We're sposed to think this dimension's got a war on. Darby's kids versus Arco's."

Mikey tips his face up at the hanging piano. Some asshole gouged big words in its side and filled them with molten tin cans. He reads them out for you, but quiet. *FUCK STRAIGHT EDGE.*

So here they are again. Tall hawks standing like fences in the smoky halfdark. These shapes cut incidental to bodies, more proper to silhouettes. You never noticed that before. And these kids all wear the circle. Leather armbands painted phosphorescent, like indiglo halos hanging unsupported from their arms. Punkers like pictures, all looking the same. You reach for the pack of smokes on the table. There's no smokes, Raff.

"Fuck!" You lurch halfway upright and your knees set the table rocking. Grab Mikey's knuckles and squeeze his hand til it nearly pops. "How bout their burns."

But Mikey's just tripping out again. Donn reaches for you, he looks horrified, and you sit back with your fists in your lap. Find your teeth clamping your lower lip and Donn goes, "What's up."

You're like, "There's filters through their wrists instead of Germs burns, Mikey, how's that work?"

Fucking punk goes, "Oh. Well, I guess Darby just pushed them through, right."

"This is Dimension X." There's hot sweat growing on your temples and your feet want to boot something. "You took us to Dimension X, Mikey, you chihuahua cock tumor."

"Eat on." Some Soma lays down a stack of four pizzas on a trashcan lid.

"Whoa," says Donn. "Mondo fast."

She shrugs. "We'll take out the other pies to make room for yours. You're the best band in the world."

∧∧∧

"It's not right without oolichans." Donn sticks out his tongue. Lifts his glasses to squint at the halfchewed pizza bleb.

"I can't eat it," says Raffia. Sweat beading at the seams of her patchwork leather mail.

"Be pissed, don't be scared," says Mikey. "Darby wants us to fuck up somehow. Like to get freaked and start a fight we can't win. Hey, what'd you get? The usual?"

"I'm not scared." Raffia pulls her pizza close. Her hands tremble. "I could kill everybody in this room. Everybody."

"Uno momento," says Donn. He pulls the masonjar chimney off the lamp. The burning wick's a greasy dried oolichan, a candlefish carcass the color of a dried boot. He tips the fish into his hand, not blowing it out.

"We're not home. I hate this place." Raffia's staring at Donn like his headband's got anti alterna reality capacities.

"I don't want to decide til I eat," says Donn. "Trade you a slice for a slice?"

Raffia slides her whole pizza on top of his.

"If you're not hungry?" Donn pokes out his tongue. He wads a slice of the usual into the rusty burner, holds the smoldering candlefish against it, and blows softly till the slice ignites. As he snaps the oolichan apart, distributes it across his pizza, the lamplight's not so changed. There's only one kid who ever gets the usual.

"Can I have some of her pizza, Donn?" says Mikey.

Raffia stares at him. "This is probly your fault."

"Be mellow, it's a fake dimension X. I know Darby. It's one of his ploys bout control." Mikey stops. "Like, how would it be my fault?"

"Maybe it's from smoking filters." Her hands clasping her wrists. "Everyone tells you not to smoke filters."

"You can't fork the time current by smoking filters," says Donn. "They're only fiberglass."

"Darby must think we're gonna freak out," says Mikey. "Just don't freak out, Raff. Don't yell, Raff. Don't hit anybody. Raff. Don't say shit bout Darby or straight edge or playing his show tonight or whatever. He's just fucking with us."

"Dude's an asshole." Donn's talking with a mouthful of pizza.

Mikey's like, "Hey, wait. He wants us to act cool. Cause he knows I'll be saying this. He totally thinks we're not gonna freak out and mosh everybody. Maybe we should just freak out."

Arco's suddenly sitting upright, hefting the golf bags in one hand. "We have to pass out these swords."

"I thought you went to piss," says Mikey. "You gonna eat your pizza?"

"No unshared property," says Arco. She stands up, steps around the table. Everybody in the bar's staring at her. Donn and Mikey drop slices on their shirts, try and grab her arms. Like trying to handcuff a wreckingball. "No, guys, I got the straight edge."

Raffia's hands snap a corner off the table.

Arco's unzipping the first bag, gathering an armload of vintage swords in makeshift cardboard sheathing, and Mikey bangs his forehead on the table and his lid slides half off his skylight, there's a quiet *PUSSSP* and a little pink spray, and then Arco goes, "Yo," and the whole pizzahut's just quiet. You can hear kids' bootsoles slide and resettle on the plated steel sewerfloor. Shit just keeps happening.

᭞᭞᭞

"**Y**ou can give these swords to your friends if you don't use swords," says Arco. Everybody's sembled in a wide crescent before her, kids testing blades against their split thumbs, slicing up the makeshift cardboard scabbards or pizza. Looking at Arco really weird. "They need to stay oiled or they'll rust. You shouldn't use gutfat less you want them to rust. Mineral oil's better. Olive oil's okay too. Or sunflower. Not chili oil. But these are the best swords in town. They can teach us focus. They can teach us tension."

"Wow," says Mikey. Softly punching Donn and Raffia's shoulders. He's leaning close to speak in both their ears. "Like, how they're looking at her all quiet. They're pretending like they didn't expect to see her here. Like this is a Dimension X without her."

"What's the point of that?" says Donn.

"I dunno," says Mikey. "Doesn't make any sense. Like, does Darby want us to see how the city'd fight itself without Arco? Cause wouldn't that make our hardcore stronger?"

Arco's making further public service announcements. Edge geometry, polishing, how to bow at walls when you're holding a sword.

Some heavy in the front, tall fat dude with binocs belted to his flak helmet and one giganto tooth growing through his lip like a narwhal, he says something quiet to his buddy. Their foreheads both scabbed up with dentical punkerscrosses and they're tilting brand new swords in their hands, the diy hardcore steel of feudal West Holly Wood. Testing grip and balance.

"You dumbass, Rock, it's not really Arco come back from the museum," says his buddy. Short fat dude with a mauve brushcut hawk and whole dead snappingturtles for shoulderpads. "Man, Darby's fucking with us. Like one of those fake Dimension X tricks." He scans the ceiling. "Darby, come out. This one didn't work."

The hanging piano kid's playing two black keys, one low, one high, really really fast. Raffia's teeth start making a sound like lawnmowers chewing each other. Like the sound of one hand clapping is the sound of lawnmowers chewing each other.

"Aw, Donn, man?" says Mikey.

Donn's like, "Yo."

Mikey's voice starts wobbling. "We're totally lost in the dimensionverse."

"I was worrying bout that," says Donn.

Mikey steps forward fast. Kind of stumbles, slaps his hand briefly on his eyes. "How'd you guys know?" he says at the crowd. "Man, we suck. I can't believe how bad we suck at acting." He points at Arco. "Specially you, Daisy."

Narwhal face sheathes his new katana and grabs two clay pitchers in his giant mitt. Tips one up to swig beer so the nother just pours down his back. His buddy puts his mouth in the stream like it's a waterfountain.

"Where's the swords from, Morgan?" says narwhal face.

"Aw, Darby gets stuff." Mikey laughs. "You know?"

Finally. Bouncing round in the tight semicircle of crash trash there's a laugh, and they're not holding their swords so high. The piano kid runs her thumb cross the board, low notes to high. Half the keys don't work.

"For sure," says his buddy, shell shoulders. "I'd of gaven mine to Darby. Like for his sword collection. Guess he already gots the bestest samples though."

"Yeah," says Mikey.

"She should do pressions at the arcore kids," says shell shoulders. "They'd go bazerk. Baldy head freaks."

Arco's back straightens. Her eyes are so fucking bright. "Do you guys think I'm somebody else doing pressions of me?"

Same laugh but a different substrate. It flares up but this time it doesn't catch at all. Mikey leans in for Raffia's ear and she nods.

Raffia's like, "Hey Arco. Stand still?"

"Okay," says Arco. "Why?"

Raffia bounces like a springloaded mountain. Unloads her elbow just above Arco's temple. Arco staggers with one foot, then straightens. Still completely still.

"Aw, fuck," says Mikey. "Fuck, fuck, fuck."

Then her eyes roll, and she starts snoring. Arco even snores econo. Mikey rubs her shoulder. "Oh," he says. "Sweet."

Narwhal face, his chin lifts. "Why'd you hit her?"

Donn steps forward. Looks like he's bout to say something completely reasonable.

Raffia's eyes are snapping back and forth across the room like they wanna break their traces and jump. You could light a smoke off the back of her neck. She's all "HIE-YAAAAH!" and uncoiling again, whirling in the air like a dustdevil. Jumpkicking the pitchers from narwhal face's hands, blasting shell shoulders with clay shards and a tsunami of palmbeer. "I GOTS THE STRAIGHT EDGE!"

Punker's eyes are slits, his lips are slits. His shirt's covered with moist terracotta particles. He wipes his drippy face with the flats of his hands. "You comed in here with a straight edge?"

Mikey's laughing, bobbing on the soles of his feet. Donn just nods and breathes out.

Narwhal face goes, "Do it, bro. Everybody's disposable. That's the circle."

"I know that look." Raffia's breathing easy. All of a sudden wearing this birthdaycore grin. "You wanna hit me in the mouth."

"Brutal idea, punker." Donn shakes his head. "That's her signature move."

"You guys aren't good nuff friends," says Mikey.

"You preach straight edge? In Ground Zero?" says shell shoulders. His hawk's standing on end. Same as before, but suddenly mood appropriate. This surly foot soldier flashes into the gallon percolator stance and it's a fucking wonderful punch. Swinging from the muscles behind his shoulder, whole body rising into it from the soles of his docs.

Here.

Raffia's chin looks like warpaint. Blood slips from the corners of her mouth. Her jaw dips and rises with a brutal grinding sound.

He's like, "Shit, you got hard bones, punker. Spose I'll go between em." Makes to draw his new katana. Then he looks at his hand.

"Mf fllf lu rf mlcp," says Raffia. A crooked lump passes down her throat. "I left you your thumb."

∿∿

There's no time lapse. That wasn't a chrono break. Just a break of emphasis.

Anyway, Raffia steps in, she dukes her browbone into shell shoulders' nose, and he falls like a fridgerator. Piano kid matches her, simultaneous headbash to the ebony lid. And Raff's started giggling again, high and sweet and shudderous with her whole body rising into it, like the fuckedest thing in the world.

Narwhal face lifts Mikey by the forehead and starts aiming shots at his solar plexus. Here. Mikey bends and shimmies his torso out of the way, left and right, and he runs his feet up punker's body, bending nearly double to heelwhack the dude's temple. Narwhal face gags and lets him fall. The piano chick's using her elbows again, and these alterna reality kids look over their shoulders before they start swinging. Mikey cartwheels over, one hand holding his lid steady. Kneeling between her legs he's like, "Hey! Arco! Chickenfight!"

Here. Arco's rolledup eyes twitch. Like the whites are tracking something. She sticks her arms straight out and drops herself on Mikey's shoulders, and he lurches upright, piggybacking her. Here. More of shell shoulders' pizza buddies are stepping into Raffia's big giant hands. She's like a windup clapping monkey, slamming two heads together. Here. Tips of two dentical hawks briefly kiss.

Donn's stepped to meet her back-to-back. He's juggling two burning lamps on the blades of his hockeystick. All these kids with their new swords, they stand back a little, grit their teeth. Flammability's such a factor with overdressed punks. Donn's like, "Go," and they're shuffling toward the exit.

"We wanna murderize these losers, though," says Raffia, and Donn's like, "No."

"Really?" Raffia lunges underhand, flattening some kid's diaphragm with a rubber tilesetting mallet. The swinging piano goes *CLONGGG* as punker rips out a low string.

"Control it." Donn's not really smiling. His glasses are entirely fireshine. "They love pizza even as do we."

The two swords on Arco's belt pressing your shoulder, Mikey. Your hand squeezes the trashbagged hilt and Arco's hand drops over yours. Hey, right on. Your first step's a stagger, your second's a swagger. Second and a half's a canter, and then you go headlong into a brick pizza oven. Keeling forward, you smash your jaw into the oven's side. Up on top, Arco's forehead whips into the hot chimneypipe.

You can hear Donn yelling cross the pizzahut. "She's fine."

Need a rest already, tourist? Mikey coughs, resettles Arco on his shoulders. Some douchebag's grabbing at his belt and Mikey stomps backward, grinding his bootheel down punker's shin. Here. Arco's hand turns under his, pulling Mikey's grip clockwise. Margin Walker unlocks clickingly from its scabbard as the trashbags around it pull and rip.

Just a leadcolored stream in the halfdark air, like a scarf caught in calzone smoke and wind. Passing twice through the chimney, back to the sheath. Arco does some of her best work when she's not even around. A height of blackened pipe clangs to the ground. Curdlous yellow smog, fed of old tires and femurs, starts unfolding through Ground Zero.

"Hey, it's Darby!" Mikey's pointing to the corner of the room. Just like that, Donn streaks the canlamp through the rising smoke, crashing orangely into a stack of milkcrates. This time his third step's a gallop. While the fighty pizza kids flash on the tumbled crates, Meatheads elbow and hipcheck toward the ladder exit.

Mikey's last up. Raffia's kneeling in the sewerpipe, pulling Arco off his shoulders as he climbs. On his hands and knees in the connecting tunnel, Mikey back-kicks the ladder off its raggedy fasteners. Stands up and he leisurely collects everybody's stuff from the coat check.

He's like, "Sorry bout the ladder."

"Fuck yourself," says shell shoulders out of the smoke.

∿∿∿

"The thinking parts aren't infected," says Mikey. Donn's holding Vauum Vauum Vauum for him to lean on. "Just a couple of the walking straight parts."

They're half a block down from Ground Zero, crossing under a stand of bobbleheaded palms. If you look back, there's this solid pillar of smoke rising from the manhole hatch. The clouds are out so hard. Sheets of rain dropping all round them like black showercurtains. Everyone's staring right at Mikey.

He's like, "Am I tripping out?"

"I really want you to take off the sock," says Arco. Big lump over her temple, but her eyes are like everclear. One hand on each sword's hilt.

"After I sit down," says Mikey. "I need to sit down and like drink ketchup tea, like somewhere where weird stupid shit isn't constantly happening."

"Let's hang at our place then," says Donn. "We got diffused lighting. Play some parcheesi."

Couple blocks to the House of Meatheads. Hardly anyone's out, and anyone's just a shape in the rain. They do the sammrye rain greet, stepping back and pointing their armament at strangers. Yuppies don't do that, right.

"Does breathing smoke kill you?" says Mikey.

"I think you can just stop, drop and roll," says Donn. "There might of been a nother exit."

"There wasn't," says Arco.

"Oh." Donn's bottom lip gets all quivery. "Fuck. I burned it. Like that time I was on acid, and Darby—"

"I don't wanna know," says Raffia. "We're not turning round."

Donn goes, "Their exit ladder was completely fine, though, like, it was, right?"

Nobody says anything for awhile. Then Arco's like, "You guys might be at our place."

"Like a wacky us from Dimension X?" They're getting close, Mikey slows a bit. His lips are pooched out some, he's dragging one foot in the mud. "I hate this weird shit."

"You love this shit," says Raffia. Mikey's like, "I caught vaginitis, okay?"

"Meningitis." Donn sighs. "Well, they might be nice to us." Raffia's eyeballing him and he's like, "Well, we're nice. At least me and Arco and Mikey." Then he's like, "Fuck, at least sometimes."

Above them a signpole's growing sideways from a building. It's slung with something like sheets of white kelp or maybe giant rollies. Donn jogs ahead with Vauum Vauum Vauum and pushes the dangling vegetation to one side. The others just walk through, soggy, ignoring this new opening.

Their side of the building, the Germs circle's blowtorched in a giant sheet of proppedup tin. Hanging against the brick facade there's a knotted rope with a black rubber kiddyswing tied to the end, the kind that's shaped like a hollow butt. The rope stretches into the grim mist overhead.

"It's just out in the rain? Does this dimension have, like, rope making machines and unlimited supplies?" Donn yanks it. Flax fibers pop out like shreds of brisket. "Man, nobody's been waxing it even." He looks at Arco. Arco shrugs. Donn gets climbing.

"So?" says Raffia, one hand on the rope.

"So he means this dimension sucks," says Mikey.

∧∧∧

Mikey has to yell. "Hey, we're in the future, right?"

"Somebody up top touched the rope," says Arco.

Donn's a couple lengths above. He stops climbing, leans back with one arm outstretched. "That warthog looking guy said Arco didn't make it back from the museum. But nobody seemed weirded that the three of us were there. So from our standpoint it's the chrono future. But it's not our future. It's not like we're the same Meatheads who lost Arco and our hardcore had us join with Darby and we just fast forwarded to it."

Raffia cranes her neck. "I hate when you talk down to us bout fillosophy."

"So in this dimension we teamed up with Darby?" says Mikey.

"Didn't we?" says Donn.

"No way. He'd be dead if he tried to force it." Raffia's hand digs a chunk from the rotten brick wall. "Or probly we'd be."

"Somebody up top touched the rope," says Arco.

"Like, for sure, time cast us out," says Donn. "But into a whole nother floor of time. Not just down the hall of time. We're pretty much time ronin."

"That sounds way trippy and dangerous," says Mikey. "What if we called our band Time Ronin?"

Raffia sets her pointy toenail into Mikey's collarbone. "We already got a name."

"Yeah, an old name and a new one," says Mikey. "Like, chrono ronin. Cromonin."

Donn goes, "No, chronin."

"Somebody up top touched the rope," says Arco.

They're like, "Oh." "Oh." "Oh."

"Band meeting," says Arco. "What do we do?"

"Band meeting?" Raffia leans her forehead against the brick. "Fucking hide, Arco!"

Arco just steps off the rope. Folding herself balanced into a windowframe.

Fifth storey, maybe the sixth. On the inside, the window's tacked over with a rubikscube bedsheet.

"Could of gotten onto a balcony," says Raffia.

"Do we hide too?" says Donn. Mikey's like, "I wanna sit down."

Raffia's biting her lips. "Fucked up time travel rope climbing shit."

Up on the next balcony, you can just see dull black steeltoes. Stiff orange trashbag socks like culottes. "Hey," says Mikey's voice from up top. "You guys the pizza guys?"

He's like, "Guys?"

Mikey slips down. Puts out his hand to Arco. She grabs his forearm and hauls him onto the windowsill. Holds him tight as he scrabbles at the slick dark moss. Ventually their asses fit in the recessed windowframe's bottom corners and their hands grab at its top corners and their bootsoles brace together. Mikey's other hand holds the rope, and Arco sure doesn't do that.

"Nah," says Raffia. "It's just us."

"And me," says Donn. "I mean, like, the royal us but also me."

"Oh, hey," says the voice of Mikey's. "I thought you were jamming downstairs. You guys don't got pizza?"

"Ground Zero's out of order," says Donn. "We think they might all of passed out from smoke inhalation. Somebody yelled they had a straight edge. Then there was a lot of smoke and swords."

Punker on the balcony, he's looking away. Claps his one hand and there's a smoke spinning in his fingers. Keeping it dry in the balcony doorframe's overhang, he hits it with a handflint from his pocket. Lights the filter end. "Huh," he says. "Guess nobody laughed."

"You still think there's no bad jokes?" says Donn.

Talking, he doesn't look so much like Mikey. Maybe when he sleeps. The muscles in his face are either too quick or too slow, and his posture's too good, and he's working maybe on a beergut. Every ragged bit of his jacket's stitched down. His skylight's a lot wider, and this Mikey's got a nice approach to the bihawk, it's diy from two lines of car antennas. Only thing is, they're retracted.

Punker blows a chrysanthemum of fiberglass smoke. The rain shoots through it. "Cowabunga."

Donn's like, "Maybe we should—"

"You guys smell like a long sweat," says the alterna Mikey. He looks down. He steps forward and his hand plays with the meteorhammer cord looped round his neck. "What the fuck's up with your hair, Anna?"

"Me?" says Raffia.

There's a little time. Nuff for more rain.

"Don't start," says Raffia. "You know I hate all this weird shit."

Punker laughs short through his nose. Like an old running joke landed on his lip and he can't blow it off. "What?"

"Hey, I'm back, Mikey," says Arco.

On the windowsill beside her, and on the balcony up top, Mikey's fist snaps tight round the air. The alterna kid's halfsmoke drops and fizzes in a puddle. He's like, "Hey?"

Arco's up the windowframe. Climbing with her fingers in the little slick grooves between bricks. Arco's on the balcony, head bowed. "I was sposed to hide but you sounded like you missed me."

Then she's standing there in her muscles and bones with the alterna Mikey's cheek pressed into hers, same way Arco always stands when you try and give her a hug.

"Hey, you got a new sword." He bites a couple of his knuckles. "How is it?"

She's like, "It's good."

∧∧∧

There's a whole scene of reconciliation, but it's boring.

∧∧∧

Their place always gets like this when Arco takes off. It's an even bigger heap of shit. The alterna Mikey's grinning, but not at any of them. Just looking over all the motorbike goggles on the xmastree and all the rotted chia pets on the coffeetable and then all the gi joes carved into the shapes of submachineguns. He's like, "Sorry." Then he's like, "Darby just collects that stuff."

They all drop into musty seating arrangements. Sept Arco leaning in the balcony doorway, she goes, "Alterna Mikey, are you keeping it safe for him?"

"He'll crash here sometimes," says punker. "Hey, sorry, I did a name switch. You may call me Morgan Donor."

"That sucks," says Raffia.

"We come in peace," says Donn. "We're from like down the hall of time."

"Can we sit down now?" says Mikey. "Wait. Morgan Donor? That sucks."

"You're sitting," says Morgan. "You just came from the museum, hey? Your brain looks rough, man."

"You don't seem weirded by our presence," says Donn.

"Don't go to sleep, hey. Hey, me? Stay up, me. I know you're tired. I got back from that trip too. I'll get you some tea." Morgan shakes his head at Donn. "When we got back from the museum, like, me and my you, you gave me antacids for my brain."

"Did it work?" says Donn.

"I dunno," says Morgan. "I'll make some tea. You gave me mergency surgery same day though." He's heading into the putrescent shadows in the far end of the livingroom.

"You're going in the kitchen." Raffia's on her feet. "What, somebody cleaned it?"

"You know Fear used that kitchen when they lived here." Mikey slaps vaguely at the side of his head. "Man, it's heritage. You better not of cleaned it."

"No, man, I just cleared a counter space." There's a broombristle torch nailed to the kitchen doorway and Morgan Donor gets it lit and they all shuffle in after him.

Arco's just sitting lotus in the livingroom floor. And fuck, tourist, you're not even gonna try?

∿∿∿

This isn't a kitchen, it's a despoiled graveyard. Or at least there's bone fragments and soil everywhere, and for some reason all these rose marble headstones piled on top of the stove. Morgan takes a square of plywood leaning up against the wall and lays it over a crustyedged floor hole. Making room, he's booting dirty dish towers across the floor, crockpots and cookiesheets glued together by unidentifiable discharges the color of burnt pus. Wormshaped flowers push from the cracks between things, squashy and completely white like cave fishies, and leaning from the broken cupboard under the sink there's a granite angel with wet eyes.

"Maybe in a thought I cleared it. You didn't really want tea, hey?" Morgan sits in a heap of old dishes. He's not careful, but they don't move, no more than his weight would move a crude old sittingplace of stones and rammed dirt. "It's good to see you guys."

"Yeah. What happened to your Arco?" Donn leans against the fridge. All the brittle astronaut magnets fall and shatter. He hangs his head, starts massaging the sides of his jaw.

"It's not even that. Us three got back with the newspaper and we thought we'd blow open this giant secret of yuppies and how Lost Angeles got formed." Morgan's big hands slipping inside each other like they belong to different kids. "Punks just said we were high. They said, yeah, we know, that's always been the story."

Donn's lips open, shut. He gropes behind him, squeezes the fridgehandle. "We couldn't change anything?"

"Man, are you lying?" says Mikey.

"How does Darby keep doing shit like that?" says Donn. He bangs the back of his head against the fridge and then he's digging in his pocket for a notepad. Punker starts diagramming something, looks like a hyperspatial flowchart.

"We never knew if we made it home," says Morgan.

Then you're in this long, weird pause where Lord Buddha plugs one nostril and blows out the other, and his danglerope of snot is the living timestream, pearlescent, and there's a nuff for every little dharma to revolve inside itself a couple times while you swing there contemplating the inevitability of not not fucking up. Finally Arco's the one who laughs. She never told anybody so, not in her life, but it's still one of those I told you so laughs.

"So I might still be kind of like you guys." Morgan rubs the side of his eye.

"Is Darby in our band?" says Raffia.

"I guess so," says Morgan Donor. "No. Meatheads never got back together after that time we broke up sitting in the tree. We all started a nother band. It's just kind of called Darby Crash Band."

One side of Donn's lip flinches. "Wait up. Did we even get back together ourselves?"

"Fuck it, Donn," says Raffia. "No meetings right now."

"You're not kind of like us." Mikey's staring at the alterna Mikey, sneering with one eye open. His head starts to sag and Donn holds it up. "You're Darby's band, you're jamming Darby's songs, standing round between songs while he pukes on our boots. And nobody even cares what you do cause it's Darby in front."

"You think you're strong til something happens," says Morgan, looking at the kitchen floor. No floor to look at, just broken plastic mugs becoming dirt. The fruit flies seem like shadows disassembling across the air.

Donn's just like, "Really? Man, what happened to Arco?"

"You could of went for him anyway," says Raffia. Getting to her feet, hands in claws. "Not just gave up."

"We didn't give up," says Morgan. "We started fighting each other."

"I'm sick of this guy," says Mikey. "I'm sick of this guy and his cleaned up kitchen!" He peels himself upright and stalks back out of the room, each footstep making a sucking noise.

Morgan spreads his hands. His fingers aren't so covered with scabbed scratches, neither. "Man, we never wanted to."

"We know we never wanted to." Donn's heading after Mikey with a white plastic tube of antacids. "We don't want to now."

ᐯᐯᐯ

Mikey's eyes look like they're steaming over. He's horizontal on the big black paisley couch. Like, it was historically paisley. Now it's mostly black from a fire. His ears are engorged bright red and other than that he's colored like the moon.

She's been staring into him deep, but now Arco lunges forward a knucklewidth, like a kid who dreamed of falling. "Mikey, I think you should take the sock out. Hey." She leans in and claps next to his eardrum.

"Oh." Mikey unlaces the halfunlaced skullplug and just yanks the folded sock off. There's a distinctive velcro sound and a bit of pinkish discharge leaping into his hair. He bends his head forward toward his lap. "Is it out?"

Donn's kneeling on the ground. "It's out, man." He slides to Mikey's side of the sofa. Presses his forehead into Mikey's shoulder. "You want some antacids? Mikey? Ah, fuck it." Then he's holding Mikey's head back, pinching his nose, letting his jaw hang open. Drops little white pills into his throat and massages them down.

Mikey belches. "Yeah, man."

Then Morgan's like, "Dudes? I'm sorry bout the balcony rail. And I guess the bathroom curtain rod too. But like." Everybody else, they're looking at Mikey, and Morgan's staring at Arco's knees. "We went through a bunch of bottles when we got back alone. I just fell on the rail and knocked it off."

Donn yawns. "I'll get mad at Darby again tomorrow. But I could help you guys diy a nother railing. I think I've got some bolts."

"No, who cares," says Morgan. "I just want pizza."

Donn's like, "I just really didn't think the Zero would be so flammable."

"What? Oh, it's cool. It's franchises now. There's like this many." Morgan holds out his fingers. "They always keep on burning down. I just, like, I'm immune to acid now and it really sucks. And I just keep on really wanting pizza, and I can't get any."

"Can't you go get some?" says Donn.

Morgan pulls up a handful of telescoping car antennas from the edge of his skull hole. Kind of shakes them out. "It doesn't work," he says. "Not even with the antennas."

Nobody says anything.

"Just be yourself, me," says Morgan. "Don't stress. I got back from the museum with that same weirdoid infection too. That's why my skylight's wider. My brain swole and it needed more room."

Arco's shaking her head. "This Mikey's forgotten. Your stress is your survival, Mikey. That's why you grow it out. Morgan must of been choked when his Meatheads got back. He fought himself against my loss. If you don't stress, you might not wake up."

Mikey's like, "Thanks." Then he's like, "Wait, I make my own stress?"

Arco crosses her legs in the chair. "How'd you rip Darby off for a Black Flag patch, bandmate?"

All it ever takes is time and distance, right? Poser. You bring up your smeary eyes and think you can watch the activity of mind ripple openly in the muscles of Morgan Donor's face. Dude looks like he popped a zit and sprayed spiders cross the bathroom mirror. Pretend you're still the right Mikey, Mikey. Like Mikey Prime or some shit. Slouching in this dank familiar space you could tell yourself this bihawk guy's a stranger. Sneaks round making plans without his band, couldn't tell the truth to heal every consciousness in town. Fucker grows out his stress cause otherwise he'd have to do something hard casionally.

"Shit." Mikey laughs, pulling himself upright. "I forgot bout that."

"Arco, I love how we're in a band together. You figured it out too!" says Donn. "Yeah, you totally stole that patch from him, man."

"How'd you know?" says Mikey.

"Darby just passed it to you and said he never checked what it was?" says Donn. "Who picks up a patch without looking at it? Cause patches are sweet."

"They're so sweet, Mikey," says Arco. "Patches are so sweet."

Donn's like, "He wouldn't just give you a Flag silkscreen. No punk in the world has one of those. But if it didn't originate with his gear, he'd of just kept it. He gave it back to get it back, like to enact a circle, and make you look like a fuck in front of us. Cause he knew you didn't wanna say where you got it, or tell us you had it. And he knew you couldn't lie to him."

"He knows you're not good a nuff to lie to his face," says Raffia.

"What the fuck," says Morgan. "Donn, why'd you never hassle me for this?"

"I wasn't there," says Donn.

Morgan starts moving his lips round something but Mikey cuts him off. Face a little brighter, or at least he's smiling. He's like, "The leather Darby promised me was nothing. He had a secret silkscreen collection. Most of it I never saw anywhere else. He said he had all history in there. So when I heard on the PA tower bout his farewell show I took off my lid and threw it. Pretended I lost it so I'd have an excuse to run downstairs. I got a Black Flag patch from his collection. It was the one time I knew he'd be busy."

Morgan's standing, he's walking around. "That patch—"

"Shut up. You sold out already," says Mikey. That voice again, like weather. Coming from the walls as much as his mouth. That thing bout how our cores are always outside us. That thing. "The Flag patch told me why they left the city. Like, there's no loading dock show. There's no curse on hardcore. The whole thing bout why we tour's a lie."

"If you got the patch, tell it," says Morgan. "Oh, you gave it back, cause you're me. You don't think Darby's still got control?"

"You never thought bout how nobody needs a patch for the tour spiel, Mikey, you fucker? Cause we still tell that one." Mikey sits up. Pulls his jacket around himself. "Punkers won't believe me. Doesn't mean he's got control."

Mikey sticks his hand up the opposite sleeve of his leather and busts it through a loose seam in the forearm. His fist gives Morgan Donor the finger. "Here. This is the spiel in the Flag patch. It sucks, there's no excitement. I still remember it."

〜〜〜

—I wasn't there. But they say Mikey of Meatheads leaned forward like I'm leaning now over the fire. He charged a spike of his hair with two fingers so it stood up and he said little kids with the talent get illustrated, wear their first leathers and sew on their first patches and back then they're sposed to be sensitive. Like they can't hardly brush a silkscreen with one fingernail and the history wakes up for them. Little space cadets. He said you're sposed to get partial munity when you get taller, but he never met anybody where that was true. More like shit merges, intermerges and interintermerges, and there's no more focus.

He said you'll just be paring bamboo and the matchflame moves for a second and you can't member if you're somewhere, that's how slipped your ego gets. Touching a silkscreen, it's not like there's a picture to see, or somebody's telling a story. It's like you turn into a shitty photocopy of a nother place. Consciousness getting wheatpasted on the outside of the world like it's a giant pin yatta, and something's missing even though it's real.

The spiel in the patch is you're looking toward four fires, said Mikey of Meatheads. I'm not there but there's still looking. Four banks or whatever in the distance, just rectangles, and there's a lot of banks in the skyline but only four are fires. It's bars of the Flag written with four tall fires, and the sun on them. All the kids are out but they're not packed in like a show. They're standing apart and just looking. And the voice of Rollins speaks from the crowd. Somebody's calling us, he says. That's a signal fire. Whoever wants to come with, they can.

There's Darby. He's standing almost separate, right. With just his friends round him. He calls Rollins a meathead and no-neck and he says it's stupid to go. He says go if you want, Black Flag fans are all the same.

In the patch, he says, you're looking toward the fires. Not at them, toward. And you can tell when punks are getting ready to go. It's the only time they're not all looking at the same place. They're looking at all the ways between.

∧∧∧

Like Morgan's talking to himself. "You make it sound like something. Even if nothing happens." He's leaning forward too.

"Who set the fire?" says Raffia.

Morgan coughs. Nobody's looking at him.

"You shit, you never even told your band, did you," says Mikey.

Arco's like, "You never would of either, Mikey."

Morgan smiles and breathes out. One finger's crooked under his lip. "I don't member if I told anybody," he says. "It's not really a remember day. Arco, do me a favor?"

"Course, Mikey," says Arco, crosslegged in the easychair.

Not looking over, the two Mikeys both go, "Morgan."

"That's Darby's name," says Arco. "Darby might of gave it to you, Mikey of Dimension X, but you can't give somebody a name."

He looks spooky for a blink, then he just shrugs. Maybe call him Morgan still. Don't wanna be confused. "Can I see your new sword, Arco? I'm not joking or whatever. If it wants blood you can cut my leg."

"I don't know what blood you mean." Arco just looks at Morgan. Biting her lip harder as she breathes.

Mikey grunts. "You forgot something."

"It's not my sword." She uncrosses her legs, slides a bit sideways in the chair. Her eyes open at Mikey. "It's not anybody's sword. Okay?"

Then she's standing on the armrests. Her eyes are closed and she steps onto the coffeetable. Her body seeming to revolve inside as she draws and Straight Edge stands from her hands like a fountain's tongue, like something only halted into shape, and it's really blue, it's actually totally blue, or else Arco's blue eyes and her blue headband were colored like steel all the way back here.

And then she shakes her head a little and stands like a normal person, and Morgan goes, "I always wanted to tell you that."

Arco's like, "What?"

"Oh," says Morgan. "You could of cut me. Or any of us. You didn't have to duck out."

"What?" says Arco. Raffia's like, "Dumbass, this is Darby steel. Rollins didn't make it. It's not the one that's all hungry for blood."

Morgan peels off the sticky sofa in a couple little tugs. "No shit?" He bobs his head and you can see his lips part. His fingers move near the sword and then away. "No shit. Tiny little stars."

"They're chunklets of suspended martensite," says Donn.

Arco's putting the sword back, really fast. Then her hands are wound in the back of her jersey. "Nie."

Morgan looks up. "You found a different sword in Dimension X. This one was really rusty. Or colored like it, anyway. You pulled it out and just looked and then you started running. We didn't know what the fuck, but you're the swiftest runner. We couldn't catch you. Pat, or I guess he was Donn then, he figured it out. It was the Rollins straight edge, the one you can't put back without blood. And it was your edge not to kill anybody. So we never saw you after that."

So no matter who you are, just stare at Arco like you're expecting the punchline. Until she goes, "Oh," and you can see her tonguetip push back and forth, once, across her top row of teeth. "That really sucks," says Arco.

Morgan glances down at himself. Pulls one sleeve of his jacket. "Uh. I missed your sword moves."

Raffia shakes her head. "You don't got to use the Darby sword."

"I just don't wanna chip it. Doing moves for show." Something flickers up and down in Arco's cheek. "How bout the easychair?"

"Nah, do the sofa," says Morgan. "It's got termites in this dimension anyway. Hey, Mikey? Man, stand up?"

Morgan swings his hand toward Mikey's shoulder. Mikey's arm flutters briefly, like something disconnected from current events. Then Morgan's blinking, staring at his fist embedded wristdeep in the drywall.

"Ask me first next time," says Mikey. He slides off the black paisley sofa. Two steps and he falls on his face. "Man, you know?"

Morgan's hand all crumbed with gyprock. He waggles each finger in turn, but stops with the third, like he's giving up. Bout then Arco's kicking her boots into a corner and Margin Walker's flicked up at the ceiling, danger point, and she's padded into the room's center and her bare foot shoves the coffeetable to one side. She's holding the hilt level with her ears, her head minutely bobbing, and then her foot sweeps out and she drops sideways like it's a slidekick, but then she's still moving.

Blink.

Big doublehelix of motion looping down her wrists, katana edge snaking into the sofa over and again and it's the blade cuisinart, the one Donn taught her from an Apple II manual the summer they all moved out together, and somehow Arco's pitched herself sideways in the air, hovering and rolling, like she's going down an invisible hill. Maybe she's propping herself up with the blade casionally, but maybe Arco can just do shit like that.

Then she's crouched in the middle of the floor, arm crossing over her hips as she sheathes the Ian McEye steel. She nods once to Morgan, and punker jumps high, tags the ceiling. Before his steeltoes touch down, the sofa shimmers and falls completely apart. Tiny dies of wood and fluff and paisley fabric, and of number they're sixtyfive thousand five hundred and thirtysix. You'd know that, if you were Donn. You'd of did the math.

∧∧∧

A big grin passes over Morgan Donor's face and it's gone. Then everybody's standing, just staring back and forth. You can probly tell why nobody looks tired anymore but you're not really sure what time it is anyhow. Rain bangs blackly at the glass door like a cataclysm of finger tweaks. The lamplight slides on Donn's glasses. So one more awkward pause.

"I wish the pizza would of come," says Morgan. "It's all I ever wanted. Not that I didn't preciate seeing you guys."

"What's my name in Dimension X?" says Donn.

"Pat Pending," says Morgan.

"Oh," says Donn. Like he's swishing the name round his mouth. "That's stupid."

Morgan's got his hands up eachotherses sleeves, clasping their wrists. "What else," he says. "You guys don't live here much anymore. Donn, sometimes you come by to see if Darby's here, and you still take care of the aquarium, but you sleep in your lab mostly. You're jamming downstairs right now. You can hear you if you listen."

"What, like jamming solo?" Donn blinks with his whole forehead. "Like Ginn in the story? What if I get bored?"

"You're the one who locks the door," says Morgan. "Raff, right now you're on Darby's shadow while he does a warehouse run. You keep the skinheads off him. They like jumping from rooftops."

"What, he needs my hardcore just cause his arm's gone?" says Raffia.

"No, dumbass. Cause Arco's gone," says Morgan Donor. "You need his." He shrugs, drops his shoulders. "What else?"

"Nothing," says Mikey. "I'll call you out if you're feeling a scrap."

"Mikey, you motherfucker," says Raffia.

Nobody moves.

Morgan tilts at the hip, then back. "You mean scrap to diy." His metalized hawks standing like pins in a voodoo doll. "I didn't know you were so pissed."

"I'm not," says Mikey. "You gotta still like scrapping though. Spose I owe you that." His brow's still super pale, and he wipes it with two fingers.

"Why?" says Morgan. He cracks all his knuckles, one motion, and the sound hangs there like thunder.

"Cause you hate this place," says Mikey. "But you can't ditch out. Cause you think your Arco might come back. So here's a way out."

"That's not what owing means," says Donn. Mikey's like, "Yeah, I know."

"They say Arco's coming," says Morgan. "All the skinheads. But they're weird bout it. They don't think she was here the first time or something. You'll meet them if you make it." He's yanking off his boots to take off the slippy orange trashbag socks. "Nobody owes shit. But I preciate it. Okay."

"Man, you got meningitis, Mikey. You can't walk very good." Donn, you're looking at the floor, Donn. Wonder if getting on your knees would help. Your wondering's one more little picture in your mind, and it doesn't help.

Mikey's like, "I never walked to a scrap anyway." He's going through his pockets for some reason. He's not taking anything out. He squeezes his lid through the pocket in his jeans.

"Can you at least wear a helmet?" says Donn.

Raffia just calls him a motherfucker a bunch more times, and she's covering her face, and Donn kind of shuffles toward her and stands there. And Arco grabs Mikey's thumb and squeezes it with her whole fist like how babies do it. You can tell when Arco's practiced something. It's not one of those.

"No headshots, okay?" says Mikey.

"Whatever." Morgan's uncoiling the moon-orange meteorhammer thong from round his neck.

"Or no brain shots, I mean." Hey, tourist? You ever seen Mikey's face when he looks out at nobody, and it's like a riddle who he thinks he's looking to?

"No brain shots. Deal," says Morgan. "Arco? If I win, will you go out with me?"

Mikey blinks or something while Morgan's meteorhammer jumps cross the coffeetable. Mikey parries with his own Fuck It, iron bulbs still wound at his wrist. Big dull clanging sound and Mikey snaps his front foot forward, he bends into a crouch.

"Ow," says Mikey.

He steps backward and his eyes momentarily unfocus, he's shaking his head fast and tight. Then lifts his foot like he's aiming for a kick, but he's jumping sideways and his other foot's plunging at Morgan's knee. Morgan steps in, catches the stomp on his bootheel, and Mikey stumbles forward. He plants one hand on the small of Morgan's back, slowdance style. Mikey takes a knee to the thigh meat, a headbang to the ear, and he's undone one side of Morgan's spenders. Fuck It's still wound at his wrist. Who knows. But Morgan slips one hand in, scoops Mikey by his underarm and hucks him into the heap of diced sofa parts. He lands with his limbs all spiderously bouncing and then Morgan's knees are on his chest.

Mikey's coughing and he cups his hand to his ear. "Did you just ask if you could be me afterward?"

Morgan's like, "No," and Mikey just sinks into the mildewy sofa chunks. "I'm not the guy to ask," he says.

Then you're bringing up your forearms like to fend a punch and yeah, Morgan's fist, it's chopping at your nose. You buck Mikey's head forward just a nuff for the knuckles to slam the naked face of his brain and fill the livingroom with breathless light colored like orange dandelion fluff.

∧∧∧

*N*o, hold on. You actually think that was you, tourist?

∧∧∧

*T*here's Morgan. Sitting on Mikey's chest in the mottled heap of sofa chunks. Lines manifesting across his forehead like a pen drawing. No brain shots. He turns his head. Raffia's standing in the kitchen doorway, arm cocked way behind her back, eyes slitted like spressionless smiles. Guess she's been there awhile.

Here's one of the tricks Raffia does just by moving her arm.

A stainless steel roofinghammer whips like a catherinewheel between Morgan Donor's shoulderblades, out through his sternum, and out the ducktaped Meatheads glyph in the balcony door. The gout of busted glass and the medusa of blood have the same shape but different colors. They race each other down.

Morgan's just sitting there on Mikey's chest and he starts grinning. He's grinning with his hands out, his eyes bright open.

No brain shots.

Arco's bent beside them. Man, she hasn't been so long there. Has she? She's whispering in Morgan's ear. He shudders, or he's just nodding his head.

"Thanks." His gutted chest's fluming like barnpaint over Mikey's face, soaking the chopped sofa fragments. "Sorry. Thanks."

"Sorry," says Mikey, and Raffia's like, "Thanks."

"Hey, you're welcome," says Morgan. He turns his head, blows a bubble of blood. It rises by magic and winks on the rusted ceiling fan. "For what?"

Raffia's like, "I always wanted to kill you. But, like, I didn't want to, too." She shuts her eyes. "Does that make sense?"

"I guess you still got your Mikey." Sitting there, Morgan leans back. He kind of points his chest so the limitless blood goes shooting to one side, and laughs. "This is pretty fucked, though."

"Sorry," says Donn.

Mikey's halfsunk in the fluff heap, his face coated all glossy scarlet and featureless like a candyapple. Light glazes whitely on it as his eyes look up. "Sorry I made you cheat, man."

"Doesn't matter." Morgan doesn't wince as he heaves himself off Mikey.

He stands and leans against the wall, hands folded behind his head. You can see ecru plaster through him, and part of a garfield poster.

Raffia's mouth slowly pushes shut. "Motherfucker. You owe me a roofinghammer, Mikey."

"Chill, Raff," says Donn. "Morgan, we're still friends, right? Are you gonna make it out okay? Like, does it hurt too much?"

Check your hands behind your head, Donn. Is it some kind of sympathetic invert of his pose, or are you fishing in your dreads for a knife? Or do you know?

What is it when you don't know?

Morgan Donor's like, "I'm okay. It's just like." He shrugs and picks at the squidshaped hole in his chest. It's not running anymore.

"Like what," says Arco.

He opens his mouth again. "It's like." There's marrow under his nail. "Aw. Like." His mouth stays like that and his shoulders stay shrugged and then the sinkhole grin of Darby Crash starts ripping cross his face.

"Mikey of Dimension X." She's not even loud. You can hear the muscles in Arco's throat, the little tight muscles moving like she'd draw her voice up from her spine to strike Morgan Donor cross the cheek. She'd slap Darby's grin. Even here. "Is that your farewell show?"

Your other hand, bled white, slips out from behind your head. Dude? You're a ghost already? No, but make a big giant fist over your tornout diaphragm so the chia pets fall off the coffeetable and all the kitchen cabinets open and slam. Morgan Donor, you could tell them thanks. Tell them you forgot. And times like these you gotta remember you're lucky. Cause this is what you train for. More than the war.

It's just.

Like.

∧∧∧

—Sometimes I try to think stuff and it doesn't come out the way I think it should, and then I get confused. And I try to track back on my thoughts, I focus real hard, but I still get confused. Because focusing still means thinking, and I try to go back to old thoughts and look, but that's thinking too. And I'm getting caught up in where my thoughts come from, cause they just come from other thoughts, thoughts diying and going round the blue circle and getting carnated as thoughts again, and there's nothing underneath. And I get caught up in getting caught up in it, *and then the circle brakes, cause there's no me to get caught up, just an ego trip of thoughts hanging onto thoughts. And then when I'm at max confusion some punk's always in my ear going, "Way to go Mikey, you're really getting over the band breakup, man, you're so strong." And I'm like, "I'm confused, let me alone, I'm trying to order pizza with my mind." And they're like, "No, your new band with Darby's gnarly, man, and you're not confused, this is the substance of the way of the sammrye. Let me just get you some pizza." But that's not the way I want pizza. That's not how I want pizza, and then I wish it could of came back and tooken me with it, like, the fuckedest thing in the world.*

And there's no shame in diying like a dog, right, if it doesn't work out the way you wanted it to. And it's not even sposed to work out the way you want. And I'm sitting in our living room and it's not our room, it's just my room, I'm just like staring at the taped up door, thinking bout thinking and pizza and how nothing's sposed to be anything and how my hardcore finally broke off and went without me, and pizza, thin crust pep and ched, and like how pizza's a circle too. And kids bring me beer and they've got millionth generation Germs burns and they're like shorter than my fucking nipples, and they're all like, "It's working out so good, you're awesome in Darby Crash Band," and I just sit there getting more and more confused, like, "How'd I join Darby's band? The fuck was I thinking?" And I would of been all hardcore bout Meatheads breaking up if Meatheads were still together, cause I could handle anything when we were one thing, and now my hardcore's missing and I don't know how I would of wanted shit to work out, cause that's what's missing. And they're all like, "No, man, it's the substance of the way of the sammrye." And I'm like, "Then the way of the sammrye must be without substance," and then they go, "Man, Mikey, you're deep, let me get you some pizza." But I don't want that kind of pizza, that's not how I want it to come. That's not how I want pizza to come, and I'm like, "Just let me chill! I'm gonna work on it myself, I'm gonna get my own pizza, I'm gonna concentrate so hard they know what my order is! Just let me chill!" And they won't let me chill, they come in all like, "Hey Mikey, I brought you some pizza."

And there's still no shame, there's no shame ever, just being a sammrye sucks sometimes. And I start thinking how maybe the substance of the way of the sammrye is subject to change without notice, and then memories of Darby Crash start irradiating my mind like Lord Buddha. "Hey, Mikey, too bad bout your band breaking up, but at least you're drunk. You guys must need a singer. And I got a vision, I got tons of creative differences, and you always played guitar like Pat Smear anyway, just join up. It'll work out." And how can you say it's working out? When I'm mainlining your liquid LSD, I'm feeling your creative differences, I'm going off for your no reason, how can I be the one who's thinking? How can I know my ego's a trip, and still be this confused?

Doesn't matter. It's probly the substance of the way of the sammrye anyways.

∿∿∿

"Yeah." Mikey looks around. "That was pretty gnarly though."

They're all going, "Yeah."

The ceiling's tiedyed bloodred, but somehow Arco's not even splashed, and she's buckling her swordbelt tighter. "I'm gonna clean up. You can help me if you want."

She presses her fingertips to her temples. Goes over with her hightops squelching in the floorwide puddle and she lifts up the dead Mikey. Then she's just standing there with him, staring at the wall.

"Don't clean up, it's not our place." The alive Mikey's not risen from his sloppy heap of gore and blackened sofa foam.

Arco turns. Punker drooping sideways in her arms like a paper scarecrow. She takes a step. "Where can I put him?"

"He was fine where he was," says Raffia. "Ground Zero doesn't even do delivery."

"You don't want to do anything?" says Arco. Raffia's like, "What'd you do today that was so good?"

Arco lays Morgan on the spattered beige loveseat. Extends the chromious antennas of his bihawk fullbore and they're brushing the ground as his head hangs over one armrest and his knees over the other. Arco finds an old tongue depressor in her pocket, snaps it in half and slides the halves under the top lip. They stick out like walrus fangs. For respect.

"My brain's bleathing." Some muscle in Mikey's leg twitches through his jeans. Arco bows her head, takes a long blink, then turns around. Her shoulders jerk around like she could use something to spring at and chop.

"I can't move," says Mikey. "Like, am I standing up, or am I, right?"

"Shit." Donn's kneeling beside him with an old dishtowel. He's pushing Mikey's hawks to the side, scrubbing his forehead, scrubbing round the burrhole. Blood keeps pushing down the stubbly scalp. "Do you want me to move you somewhere?"

"Everything's fine where it is." Raffia rubs the side of her face.

"Did you know you're hemorrhaging from your eyesockets?" Donn absently flings the soaked dishtowel over his shoulder.

"Yo, I wondered what that was," says Mikey. "Raff, I know you hate redecorating, but can you let Donn straight my arms out?"

She goes, "No." Donn straights Mikey's arms out. Then she's like, "Wait, are you fucked?"

"Donn, am I fucked?" says Mikey. Arco tosses Donn a spare sock from her belt while Raffia's going, "I don't want to have no Mikeys. Just two is a lot, you know?"

"Yeah, I like you too," says Mikey.

Donn's blotting blood off the naked brain, wringing out the sock, scooping off chunks with the crunchy toepart. The membrane's ripped like a showercurtain and underneath in the brain matter there's a big crumbly sloppy gouge like somebody wasted a brick of pink styrofoam with a table leg.

"Darby Crash. Sorry. I mean, like." His face wrinkles up. "How are you even alive?"

"Every time you touch there, you go up and green." Mikey pauses. "Starts slinkying without moving your face. Faces."

"Hold still while I disinfect it." Donn tips a shot of rum onto the brain trauma and Mikey shudders and grins. "You were a yuppie, you'd be down," says Donn.

"I want to see," says Raffia. Then she's like, "Oh, fuck."

"Arco, your sword can cut round individual neurons, right?" says Donn.

"Yeah," says Arco. "What's neurons?"

"Raff, get the table outa the way," says Donn.

Raffia moves the coffeetable. "Fuckoff."

"Okay, so don't worry, man. Everybody wins this one. I just gotta start thinking really fast." Donn's chewing on a handful of pills from Mikey's inside pocket, and there's Morgan Donor across the room, head lolling off the armrest, blood getting tacky round his lips. "We gotta keep his brother awake," says Donn.

"Fucker's dead," says Raffia. She prods his eyeball with her thumb.

Donn's turning all around, squinting into the junkstrewn corners. Absently spinning his purple cellophane shades in two fingers. "We need better light. Mikey, gimme a hand."

"Out order of," says Mikey.

"Use your jaw muscles." Donn lobs a cranktorch over his shoulder as he jogs out the door. The pump lands in Mikey's lips with a gentle plopping sound.

"What?" Mikey's voice muffled round the plastic handle. The round lightbulb flickers as he starts chewing.

"Brain transplant," says Donn. He's already in the hall, he's talking to himself.

∿∿∿

The lab's still down the hallway, past the tank tread storage closet. Same ad for Spirograph on the door. Bright crayon colors mummified in layers of powdery sealingtape and bordered with a potpourri layer, clove nubs and allspice and splinters of cinnamon bark. The ginormous padlock's new.

Arco's like, "We do suck in the future."

"Why don't I want friends visiting my lab?" Weird squiggle under Donn's voice.

"Yeah, nobody understands your science in whatever dimension," says Raffia, coming up behind them.

Donn tilts up the lock. Without looking, he goes, "Raff, do me a favor."

"I'm not horny," says Raffia.

"What the fuck?" says Donn. "Like, like, like, just get some extra blood into Mikey. I mean like Morgan, not Mikey. Or alterna Mikey." He flings his hands up. "Make sure Mikey's not dead, but also get a flow of blood into Morgan, and make his lungs work manually."

"I ripped his heart in half," says Raffia.

"Yeah, you need lots of blood," says Donn. "Use the rain. Arco, do the lock? Raff, the heart doesn't matter, there's a pump in the fishtank. Arco, here's a single ordinary spoon."

"What, I can't do the lock?" says Raffia.

"You'll blow the whole door down and break the subsonic acoustic mikeyscope," says Donn. "And remember the blood doesn't rain down properly oxygenated. Use the airbubbler too."

"Why?" says Raffia. Arco's like, "Bandmate."

"Mikey might not be okay," says Donn. "And dead guys are harder to wake up the longer you leave them. And severe brain wounds are fucked. And nobody's ever done this operation before, I need to stress reduce."

"He's still Mikey," says Raffia. "Brain'll live for days." She starts shuffling backward down the hall, picking her asscrack with a thumbnail. "Gonna get better. Like how you leave pizza out."

Arco's cupping the padlock, it's bigger than her hand. She blows on it, rubs her thumb in the humidity remnant. Touches her forehead to it, and then she's like, "Yeah."

"Yeah?" says Donn.

"Yeah," says Arco. She swings the single ordinary spoon against the lock, one smooth arc like one beat of a gull's wing. A low harmonic echo starts to spread.

Arco takes a step back. "Sorry," she says. "But you have picks, right?"

"What?" says Donn. "You got it, give it a second."

One microdot of sweat stands up on Arco's forehead. "I got the straight edge, no measures of—"

"Fuck, sorry, whatever," says Donn as the ringing sound terminates with a crunch. Broken lock guts trickle from the keyhole like sand. "See? Now, like, help out."

Arco pushes through the door. Strings and strings of xmaslights snap on and there's a barrage of clicks and Arco's voice comes from a ceiling speaker. "Hey, what's up Pat, oh, if you're not Pat, thanks for turning around now, man, this is the private workspace of Patricular O. Pending, all rights resevered."

There's a dialstudded shoebox tacked to the wall, and the real Arco's cooly menacing it with Margin Walker. "Chill out," says Donn. "That's a buddy. Lets you make free long distance calls."

Arco's like, "Where'd my words come from, then?"

"I dunno, I must of missed you in this dimension, and like modeled a robot of your throat." Donn stops. "Is that creepoid?"

His lab still smells like ozone and potpourri and crayons. Maybe there's a couple more burnmarks on the fake wood paneling. Shit's all fuzzy under these xmaslights. Donn whips around the workbenches, stopping everywhere to pet the gear with his fingers. Arco follows him around, staring at the back of his head.

"Looks like the termitepowered methedrine generator still works. Shit, that grill? Does that do both sides of food at once?" For some reason Donn peels off his purple raincoat without unzipping it, balls it up and throws it into the hall.

"Focus, man," says Arco. "What's the mikeyscope like?"

"It's made of a ghetto blaster. What about those, can I use their model numbers around you?" says Donn.

"What?" says Arco.

"You're looking for a JVC RC-M90 modified for triple wattage with cryonic bass condenser coils mounted externally and a lectrostatic vector monitor stead of a tape deck," says Donn. "D cells can't push out a nuff lectricity for the lectron gun, so I've got it running on kerosene."

"Is that it?" Her swordpoint's poking a huge silver boombox under a table. The cassette door delicately chugunks open.

"No, that's a Sharp HK-9000." Donn kneels alongside it, pointing. "It's so completely different. That part's an EQ. That part's the logic controls for the clock."

"Okay," says Arco. Her head snaps ceilingward and down. "Is it up there?"

Donn's eyes track and get pinned. "Uh," he says. The ceiling's covered with dinnertables and ironingboards covered with dissected chunks of technology. There's lava lamps up there too and a beanbag chair, and the posters on the top half of the wall are flipped. Donn flips a washer off his thumb. It lands on top of a ceiling table and sits there.

"Is it up there or what?" says Arco.

"You don't think this is evolutionary?" says Donn. "Oh. Fuck. Yeah. It's up on that table."

"I don't know," says Arco.

Donn's moving toward a terminal with a buzzing green monitor and a vertical rack of fluorescent tubes half full of sloshing mercury. Purple waves of lightning sleepwalk up and down the tubes like something from a cheapo stoner toy. "This probly flips gravitons. I was thinking bout this." He slides his fingers over the keyboard. "Okay, these look like quadraphonic Poincare tables. I just gotta figure out how to condense them."

"I can condense this table." Arco's standing on two towers of milkcrates. A stray piece of lint falls upward from her fuzzy scalp as she grabs the sides of the cardtable and squeezes til it cracks inward in a v shape. The mikeyscope slides heavily up to the ceiling and sits there in a pile of cardtable chunks.

Donn's looking at her sideways. "We need some sleep. Come help me with brain surgery."

∿∿

Raffia's squatting by the loveseat, rhythmically slapping the corpse of Morgan Donor in its jaw. Forehand, backhand, then there's a splintering sound and the head's dangling sideways. She frowns and holds the neck steady with her free hand, she slaps it some more.

"Fuck, you're not even stiff." She squints at Morgan's eyelids. "Stop being dead. En. Core. En. Core." Slap with each syllable and then the ceilingfan tilts and the candleflames start skipping orangely in the cans on the walls.

—*I did this giant encore. I made everything okay, Raff, you asshole. I wanna sit by the bonfire.*

"There's really the bonfire?" Then Raffia digs her thumb into the lukewarm cheek. "No, but stop being dead. Stop being dead."

—*Ghosts don't freak you out anymore?*

"I'm cool with you," says Raffia. "Look, I'm kind of sorry I killed you, man. But we need your brains for a trance plant. If you don't stay up they're gonna go bad or some shit. Mikey Prime's bleeding to death and then our band's broken up too. He's almost as dead as you, man."

Mikey spits the cranktorch onto his chest. "Hey, man, there's really a bonfire in their basement?" He coughs and dribbles. "Man, being a couch surfer sounds totally tubular."

Raffia's pointing a clawhammer behind her. "Mikey, last warning, shut the fuck up. Morgan, you're coming back, fuck it or not. And open up the arts and crafts cabinet."

The little door in the side of the coffeetable swings open and bangs shut and swings open again. Raffia grunts. "Cool." She reaches inside for a packet of red striped bendystraws, takes one and starts to palpate the side of Morgan Donor's throat, squinting. Then she's pinching the straw, getting a corner on it. "GRULT!" She punches it into Morgan's throatmeat. Wiggles it in on an angle til the bendy join's half tucked up inside him. The punchwound doesn't leak. There's nothing left to leak.

"That was your carotid, right?" says Raffia. "Not your jugular? Morgan? Ah, whatever." She starts sealing round the entrywound with white elmerglue.

"Worst arterial shunt I ever seen," says Mikey from the nest of shredded sofa. Head turned sideways, eyelids halfdown.

"Fuck it or not," says Raffia again. She stands up with a groan and kicks out the rest of the jagged doorglass. Then she clasps her hands, mutters something, and stomps over to the fishtank instead.

No, Donn's had the fishtank since they moved in. You must not of been noticing. It's long and low against the short livingroom wall, seeping with synthetic crimsontoned moonlight. It's full of blood, what else? Grain alcohol's clearer, but fishies can't breathe right in that. Stripey black and gold gouramies shoot along the glass front as Raffia leans into the tank, her leather sleeves rolled up. A mess of brown silt starts furling up as Raffia pushes coral around and unhooks the airbubbler and the suck and blow pump tubes from the back of the tank. Somehow the lectrical outlet behind this thing never stopped going.

"You gonna clean out the filter?" says Mikey.

Raffia shrugs. She brings the pump and the airbubbler over to the loveseat with an extensioncord. Sits them on the sofa backrest, mounting the intake hose and the bubbler in an empty choppedoff milkjug. Then she sticks the blownozzle from the pump right into Morgan's bendystraw arterial shunt and seals it with a bunch of black hockeytape. How to diy.

How to diy. She steps through the doorframe out to the balcony. Over her head, the tarp canopy's bellied in with rain. She's like, "Okay, keep going." Two fingers pressing between her eyes. The pineal gland under her skull. "Okay."

There's a fairsized bamboo plant spindling out the side of the building. It's climbing the brick siding with its rootlets going everywhere like a mat of mushed daddylonglegses. She snaps off all the longest stalks and chops the tops and bottoms flat so she's got tubes, and scrapes the foliage off the sides. One by one she raises them to her lips, blowing out the baby scorpions.

"Can't even see the care I'm taking bout baby scorpions, Morgan, you fucker." She starts wedging the skinny burbsides of the bamboo tubes into the fat coresides, screwing them tight. When she's got a bamboo pipe a couple times as tall as her, she takes it into the livingroom and sets it propped in the plastic milkjug. The pipe's going up diagonal through the smashed balcony door so it pokes the overhanging tarp. Raffia goes back out there and reaches up with a nail and stabs a little hole. Skyblood starts plupping down through the tarp, and she squints one eye and fits the narrow end of the bamboo through the canopy leak.

So inside, blood's sliding down the pipe, filling the milkjug for a pump reservoir. Raffia spits on the ceiling and laughs and flicks the pump and bubbler on. They rumble and choke and then frothy red juice starts shooting up the yellowed plastic pump tube, into punker's carotid artery.

"What the fuck," says Morgan Donor. The hole in his chest is drooling again. "Brain activity."

"Lucky," says Mikey. That one muscle in his leg aimlessly twitching. "Dude, listen, I'm really not pissed no more. I feel like we worked it out and stuff."

Raffia sits heavily on the floor. "Anybody got smokes?"

∧∧∧

Arco and Donn padding through the doorway. He's got a milkcrate full of audio cables and surgery gear. She's got the mikeyscope. All hard silver plastic and soft chrome, size of a suitcase. Bedight with knobs and sliders, interlocking bezels, webs of forking collapsible antennae, and on either side of the main woofers there's curling black trumpets like hypertrophic goathorns.

"Right here?" Arco extends four struts from its base, sets it down on the carpet in front of Morgan. They squoosh in the gummy sargasso of blood. "Hey, sorry we needed to bring you back, man."

Morgan tilts his head. Grim bags under red eyes. "Nothing means shit."

"Good resurrection job," says Donn, fumbling with adapters for a couple microphones. "How's Mikey?"

"What?" says Raffia, chewing something.

Donn says it again and she spits a chewedup mallburrow slim against the wall. It sticks like a turdcolored loogie, pearled all over with mini bubbles. "He passed out."

"Fuck do you mean?" says Donn. "You don't let somebody sleep with a head injury! You keep them up for days, don't you remember with Mindy?"

"That was medical?" says Raffia. "I thought we were just being assholes." She wipes her brown tongue on her shoulder.

"Now his ears are leaking," says Arco. She takes the torch off Mikey's chest, pumps light on his face as Donn leans in. Punker's lips are mumbling dissolutely and there's two darkish treeshapes of blood under his head.

"We need to go really fast," says Donn. He belches. Spits out a pill casing. "Like so fast."

"I'd take over for your guy, just trance plant me his torso," says Morgan. Blood's running down from the hole in his chest and soaking his jeans like he peed.

"We did you a favor, sellout," says Raffia. "Hey, is Mikey alive?"

"I dunno, check if he needs to be returned back to life," says Donn.

Arco lifts Mikey by his armpits. Pulls him up droopy like a kittycat and his lips gradually fall open for a snore to come out as she drags him onto the loveseat. Him and Morgan side by side like bible buddies.

"He might. Just. Be tired," says Morgan. Gray shadows under his face. Beard fuzz like inept pencilcrayon scribbles against the sallow cheekbones.

"Mikey." Arco just says it once, right in his ear. His eyelids shudder and a pinkish fluidic bubble appears on the curve of his brain. Nothing else happens.

"He's not really sleeping," says Donn. "He needs a constant series of kundalini infusions." Tipping a plastic bottle of kerosene into an canteen mounted on the back of the mikeyscope. "Arco can't do it, I need her swordhand for surgery." A spiraling copper tube leads from the canteen into the old battery compartment. Donn yanks on a starter cord and the mutoid boombox coughs. "Raff?"

"This is fucking stupid," says Raffia. Morgan's laughing silently, strings of chewedup muscle whipping around in his chest cavity.

Donn's like, "So you've got a better technique?"

ᔕᔕᔕ

"Man, I can't just play a tape." The scope's purring like a lectric can opener, glowing purple round its buttons and dials. Donn keeps scribbling diagrams on a big flat chip of drywall. Dreads hanging over his eyes. "I swapped out the tape deck for a lectrostatic monitor. Or you couldn't see what it was magnifying."

Raffia's got two condenser mics stuck to her chin with tape, cables leading to the back of the mikeyscope. She shows Donn one tooth. She shoves. You can hear Mikey giggle and yelp.

"The baseline sound's gotta come from somewhere," says Donn. "It's an acoustic scope, it looks in Mikey by measuring variations on sound waves. We're just lucky this scope's got jacks for auxiliary in."

"You keep the best time," says Arco.

Raffia glares crosseyed at the chin mics. "Thurrrrrhhg." Her voice rumbles through the mikeyscope's bass condenser coils, and some brief white lines flicker on the scope's display.

"Tubular." Donn goes for the bass knob but it's turned all the way already. "But lower, though. Use your core muscles. Like, magine you need to take a dump and it's stuck."

Raffia goes, "Brubbbbbbppp." The monitor flickers again, then resolves into a black-and-gray line model of the two Mikeys on the couch. The aquarium pump in Morgan's carotid makes blurting noises. She shoves again and Mikey squeals like a cat.

"Okay, keep doing that," says Donn. "But don't let Mikey's awareness slip."

She goes, "Bppbbppbbthubbbbb."

Mikey's seated with his jeans bunched at his knees and Raffia's hand under his ass. She thumbs his prostate again, and he yowls. Gulps a huge breath and smiles weakly.

"Can I get a turn?" says Morgan.

"Don't stop," says Donn. "Get comfy, Raff. You might be doing this for awhile. I never did this complex of brain surgery before." He tweaks some EQ sliders. The scope's perspective lifts and turns, showing the top of Mikey's head. "Hey, Arco, do his meninges?"

Arco lifts her arm. Her nostrils flare slightly as the point of Margin Walker skims round the inside of Mikey's burrhole. "You served the universe with distinction, dura mater." She pinches the leathery membranes, lifts them off. They make a gentle *sssh* noise in their going. Underneath, his brain's marbled pink and gray, like a bleb of limestone and congealed peptobismol.

"Do we need these?" says Arco. In her hand the dura mater resembles a skein of bloody, phlegmy saranwrap.

Mikey's like, "I think I might need that shit for my collection."

Arco sets the meninges down in Raffia's lap. Margin Walker turns in her hand, light as a coin. "What do I cut?"

Raffia coughs. "Dude? Do you got a crush on your own fucking weakness?"

"No, but you're mouthing." Mikey coughs. "Her off while she's got swords in my brain."

Don's like, "Straight Edge would be sharper. Like, Margin Walker's hella strong for fighting and stuff, but nobody ever did this before. It doesn't matter how good your moves are. Based on any conceivable medical knowledge, it's not even a good idea. We need to cut in the spaces between Mikey's neurons. Nobody cuts that good. Not sept in stories."

Raffia's not looking up. "None of us would tell."

The tail of your headband's hanging in your eyes, like raggy gristle as much as tshirt cloth. "What if someone sees?"

You gotta whip up Margin Walker so it doesn't punch through Mikey's cortex, cause Raffia's getting up, hoisting him half off the couch. Her eyes get small at you. "Why are you even straight edge?"

Mikey's like, "Urrairgraughblag," and you grit your teeth and don't step back or say shit.

Don's like, "It's how you said. We need the sword from the story. The one we ventured for." He bends his head in. Speaking to like a point between your eyes. "Fuck, Arco. We know you run on auto sometimes. Your muscles just do shit without needing to look first, so does your brain, and that's how you're all tough and excelling at hardcore and shit. But the part of you that's reluctant about wielding this sword? We all know that part's not cruise control. You need to know that too."

You're like, "What?"

Don's like, "Arco, if there's some weird judgmental process in your mind right now, pretending you're a tourist, it needs to fuck way back right now. Head tripping doesn't own its own head tripping. You're not a tourist, Arco. You're Arco, Arco. Nobody else is even good at swords."

Arco's like, "What?" But now the Crash steel's in her hands.

"You missed this shit," says Raffia to the halfcomatose alterna Mikey. "You missed it."

ᗰᐯᐯᐯ

So hold on, check out the lamplight scattering over the blue steel. A fingerwidth out of the sheath, it's grained like ripples in an old pond, or ripples in fake maple paneling. If you tossed a rock in the side of your dad's stereo cabinet and it splashed and echoed. Like that, but a sword.

ᗰᐯᐯᐯ

Donn's like, "Okay. So hold it right there. No, like with the edge right in the sound beam."

"Won't it cut the sounds?" says Arco.

Donn just makes a really sad face til Arco holds it there. Raffia's going "RRRRUUUUPPPP" into the mic and it pours out from the subwoofers into their trumpetmouthed condenser coils, the infrabrown note, bass like one slow throb of a mudmonster's heart.

"The edge geometry's really bamboozling." Donn touches knobs, staring at the tip of Straight Edge magnified in the vector display. "Katana blades are just chisels up close, doesn't matter how sharp. I can't find the middle of the edge, though. Like the part where it's blunt. If the edge was really this thin? It'd chip when it hit, like, a birthday cake."

Mikey snorts. A chunk of spit rolls off his lip.

"Only bad swords hit stuff," says Arco. "Good ones just keep going."

Donn spins the volume knob forward, magnifying. The nie expand like amoebas, then distort and fractalize in the bright monitor. "No, there must be some burnt memristors somewhere. Like, this level's molecules." He dials further in. "This one's atom level. Here's subquarks."

Straight Edge burns white in the monochrome screen. Just a line and nothing else.

"It's cause Darby beat down the steel so many times when he worked it." Arco tilts one eye. "It's not just to burn out the crud. The atoms get flatter every time you fold and hammer. So you got a grain of atoms all thin on the cuttingplane, way thinner than prefab mainstream atoms. That's how come diy hardcore carbon steel cuts so good."

"That's not how blacksmithing works, and topological physics and materials engineering and, like—" Donn rubs his finger on the display. "That's not how anything works. Like, particles of any one kind are all the same. Cause they're not the parts of things, they're the parts of the universe. And on the screen they look like little milk crates. If this sword's not made of the same stuff as the universe, how can it have an effect on anything? Darby fucking Crash, it's the same thing as consciousness, right, it's like a dharma that's marooned from the wheel of interconnectionality!"

"Man, that sword looks so badass on the screen," says Mikey.

"You can't even see it from there," says Donn. Mikey's like, "Oh yeah."

"You guys shut up," says Raffia. She reams her thumb round in Mikey's asshole. He squeals again.

"Oh. Yeah." Donn peels himself off the monitor. Muted sigh. "Okay. Number one reason for brain surgery disasters is the blade's not a nuff sharp. So we should be good here. First thing is we gotta fix classic Mikey's brain. A lot of the brain cells are gonna be ripped. So we scrape those ones off, make room for the new ones to hook up. Then we cut a chunk out of alterna Mikey's brain to fit the hole, and we screw it in there."

"What are you sewing it with?" says Mikey.

"I got some pink thread," says Donn. "It won't really show."

"Man, meetings of the friend club," says Mikey. "Eeeeroik! Fuck, Raff, that was deep!"

"Okay. Arco, I'm gonna steer your cuts, okay?" says Donn. "Wait. You can do these cuts onehanded, hey?"

"Any two things are the same," says Arco.

"Sounds good." He sticks out his index finger. Arco closes her fist around it. "Cut the way I twitch."

Arco's positioned the katana pointdown in Mikey's brain wound. Donn steers it down and in, other hand spread across the mikeyscope's fine adjustment knobs. "Slower. Okay. Slower than what you got now. Slower. Bout half that. Yeah, okay. Like that."

Raffia snorts. Jams his prostate again. "I don't need structions. I know how he likes it."

Onscreen, burning in the thicket of maladapted punk rock braincells, the swordpoint's just a point and nothing else. It noses in the tangled roots of Mikey's axons, unraveling and pushing them aside. Lancing the infected bits, slicing the ripped bits off their bulblike moorings, letting them drop.

"Your brain sucks for this, man," says Donn. Mikey's like, "Oh."

Or maybe he's just breathing out.

ʌʌʌ

Member there's no fast or slow, just rhythm. It's a while. Raffia working lifesupport, pushing, pulling, the leathery dura mater drying cardboardcolored onto her lap. The Mikeys making disjointed wisecracks with nobody looking at them. Donn's tongue between his teeth, he's tuning control sliders, sketching spiderous neural diagrams on the drywall. Arco's body shivering up and down like radio waves sept her one hand high on the hilt of Straight Edge, seeming fixed and immutable while her wrist makes mikeyscopic adjustments.

"We got the wound cleared out." Donn snaps his fingers at Mikey's ears. "You sleepy?"

"Like. Uh." Mikey smacks his lips. "Does sleepy suck?"

"Might be your autosomatic system going into death shock," says Donn. "Or you might be sleepy. I'm sleepy. But you don't smell a campfire. Like. Do you?"

"Bout that," says Mikey. "Maybe pills?"

"Okay." Donn gets up, he stares at Mikey's face from a couple angles. "Your breathing sucks. Your eyes are different sizes, but your swallow reflex is fine. You can kind of talk. I think you should be prescribed two antacids." Donn starts picking caplets out of his ziploc pocketprotector while his other hand steers Arco out from the incision.

"Here, I'll do it," says Raffia. Whips her hand out from under Mikey's ass. There's blood around her ragged thumbnail, and all these clayish dingleberry streaks, and so many krinkly pubes. The pills stick to her thumb.

"Remember you're saving my life," says Mikey. "I'll be around for revenge— GLUMP!—aw, acccch. Acccccch. Accccccccccch. You wouldn't believe it."

"Believe what?" says Raffia. Mikey's like, "I can taste the cat."
They keep going.
Raffia's like, "Must taste like your mom."

〰〰〰

Nobody ever learned compassion from something good that happened. So
your head rocks on your numb crunchy spine. Donn said he couldn't look at
you sept in the scope and he said he was getting way sorry, and you remember
being like, It's okay, and thinking your smile wasn't a fake. And Arco's tooken
off the whole top and now your skull's hanging sideways by a little hinge of
skin. Meetings of the friend club. You can feel a really warm draft everywhere
above your eyes.

No, sure you're sick of Mikey, but be Morgan for awhile. He's sick of Mikey
too, and it's never too late to sit and focus. Were you ever bad at that? You
don't member. It's way simpler when you're actually diying, cause then you
don't gotta pretend. The straw pulls in your numb throatmeat and for some
reason everything's okay. The lamplight frisks and recedes, the room gets
huger and huger in pace with the beat in your brain. Man, are you sposed to
smell bonfire yet? You might not have smelling neurons left. You can't picture
the House where couch surfers land. Was the other Mikey just fucking with
Raff? For some reason there's still time left.

—Hey Mikey. Sike hard on your racecar. No, I mean the other Mikey.

The little orange racecar's sliding across the sofa armrest as Donn's stubby
fingers lift away. Sliding in framesteps backward, like the filterpump beat in
your brain. It's got to be your racecar, it's out of wheels, it's sliding. So Donn's
talking to the Mikey from the alterna future.

You're like, "Oh, okay. Why?" You're the one talking. The one from the
future.

—Cause we're amputating your brain now. But you can't trance plant expired
brains. So you gotta sike really hard, keep your consciousness up. Even after you're
disembodied from your skull. Hold onto the hockeystick. We'll cut when the meters
peak out.

It's the oldschool Vauum Vauum Vauum, just two rows of purple and no
graphic equalizer, and the meters are already peaking, but it's growing new
lights as space blows out like a balloon.

—Shit, Arco, don't cut without me.

—I carved the hole, I know its form. We need to go fast.

—No way, punker's more fuckeder than classic Mikey, who knows what extra brain damage he's got.

—I'll go really fast.

Saying something bout the racecar. It can't be popping wheelies between your hawks, there's no wheels, just little rusty axles. Some kind of dashed purple stripe on the map, blue and purple roadlines scraping your brain, sept the car's over on the sofa armrest.

Oh yeah.

—You shouldn't grab somebody's arm while she's doing brain surgery, Donn.

You land in the orange racecar. Not orange like the orange rust continents on your chassis. Not like your diyed orange jacket or the butterous lamplight. It's so light here. You can still feel the light, how you sat in your pocket.

〜〜〜

There's a dashed line of charcoalpencil cross the hollow of Morgan's throat. Donn's standing on the sofa with his hands extended into punker's halfempty skull. You can see Morgan breathe in and breathe out. In between, Arco's slipped the point of the blade through the charcoaled line.

〜〜〜

And sitting lower now, tilted to one side, cause your stub axle's kinked over like a knee. Your hood tickles, but you can't move your no wheels to scratch. If you were here before you didn't learn fuckall that time either. All you ever saw in your life was the edges of things and this death's not different, tourist.

All the edges weaving in and out. Inside, heartside, light in your pocket.

Finally there's no time left.

〜〜〜

Donn's face wrinkles as he draws up the pulpous coresample of Morgan Donor's brain in its gray and crimson striations, and the brainstem like a hunkering maroon testicle trailed by a length of slick, jointed spinalcord. He flips everything vertically in his hands, turns, and in one motion lowers the whole assembly into the negative space between Mikey's drooping hawks.

Then gripping the spinalcord he rotates the whole thing a fraction, like somebody gingerly twisting a hot lightbulb in the socket.

They say it's bad when one thing becomes two. Shit like this, who knows.

"That should work," says Donn. He glances at the schematics on the bloodspecked drywall slab. The imported spinalcord tilts forward slightly just as Morgan's carcass sags.

"I doubt it," says Raffia. She does the thumb thing again. Mikey's mouth hangs slightly open and his eyeballs shimmy behind halfshut lids. Then Raffia pulls her hand out and just looks at it. She just looks at it. She wipes it on the carpet behind her.

Then she's like, "Donn? Why'd you take so much out?"

"Oh." Donn's still looking at the schematics. "You need to maintain connection with the deep brain bits as long as possible. Like the medulla alligator and shit. You whittle out what you don't need so you can get deeper."

Arco's cleaning off Straight Edge with some yellow mcdonalds napkins.

Raffia's got pinkish brain guts all over her lap. "So you don't need this shit anymore?" She carefully wads up the squibs of braintissue on her palm. Looks like a crenellated squirt from a strawberry frogurt machine. "That's Mikey's brain," she says to herself, and whips it overhand. It explodes against the wall. A foodfighter's hi koo.

"My head feels heavy," says Mikey. He kicks his leg forward. Then the nother one. "Hey, weird."

"Did it work? Oh, dude, sweet," says Donn. "You can bust off the spinal cord and extra hindbrain and shit after you get better."

"I might start liking it too. How long til I'm better?" Mikey sticks his arms out and starts tipping forward. Donn pushes him back into the sofa.

"It's your brain, it shouldn't take long," says Donn. He bends to pick up a square of dura mater. "Hey man, spit on this? It's kind of dried out, but I don't want to get my germs on it."

Mikey looks up before spitting. "Do you want some loogies too?"

"Shouldn't be necessary," says Donn. He takes the meninges back, cuts a little cross-shaped slit in their center. "Yeah, recovery won't take long. It was actually a great fit."

"Like I didn't change as much as I thought?" says Mikey.

Donn slips the dura mater like a tarp over Mikey's new alicorn of spinal bone. Tucks the edges under the rim of the burrhole. "Nah. Didn't change at all. I think you were just super bummed."

"Weird," says Mikey. "Oh, hey. Thanks Donn. Thanks Arco." He just grimaces at Raffia. She grimaces back and they both start to giggle.

Donn's like, "Whoa, don't get up yet. I still need to sew it down and stuff."

ʌʌʌ

Kind of futile trying to scoop blood off a carpet with plastic dinosaur mugs. But the sun's finally halfrisen and there's Donn and Raff and Arco on their knees. The floor's so soaked it's developed sinkholes and you can't possibly magine these kids know how to clean up after themselves. Mikey's just cracking his back and whistling.

"They'll still have to move," says Raffia.

"We could get them new carpeting." Donn cups his hand in the floor. His eyes drift shut and clots slop out his fingers like incompletely set jello.

Arco's like, "Nobody lives here now." She gets up, rubbing her hands on her pants.

"Wow. No, you're right." Raffia hucks her red try scaratops mug off the balcony. It flies in a line like a superhero.

"At least you kinda still live here, Mikey." Donn shifts into a crosslegged position, gore splashing around. "Cause part of the other Mikey's alive in your skull now."

"He was a dick," says Mikey. "Wait, like. I resemble that remark." He lowers his head and briefly shuts his eyes. "I dunno. Should I have alterna memories? Or like double thoughts? What's double thoughts like?"

"Nobody ever had this before," says Arco.

"Either way I want to live with you guys," says Mikey. "Not a bunch of futuristic sellouts. Is anybody else sleepy?"

Raffia's just staring outside, elbow resting on the windowsill. "I still gotta kill Anna Complice. Donn's got Pat Pending. If their Arco comes back, ours can kill her. Plus we still gotta take care of Darby. Probly everyone's going down honestly." She pushes her forehead onto the pane. "Man, I'm so sleepy. Arco woke me up. And my hand smells like your ass."

"Back home they must think we're on tour." Arco's shaking her head with a thin tight smile. "I'd have a nap if you guys want. Or a meeting."

"Nap. Hey Donn." Mikey points at the floor. "Are you still jamming? It sounds different."

"Oh, weird." Donn reaches for a clean couchcushion. He lays back on the flooded carpet, hands cupped behind his ears. "Man. I think I'm listening to Yes. Where'd I get this?"

"What?" says Arco, and Donn's like, "It's an audiocassette. I've got a couple copies, like the me who I am has them, only they're mostly rotted. I extensively studied the remaining fragments with near-infrared spectroscopy, though. This one was known as *Tales from Topographic Oceans*."

Raffia's jaw trembles. "Rollins would of split their bones and sucked the marrow."

"No, who cares," says Mikey. "I just thought he was busy jamming."

Arco points up. Pat Pending's hanging from the ceiling. Maybe foot harnesses or suctioncups, no visible means of support. The same messy pencilthin dreads strung with tools, cellophane goggles and the hockeystick slung on his back like a wizard crook. Punker hasn't even changed.

Nah, the circle brand on his face, that's new. A deep scar rubbed with blue tempura paint, overlapping his eyelid. His face has no more spression than a knot of wire and one arm's crossed against his chest, the palm turned in so you can see the filter jammed through his wrist.

Pat drops and lands headfirst on the coffeetable. Balances for a beat, no hands, then he's upright in a complicated movement. Arco's lips are slightly parted, her fingertips sketching in the air. Like she'd trace what route his muscles took.

So look around yourself. The excessive blood, the shredded sofa, the busted balcony door. You're that, too. The dead Morgan Donor with the top of his skull dangling to one side like the lid of an empty fruitcup, and the hammer missing from the top of Raffia's bandolier. You're that, too. The spinalcord waggling at the crest of Mikey's dome. The subsonic acoustic mikeyscope striped with crimson spray. The two blades scabbarded in Arco's belt. The bamboo transfusion pipe and the quiet of the pumpless fishtank. You're that, too.

Are you in trouble?

Pat's head's nodding slightly to the muffled drumline and he lifts his hand off his chest, waves his filterstuck wrist cross the room like a videocamera. The way a camera takes your soul.

"You could of come down and said hi," says Pat Pending. Nobody does anything. He bites his lip and looks out at them very clearly. Nobody does anything and his feet leave little paddle wakes where he walks. He steps through the broken door. See its jagged margin around him. Look, he's got the top of Morgan Donor's skull, he's holding it. Running fingers round the sticky inside of the bowl, the smooth-edged stripe of skylight. He sets it down.

"No matter what. That part doesn't hurt. It never hurts to say hi." Pat's standing on the coiledup ropeladder. They just look at each other. Somebody might be bout to step up and he just looks like Donn and he's falling backward off the balcony, both feet at once, into the rain. The panes of his glasses flash lamplight and he drops backward with his hands folded behind his head.

Downstairs the tape turns over and starts playing again.

THE THNEEDING OF THE 5000 // IN GOD WE THRUST, INCARNADINE // THE SHAVE OF PUNK TO COME // DARBY CRASH WRITHES AGAIN

Responsibility makes me quit.
Sick of this motherfucking goddamn shit.
—**Poison Idea**, "Just To Get Away"

Because I cannot touch the moon, is it therefore sacred to me?
—**Max Stirner**

Hardline allows for recreation.
—**Sean Muttaqi** answering letters in *The Vanguard*

—You know what coreward means. There's always somewhere closer than your house. You could be home, and somewhere'd still be closer. Keep going. That's what coreward means. Coreward means keep going.

Just that's not a spiel.

There's gotta be wood if the fire's hungry. There's gotta be beers not drunk. This concrete's cold as all fuckall, the sun's never getting down here, my eyes don't work for shit since Donn and Arco borrowed half my midbrain for a patch job, even the joint's dead and you weren't there and we still need something passing round the fire. So this one's the old timey Oki Dog spiel. The show me your hardcore spiel.

So he showed up late to the Zoom Lounge, Lord Darby. He missed the first band and the tear gas. The barfront window was all closed with metal shutters that told GI SOLD OUTS in halfwet spraypaint. Some kids conked on the ground with their jaws bashed in and citation stubs pinned to their jackets. Darby stood and tried to smoke. Then he put his forehead on the shutters and retched.

Block away Pat Smear was hiking limping down the dark sidewalk with his guitar stuck half out his backpack and some kid's amp propped on his free shoulder. He knew how Darby puking sounded and he turned back for it. Pat shoved him into a gray puddle of needles, didn't even put his gear down first.

Darby spat thick stuff that hung down his chin. When he turned over, needles broke off inside him.

Aren't you in the band, said Pat.

I didn't get here yet, said Darby. Or like. You're mad at me.

Don't try to define it, said Pat. Germs can't play without Lord Darby. Your fucked fucking fans pulled the fire larm and kicked the toilet bowls in. Some arcotect's daughter from Encino put her head through the fuse box. What were we sposed to do, give out free funds? We drank the door money waiting for you.

Darby's eyes closed and he fell back on his stomach. Yet somehow you're not drunk?

Fuck I'm drunk, said Pat Smear. I heard some punk say reconvene at Oki Dog. So fuck off.

I'm gonna kill myself, said Darby. You think you know I'm drunk.

His hand went out and found the gray mud puddle. It was all burned papers from the news box slopped up with smashed beers. Some of the blood there was already his. Darby rolled over again. He rubbed his muddy knuckles through his eyes.

You think you're so hardcore, Pat. Gimme one of your beers.

Darby licked his finger and spat a piece of glass. All he could see was red shapes *sliding like the mucky ashes and little bright chunklets like the broken bottleglass. Even after he wiped his eyes again, that was all he saw.*

He said, I might be drunk but you're all just figments to me.

So he went going to Oki Dog, Lord Darby. Walked on the edge of the street and the curb. One foot dragging in the way and his eyes swollen down to cracks. When he fell over he'd crawl for a while, and sometimes there'd be car horns all round him. He took it coreward til he put out his hand and some punk put a beer there.

Kids were running in, crowding round Darby. He curled on his side and retched out foam. Mustard dropped from somebody's pastrami burrito to make spots on his face. The whole drinking lot was tainted pink from the rainbow shining off Oki Dog.

Your eyes got the severest look of hardcore, said some punk. You must of been going siko up there. Now I wish I didn't miss the Germs show.

We never played a show tonight, said Darby. Guess you don't care if I kill myself. Hey Pat? Just gimme a beer, Pat.

Casey Cola was tipping wine into her hand, it looked like hot dog juice in that light. We all must of missed it, she said. And you just stood there singing while some beach district meathead clawed your eyes? Germs are so hardcore.

She tried to clean out Darby's eyes with pink wine and he punched the ground with his knuckles.

You guys keep on going hardcore hardcore, said Darby. And not listening. You guys are the same as my eyeballs, you probly have no independent reality. Show me your hardcore or else stop talking.

What'll you do with our hardcores, said Casey Cola. You think you can chill them out?

So he kicked and flailed on the ground of the drinking lot, Lord Darby. Show me. I wanna see them. Whosoever shows me their actual hardcore? They can become me after I commit suicide.

You should know he doesn't even like rose wine, Casey.

It was Gerber talking. Darby stayed still on his back. She held out two smokes burning to him and he didn't take them.

You don't need to talk now, Darby. She crouched down and scootched a little forward, so his head pushed in her lap. His cheek stuck to her black latex skirt.

Show me your hardcore, Gerber.

I'm so sorry I didn't go to the show, said Gerber. I just thought I'd get too drunk if I went. And then I wouldn't be able to make it here and take care of you. Cause I figured if you ended up at Oki Dog again you'd want to shoot up puddle scum again. I really wanted to make the show but I'd rather I could keep you okay.

You can't become me, you're a figment. Darby stood up and took a step. *You're only my soft lap waiting for me.*

So he put out his arms and took it again coreward, Lord Darby. The crowd split to make way. Kids stuck their feet out to trip him and other kids jumped on them, and fights rolled back and forth on the ground. Then Hellin Killer was holding Darby by his shoulders. He went slack and his head bobbed against her tits.

Show me your hardcore, Hellin.

Do it or don't, said Hellin Killer. But stop saying you will. I'm trying so hard not to give a shit. You think I don't feel it every time you say you'll kill yourself? You keep talking bout circle plans and how suicide's the best way to define history and I try so hard to accept it, Darby, and I know you're smarter than me. I know Germs are a plan, you standing here's a plan. Just I wish you'd stop bragging about it. I can't connect with anyone now, I'm waiting for one thing to actually close.

Hellin shoved Darby on his ass. She crossed her arm over her eyes and walked cross the street. Lots of the crowd came with. Germettes with tiny skirts and knife heels were waiting to smoke with her there.

You can't become me, you're a figment. Darby stood up and took a step. *You're only my hands pushing me away.*

So his circle kept moving, Lord Darby. One boot was gone and his sock was all blood. Then he banged into Greg Ginn's merch table, spilled on the ground with a bunch of Germs shirts. Ginn was all practicing with his back to the table, fingering riffs on this sawedoff and soldered guitarneck he had.

Stop saying you will, said Darby. Just show me your hardcore. Or you actually want me to commit suicide on the toilet?

No, I'm Greg Ginn from Black Flag, man. Maybe this is a bad timing, but I was thinking Black Flag should play at Darby's funeral. Hey, you're Darby. So I phoned all these funeral places and wrote down the private party rates. Could your mom stake the extra deposit? Here, look at these flyers I got made.

You can't become me, you're a figment. Darby stood up and took a step. *You're only my mind turning deals.*

Nobody was around him then and he fell sideways into a road divider, Lord Darby. Every way's always coreward. You can either forget that, or forget to know you're going. He ripped his chin open on the asphalt. He saw the same glass twinkles and the same red sliding shapes.

Show me your hardcore, Pat. And fuck you for not saying I was falling. You're drunk too, Pat. It's not like you can make fun of me. Not like it has an effect. You know you look scared, right? Just following me at the Oki Dog and not answering when I ask. Gimme your beer. Gimme your fucking beer.

The bright car horns were all round him again. Somewhere kids were yelling, and his hand still had that beer some punk gave him. The can was part crushed but still full. That's not how it ends.

Lord Darby, I got you a beer.

∧∧∧

*H*is dark jacket laved in auburn torchlight. His shoppingcart wheels dragging in the muddy cobblestones. And he just looks the same. Stay back. Remember you're a tourist. Darby Crash stands in the overgrown aisle of the toysrus with reeds poking up round his boots. On each side of the aisle, brown warehouse shelves tower to the faroff ceiling, less they're dead oaktrees twisting themselves into scaffolds. The light here sucks.

He points at something far up. "I can read that crate. My Tressy's gonna be there. Gimme your shoulders."

The other one's Raffia, mostly. She kneels, leaning on her plastic tikitorch. Musclecolored platemail tiling, sawn from olden dumpsters, screaks against her back. Get down on her knees if you want, stare through the tangled shelves. Shrooms glow like nightlights from the mooshy plaster hillocks beyond the aisle, and the aisle winds on and on.

Darby steps back a little. One boot treads on a dead giraffe in a red pinstripe suit. It's colored the same ocher as the luminous shroom stems, and somebody did its face with a sledgehammer. Fuck are you staring at it for? The tawny flesh coming apart already, delisquescing like an infected slime mold. One big white plastic eye rolls and points up at the legend like a pitiful accusation and sinks further into the slurry.

For serious, tourist. Stop looking that way. Don't think his mind's on the slurry giraffe. Don't think it's on the scaffold of crated toys. You can't just reach out and get to know Darby Crash. He'll see you in himself, he'll catch you in the fingers of his mind and blow you into nothing.

You know you're a story. What you can do is watch the whole wheel from behind, so even if you don't got weight and volume, you can make believe you're running the works. You can postulate bout levels in levels in levels of dreamtime, and cheer when shit's rumbustious. You can guess how a punk's feeling and live by those guesses, same way they pretend to fit in with themselves. That's it. Sept if you try showing Darby Crash empathy, you can get your mind fucked to death.

Stay back.

NOAH WARENESS

His teeth flash. "Kay. Get up there, Waffles." The legend's sucking his lip, sawing his head back and forth. His shirtfront's sour with vodka. Some punk or something waddles out of the dark, jaws wound shut with a whole roll of ducktape. It's standing attentive and sunkenchested and pantsless in a gold velvet smokingjacket. Somebody's sequined *WAF* and *ULS* on its cheeks. It waves its arms theatrically at Anna Complice and climbs onto her shoulders.

She just goes, "Fuck, Darby." Pushes herself standing and the yuppie's balancing on her, pawing its hands in the air.

Sweat glints under the legend's eyes. "I don't got a lighter one. You know they can't bite with their teeth taped up."

"It doesn't matter," says Anna. Her teeth are gritted, her hands are clawed at nothing. Waffles tips minutely on her shoulders and she jerks the other way to straighten it. It reaches and grabs the overhead shelf. Darby's chewing his finger. Sweat crosses down his beardless cheeks and runs to the corners of his lips as the yuppie reaches and swings itself up. Now it's sitting on the scaffold, picking its nose.

"Okay," Darby's nose twitches. "Sike something for a decoy. I'll get the Flintpope up there, but I'm gonna go mental running two yuppies."

Anna's staring evenly at the ceiling. "We could do the whole thing ourselves. I got rope."

"That's not the game," says Darby.

She sighs. "Put your mouthguard in. If you bite me, I'll kill you."

"No, cause you can sike." And the eyes just roll back in his head.

Anna's breath hisses in her teeth. She grabs a foggy white plastic trashcan off the lowest shelf. It splinters in her hands, it's full of monstrous little wrestlers colored like sticks of gum. You counted ten, tourist. If you were Raff you know you'd of seen them appearing everywhere in millions, all fucky and lurky and spilling out your hands. But shit, you're not even Raff, Anna. You're Anna.

The monster in your hand looks like you, sept it's wafflepatterned and colored like corn cobs. Don't think bout Darby, don't think bout yuppies, mind works better busy, no, no it doesn't, but still. Stick the little bruiser in your teeth. Fucker tastes like polyvinylchloride and your tongue pushes a little perforated plug free in its chest, where its heart should of been.

Darby's started drooling and there's a nother yuppie with a tapedup mouth coming out of the dark. The fucking pope hat's come half unstapled from its skull and all the flintstones stickers are peeling off it.

"This isn't fucked for you, is it?" says the Flintpope's mouth. It sounds half like Darby, half like a squeaky car door.

You look at it and it coughs and pretends to try and wind the ducktape back round its face. Did you just see a burn on its wrist? Then it's grabbing hold of your topknot and hauling itself onto your shoulders. Feel the weight lighten as Waffles pulls it off you and it's fucked how they're both Darby, but don't even think. You're in the wrestler. The wrestler trying not to think.

Fuck, you fucking taste like polyvinylchloride.

Darby's started to make gargling noises. He's snapping at the air and Anna pitches you down the aisle. You're going woosh, woosh, end over end like a stupid starfish.

∧∧∧

Anna stares at Darby's body sprinting into the dark. Her hand tightens on the tikitorch while the muscles in her forehead flex and harrow.

There's the two yuppies, balanced on scaffold near the ceiling, shoving at a gigantic crate. It tips off the edge, spinning like a die in the air, and smashes in the mud. Wood splinters spray and dolls spill nonymously across the ground, all torsos and flapping rayon dresses coming to rest against Anna's boots.

"See, that was alright." Darby's sauntering back into the torch radius, holding the rubber wrestler up to his eye. You can't see anything through the little round hole in its chest. "Don't swallow the heart piece. I gotta fill out my collection. Hey, watch out."

Anna? Anna. You pivot as the yuppies drop at you from the scaffolding. Facefirst and snapping, it's really not elegant. Darby sags in every muscle. His eyes flip to blank lines and the Flintpope and Waffles grab each other's armpits in midair and drive their foreheads together with a crash like sea urchins hitting concrete, and meanwhile you're diving sideways, hauling Darby with the crook of your arm as the blownout yuppies slam into the dirt right where he'd been standing.

You totally swallowed the heart piece.

∧∧∧

Anna turns herself over, cumbersome in her lashedon platemail. She's sunk half in the spilled dolls like a mountain of garden mulch. Her hand's still on the burning tikitorch.

You can hear Darby yawn affectedly from somewhere. "Bummer. Those yuppies were choice."

"That wouldn't of been a good death," says Anna, after awhile.

He's like, "So tell me bout the good ones."

She stops one nostril with her thumb. Blows a plug of redthreaded snot cross her hand. In this teacolored greaselight it looks like a fortunetelling. "If your hardcore was death by misadventure, you'd of got it already."

"Your job's not to protect me," says Darby Crash.

She thrashes her arms behind her, clawing upright. The dolls catch and tumble against themselves. Torchlight finds the legend sitting on a crate on the secondstorey ledge. There's a plastic Darby sitting in his hand. A black leather key's spinning in its bellybutton, autonomous, and his thumb strokes its hawk while it grows.

∿∿∿

What can you do?

You'd stand there for awhile, you'd work your lips like something'd come out, glancing at each other's knees. If you had them you'd spin your battered cardboard shades in your hand. Or rub the scabbedover zits on your forehead. You wouldn't know if you were even crying.

Raffia clenches her jaw and pushes her bare foot sideways through the mire of lumpy blood. Mikey's like, "What's up?"

She kicks the blood further. "We don't have a broom."

"Oh. Is that what we're doing?" says Mikey.

Arco's like, "I guess so."

They all look at her, like nobody else should know better. Everyone starts trying to kick blood out the door, and it doesn't really work.

∿∿∿

So then a yellow tennisball comes streaking through the smashed balcony door. Arced like it came from a lower balcony cross the way, it's trailing a super long foxtail of knotted nylon scraps. Arco picks it up from the air without looking. The nylon line stretches from her hand out the door and down into the moody rustcolored evening. Then it goes tight and her arm muscles tight up too.

"Watch out," says Arco. "This is something fucked."

But they're already fanned out and mustering gear. Mikey's swirling his hands round, doing experimental little feints and chops. The inverted spinalcord bobs and jiggles sympathetically from his skull.

"Man, you can sit down." Donn's mouth only moves on one side. "Don't need to work all your new cortical tissue at once."

"Wasn't my idea." Mikey laughs. Hops once and does a sweet backflip. He comes down with one hand cupped round the spine, holding his brains in.

The taut nylon braid's moving against a sharp glass chunk in the doorframe, and it parts with a plaintive little sound. Half a heartbeat and a dentical tennisball shoots through the window. Arco palms it with the same hand.

"Should we put the ladder down?" Donn doesn't move. His hands tighten on Vauum Vauum Vauum's shaft. The purple spectrum analyzer flickers lower as he juts out his jaw.

The foxtail's pulled tight against the balcony's edge. Now there's some fingers coming up beside it. They're missing a couple tips and scribbled all over with complicated tattoos like the bottom of a cup of hair tea. Now some punk's hauling himself up. His floppy blue ballcap's cut through for a dark topknot to protruberate like existentional reverb of Mikey's extra spine. Windowpane eyes underlined with broad streaks of charcoal, gray jersey camopatterned the same. He's got three katanas swinging at each hip, sheathed with tarp and twine.

"Hey, Arco, it's your friend," says Mikey.

"No friends," says Arco. "I got the straight edge." She looks over. "Sorry. I didn't mean. Like." She's pressing one arm to her torso, like trying to give herself half a hug.

The ballcap kid's standing half off the balcony edge, weight balanced on his toes. His fists tremble against his solar plexus. The nylon line's still taut, running between his legs, and he plucks on it some times. Steps up and stares at Arco. He's got four more blades, long puppies, crossed over his shoulderblades. Dude's all like, "Arco."

"Hey," says Arco.

Ballcap points his chin up. "Hey," he says to himself.

Nother arcore skinhead pops up. This one's got a massively bruised eye, plumdark and streaky like a heirloom tomato. Short and wiry, no middle fingers. Sleeves cut off the shoulders of her black rubber rainjacket and her arms layered with some kinda breathable titanium mesh. And a bunch more swords.

She stands beside ballcap. Ballcap's like, "Arco greeted me hey."

Both the arcore kids go, "Hey." Nodding with their folded hands. All their katanablades wag back and forth.

"Hey," says Mikey. The skinheads don't say anything.

"Hey," says Donn.

Arco's looking cross Meatheads. "I guess this is something you want me to handle."

"They're your clones," says Raffia. "If they were my clones, I'd handle them."

Mikey's bending the spinalcord forward. Like the bending of a recalcitrant symbiotic eel. "Get a good look, Morgan?"

"Dude, respect." Donn's got both hands on Mikey's elbow. "That shit's still independently conscious."

"No it's not. Is it?" says Mikey. Donn's like, "Well, how would we know?"

"We heard you might of come back." Ballcap's speaking straight ahead. "We got the swords."

"I gave them away," says Arco.

"We didn't say we got them back," says bruised eye. "We just got them." The rebar in her voice, the falling leaves. That much like Arco anyway. "We'd like if you stayed at our house."

"We never found Straight Edge." Ballcap's voice comes fast, overlapping his friend's. "Is that Rollins steel at your belt?"

Arco shakes her head. "We're forms of Dimension X. Not the Meatheads of your seeking."

Bruised eye doesn't turn to ballcap. "No eagerness, arco. Arco wouldn't be eager."

Ballcap draws his face away and nods. Bruised eye pauses slightly, like a line skipping on a piece of paper. Her fists grab themselves. "That chastening could of come from hardcore but it didn't. I felt better than you for a bit."

Her buddy shrugs. Graceful, symmetric. "You can take it back, arco."

"Arco, your clones are fucked, Arco," says Raffia.

Arco's pointing behind her, the carcass on the loveseat. "We owe this lost tourist an owing."

"Bring it. Whatever. Just we've never had people over. Our house is called Arco House." Ballcap's scoriated fingers work and work like airguitar. "We named it after you."

"We're forms of Dimension X," Arco says again. The skinheads just look at her. "You don't need me at your house."

They just look at her.

Raffia shoves Donn's shoulder. "It might be dry there. Do they got beds?"

"Should we even talk to the non-Arco Meatheads of X?" says ballcap.

"I wanna stay at their stupid shitty house," says Raffia. Donn's like, "Yeah, me too."

"Me three," says Mikey. His eyes glance up. "Or like four, I guess."

∧∧∧

"Somebody just came in the front." Darby pockets the doll and jumps. He lands crouched with knuckles pushing through his scalp. His hair's crowcolored, glossy. No more veins of gray.

Anna's on her feet. She angles her neck a couple degrees like she's halfheartedly stretching, and she nods her big flat face. Stands the tikitorch in the mountain of dirty dolls. When she turns around there's a couple nailstudded twobyfours nestled in the crook of her arm.

"Traitor. I got two pointies here for you." She lobs her voice down the aisle. "Hey. Two. Count em."

Some arcore kid drops from the lightless ceiling levels. He lands rolling, it's picturesque, he's coming in at a quick jog. Charcoalrimmed eyes reflecting flatly in the low tikilight and he says something bout doing whatever's necessary. His lips shut before he's done talking, like he got dubbed.

Anna looks over to Darby. He's not there.

"One," she says.

She hucks the first twobyfour at the arco kid. His wakizashi ribbons up from its sheath and clips the plank in half. Wood pieces spin past the sides of his head.

"Here's the second one, cause there's two," says Anna. The kid's closing, blade leveled on a slight diagonal. She grabs two more boards from the crook of her arm. Gripping them pressed tight like disposable chopsticks, she loops them in overhand. The arco kid effortlessly halves the one in front. Pares bout a quarter from the one in back. It rolls in the air and sinks spikefirst just atop the kid's eye.

"There's others," he says, still coming forward. The ungainly plank stuck tight to his head and his eyesocket flashing blood. His free hand pulls a katana while his ankles weave together. Anna boots the plank as he falls.

"I liked that," says Darby. His two fingers resting on her hip.

"They're too stupid for yuppies to smell," says Anna. "It's not meditation."

"Everybody's stupid." Darby strokes his lips. "Go through his pockets, Anna."

She's kneeling by the body. "He doesn't got pockets. I can give you his swords."

Darby's like, "Must of been what I said."

The blades are a matched pair, quenchlines whorled like winter breaths. Darby brushes the kid's jeanscuff with the katana. Safetypins parting as easy as the fabric.

"That's not our work. They made it pretty." Anna's thumbprint leaves a blurry trail under the quenchline. Right by the hilt, the edge's chipped where it fell on a pavingstone.

"History," says Darby.

Anna just looks at the air. Her back's really straight, and Darby's like, "So you puncture a yuppie's brain. And the existential paths leak out, every life choice it never made. And one takes over for the old universe, but nobody knows. Cause now it's always been that way." The wakizashi hangs from Darby's curled fingers as he scratches his jaw with his thumb. "What if that just happens in a finite circle."

Anna hawks and spits at the ceiling.

"Magine. An x dimension spins off from the classic universe," says Darby. "With that blownout yuppie as a center, maybe a couple blocks wide. And whatever's near a nuff in that moment, it all gets sucked to Dimension X. Magine. Cause we're only quenching yuppies near core. Nobody ever leaves the city far, not sept to go on tour. So punkers wouldn't know if the whole dharmic network had reshaped round them. They'd have nobody to compare home dimensions with."

The loogie hits behind them with a flat slapping sound. Concentric shockwaves reverberate cross the bright puddle of giraffe flesh. Circles, circles.

"Nah," says Anna. Darby's like, "Oh?"

"Nothing changes when you kill a yuppie. No more than killing a rat. Cause you wouldn't even know," says Anna.

"Occam's Razor," says Darby. "I invented that in high school. If there's two ways for truth, it runs down the shorter path."

"It's all words." Anna's jaw works minutely. "You wouldn't even know."

"If somebody came back to us from outside." Darby's tilting the blade so his reflection looms in the foggy steel. "They would know."

Anna finally turns and looks at him. "How bout when you went way past the fence for no reason sept to slay yuppies, and a tiger bit off your arm?"

Darby just stares til she turns away again. "Like you know where I came from. Like you know."

"She's not back." Anna's got her foot on the dead kid's jaw, renching out the plank. Even her feet are laced up with platemail. She's like some weird iron rendition of a pangolin.

Darby goes, "Some arco kid showed up at Ground Zero with fortysix vintage sammrye blades in four golfbags. And my band for a crew. She handed out katanas like a soup kitchen. Then after the arco kid armed all my moron groupies with the best swords they ever held, the Anna kid started a brawl for no reason, and they beat their way out the middle. Sure sounds like the Confused."

"The what?" says Anna. Darby's like, "Sorry. Meatheads. I can't keep up with all these new bands from Dimension X."

Looking at him, she breathes in. Then she breathes in again, nothing in between. "Some jerks found swords someplace. Who knows. You didn't hear bout Straight Edge. If she could of put that one down, she wouldn't of fucked off."

"The Rollins straight edge." Darby shakes his head. "You say you know Arco's not coming back. How?"

Anna sneers. "I let her go in my heart."

∧∧∧

Bruised eye scoops up the tennisball and its heap of scruggly nylon foxtail. Knots the line to the doorhandle and cocks her head and pitches the ball down into the grainy marscolored evening. The foxtail uncoils and coasts weightlessly behind it like the ragged contrail off a tiny, filthy starship.

There's a couple dents in Donn's lower lip where he's been biting it. Shit, no, you're Donn again. Touch the dents if you want, check for blood. "Hey? How bout me?"

Mikey's on your retinas. He looks taller, looks like he could walk through anything. Is he even tired? The new spinalcord's already tightening, drying the color of particle board. Like a curved plungerhandle standing between his hawks. He's talking and all you can feel's the dents in your lip.

"Like Pat Pending?" says Mikey. "Look, man. I don't know how to say this. But he must of been like majorly depressive already. And this whole trip is getting fuckeder and fuckeder. Can we just let his crew take care of him?"

All you can feel. At ground level the drinking lot's just rain and brown rubble. The halflight makes it indistinct, murky like an underwater polaroid. Did there used to be those? You're like, "Why did I jump off?"

Nobody says anything, and then you're like, "Would I of been okay with them leaving me here?"

"What, them like us them?" says Mikey. "Dude, you're you."

You don't say anything else. Raffia's nodding, not looking, and the tennisball must of caught on something cause now the line's taut from its mooringknot on the doorhandle, sloping down through the air over the street.

Bruised eye starts unfixing carabiners from her belt, passing them out. Ballcap swings his legs over the side and hooks his carabiner to the stretched rope. He knots his fingers round that and just pushes off, sluicing down the cord like blown smoke.

Raffia's down on one knee, peering cross the skinny tightrope. Its endpoint inconclusive in the foggy dusk. "Aw, fuck it. Fuck it." She slides down after ballcap. The rope bobs, and listen to her yell. So clip on and follow her down.

Are you still Donn, though? Feel your face grinning as the velocity pulls it back. If it was a real grin of feelings, you wouldn't need to feel yourself inside it. What are you, tourist? Like some kind of joke. Like there's nothing but the muscles as they move.

∧∧∧

No, you're Mikey. No, open your eyes again. You're not that Mikey. You're just tired. You're sitting on the balcony edge, watching Arco stand in the rainshadow with a corpse of you slung over her shoulder. She's sharp and thin as a short-term memory, shaking her head mikeyscopically, shading her gaze with the flat of her hand. No, open your eyes again. Is she even tired? You know she's good with baggage. You know she's good with crossings.

Turn your head. "Is your crew at war with Darby's crew?"

Bruised eye doesn't say anything. You reach over and scrape a dead leaf off Arco's ancient tennis shoe. Feel it between your fingers, kleenexy with the beginnings of rot.

"Cause we're not with him," you say. "We're still the classic Meatheads lineup. We never lost Arco."

"That's bullshit," says the hard little skinhead with Arco's voice. You start saying something and then she's like, "I mean, it's probly true, whatever. Things like that are just bullshit. You're with Arco. You can pitch in if you want."

Fuck, man, just clip onto the rope.

They say nothing you can't practice is real.

You're lacing your fingers round the rough metal clip and her boot pushes your shoulder. And you don't get killed on the way.

ʌʌʌ

Did there used to be a building here? There might not be one now. The burbside of Arco House is a giant nondescript mound on the edge of the fence, all papaya thickets and mossy plaster flamingoes and concrete shards like giant petrified hotdog buns. They slide right through a glassless windowframe the size and shape of a humpedup punk sliding on a rope.

The entryhall's a grove of scruffy potted trees under hidden skylights. It's hard to see all the way to the walls, if there's walls. If there's a floor, it's knuckledeep with dirt and pats of shitmanure. At the end of the sliderope there's two really sturdy bamboos growing through the floor. Two stalks braided in a doublehelix with the foxtailed tennisball hooked and knotted all round it. For serious. Call it a pretty good throw.

So ballcap's standing, staring out the window, and Meatheads shoot in one by one. After they pry their knuckles off the carabiners they just sit in the floor, blinking at each other. Bruised eye slides through a breath after Arco, and the little skin's holding ballcap by the shoulders before Arco even slings down her corpse luggage.

"They're really tired," says bruised eye. "We can talk to them tomorrow. Okay?"

Ballcap's about to say something but his eyes close and open, and he nods. Bruised eye takes his elbow. Hauls him to a nother, thicker bamboo pole. Ballcap climbs through a hole in the ceiling, stopping once to stare backward. There's no lamps in here. It's getting pretty dark.

"There's some couches that way, past the hedge," says bruised eye as she's climbing. "We hold a no blanket straight edge, though. Sorry. And some of us might come in before you're in a state of readiness. All the doors got tooken off in the reno." The pole's at her back, she's gripping it with just her ankles, she bows to a place equidistant between Meatheads. Last thing you see, she punches herself in the eye.

Past the hedge it's pretty similar. Dense with clay pots of miscellaneous plantage. Redwood saplings, guava, yellow kale. Raffia kicks pots aside as they walk. There's a profusion of clay tablets fixed to the trees, grids dense with pictographs of carven punks sweeping, watering, washing out mugs. Spose they're chore charts for kids who don't read.

The couches are actually coffinsized planters full of damp oystershrooms. Donn's like, "Yeah, they never had friends over."

Hard to tell Arco's tired. She's got the dead Mikey on a couch. Her face set like clay, she's splitting the chest down with a huge square cleaver. Her arm freezes midchop as the live Mikey reaches into the cracked sternum. Punker idly rubs his finger on an edge of rib bone. "You still got your sword?"

"At my belt." Arco passes the cleaver's edge between her fingers.

Mikey's like, "No, the one from the museum. Dude, you're all stressed and shit."

"It's in your backpack, right?" says Donn. "You wouldn't of lost it."

She doesn't answer at first. Her eyes get really wet and shiny. Coming from Arco, that's really weird. "I've got it," she says. "It's not anyone's sword, okay?"

"You don't have to tell them," says Mikey. "Just don't. They're hung up on you a nuff already."

"Are you acting fucked cause you're keeping it secret?" says Raffia. "You're not straight edge anymore even. You broke it already when you didn't tell them."

"No, they asked me bout a different sword," says Arco. Raffia's like, "You're still hiding a secret. Your whole edge is gone already."

"Ease, asshole," says Mikey.

Raffia's like, "What? I'm trying to make her feel better."

Arco sounds like there's a thumb on her windpipe. "Do we want to have a band meeting bout it?"

"Can we sleep first?" says Mikey. Arco just starts nodding.

"I'm really sorry," says Donn, and Raffia goes, "Then do something."

They stare at each other in the dark.

"Why the fuck is Arco straight edge?" says Raffia. They stare some more. She's like, "No, you tell me, Donn. Why?"

Donn's finally like, "How do I know?"

"One stupid fucked problem at a time. Okay?" says Mikey. "We gotta talk his ghost off the bones. Nobody else can do that."

Raffia keeps staring at Donn. "Pat Pending could of done it. Sept he jumped off, like a wimp."

"Go to sleep," says Mikey. "You know when you said we keep you level? And you would have been slain by now without us?"

Raffia starts laughing. "I'll still be like this tomorrow." She falls backward onto one of the springy shroom planters. You know what, there's four. She's like, "Arco?"

"Yeah?" says Arco.

Raffia's like, "Why were you holding straight edge?"

Breathe.

"Cause it was easy," says Arco.

"That's so heavy," says Mikey. "That's so heavy, dude. That's so heavy."

∧∧∧

His hand's still in Morgan Donor's split sternum. Mikey looks down and dabbles his fingers round. Pokes the deflated lung in its bluegray sac, leaving a dent. "I wish I spent more time magining myself doing this."

"To yourself?" says Donn. "That's pretty heavy too."

"Anyone want a nic fit?" Mikey's looking nowhere. He slides his ass to the end of the planter couch and rips open a mallburrow slim. Fluffs the tobacco into a popcan pipe and draws. He's started to cough out a plume of formaldehydecolored smoke and an unripe walnut drops from the ceiling, knocking the pipe from his hands. Punker just stares upward, baring his teeth. "Fucking ceiling's got the straight edge?"

Arco's like, "He's ready, I guess. If you wanna help."

Mikey goes over and squats by the Morgan carcass. "You ever get that feeling? Like you forget which one of us you are?" He pokes the dented lung again. "Is it even my hardcore to talk the ghost off? I mean, it's my ghost, right?"

"We're all his band. We're the same in this." Arco's crosslegged. She briefly presses the soles of her shoes together. "But you're the best at it."

"I couldn't miss me if I was gone," says Mikey.

"Do you member who you used to be?" says Donn. Mikey nods, or just holds his head down, and Donn's like, "Do you miss them?"

"Him, not them," says Mikey. "Or. Fuck. I get it."

The wind smells like spam and ozone, tonguing through the ragged skylights in the side of the hollow mound. The wall's lined with bamboo and popcans and clay. Arco stands up. Mikey's standing beside her. Saying this is off the name line. It goes from intro to out.

"Sometimes it bends in the middle," says Mikey. Says Mikey in Mikey's voice. "Or it dips round. You go under to stitch a patch. The name line dips like that."

Donn's like, "What was your first name?"

"I dunno," says Mikey. "Can I make it up?"

Raffia rolls over. Cracks her eye. "Fuck," she says. "Might as well."

Cross the room, there's arcore kids filing through the doorless wallhole. Stepping among the plantpots, lining up against the far side of the guesthall. Eyes like the middles of zeroes and never looking away.

Mikey's like, "Sweet fuckall shat Mikey D'Angelo."

"What's D'Angelo mean?" says Donn.

Mikey goes, "It's a word from the dead yuppie language."

"Is not." Raffia's lips are barely moving. "Man. You're hardcore."

"It means one of Angeles. Lost and found." Mikey stands up to face the skinheads. You know, he's already standing, but there's this vibe. Like something stands up inside him. "Mikey Foretrack ate Mikey D'Angelo."

Arco waves her groupies over and they're padding in, soundless. Then for some reason they've all started doing extended finger pushups. You can smell the meditation coming off them. Makes an old and lonely mountain smell like a plugin air fresher. Some punk's like, "You can't eat people in here."

Then some punk's like, "Why are you always Mikey?"

"Hey, listen," says Donn. "Mikey can't come to the phone right now. He had more names than any punk I ever met. In our time zone, if you diy by getting killed? It's on your friends to do the list of names. You can't stop half down the list or you might get lost, you know? And then we talk bout our feelings. And then we feast out on the meat, and diy with the rest of the parts. Oh. And Mikey always keeps a form of Mikey cause it honors how Arco's always Arco."

They're all still doing pushups. Listening with their chins up, bobbing their heads onefully, meeting his cadences with their eyebrows. When Donn's words run out, some punk's like, "Crash trash eat that stuff in every dimension. We don't do it. We got the straight edge."

"That's okay," says Donn. Raffia's like, "We're not crash trash."

Some punk's like, "No, you're in our house. You gotta eat him outside."

"—ate Mikey Trashbaginhaler," says Mikey. "Shit, hold on. Listen, arcos, we really preciate how you're putting us up, and your intense ethic is like inspiring, but we've got to do this. And we've been awake way long, like just fighting and having ventures, and crossing the time stream, we're still drying off even, and like, hosfatality—"

"Eat it in the rain," says the same kid.

Raffia's like, "Fuckoff." Eyes heaving back open, she jackknifes upright from the planter.

"Any one of us could destroy you effortlessly," says some punk in the back. By now the shadow kids surround them entire.

"Mikey? Do we gotta finish the spiel before fighting?" says Raffia.

Ballcap talks out from the crew. "Arco."

Arco goes, "What?"

Some other skin sounds just like ballcap. "Why are you hanging out just watching them break edge?"

"They're not edge even," says Arco. "They're my band."

Some punk clobbers ballcap on the ear. "Arco'd kick out the non-Arco Meatheads of X. Arco wouldn't just talk and watch."

Ballcap turns round with a headbutt. "Arco'd splain what was up first. Arco wouldn't go too fast fighting. Arco wouldn't be an asshole."

"No shit?" says Arco.

Mikey's mouth opens and there's a steeltone whisper. Margin Walker rousing a little from its sheath. His lips peel back and he's grinning.

"We don't eat anybody here who might of ever thought impurely. We got the straight edge." Ballcap's bleeding from his forehead, his buddy's tooth embedded in the wound. "Thoughts of fucking, doing math, trippy thoughts, overly recursive thoughts. There's a list if you want."

"No," says Arco.

"So, like, how do you know my thoughts weren't all pure and shit?" Mikey toes the Morgan Donor carcass in its vacuous grin.

"No, for we were acquaintated before Arco's passaginging, Mikey of Meatheads." Some skinhead's pushing sideways through the crowd. He presses his amputated fingertips together. "Jointly we buzzkilled the pacificationation of our senses!"

Mikey's like, "What?"

Punker climbs onto a couch. Fingers still joined together, looming over Mikey like he's ready to spring. "Like that time after the Man on Rye show when I injected rum in your vagus nerve!"

"No way, you're Matt Finish?" Mikey reaches up, splays his fingertips across the kid's cheekbones. "I didn't recognize you without the poptop tabs in your eyesockets."

"We took off our names." He's pulling outa Mikey's grip.

"You still got that pet newt?" says Mikey. He starts walking a hand through the air. Lands on buzzkill's hip bone, keeps moving. "You and that newt were inseparable."

Buzzkill's like, "I ditched the newt."

"Mikey of Meatheads of Dimension X means to work you," says ballcap. "But he just had brain surgery, arco. You shouldn't butt his head."

"Saaaiin brurgery, duuu-huuu-huooy." Mikey's working his hand down the back of buzzkill's jeans.

"Shut up. It's not. It's not straight edge to keep a newt there." Buzzkill's eye tics twice. He tries to back up but three of his friends are already standing disinterestedly on the planter behind him. "Fuck!"

He whiplashes his whole body forward, ploughing his forehead toward Mikey's nosebone. Mikey bends forward and catches the hit brow-to-brow. Giggling while they grow identical mauve hematomas. He's like, "I missed your good headbutts, man."

"So who do you guys eat, anyway?" says Donn. "Doesn't it smell like spam in here?" He pinches his lower lip. "You can't eat pigs, right? They always think bout fucking."

By now the arco kids are pressed in so tight, Meatheads are back-to-back among the planter futons. Raffia's sitting on Morgan Donor's stomach, making the dead punker's dick puffenate and stand half up.

"We eat yuppies that never had impure thoughts in life," says ballcap. "Like with their brains messed up. Those big head wheelchair yuppies you find sometimes. Sometimes we eat one a nother."

"Okay, so why aren't you super skinny?" says Donn.

Some punk goes, "We eat beans and shit to keep from starving." Then the crowd parts to let in some heaving dude with a bathtub wheelbarrow full of katanablades. Some in their original tarp and cardboard scabbards, some in greasy banana leaves. One motion, he tips them into a pile round Arco's feet and bows.

"Arco? Arco? Arco?" says heaving dude. "Like, if hardcore were liberated from mind? By what method would it operate?"

Arco's up to her shins in the spilled blades, breathing heavy. She whispers something despairing. No words you know. Her hand's moving at arcospeed, drawing steel from the pack behind her.

∿∿∿

Here.

∿∿∿

So heaving dude's leaned into her stroke, right? Caught the bladeflat sideways across his skull with a broad crack to match his spreading grin.

Or else Arco twisted her arm on purpose. Or this swordblow itself exemplifies the operation of hardcore liberated from mind. Or else that pale blue steel jagging like a milk thunderbolt, back in her venturepack already, that's Straight Edge, nobody's blade, refusing to cut lightened flesh.

Or else it's fucking everything at once.

Heaving dude's eyes cross and he's all like, "Thanks." He crashes backward into the bathtub wheelbarrow and the arcore kids whoop and lift it on their shoulders. Someone goes, "Here's my hardcore, can you make it mellow out?"

Now bruised eye's pushing through them. Little and wispy, utterly focused, like a punk congealed of smoke. She leaps and punches the bathtub wheelbarrow's underside. Everybody freezes and all the shards of avocado paint flutter to the floor while the tub rings like a belching gong.

"STAND DOWN, POSERS!" Her fists balled in the air, her choppedoff middle fingers standing clear as bars against fuckall. "NOBODY'S BETTER THAN YOU!"

The arcore kids all step back, collectively muttering. She's like, "YOU'RE SO DESPERATE! YOU THINK ARCO EVER GAVE ONE BOUT THE FUTURE? YOU THINK YOU KNOW WHAT WAY SHE CAN HELP YOU? YOU NEVER EVEN SAID HI! STAND THE FUCK DOWN, YOU WANT MEATHEADS TO MURDER YOU? CAUSE THEY'RE CHRONIN, THEY'RE HARD AND SHIT!"

Raffia's bent over herself. Her laugh sounds like birds shattering against the high keys of a piano. All the arcore kids start backing into the doorway and the hall, and then bruised eye goes over with the volume down and says Arco and her crew from Dimension X need a good night's sleep, they're really tired. So these kids ventually file off to do more pushups or whatever.

Bruised eye's standing by the doorway as her crew peels out. "Hey, arco." And it's the fuckedest thing. Arco doesn't even turn her head, but the form known as ballcap comes back in.

"Bandmate," says bruised eye. She takes two steps and she smashes ballcap in the eye. He staggers once, straightens, bows.

As he's walking out he touches the flesh beneath his eye like in wonderment. Punker's got a fist like a carved amber knot. Like something to wear at your throat. Something to remember, something to pass down the line. You know what, don't worry bout it right now.

∧∧∧

"Part of me likes you," says Raffia. "You're such assholes."

"Back then when I was yelling? You were the asshole of my mind." Bruised eye stops, and then she's like, "I'm sorry for my friends. I hope you don't think I'm a leader. Like, I hope it too much. Do you want to finish the name line thing and consume Morgan Donor of the Darby Crash Band?" She crinkles her eyes. "I thought bout it. It's you eating him, it's not us. So it's not actually an edge violation for you to eat him in here. We just never had friends over before."

Mikey's like, "We're pretty sleepy. But yeah. Sleepy helps."

"Yeah," says bruised eye. "I can't, like, watch, can I?"

"I think that would be really cool," says Donn.

"Okay. Really?" Her fist pushes her thigh. "Arco? Can I just touch you?"

Arco's like, "If you want."

Bruised eye stands on tiptoes. She touches her forehead, soundlessly, to the other. A smile washes and recedes on punker's face. Say rock, say roll.

"The fake zits piss you off," says the little arco.

"Yeah," says Arco. "It's just my ego, though. You're not pretending to be me."

"We're practicing." The smile's there and gone again. "You showed us."

"Arco?" says Donn. "What are you always practicing? You know, like when you're. Like. When you're not practicing anything else."

Arco takes so long to answer, you think maybe she's tired after all.

"I have to be ready. In case I show up."

Guess that's pretty heavy too. But then bruised eye stands way back, and they get going.

∧∧∧

If you had time you'd use down every bit of him. String longbows with the troutcolored tendons that run down from the cheeks of his ass. Push out his ribmarrow with a coathanger, spread it on crackers and diy birdcalls of his hollow bones. His tanned eyeballs caddies to ride the edges of cerealbowls. Toast the septum for a pocketsize coke trowel and the scrote a dicebag in your scabbard pouch. The brains to tan patches from the tough hide on his shoulderblades and the cavitated black toothaches to stain diy upon those patches glyphs of bands you'll never hear again. *FEAR. BAD BRAINS. MDC.*

MIKEY DIYED CONFUSED.

You've got his graybrown lungs spitted over the hot burnbarrel coals. Ripped into nodes, they look like fern fronds sculpted in sausage meat. So bite open an ancient paper tetleybag. Sprinkle the black dust down.

You don't have time for shit. You're on the road.

"Punker never even tries to be real," you say. Slide one prong of your corpse's antenna bihawk up and down.

You're like, "You mean you, right?"

They say to diy every part of a yuppie too, but that's not for respect. More just to keep the buzz going, same way you drink every part of a beer. So it can't be the steak body you're honoring. Not punker's old spiels and memories, the mind steak. They're your band anyway, not tied to the dead, and you'll use those down the same.

You're like, "I hate that. He won't stop looking for the best way to feel. Til it's not bout what happened. Believe something new like putting a shirt on. Man, I shouldn't of let Darby tell me I deserved to know the truth." You stop. "I should of just ate the sandwich."

"You are talking bout you," you say. "Dumbass."

You're like, "It feels gross knowing I'd ditch and run off just outa stress."

"Forget it. There used to be dinosaurs." You squeeze your wrist. "Right here. Right here, there was dinosaurs."

"Yeah?" you say, and you go, "They were roaring."

It's not your bandmate's consciousness you honor. Cause that part's threaded cross the whole universe, not even running down, and you can't hurt it and never ever help it, and under the mind steak that gives it form, it's nothing special at all. Not the history of a friend, cause the past won't ever bow to your respect, not til it's too late. Not til history's gone.

There's not a nuff for a meal, but this part's not sposed to taste good anyway. You pull the charred and shriveled nodules of your lungs apart. Hold them in your fingers, tearing clumps away. The emphysema vacui pop in your teeth like fish eggs, squirting orange grease.

You're like, "Hey, there's something stuck in mine."

"Fuck is this shit?" you say.

You're like, "Sorry."

Is there gotta be something you honor? Maybe it's all a sploratory mission. Looking under and under for whatever's left after we diy. The joke we came from.

"Dude?" You chew and chew. "These are so stale."

"I thought they were tumors." Spit one in your hand. "How'd you get filters in your lungs?"

You're feeling underneath your leather, greasy fingers probing your ribs. "Sorry."

You're like, "Nothing in my straight edge says I can't chew filters outa my friend's lungs."

You pack the fat orange headband and the meteorhammer and the patches off your jacket. Crack out the dozenous car antennas from the little boreholes down your skull. You're the only one who swallows the filters, and your reasoning's obscure. So here's a nother secret. For once the legend doesn't even know. Nobody decides to go on tour. You don't even stop deciding and go. All you can do's notice the road, and if you could honor hardcore, that'd be how. You're already on tour. You're already on tour. Your hardcore's already gone by.

〜〜〜

"Hey, I just thought. We didn't do a band reunion. Right?"

"Fuck. We forgot."

"I remembered. We were just busy."

"Darby's gonna come."

"Whatever." And then punker's like, "Meatheads."

"Meatheads."

"Meatheads."

"Meatheads."

You're the one broke up the band this time. So they all get to spit in your eyes while you laugh.

〜〜〜

In the bedroom, since forever, there's always been this walnut bookcase. It's stuck down with fingerlength rivets, slanting wastedly with the grade of the sunken floor. Nobody lives here now. Donn's old ace doubles and microfiches and integrated receiver schematics are sprawled all over the floor, and Darby's sitting in the top shelf, still and chill as a painted wood junkie, solo hand gripping one side of the wood.

Anna's leaning on the other side, slitted eyes on the doorway. But it's her who talks. "I never used to have to change my mind." She puts a hand out flat, like to shade out the view, then brings it down to her hip.

Darby's like, "Say it."

"I mean that's brain surgery leftovers on the wall." Anna Complice points through the doorway. "They are back. That's what I mean. And I'm back too."

"Yeah." He's got a gravitybong clutched between his knees, a plastic halfbottle mostly submerged in a bucket of blood. There's a little clay pipebowl caulked into the bottlecap. "Say her name, Anna."

"Fine," says Anna. "Raffia. Raff. I hope they're talking out Morgan's ghost. We couldn't of done that right. The fuck did you bring me here for?" She fingers the cord loop holding her topknot. Braided palm fiber, nothing peculiar. Just a raffia tie.

"You get anxious when you can't act. I wanted you to feel that." Darby's biting the corner off a little bag, pouring powder into the bongbowl. It's a dimebag of cake flour.

Anna slams her head backward into the wall. Plaster buckles tectonically, the bookshelf sways, and Darby's like, "You came to me when your band selfimploded. You said you had nothing left to be. Now leave if you like, and stand with them. I put out the call to pick sides. You're not free of that call."

"You're full of shit," says Anna. Darby's like, "Light."

Anna scowls and digs out a red bic lighter. She snaps the flame over the bongbowl. The powdery flour flashes orange and holds it, a monochrome dust of fire. Darby's slowly pulling up the submerged halfbottle so air sucks down through the bowl, filling the bottle with dense smoke.

"Ask me for something," says Darby. Anna's like, "What?"

Keeping the bottle's cut edge barely submerged, Darby unscrews the bottlecap bowl. The heavy smoke bobs and rocks inside the bottle's rim. He bites down round the bottlemouth and lifts the bucket with his hand, forcing the bottle back into the bucket of blood so all the smoke floods into his lungs. Then he tips the bucket off his lap, and everything else floods on the floor.

"Fuck," says Anna.

Darby's breathing out and he's still breathing out this seemingly infinite cone of moldylooking smoke and flour flecks. Like, this gaseous dough. It fills half the room, growing larger as it disperses. His eyes are drippy red. He wipes his nose with his wrist and he's like, "No, you never asked me for anything. Not even smokes or a place to crash. Ask me for something."

Anna just bludgeons her head backward again. Moderately affecting the exposed concrete. Darby says, "You have to."

"Tell a story," says Anna.

Darby licks his lips. His nostrils are caked with flour. "You're finally grieving Morgan. You wish you never stopped partying with him." Sends out his hand and grabs a red raindrop as it leaks from the ceiling. His fingers smearing the rain like a bug. So many floors stacked above. "But do you want bullshit? Or something how it really was?"

Anna pauses. Eyes closed, head tilting back. Like a breathing exercise, but she's not breathing. "Who cares what I want," she says. "Tell me something that happened."

"Sit with me," says Darby.

Anna just stands with her hands behind her. "Not like that," he says.

So she sits against the side of the bookcase, where she can stare at the doorway as he talks, and her fingers can play on the leatherhilted roofinghammers in her hands.

〜〜〜

"I told this to Mikey once." Darby's mouth stops, like something delicious flew in. "When? Must of been I told Morgan. I got this acid connection from a phone number on a wall in the school library shitter. It was the girls' room. I had this thing where I'd kick down the kotex machine and sell the tampons during lunch hour. I've totally still got three hundred and forty kotexes somewhere."

"I use dreadlocks for that," says Anna. "What's a phone number?"

"You don't know what a phone number is?" says Darby. She's like, "I never paid tension."

"Every number you put in a phone, you'd get somebody different," says Darby. "Didn't matter if you knew the number. Their phone goes off, right, and then you're talking. Even though they're not there."

"Ghosts." Anna shakes her head.

"This number was six six six—ah, you don't like numbers," says Darby. "I didn't know it was an acid number, calling. But that's what I wanted so I asked for it. In a convincing tone of way, you know. I told the phone voice John said I could have unlimited acid. Strictly for testing purposes."

"Who's John?" says Anna.

"Oh, that's just the name for a yuppie," says Darby. "He asked me how I got the number and I got very catty. I cut in every time he stopped to think. Kept saying the name of John, right. I said I wanted this deal set up where they left ten sheets of acid a week in the kotex machine. I said I didn't care, get a key cut for it. So he said he'd check with John. I said if I had to go over John's head and talk to the McReagan ministration, there'd be complications. It's easy, right. It's the same as hitting somebody. There's always this point where they stop to think. That's where you hit them again.

"So, like, I'd still accept free acid off my other connections. Cause I liked the attention, but ten sheets a week, I finally had a nuff to teach my own classes at Uni High. You know? I didn't have as much time as the stablishment, cause they set the schedules, but acid's nice for compressing time. We'd stand out by the dumpsters and I'd plant specific thoughts in peopleses minds. So they couldn't pay tension in corporate ethics class, right. But couple months down the line, Pat comes up to me. I mean Pat Smear, not the bass player Pat or whoever. He found the advance placement chem teacher's briefcase, it was under a desk or whatever. We broke the lock together and there's ten sheets of blotter acid held with a red paperclip. It was so fucked we started laughing. The principal of Uni High was John that year."

"That's what you're like. I know what you're like," says Anna. "I should of asked for something that made you give a shit."

There's a breathing quiet in the room. Darby Crash nods with his eyebrow.

"Cause this'll go down fucked. You act like I don't know what our names mean," says Anna. "But they'll come like you wanted them. They'll never not be sammrye. And I'll diy in your service soon, I'll welcome it. You think there's no reason I never asked you for shit?"

"No." Darby laughs. The bookshelf wall, it's broken where he touched it. Where he just touched it. "Hardcore of dead times. Burning solo, four in one. It's all I ever wanted, to see that again."

Anna's like, "You want all sorts of shit, man. Fuck knowing what happened. I don't even know who you are."

He's still laughing. Then he stops. Darby brings up one leg, circles it with his arm. It's the first time he looks at Anna Complice. "You would say I know?"

"Was Pat Smear even real?" says Anna.

"Yeah," says Darby. "Yeah, of course. Course he was."

Anna stands and lays her fist into the dented wall. "So then he was your best friend."

Darby's like, "I don't know actually. Sometimes. Mostly in high school."

"He'd of said he was?" says Anna, and Darby makes a weird motion with his hand. Like he reached for the other one. "Most of the time."

"You told Mikey you called Pat Smear from the morgue phone that time you and Casey Cola tried to OD," says Anna. "Not any of the fatass valleygirls you were using for car rides. Pat didn't even have a car, but he drove up with new jeans. And you didn't ask, but baby wipes too. How'd he diy?"

"Fuck." Darby looks at the ground between his legs. "Fuck, fuck, fuck, fuck, fuck." Like there's different definitions, every one. "I can tell when somebody thinks they're getting strong. Not cause they go their own way, or try to take my place. They think they see through my kung fu. They think it's, like, this game I play. Like the real me's underneath. They try to pity me."

"I—" says Anna, and Darby's like, "I know you serve. Kids get to thinking they know me."

Then Darby's bounding up from the bookshelf. As he stands, his one leg shoves behind Anna's knees. His shoulder decks into her collarbone, side of his head smashes her chin, and she's tripping backward into the blanket pile. Darby halfstumbles forward with the momentum, stands over Anna with his toe planted in the pit of her throat. Her face is always kinda red. Still, it's turning red. Capillaries in her eyes slowly exploding. Her shouldermuscles bulge and she grabs for his ankle. As he's bending forward to put more weight on, her hands drop, she tucks them behind her head. And her lips say, soundless, "Do you want me to fight back?"

Darby steps off her. Just as soundless. He sits on her belly and closes his eyes and starts rubbing his own scalp with his fingers, like the outro to a fancy haircut. Anna's upper torso convulses once. She pops her larynx back into place with two thumbs, then she coughs. Coughs again.

"You're okay," says Darby.

"Yeah," says Anna. "Donn and Mikey. Used to go off bout compassion." She coughs again, harder. Red foam at the corners of her lips. "I would always think, what's the point."

"You do it or you don't," says Darby. "If you showed compassion, it'd be through fighting anyway. Fighting on my terms or yours." He looks up, but not at her. "Don't worry bout compassion, golden girl. You're not responsible for that. Something got fucked. Not with you. But like way long ago. Other kids have reasons for their weird trip. But I looked. There's nothing under me."

"Looked where?" says Anna. Darby's like, "Here. I'm gonna show you the hardcore of the universe."

He stands up and pulls his wallet. It's just a leather flap the color of skidmarks and lint. He unzips a pouch and pours out a handful of change.

"Heads," he says, and then just throws the coins all over the ground. Anna's not looking at first. You can float in and count them. Tails. Tails. Tails. Tails. Tails. Tails. Tails. Tails. Tails. Tails. Tails. Tails. Tails. Tails.

"Arco could of done that. Sept she'd of called it right." Anna sneers, but underneath it's a shiver. Anybody could see.

"Nobody could of done that," says Darby Crash. "Like, a lot of kids have the same mistake, Anna. They think the universe is some particular way. As if some ultimate principle could clarify action."

"What, you're gonna read sections from your diary?" says Anna.

Yeah, there's some space.

∧∧∧

They pushed the four planters together, undid a couple tarp scabbards from the swords. Hung one tarp up over the doorway, wall twigs pinning fast its rusty eyelets, and more tarps for sheets and tarps for shitty blankets on the giant mushroom bed. Meatheads curling together, their pillows split logs. There's a low fire set in a clippedoff burnbarrel, dried tree boughs and goops of the dead Mikey's fat, and to make it smoke nice, cinnamonsticks and fingerbones.

"Out there nobody talks bout hardcore. Like there's nothing to talk bout." Bruised eye swigs from a narrow clay bottle.

"We talk bout it," says Mikey. "Arco won't shut up bout it."

"That's the one, but not." She's sitting on a flipped plantpot, arms crossed low over her belly. "Hardcore means how punks do things." Bruised eye shrugs. "Diy our gear out of scraps, fight in the drinking lot. Blow up stories to honor our friends. Spikes in our hair. We talk bout that hardcore. The word Darby came up with in history. But past that. There's the hardcore you're barely good a nuff to feel."

KISSSH-KURSSSSH, says the flaming barrel. Raffia looks like she'd say something but then she rolls over, face into Donn's armpit.

"Sometimes we'll say our hardcore moved us," says bruised eye. "That's the hardcore outside your mind, the one we don't talk bout. To found a band. Or commit to an edge or to break it. That's not the same as standing up your hair. Nobody invented that hardcore. Or if Darby did, we have no chance at all."

"Arco won't shut up bout that one neither," says Raffia. Voice muffled in Donn's dry armpit. "It's there. Stop talking."

Bruised eye nods. "Everything's beyond talking though. A million words won't get you one rebar. You can't get any spiel perfect, but you can work on it. Why's hardcore different?" The little arco swallows something. "This tarp's shitty as a blanket. Looks like it works though."

"Weird hardcore, to be a shitty blanket." Donn smiles. His cardboard goggles pushed up on his forehead.

"As an old tarp it's prefab," says bruised eye. "As a shitty blanket it's diy. It's simple to line out the hardcore of something we've made. A tarp's got no ego to get in the way. Hey, Donn O'Aural of Meatheads of Dimension X. Can I ask you a question."

He's like, "I'm just Donn. I'd only be Donn of Meatheads if we were on tour."

"That's why I said it." Bruised eye looks into the smoke. "Donn? What kind of thing is a punk's hardcore?"

—On your way out pay a nother dollar.

This is the only one.

You're not gonna see it again.

Donn shakes his head with sudden force. "What, really?"

"Course," says bruised eye. "Sorry it's a non smoking house. I remember how it's good to smoke when you talk bout hardcore."

"Wow. Yeah, I guess. It's like a blade," says Donn. "I mean, mind is. Or, you know, everything is. But mind is more like everything than anything. There's an edge that leads it."

Arco's eyes are completely clear. Sometimes that means she's asleep.

"Like, there's consciousness moving forward against time. They talk bout diying every breath and always being new. Part of that is consciousness consolidizing into memory. Cause consciousness is like the cutting edge of memory," says Donn. "Hardcore's like that. But it's further ahead."

"Like the edge on the edge. You're trippy." Mikey sits up and reaches into the burnbarrel with his hand. Fishes round and comes out with a scorched middlefinger, knucklebones and flesh shreds held together by Morgan Donor's sinew. There's a flat orange ember for the nail's bed. Mikey gives Donn the finger. Diy every day.

"It's the swing that's really out in front," says bruised eye. She swigs again from the clay bottle. Licks red all round her lips. "Anybody want some blood?"

Donn tokes off the crooked, bony finger. The nailbed glows and hollows, speckled by a lattice of ash. "Well, like, say consciousness is the moving edge of memory. So it's the present, cause it's the difference between the past and the future. But consciousness can't make things happen. The forms of the universe morph across consciousness while it just hangs out and beholdenates like a tourist." Donn stops for a really long time, spinning the finger in his hands. "Sorry. I just never talked bout this before. It's just. Like. Like, there's a nother edge makes things happen. It's the edge of action, and it's just close a nuff ahead so sometimes you can feel it. Sometimes. Only when you've been diying."

Raffia turns over, covers her head with the log pillow. Then Arco's like, "No. Keep going."

Doesn't Arco not give orders or something? Whatever. Punker never stopped going anyway. "We think mind moves forward," says Donn. "But memory's the only thing it actually has to work with. Mind's only facing backward, ever. Cause perception's only bout the past, same way as memory and night skies and stuff. Mind can't keep up with what's coming, it just moves back and forth in the past, and we think we follow our hardcore. But hardcore's the only thing that's even moving itself, and it feels to us like the skinniest ghost. But that's cause mind's the ghost, and hardcore isn't part of it. Not part of us. It's always in the future." His eyes are opening and opening. "We're not with hardcore. We don't know what it wants. That's what they call 'you weren't there.'"

You just hear Raffia growl. "Don't talk bout hardcore."

"What, Raff, you got a spiel bout it?" says Mikey. Hands behind his head, staring at the ceiling. "You gonna tell us?"

"I actually like that one," says Donn. He's still puffing on the finger. It's crooking harder, bending in on itself.

"Yeah, I do too," says Mikey. "Aw, Raff, you got a favorite story? You gonna tell us your little favorite?"

"She's asleep," says Arco.

Everyone just stares at Raffia. She's growling and gnawing at the log pillow with her teeth. Then she calms down and drools out a mat of crumbled wood. Her eyeballs jiggle behind shut lids. "Don't. Don't talk bout hardcore."

"No, no, okay, check this out. Totally gonna work this time." Mikey stretches his arms over his head, flexing his knuckles. You ever wonder what happened to Mikey's missing finger?

Bruised eye's staring hard at Arco. "I kind of need to, like—"

"It's actually a rad story." Donn yawns. "Raff can just be kinda shy."

"You weren't there." Mikey's putting on a voice like Raffia's. He leans over so his lips graze her ear. "You weren't there." Breathing in sharply, he sticks his fingertips in the corners of Raffia's mouth. She doesn't bite, she just gurgles a little. "You weren't there," he says, moving her lip muscles to sync with his voice. "You weren't there. You weren't there."

"Weren't there," says Raffia.

Mikey pulls his fingers away, staring wondrous at their tips and then Raffia's like, "You weren't there. You know those places you can't even get to."

∿∿

—You weren't there. You know those places you can't even get to. Old people talk bout places you can't get to, not even if you go there. Cause you go there and it's all fucked.

—You mean old times, Raff.

—Donn calls them old times cause he's a scientist. So this one was called Lost Angeles. Same name as here, only that place was too. One fucked part, the shitters had water inside. Nobody was sposed to drink it but sometimes punks did anyway. You'd pull the flusher and the water carried your turds to mcdonalds. Every five million flushes Ronald McReagan would call you to say thanks for being amerikan. A nother fucked part was tours. Bands would come back alive from tours cause yuppies were on an Oki Dog diet and not eating punk steaks. But the fuckedest thing, they weren't posers in Lost Angeles, they really didn't talk bout hardcore. So they didn't need a don't talk bout hardcore spiel.

But anywhere there's punks, anywhere, there's the House of Anything Goes. And this old chick was older than Darby Crash there. She lived in the front attic where she set the floorboards herself. She didn't specialize. She never said shit. She just lived with her hands facing out. The knuckles all pointed fucked ways and there was more scars than skin.

She didn't talk bout hardcore.

So this one afternoon she was sleeping with a beer on the kitchen counter. The phone was her pillow so she woke up. Ian McEye of Minor Threat was talking.

Hey, I think I smell beer through the phone, said McEye. Goes Anything House is straight edge, right? No idea why I'd call you if your house wasn't straight edge. So like, we're on tour. We need a stage for tonight. At least twenty-three feet square. Then we need a nother like nine hundred and seventy feet square for our crew to sleep on. We all got the straight edge and we heard you have the basement where couch surfers go. Minor Threat would play the Whiskey but Minor Threat can't play the Whiskey cause last time our crew physically bliterated it cause of the name Whiskey. We all got the straight edge. We'd go somewhere else but we threw out our address book. Somebody put a bad sticker on it.

How are you on the phone if you're driving, she said. But McEye was gone.

The old chick woke up the living room for a mergency Minor Threat house meeting. Those shows pulled such a big crew, they'd leave all the county's orange groves and chip factories barren for years. They'd plug every shitter and dry out every sink, and if a dog licked one beer puddle anywhere, they'd hold a community court for it. Every venue they ever had became a crusted crater.

I like Minor Threat, said the old chick. They're fucking fast.

Some punk kicked the TV and it started talking news. After a lengthy appeals process, the bliterators tooken into custody at last week's Minor Threat show are getting lectric chaired tonight, it said.

While the House was waking up the old chick did all the dishes. She took back the mountain of bottles behind the washer and dryer and spent the empties money on baby pickles to plant in the bongs. She hid all the sausage patties in a vegetarian broccoli box, she turned the serial killer posters backward and wrote YOUTH CREW and FUCK YOU DO YOUR OWN DISHES on the blank sides. She put new screens in the sink faucets and got the mower engine working on old deepfry oil. Down in the unfinished basement she painted straight edge Xs on the wrists of all the fuckups and bums and new travelers sleeping by the campfire and on the basement stage. Then she woke them all up running over soupcans in the mower blades.

She didn't talk bout hardcore.

After that she sat with the tired bikes on the front porch and smoked. It looked like the House of Do Dishes and the House of We Got The Straight Edge and the House of What We Say In This House Goes, but Minor Threat hadn't showed up.

Then something like a thunderclap hit. She saw this fat glowing bulge shoot cross the powerline, running toward downtown. The transformer tower down the street leaned over and started melting, and flies dropped all over the sidewalk like burning marshmallow bits. Lights started snapping out all through the House, from the green xmas stars in the attic to the giant halogen floodlamp over the stove, and then the streetlights. They came back on shining brown like shit soup, so brown you couldn't tell where anything was.

Everyone climbed the rope ladder to stand on the House's back, where her fists would pound shingles to keep out the storms. They watched the brownout wash cross the burbs of Lost Angeles, oozing brown light like a mud flood up to the roofs of all the houses. Cars were smashing and honk horning all down the block, and over top the brownout, millions of fresh straight edge ghosts streamed round in the dark like kids of lectric gray graffiti.

Could of spaced out the lectric chairings, said some punk. Do we even got room for that much couch surfers at once?

So they had a mergency brownout house meeting in the living room. Passing round a spoon and a peanut butter jar, and flashlights for under their chins to cut through the brown when they talked.

Minor Threat might be so edge but even they can't find their way in a lectric brownout, said some punk. Pass the peanut butter. Ronald McReagan like cancelled the show for us.

Pass the light flasher, said some punk. No, they'll come when the sun's up. You know what, you can't outstorm straight edge, but you can outconfuse it. We need to retrofit the house. We'll bury the bottles in the side yard and put up chore charts and signs. We'll give them a house of orders and regulations.

I already did that, said the old chick.

No, I still have the light flasher, said some punk. We can present rules and ramifactions so impacted they won't know how to step, and then we say their pants are in opposition to us or something. We can outedge them and ban them from LA for infractions, so they won't end up wrecking us to the ground.

I already set up the house with fake order, said the old chick. But to make them feel chill bout playing here. Fuck, I like Minor Threat. Pass the peanut butter.

So they pushed her out the front door and locked her out on the porch. This is a valuable lesson bout cooperation, somebody said through the mail slot. Come back when you're ready to agree.

She sat on the porch rail and smoked and ate peanut butter and looked at the night. The straight edge ghosts were linking elbows in the sky and moshing out boring new constellations. The X, the Apple Juice, the Double X. Then she set the couch cushions on fire. When the porch was burning hard, she put her lips to the mail slot. I'm ready to agree, she said. Now Minor Threat can see us from far away.

Everybody got out and they sat on the yard for a mergency arson house meeting, edging off from the hot burning porch. We should have one of these every brownout, said some punk. Beats not seeing checkers in the dark, and fuck our tape collections.

I was feeling really threatened by the dishes posters in the new house, said some punk. And the best part is Minor Threat can't play here now.

What? Fuck. If you're really not willing, I gotta find them a nother venue, said the old chick. She went through the milk crates under the porch steps and got a bottle of hibachi fuel.

She didn't talk bout hardcore.

You couldn't tell where anything was and the dark was hot and brown like shit soup. *The transformer tower slipped on its side in a puddle of sparks and molten steel. The porchfire lit round her edges like a cutout as she went fucking off with fuel in her hand. That was how it was the night Minor Threat came to LA.*

∧∧∧

The floursmoke's still drifting and drifting. Darby snaps his fingers. There's no sound. "Tomorrow night I think I'll have a reunion show," he says. "With Meatheads of Dimension X. Like, the classic lineup from that night they bit off my arm."

"Get what you want," says Anna.

Now Darby's hand has a budweiser, the tallcan like a painted joint of bamboo. He bites the pulltab open. Stares down the dark keyhole, then passes Anna the undranken beer. "It's a farewell show, too."

"For who?" says Anna. Darby's like, "Probly everyone who comes." She's like, "I know."

"You really don't mind getting killed," says Darby. "No fear."

Anna swigs the entire can, spits hard in the hole. "So?"

"Just it comes to you natural," says Darby. "I like that. Do you wish we could of had a real band? Germs and Meatheads were both way better."

"It'd be different if I wasn't fighting," says Anna Complice after a breath. "I keep my hands going. Are you headed to the House afterward? Or are you gonna stay lucky?"

Darby's like, "I'm gonna try."

"Try for what?" says Anna. "You never try." She spits in the can again. It's sloshing full. "What happened to Pat Smear?"

"Yeah," says Darby. "There was—"

"No, you know what? I don't care anymore." She's walking away. "I'm actually gonna get killed at this show. I should at least try and smooth my thoughts out first."

Darby's shaking his head. "There's no karma, Anna. But get what you want."

"I'll see you tomorrow," says Anna. "Where's the show?"

"Disco hell," he says.

Anna stops for a while in the doorway. There's a noise as she grits her teeth. Louder than the creaking of the dumpstered diy platemail as she shakes her head. Then Darby's alone in the quiet. The muggy night lapping through the window, and the wind. He looks down at his jacket, one completely blank patch among others, and he laughs. He goes, "You weren't there the night disco diyed," and he laughs.

You know how punks don't like to talk bout hardcore, or where you get the milk for pizza cheese. They don't talk bout what yuppies were for real, back in history, their lives. The azathothic grins that split the faces of the dead, or how it makes you feel when Darby laughs.

ᐧᐧᐧ

You weren't there the night disco diyed. It was the olden days. We were smoking weed on the bank helipad, roasting marshmallows on the wind, and Mike More got up there with a grapplinghook. His face was red from climbing.

Bandannas tied on his bandannas. That machete name of Sorry swinging sheathless from his beltloop, it was always chipped from dragging the ground. Siko Miko of Suicidal, his jersey torn open. There's gnawmarks on his collarbones. It was dark but some h-bombs were blowing in the distance, so it was light too. We all thought Mike was gone.

We came up with farewell shows the night he sealed the gates of disco hell. And I don't know who came up with diying like a dog for no reason, but his way was the best. Every punk has to be super afraid of one thing. Mike gave us a good clear pick.

But anyway, he sat down heavy. He was like, A coyote bit me.

His collarbone was ripped up, punks got in there with bleach and bandaids. It looked like stray bone chunks at first, but nope, teeth stuck in there. Silver fillings in them even. So we all jumped back, pressed armament to his neck.

I guess maybe it was a pet coyote, said Mike More. Or like some dentist's pet coyote?

We just stared at him til he was like, Or, okay, fine. Just chop off my body. It was worth it though, I pulled a great joke.

You might not have a ton of time, says some punk. Can you feel your neck where I'm poking it?

He's like, Stop standing there, chop off my body. I don't wanna sell out. Fuck turning into a yuppie and doing taxes all day.

We were all like, You're not thinking right. You need riffs to think, remember?

He said, I thought you guys were my friends. I'll do it myself. So he stood up and unhooked his machete name of Sorry, it was always chipped from dragging the ground. Everybody ducked, that blade was longer than your arm. He swung sideways into his neck and banged the neckbone. And he was like, No, I got this.

Next swing and his head hit the ground stumpfirst. His body was standing there shooting four lines of blood out its neck veins and artery veins. The rest of this shit happened while the body just stood there shooting blood.

Okay, now I can relax, said Mike More. Whispering though, cause he was a head. I put a bikelock on something. I don't remember where though. Can you guys do riffs?

Mike's mind always needed riffs for basic thinking. Back in history his parents sent him to all these sikiatrists offices, but all he did was bite his shirt collars and scream. He got all these low bottomies and nothing helped until his grandma phoned at practice to ask if he wanted to talk about anything. Finally there was riffs so he could think. He figured out his problems and somebody recorded it for the album.

The guitars were on the other side of the roof though, so we just played a tape on this radio behind his head. He didn't turn round to look or whatever. His head was all like, All morning I was staring at that dumb disco tower down the way. It felt weird to me how civilization was burning, but the strobes were still going in the windows and I could hear the bass. Like those disco fucks had backup generators, they were still enjoying stuff. So I was frustrated.

I didn't want to ask anybody for armor so I just went out there. A yuppie bit me in the leg but I said it would be okay. It was dark all through the disco palace, just a bouncer voice in my ear. Asshole said it was a private party. Like, they were disco dancing waiting for the copters, and if you were on the guest list they'd fly you off to Mcdonaldland. I couldn't see good in the dark, and I went down cause they were hitting me in the groin with tazers.

When I got up outside, my leg was sleepy and some asshole in a flight attendant uniform was biting on my chest. So I was like, There's no right to disco. I picked up the flight attendant and I opened the door with my nother hand. She might of bit me some more while I threw her in, I dunno. I put a bike lock through the handles. Went round and did the fire exits. Nobody has the right to disco. By the end I could hear lots of screaming.

That's awesome, somebody said. Lit up a nother joint. I'm glad it was worth it.

Yeah, I guess now I'm on disability though, said the head of Mike More. Do you think I can still use my machete? Like maybe I can hold it in my teeth, and somebody picks me up and runs at shit. And I can still sing if I've got riffs.

Somebody said, No, you need a body to live, Mike More. You shouldn't of dropped biology class. And the head was all like, Listen, man. It was a ninstitutional learning facility. I didn't drop out, I busted out. And all I need to live is that Pepsi there. Turn the riffs back on.

Nobody told him the volume's already on max. But the eyes kept goggling over this sixpack of pepsi sitting under a deckchair. Can I just get one pepsi, said the head. Like, that's really all I want right now.

Nobody got up, we were all high. The body kept standing there, bleeding like a lawn sprinkler. And the head started going, CAN I GET A PEPSI! ALL I WANT'S A PEPSI! I THOUGHT YOU GUYS WERE MY FRIENDS! YOU WON'T GIVE IT TO ME!

Some punk was like, Sorry, this is just kind of fucked, you know? Cause I'm high? But she reached her foot under the lawnchair and slid the sixpack over to Mike More's head. Do I need to open it for you?

The head started rocking back and forth. Tipped onto the pepsis and started chewing the metal apart with its teeth. Slurping and burping. You could see the trachea hole shitting jagged pieces of popcan metal, and the throat veins pissing out pepsi. After it demolished the sixpack, the head of Siko Miko kept telling us to go away and leave it alone so it could think. Ventually somebody put on oven mitts and threw it off the side.

We did some thinking too. We figured there needed to be some kind of procedure for proper farewell shows, or else this kind of shit would keep happening. And not everybody's as hardcore as Mike More, so we should probly capitate them right when they sell out, not before.

They say the bikelock to disco hell's gonna pop at the end of the world. Kids just mostly repeat whatever crazy shit they hear, but they hope that's how it ends. PS, the next day a forage crew found his head. They reported no signs of entry, but the brains were missing.

∿∿∿

"That's not how it—" She snorts and coughs, blinking awake. "What?"

"You felled asleep," says Mikey. Raffia's like, "No I'm not."

"Sorry I've been so fucked," says Arco. "I used to think I got your crew."

"Nobody gets it. We don't." Bruised eye shrugs. A shudder moves at the back of her neck. "It's really okay to act fucked to us."

"Why aren't you freaking out bout Arco?" says Raffia. "Your friends are."

"I kind of am, inside," says bruised eye. "I dunno. There must be something wrong with our teaching. I try not to push it."

"So you don't do the leader thing?" says Mikey.

"Arco leads us," says bruised eye. "We talk bout what Arco would do. But we're not talking bout what you would do right here, Arco."

Mikey goes, "Cause she's from Dimension X?"

"No. No way." Bruised eye presses her knuckles to her mouth. "The Arco made of meat wasn't perfect. Just far along. Arco's a word to us. We talk bout Arco to get our hardcores in mind."

Donn's curled to one side, not at all sleeping. "You wouldn't say that if you knew her."

"Tell me," says the little skinhead, and Donn slips his open hand from under the covers. "She shivers when you blow on the back of her ear."

"Really?" says bruised eye. Donn's like, "Any of us could say a million things bout Arco. I picked one from the middle. We're a band, dude. Like, we're not ideas in your fillosophy."

"You're saying her name when you could mean anybody," says Mikey. "It's kind of cool, but it's still bullshit. We know her better than you. First time we all met, we could hardly walk. Not cause we were drunk, either. All that intense sammrye shit, she puts it up to cope. Cause it's hard when kids look up to you."

"You can't stop loving somebody," says Raffia. Arco's looking at her and she's like, "What?"

"I met her one time." This time the little arcore kid shows some teeth in her smile. This time it holds. How old is she? She doesn't even have boobs. "We teach that Arco will arrive. Arco's not here yet. We don't mean the one you love, who taught us to prepare."

Mikey's saying something else, but Arco's voice cuts in like a sinewave. "That's why I can't give it back."

"When she's arriven in herself, the million things will be gone," says bruised eye. "And you'll still love. You'll love a story of words or an idea of something gone. But there's substance in this. The idea of Arco to reach your own hardcore, which loves."

"Like we're using her like you are. Fuck you guys." Mikey laughs and shakes his head and draws the tarp covers in. His hawks peek from under the blankets, downy, snarled. He's like, "I don't mean that in an angry way, right."

"Sorry for keeping you guys awake," says bruised eye. "I just really need to transmit this special teaching."

"No," says Arco. "It's just the other kids thought they'd get lightened off me. You just wanna talk. We got lost and you took us home. You're smart. You can talk if you want."

Bruised eye hunches forward for a breath. When she talks again it's slower.

"Darby Crash says he knows the hardcore of the universe. What happened to your brain, Mikey?"

Mikey opens his eyes again. "I had this cortex, right. It got punched in a fight and I needed a brain boner."

Donn's like, "Donor."

"You remember that kid who fell off the ladder getting Darby beer, and his head swelled up? And it swelled down and his one arm kept punching everybody, even when he said he didn't want to anymore? Donn, you probly know," says bruised eye. "That part in the middle got broken."

"Yeah, his corpus cavernosum," says Donn. "It's like, a punk has a two hemisphered brain, and each hemisphere handles half the punk with the cavernosum talking between them. That part got blocked by a scar, so the brain lobes couldn't figure out what they wanted."

"Like how you keep Mikey and Raffia talking," says bruised eye.

"Do you?" says Raffia. Donn's like, "No shit I do, Raff," and she covers her head with the split log.

"He had two hardcores," says bruised eye.

Donn shoots upright. Standing on the bed. "Two hardcores?"

"I know, right," says bruised eye. "But busted hardcores perma. They can't get what they need. Cause the hardcore of each side's made in that scar."

"And it's to talk to the other one." Donn's bouncing. They all look at him. He's actually bouncing on the shroom futon. "You mean lightenment."

"Sure." Bruised eye coughs. "Words."

"Like something's lightened if it fits its local environment seamless, right?" Donn sits back down, hugging his knees. "Like some punk fights herself for years trying to bust out between her mind and the world, but her brain's been lightened all along. Cause her brain, or like the nerves of her brain, they do everything they're sposed to do. It's just her mind that got confused."

"I think you're smart too, Donn." The lid on her good eye momentarily dips. "Sorry. I'm really tired. Like, in a sword. You don't talk bout the tang and the edge and the hilt working together. They don't have to work together. They're a sword. Nothing to talk bout til it breaks. We don't think anything's ever hit full lightenment. Cause if one thing does, it all does. We say Arco for short. Cause at a certain moment, she seemed like the closest. That's all. But we mean whatever arrives. Might be a youth crew, or some pro teens. Two dogs fucking. Half of some punk's brain."

"Farandolae," says Donn, really quiet. Staring at the mussy hairs on his arm. Don't worry bout it.

"Darby Crash says he knows the hardcore of the universe." Bruised eye shakes her head. "But nothing's built right. It's all like that scar."

"Arco's built pretty good," says Mikey. "She's got good arm muscles."

"Yeah, I know," says the little arco kid. Motionless now on the flipped clay pot. "All this shit we're saying? It's probly wrong. I'm gonna pass out sitting up. I hope you guys get a really good sleep. You should pass out too. Tomorrow's gonna be hard. If Darby can't find someone, he knows they're here."

ΛΛΛ

"Sorry I'm such a tourist." Bruised eye turns her head. Her face blurs and drifts in the emberlit dark.

Your band's snoring and breathing. Your eyes are open, spose you weren't dreaming. Your voice rings in your head like a thought. "I'm the tourist. I hardly spoke. What you guys said bout hardcore. I never knew there were words for all that. I was just sitting, going through it."

"Words aren't for anything. I'm the tourist. Sitting and bringing things up with words." Bruised eye's leaning forward on the clay pot. Her lips are loose, hanging apart. Her teeth are really dark, or else they're saturated red. No, she's totally bleeding. Something internal. "No matter what you say. It comes out fucked. That's why we don't talk bout hardcore." A dark glossy line runs down the side of her chin. She licks it away. "I just thought I'd try. Cause I can't stop from thinking."

"No, I'm the tourist." You reach down from the planter, touch your backpack. Running parallel to the left shoulderstrap, the sword's long outline in its bullhide sheath. "I broke edge. I must of broke it a lot on the trip. I got all stressed cause they weren't going fast a nuff for me. My mind was hungry and I don't even remember all the places I broke it. I was speaking measures of time. I was staring right at signs of words. Think I even told Mikey an order. It's just. Like. Now it's a nother secret."

Bruised eye straightens up. She's looking right at you with this wide streaky smile. "That's so cool."

You're like, "What?" and she goes, "I never met anybody who broke edge before. I wouldn't ever have the guts. You know it's alright, right? You and like Meatheads made it back from the burbs. You were the only ones. Even if you never did anything else, that'd be a nuff."

"I've got all these secrets now." You're holding one arm low across your stomach, Arco. From hip to hip. Same way she is, see? She's not copying you. "Like, how we're trying to bring down Darby Crash. And we're hiding here. And the having secrets secret, and the secret of I'm not edge anymore. And that one means it doesn't matter if I tell them or not. It doesn't feel like it should be anything anymore. But it's bigger than ever."

You breathe in. Find yourself smiling in the shape of her smile. Think bout the blood she must taste, Arco. The soft blood rising like heartburn in the back of her throat. You're like, "Can I tell you something?"

"I really want you to," she says. "You're carrying Crash steel, right?"

Now her smile hurts you in the belly. You let down your head. "Do they know?"

"My roommates? No. They didn't get to talk to you." She's shivering, shimmering. Only her eyes are steady. "Is it true? It won't cut a punk without desire?"

"I never tried it for that." Your hand's still on your pack. Your hand doesn't move from over the sword. "I only really used it for brain surgery once, and I had to concentrate."

"Arco," she says, and stops. Like your name only means wow and fuck. "Is the blade really laminated in seven different panels? Like soshu kitae style with sendust and elliptical grind?"

"I can't tell shit from the weighting. When I hold it, my arm feels lighter." Your teeth move against each other. "If I let people know, they'd think I was gonna save them."

"No, we know that. Cause you already saved us." She touches under her eye, the taut red bruise. "We'd just get super annoying bout it. I'm sorry, I'm being such a tourist. It's just. Like. I knew you'd come back. I'm not gonna ask to see it or whatever. Straight Edge would cut me though. Either way. I used to think I didn't have desires."

"Yeah." Hands on your knees. Look out into her. "Guess you finally feel differenter from your roommates? Like something special's gonna get lost when you bleed out?"

"Fuck." She doesn't stop shivering. "I wish you didn't guess before I showed you. But that's ego too." And she finally uncrosses her arm from her stomach. Letting go. She makes a little gasp and the shoosh of her blood as it pours from her lap, pooling on the dirt floor. Rolling from the sides of her smile, too dark to be the dark.

"You did the gut cut and sat and spoke the Dharma? That's the hardcorest thing I ever saw." Your band's asleep. Snoring, breathing, they kick around and mumble. You cup your hands together, Arco. "Punker? All changes are irretrievable. A million special things get lost every second, no matter what anyone does. You got to feel this, here. That's what we all get."

"That's not a nuff," she says. "I'm sorry."

You're like, "I'll make sure we remember you."

"Yeah. But I wanted you to do something. Or I wanted to show you something. I can't remember." Her jersey's soaked tacky and black against her stomach. She pulls it up over her belt, and the knifecut beneath, it's longer than Mikey's hand. The ropes of her guts glisten inside her. A bundle coming undone.

"You're okay, right?" You lay a finger against the side of your own neck. "I could use the sword if you want."

"Oh, no, no way. It doesn't really hurt anymore. Just cold. I'd rather hang out as long as we can." She swallows and more of the dark spills from the wide cut under her navel. "Could you touch me?"

Your arm jerks a little. Punker? Were you reaching for your backpack again?

"Anywhere," she says. "I'm just feeling really fucked bout this."

So you touch her shoulder.

Bruised eye leans into it and grabs your arm over and under the elbow. Feel her collarbone move under your fingers. Her fingers leave cold sticky tracers on your skin. She gets down from the plantpot so she's kneeling next to your bed. Presses her mouth to the crook of your arm and just holds there and nuzzles. Her tongue's all cold like a dog's nose. The puffed flesh round her eye's the only thing with a bit of warmth and there's this hum in both your ears. It doesn't come from anywhere.

"Could you touch me?" she says again.

"I am. Sorry." You put your free palm on the small of her back, where her jersey's ridden up. Her back's narrower than yours. Your whole palm strokes in toward her hip.

"Sorry. I'm such a tourist." She laughs with her mouth shut. The breath chuffing on your arm. "I just never did this before."

"I used to be all straight edge. I never have either." No, that hum in your ears, it's a sound she's making. Like she's happy. And your fingers trace inside the wet lip of the knifecut and she's like, "Anywhere."

"It's not even ragged. You cut so smooth. You're so fucking hardcore, arco." Get on your knees to see closer. Here. The ducts of her guts. She arches her back and they push like secret ribbons cross your lips.

She leans down. Her hand brushing your cheek, she puts her bloody mouth on yours. It tastes different from rain. Thicker, more numb. Like this impossible concentrate of sweet fuckall. She starts shuddering and you pull back a little. "It really does smell like bonfire," she says.

You're like, "There's a bonfire."

She nods. "Right." Shuddering slower as you hold her. Like a tide's lapping inside her.

"What are you thinking bout?" you say, after a while.

"Sorry," she says. Her eyes are still so clear. "Bout jumping off a ledge."

You're like, "Hey?"

"We teach this thing." She's easing her back straighter. "We heard you said once. It's never too late. To do the meditation on diying."

Her eyes are still so clear. Like nothing's far away.

"I wanted to tell you at your show," you say. "You had the raddest band. Happy birthday."

ᐱᐱ

Then Raffia looks over and she slams everybody alert and breathless with two spazzing arms. Look through the skylights, it's gotta be noon.

"I didn't want to wake you guys," says Arco.

Bruised eye's sitting in a sunbeam, legs crossed under her. Her back's so straight. Big flies sputter through her lap. She's holding there a pool of stagnant blood, it's colored like the dead bruise on her washedout face. Her back's so fucking straight, her face's one more verse of Darby's grin.

"Fuck, this is real." Raffia's eyes are stuck shut with sleep, but she's testing a hammerclaw with her thumb. "You think we can take everybody?"

"Chill, Raff, it doesn't look like we did it. Like, our style's distinctive." Donn burps, rubs his mouth. "Man. I just thought we'd all be friends. Was she really bummed? I didn't get that from her."

Arco's like, "Yeah. It's really weird."

"Donn, they'll still blame us, these kids are all stupid." Raffia blinks. "Sept for her." She blinks again. "Now they all are."

"So heavy." Mikey's crawling out of bed. He sits on the edge and stares through his latticed fingers. "Man, that stupid smile. Man, why do dead punks smile like that? I hate that smile, man! Makes them look like Darby!"

"What, you never noticed that?" Raffia's pinching hard amber sleepchunks from the sides of her eyes. She yawns and when she throws them cross the room it sounds like a handful of aquarium gravel.

Mikey goes, "I don't wanna look at Darby! He can probly see us through her mouth!"

"Man? Mikey?" says Donn. "What in the combinatorial fuck are you doing?"

Mikey's got a giant katanablade from the heap on the floor, and he's bearing it overhead, both hands. Lips pulled back like a dog concentrating. Hang there for a bit if you wanna contemplate the ineffability of the quenchline. Then he's like "MONDO!" and hacks diagonally down into the corpse's nose. Sinusbones and sinews part like glass and Mikey's stepping away with his hands at his sides. The sword just hangs there, bedded underneath bruised eye's collarbone.

Just above the top lip, the entire grinning mouth slips off her face. Like you hucked a steak at a fridgedoor and it stuck there for a sec. It drops into the blood pool in the corpse's lap. There's one leaping symmetrical splash, and a littler one a halfbreath later, as the tip of her nose falls off.

Might as well write a high koo.

"Arco?" says Mikey. "How do you clean swords?"

"I'll do it," says Arco. She sighs. Reaches out of bed and works it free from the body. "It's a really nice sword."

"Wow. Oh. Wow." Raffia grabs her chin like she'd tear it free herself. Like she'd fling it at Mikey to demonstrate approval. "We're gonna go down, right here, no drama. Just throwing swords."

"Yeah. Our style's definitely distinctive." Donn holds a deep breath, starts cracking his fingers out. "At least we're slept in."

Arco's stroking down the sword with some old underwear. "I'll talk to them."

"They can talk to our split bones," says Raffia. "We gotta hit first. If we pin them in the doorway—"

"I'll talk to them. It's just. Like. She's the only one didn't think I was Lord Buddha." Punker holds out the katanablade, squinting down the edge like a riflescope. No chips you can see. But are you still Arco or what?

"Dude, she totally did too," says Mikey. "Hey, I think Morgan was in my dream. He said he was happy we got to hang out and stuff. And how we talked my ghost off? He said he was glad I talked bout what we couldn't stand. Cause otherwise it's ego."

Arco looks up. "That's ego too."

"I guess so," says Mikey. "Man, now I'm like depressed."

∿∿∿

They pack Morgan Donor's chest cavity with garbage, tape him up and put the pink tshirt back on him. Wipe their hands on the backs of their jeans and rip down the tarp door. All the arcore kids are squatting in the hallway with ketchup squeezers and little tupperware lid saucers. They're participating in some unfathomable ketchup distribution saramony.

"Arco wouldn't do it that way." Some punk swings the weathered plastic bottle. Her roommate takes it in the temple, keeling over graceful, shielding her plate of ancient, brackish, immaculately squozen ketchup.

"Be the ketchup. Be the ketchup. Betheketchup. Be." Blissing into the humming silence, some punk splurts ketchup into a saucer. "Arco? Is this—"

Arco scrunches her face up, staring. "You're not putting it on anything?"

Some punk stands up, plastic squeezer swinging in his scarified fingers. You know this kid too. The dark topknot bunched with wire, how it spikes up through his cut ballcap. See where his best friend socked him last night. A special transgression outside the scriptures. You can't ever tell what comes true.

"Can we have her body?" says bruised eye.

Raffia's humping forward like a legged anaconda, twin roofinghammers gleamless in her hands, and Mikey jumps on her back, she staggers and he's trying to do a chokehold and she's like, "Damn it, Mikey," and she's worked her elbow behind her for the exact same hold while Arco steps forward going, "Your friend did the gut cut yesterday at dusk. She went out with utmostest honor."

"No, we know." Punker traces the rim of his fresh hematoma. "She wouldn't of killed herself without talking it over first." Inside the smashed red of his sclera, the pupil's impressively clear. "We hate drama."

Mikey's easing off Raffia and she grudgingly unlocks her elbow from his throat. She's like, "You don't think we did it?"

Bruised eye presses his tattooed hands together. "You're not fast a nuff to take us."

Raffia's like, "Mm." Raises her eyebrow. "Bet you think you're ready for this." Bruised eye breathes in and Raffia loops a right hook toward his cheekbone. As his hand steps up in the air, she swerves to punch him in the palm. There's a plainly visible shockwave and his arm telescopes backward from the wrist, like an example from a physics textbook.

"Raff?" says Mikey. "How've I never seen that before?"

"I got a really good sleep." She cracks her knuckles like she's fluffing out a pillow.

Bruised eye stares down at his arm. It's way shorter and wider than before, and evenly sweating blood from fingertips to elbow. "Dude, I just achieved lightenment, dude!"

All the arcore kids start cheering.

"What?" says Raffia. "I didn't get shit!"

"No way you could hit me again," says bruised eye. His pores are dripping blood into a potted fig. "It'd be like punching at Arco."

Arco looks over at Raffia and steps between them. Donn pins one of Raffia's arms, Mikey the other. Bruised eye goes a few steps into the room, and then Raffia's dragging them both behind her.

"She held edge to the moment of dissolution," says bruised eye. Not a question, but Arco nods two times. "We weren't sure why she wanted to do the gut cut. But she was making a point to you. Did you get it?"

"Was I sposed to?" says Arco.

Ballcap bows. He grabs his messy wrist and pulls it back out, eyes momentarily unfocusing. When he wipes it clean, it stays clean. "Honored," he says to Raffia. Then he finally looks at the corpse sitting on the plantpot. He seriously bounces forward like a grasshopper to stand before the dead kid. "Her mouth," says bruised eye.

"Mikey? Donn? Could you let go yet?" Raffia sighs. "It's just now we're surrounded."

Bruised eye drops to his knees. "She defied Darby's grin." Lifts the wedge of soaked mouthparts from his dead buddy's lap and holds it by his ear and clacks the jaws together once. The arcore kids are filing in around him, and he stands and presents the relic. "Punker chopped off her own fucking mouth!" He tosses it to them, checks out the katana sheathed by the corpse's side. "And afterward she greased the blade!"

"Yeah! Yeah, she was pretty hardcore," says Mikey.

"Arco, we have a finity of questions for you," says some punk in the back. She shakes her head. "We'd help make breakfast."

Scooping up her buddy's stiffened carcass, some punk's like, "Can we observe your breakfast making and eating techniques?" and Arco's like, "Sure, I guess."

"What, like you can eat your friends, but we can't eat ours?" says Raffia.

Donn goes, "No, I kind of get it, but could we all share, though? We haven't had any breakfast, and midnight snack last night was limited to—"

"Stop talking, Donn," says Mikey. Bruised eye's like, "No."

∧∧∧

At a little cardtable on one end of the foodhall, like the kids' table at thanksgiving dinner, they're munching beans in big unglazed clay bowls. The kind of bowls so diy, you just stroke them with your fingers and every throwmark in the clay meets your mind halfway. The kind of beans so halfass they crunch in your teeth like gelcaps. Figure they meant it that way. Farting means you live in the moment.

All these kids with shaved skulls and greasy lips taking turns coming over, trying to pass Arco a bowl of human flesh, chopped close and fast and salisbury seared. Arco's just keeping one palm held up stop.

"What, you're mad cause there's no sauce?" says Raffia.

The main table's diy of some really old diy bleachers, loominum scaffolds with plywoods laid on top. There's no chairs, these kids stand on the table to eat. One's up on tiptoes, hands folded on his stomach and his clay meatbowl balanced inscrutably on his head, he's going off bout someone called the one who arced out. How she always totally inspired him with her posture while she was doing something called taking out the garbage.

"See, Raff, they chopped her so fine cause she was totally buff and chewy." Bean fragments spray from Donn's mouth as he talks. "You'd be bout like that."

When bowl head's left his tiptoes, Arco just tilts her face slightly. Whoa, all the arcore kids sit down like dominoes. Her brow briefly manifests a crease, the size of the side of a dime.

"Your buddy taught me a lot for somebody I only met once," says Arco. "Even her fuckups were good a nuff to be somebody's guiding principles. She killed herself kind of to impress me. It would of been even awkwarder sept it totally worked."

Some punk's like, "Arco? Is that good or bad?"

Arco shrugs. "It was her hardcore." Meanwhile Mikey's waving his hands, saying the same thing in a big dumb version of Arco's rivery voice. Just that friend mind meld shit. Donn and Raffia bust out giggling, and even Arco grins a little.

Some punk points a finger. "Arco wouldn't do her voice like that."

Meatheads start convulsing. Chewedup beanstuff falls on Donn's leg and he slaps at it, making the bowls rock on the cardtable and then cross the room, somebody's head shoves through the window.

It's hanging in the square of light, mottled and bloodless with a bruise floating blue as a burn round one eye. There's no mouth, just a blunt crevice, this oval cross-section demonstrating layers of stringy muscle and sheared red cores of bone. A stub of tongue droops under the face like a mushy gray eraser and Mikey's pointing, still laughing. "You fuckers all look the same! And like, you cooked the wrong one!"

The skinheads all set down their plates, one sound, one motion.

"Dude, that doesn't explain the sitch," says Donn. Mikey's like, "What?"

"We saw her dead, dude." For some reason Donn's counting on his fingers as he talks. "Why's she at the window?"

"No, what's a sitch." Mikey's looking straight ahead. Fuck It flings in the air like a copter blade.

"Situation," says Raffia. Teeth clenched.

Donn's like, "It's for short, right."

"He must of stoled her head from the kitchen," says some punk at the big table. "He loves fucking with us."

Bruised eye's head pushes further through the window. Shit, that's not a long jointy neck. Head's on the end of an arm. It falls and rolls, denting the clay floor, and then some asshole tips forward through the window to land on five points, palms and feet and chin. Punker's naked and built like a coal golem, skin raggedly callused and stained in layers of soot. Just balancing there dead steady, nose mushed to the ground, ass up in the air. Muscles pull and bunch unevenly cross the wide shoulderblades, but nothing happens, nothing else moves.

No, but Donn, you met this guy. He moshed you over playing sewer hockey once, he picked you up and put you back in goal. And Raff'll talk bout him when she's drunk, how he'll splain the structions of things all these times and bend her fingers to show them the right way. How he knows she can't see far. You put your hand on Raffia's shoulderbone and swallow nothing.

Two arcore kids step backward off the big table. Their paired images jogging careful cross the foodhall, leading with vintage steel.

The visitor cocks its head sideways, setting one cheek against the floor. "I heard the band's back together." Each word discrete, artificial. Like a sculpted cough. "Am I talking okay? Try to chop me if you can hear this."

As the two kids close, it lopes forward on one arm, one leg. Dragging like a broken spider. It's like, "No, wait." Then it's squatting on its haunches, catching a bladeflat on each of its palms and the hard little skinheads stumble. Blink. Each one's speared on the other's katana, and the visitor pushes them over. "You'd do that anyway. Just stand there if you can hear me."

Raff's squeezing the clay bowl so hard her nails are white. You're staring there, Donn, you can feel her whole body shudder. But you're that, too, Raff. Wanting the bowl to crack, so you can stand up and kill something. Feeling the blood thunder in back of your eyes. "Darby, you pointless fuck."

"I can't see either," says the visitor. "It's hard to see in a yuppie. All you can feel is oscillating consciousness. You guys just have to be Meatheads though." It splays out the fingers of its hand, pointing four ways. "You guys have like zero lightenment. No offense. That sword's sure bright, though, Arco."

Eight more kids start rushing the yuppie. Arco's like, "DUDES!" and they freeze. Her hand's in her backpack but then it's not. You stare at her, you bite blood from the inside of your cheek.

"You're right. He's just faking us out," says one. His hands rubbing his forearms. "Who knows where he is."

"Darby can sike into yuppies now and move them?" says Donn. Bruised eye's like, "It kind of sucks in this dimension."

"So we're playing tonight," it says. "Disco hell. Don't worry bout setup. Doors at sundown. You can stinguish the Bo yuppie now."

The stubby stained hand reaches up, taps the side of his nose. Then Bo's upright, streaking for the skinheads just like a yuppie would. Arco's in his way like she never even had to move. Taking him apart with fucking Margin Walker, zigzag slices like he wasn't even there, the wedges of his flesh falling and not bleeding as you're careening forward with your arms out.

Fall on your knees. Shivering, trying to breathe. You're trying to sheathe your own hand, shoving your hand among hammers in your bandolier. Don't look at her. "Fuck. You could of let me deal with him. You weren't friends even. You didn't know him even."

"Sorry." Arco dips her head. "I've got too many reflexes."

"We're playing the show, right?" says Mikey.

Arco's like, "Well, we could use the practice."

∿∿∿

They're eating crunchy beans in handfuls from the big bean tureen. It's almost like they need energy for something. "You know everybody at the show's doomed," says Mikey.

Donn scarfs and swallows and turns halfway round. Stretches his twined arms over his head and his arms do stretch, tourist. Maybe Donn's bones are actually sewn together with rubber bands. "Nobody's doomed," he says.

"Darby just wants closure," says Mikey. "He wants the biggest farewell show so he's throwing in the entire decline of western civilization."

"Who cares?" says Raffia. She's holding Bo's hand, she's smeared her eyes with his soot. Gnawing at the raw wristjoint and breathing through her teeth. The arcore kids glaring, keeping way back.

"It's okay to diy like a dog without achieving your aim," says Arco. "We don't even aim, Mikey. We're ronin. Remember we want the same as Darby."

"Fuckedest thing in the world," says Mikey. She's like, "Punker." She grabs the crook of his arm really really hard. Like a reassurance, almost. But you could sew a wallet with the bags under Arco's eyes.

Donn goes, "Hey, arcos, how'd Darby get in here for the head?"

Bruised eye shrugs with his hands. "We strive to practice due diligence. But we're still us. Darby Crash invented consciousness and made Lost Angeles diy."

"You really believe that?" says Raffia.

"No, look," says Mikey. This with no scorn at all. "Do you believe that?"

Bruised eye shakes his head yes, spooky and slow. "Arco? What did he say bout a sword hardcorer than you guys?"

"Margin Walker?" Arco unsheathes a couple fingers of pencilcolored blade. Shit, she forgot to clean it. Her eyes jerk to Mikey's.

He leans forward before bruised eye can say anything. "Sweet sword, hey? It's vintage jewelsteel, like from the vegan smithworks of Ian McEye. There's sposed to be a single piece of crabgrass running down inside the blade, like for balance. That's probly why it burns so hardcore to yuppies."

Mikey boots Arco's ankle. She nods and he's like, "She needs it for tonight's the only thing. Or she'd let you borrow it. But hey, we gotta go. We gotta practice."

"Really? Ow, my ankle," says Donn. Raffia's like, "Yeah. We gotta go. Bye."

"You guys are coming to our show though, right?" says Mikey. "I mean, if you're down with couch surfing afterward. And like, the possibility of no afterlife of course. It's just gonna be a really good show."

"Are you shitting me?" says some punk, and some punk's like, "No, you guys are such a big influence. Not just cause you're Arco's band. I saw you once." Her fists at her sides and she looks back and forth like she's daring somebody to doubt her. "I saw you once."

"Good," says Arco. "We probly need your help."

"Even if you get killed tonight, we'll help you somewhere else," says bruised eye. "We're like you guys and Darby. We're in every Dimension X."

"How the fuck do you know that?" says Raffia. Bruised eye blinks. He's like, "How could it be any other way?"

∿∿∿

"**F**uck's sake." Raffia's bare feet pound the cement stairs. "I won't even be here."

"She might be," says Donn. "Like a chance. What else would we do, hang out with people? Practice?"

"I don't wanna practice either," says Mikey, and Arco actually nods.

"Anna Complice." Raffia's voice sticks to the grotty black stairwell walls. "What kind of loser lets Darby pick their name."

They climb a nother couple storeys. When they hit the right landing, stead of a fire door, the rest of the building's missing. Like somebody took a can opener and peeled it away. Meatheads standing there like matchsticks in the little scoopedout gully of landing. Plumed brown ferns and fiddleheads thatch out all round them, rusty in the monotonous sun. The ropebridge's gone. Cross the air, the pizza hippo's burnt black on its concrete wallmount.

Mikey kneels, points at this bridge a couple storeys down. "Think we can jump and go from there?"

Raffia's like, "You're an idiot."

"Wait, is that you up there, Raff?" Donn's pointing at a condo deck, scorched and halfcrumbled, way above the hippopotapus. "That kind of reddish formation? Like, is that you having a nap?"

She's like, "No way that's me."

"Hey Raffia. RAFF! I mean, like, ANNA!" Mikey turns to her. "If you, like, changed your name to something dumb, and then your old band came to visit you between dimensions, would you rather be called—"

Her filed teeth work between her lips and he stops talking.

By then Arco's done working up a slingshot. Not much of a cranium partitioner, just a rubber band on a branch. She licks her finger, crinkles her nose. Lifts and pulls and shoots, all one thing. The pinecone spins languidly, getting smaller, thunking the side of the red shape in the bandoned Ground Zero entrance. The shape stirs. It makes a sound like a haunted lawnmower.

"Hey, how'd a hugemongous crust hog get up there?" says Donn. The hog takes two hops forward. Backs up, two more hops forward. Arching its chest, gobbling threats cross the gulf. Its multifarious bristles and tusks oscillate outrageously and Mikey's like, "Tag it again."

Arco's like, "Yeah, if you want." She whips a nother pinecone through the distance, catching the hog's upper lip.

"Wait, don't shoot it again," says Donn.

The crust hog backs up again, then rushes them as if a bridge existed. It blows out the rusty deck railings and knocks the iconic hippo glyph wheeling earthward and it's dropping toward them, snarling, and Arco's arms blur from shoulder to fingertip as she drops the branch slingshot and hauls out the real thing, slips a lead fishingweight from the pocket of her cheek, she's loading, drawing, and between the hog's red tiny eyes there's a nother eye, redder, and it's still soaring its arc unchanged, the jowls billowing like vacuum cleaner bags, and just a couple handwidths under the landing's edge its snout cracks on the wall and it tumbles down the condo face til the skunky vermillion undergrowth rises like a shrug and gathers it in.

"The fuck was that?" says Mikey.

Arco's like, "I wanted to be kind."

Donn's on his knees, staring down the edge of the building. A spit strand hangs from his mouth, then rises like a yoyo. He lays on his back. He sits up. He's like, "Does anybody know why compassion's always just finding kind ways to kill stuff?"

"Cause fuck this shit," says Raffia. "Wait. Wait." She turns and cracks the wall with a roundhouse kick. "You guys thought I was that? Fucking crust hog? You thought I was that?"

"My mind fell with it." Arco's got thumbs in her beltloops, her headband's coursing out in the wind. Back so straight it looks customized. "You guys feeling ready?"

"Thanks for not pushing the practice," says Mikey. "When I prep for diying I start holding on." He takes a step forward. "It's like punker said though. This is what we trained for. More than the war."

Raffia's spitshining her hammers. Staring at various parts of her big giant arms like an inspection. The way she's breathing heavy through her nose, she really does sound like a freshly awokened crust hog.

Mikey squats. Rests his hand on Donn's neck. All you can see is the flaky black dreads, like a bag of expired snake jerky. "What's up, man?"

Donn looks up. He tilts his cellophane shades. "I'm not holding on, if that's what you mean. Less freaking out counts." His eyes are colored purple under his paisley jogging headband, how long's that been going on. The color of empathy blobs rising in a lava lamp. The color of bamboo sticks from the purple dimension. "At least if we lose. We'd lose together."

"I know, right." Mikey smiles. "We're all kind of shitty alone."

"You guys dropped your pig."

Hey, Anna.

∿∿∿

She pulls herself up over the edge. Turns her grapplinghook in her hands. It's cut from the hog's red pelvis. "Fuck it," she says, and pitches it off the drop.

"How's it going?" says Donn in an even little voice.

"It sucks," says Anna. "Your name still Donn?"

He nods. "We've been having some pretty mad adventures actually."

"I don't bet you meant to come here," says Anna. "Kind of a fuckedapart place."

"We were fighting over if you'd be at Ground Zero," says Mikey.

"It burned down, patchbrain. I was waiting in the lookout tree. Where Meatheads broke up." She points her thumb behind her, the massive papaya on top of the ruined spam works.

"We were just there." Mikey closes his eyes. "Donn knew you'd be waiting. Hey Anna? Are you on Darby's side?"

She's like, "No shit I am. Donn, catch him."

Anna shoves right through Mikey, ploughing him off the edge. Your mouth opens and you're plunging forward too. Hear him going "RADICAAALLL!" while your knees slam the concrete and your hands shoot out to close round the straps of Mikey's spenders. You're tipping forward, he's got more weight than you as he pitches sideways in the air. Where's fucking Arco?

Mikey bobs and scrabbles against the building's side. He hooks his toe on the edge of the ground as you rock your whole self backward. You've got him, you're heaving, dragging him up. Under your shoulders, the infraspinatus muscles feel ripped and numb. Man, you've got a show tonight.

Mikey's hauling his giant lanky body into your lap and you turn your head halfway, Anna's not even looking at you. Your lip curls back, but now you've got time to be Donn again, and cause you're Donn you flash on the systems of other people's minds. Was that compassion, man? Giving you a buddy to save?

Anna's on her tiptoes, jamming her face into Arco's. "You never needed to leave."

"I'm right here," says Arco. "We can't let this get to a fight."

Raffia finally turns. She tips up her head. "We so can."

Mikey's leaned against the crumbling wall, dry heaving over the edge. He rubs at his back. "Not the same Arco, keep your shit together, Dimension X Raff."

Anna blocks at Raffia as she stalks closer. Throwing a palm against her face, not looking. They're the exact same kid, their arms the exact same of long, but somehow Raffia's swings can't reach. Anna's going, "You found the blue sword instead, right? The super sharp lightenment straight edge?"

A tendon twists in Arco's throat.

Raffia's cheekbones are litebrite red, but she's given up swinging, and Anna's like, "Fuck, I called it! You fucking sellout, Arco! Everything was the same til the sword!"

"Punker?" Donn's sitting on the edge, swinging his feet out like some kid fishing off a dock. "How'd you know that?"

"Cause I know her!" Even this, even this, Anna's yelling direct in Arco's face. "You only stayed with Meatheads cause nothing else came up! Listen, the straight edge in this stupid shitty dimension was the pissed off Rollins steel, man! And why the fuck did you guys slay Mikey?"

"He's okay," says Mikey. Rubbing the bulge of transplanted brains like he's working out a muscle knot. Nobody pays any tension.

"Our Arco pulls the sword," says Anna. "And then she's like, I need to take care of this. Cause it's the sword from Mikey's stupid silkscreen, you can't put it back without blood! And she's like, I can't kill my friends, I got the straight edge against killing anybody, I got the straight edge! I'll just wander the fucking earth holding out my straight edge!"

"Wiping a yuppie wouldn't of helped," says Arco. "That's not real killing. It's like cutting up a sofa."

"That's what the other you said!" Anna shoves her in the midsection, and Arco's neck actually cords up. "You're so fucking stupid! You're so fucking stupid, Arco! You never even tried a yuppie! Or you could of cut somebody's finger!"

Arco's like, "Really?"

"No, you fucked off to wander the earth cause you never loved your band!" Anna's pulling Arco's jeanvest collar taut. Seams stretch and rip and now Raffia's sprouting this crazy surly grin, like a shark just freebased a little blood. But then what happens is Anna looks down at her hand, all the little scabs and knurly standing veins, and she lets go and takes a step back. And she's biting her lip. "This won't even help."

"What the fuck?" says Mikey.

"I had to learn how to think comparatively and do deep breathing and like self control myself without you," says Anna. "Isn't that fucking pathetic?"

⋀⋀⋀

"No, gimme both." Anna grabs two smokes from Mikey's fingers. Lights one, sticks one in her nose filterfirst. Lights that one off her mouth smoke, and her free nostril blows a weird double stream. The vein in her temple ticking hard.

"You're with Darby," says Mikey.

Anna's still looking right at Arco. "We needed something to do."

"You mean you needed," says Arco.

"I mean us without you, punker. We trusted you so hard we didn't even chase you." One smoke's already a stub. Anna grinds it in her palm. No burn, just a sickleshaped tar stain. "You ever not had a band, Arco? You get lonely. You get so fucking bored."

"It's okay," says Arco. "You're—"

"Don't say what's okay," says Anna. "You think I'm strong a nuff to stay okay? You fall in with Darby Crash and nothing's funny anymore, and no matter what you do, he's got it so you're trying to impress him. Like you learn everything leads to him for real in this fucking place, and you can't take that back. Morgan was probly happy you slayed him."

"I can't get your forgiveness," says Arco. Anna's like, "You wouldn't ask either way."

Donn's still not looking up. "Why'd you come here at all? Did he send you?"

Anna doesn't answer at first. Mooshing her fist muscles into her cheek. "I wanted to see if I'd try and kill Arco."

"And you can't even try," says Raffia. "I hope I never turn into you."

"Shut the fuck up while she speaks," says Arco.

Raffia blinks hard. Who knows the sound of a straight edge breaking?

"I broke ranks. I came here on hardcore," says Anna. "But I know Darby wants this show a lot. And not just to kill everyone. That time the five of us played? He never stops talking bout it. And I thought I might of been able to sault you, but I can't. It'd fuck up the show."

"You never could of dropped me," says Arco, the blood all pale in her cheeks. "Not before the sword, not after."

Anna's like, "Sword. Lemme see."

Arco draws herself up, and Mikey just goes, "She's in your band, dude."

So Arco unbuckles her venturepack and sits crosslegged into some ferns. Her teeth grind a little. Probly no one but you can hear. Anna takes Straight Edge from Arco's hands and she barely even looks. Just drags the edge cross her forearm, two times, propulsive, like sawing a cello. Arco's jumped up and they're all bugging out but no blood even comes.

So Anna just bows her head. Who's talking? Could be you if you want, tourist. Could be the standing spine between Mikey's hawks, sending out radio waves. —*Those swords don't stop on sweet fuckall sept the skin of a punk without desire.*

"Maybe that's why I showed up." Anna's turned to Raffia for the first time. "Think bout if you want this."

"Dude, you got lightened?" Donn's excitedly feeling her arm meat. "Did you know before you did that?"

"I serve," says Anna. Pulling her arm away. She takes one step down the stairwell. "Darby thinks you've got the Rollins blade. He can see through the burns for real now, it's not just bullshit. I covered mine up." Nother step. She turns the knotted red bandanna at her wrist. "He thinks he can goad you into drawing it, and you won't have anywhere to run, and you'll have to break edge and kill him onstage." Nother step. "I keep secrets, Arco."

Arco goes, "You're in his band and you ducked out to tell us this?"

Nother step. "He wants a fuckedup death. It's fuckeder what you don't see coming." Nother step. "I'd of done it for you too, asshole."

∧∧∧

Mikey bolts down the stairs, holding his brain in. Loose bootsoles flapping. He only catches Anna cause he starts jumping down whole stairflights in the dark, or maybe she's stopped and turned round.

She's like, "What're you about, Mikey."

He's like, "I need to ask you. Arco's keeping the sword thing secret. Like even to her clones. She won't talk bout having it to anybody and she's all tensed up and going siko."

Anna doesn't say anything. You can hear the soles of her feet shift.

"I didn't get a chance to talk lone with Donn." He pulls at the meteorhammer weights at his wrist. "But everybody's really freaked out."

The sound coming from Anna could be one more condo wall caving in. "Same straight edge," she says after a while. "She thinks they'd expect her to lead. They would. Did you just come down here to bitch?"

There's a nother while.

"I guess," says Mikey.

"No, that's cool. You used to do that," says Anna. "I thought bout it, though. You're not doomed, not less you want it. We were all so hardcore together."

"Oh," says Mikey. "Hey, we're still friends, right?"

"Me and Morgan weren't," says Anna. "We can be, if you want. But that makes it worse."

So she's gone.

∧∧∧

"You ever see something a million times and you still can't think it's real?" says Donn.

You can tell when Arco's thinking. Her fingers move on nothing. "Mind is unreal."

There's no bridges go here, and nobody ever trimmed the bamboo here, not once, and it scraggles all round the tower of disco hell like an bathmat gone to seed round a toiletbowl. This monolith prefab of windowless, unmitigated black plastic, and you can still run your thumb down the moldlines where some asshole poured the form.

And now it's dark.

Rain on their lifted faces and on the puddles rain and rain slamming the jagged windowpanes of the sky, and nothing, nothing is a metaphor, not ever, and what's growing in the puffy stucco sidewalk isn't flowervines or slime mold but a net of thin, unremarkable veins.

Mikey pokes out his tongue, bites it through his smile. Punker's shaking like a werewolf. "He means when shit's actually there."

There's a fresh road through the punkgrass snarl, hacked and trampled. Here and there somebody impaled yuppies into the bamboo. Hanging pierced from taints to shoulderblades, with bonfires skipping in their chest cavities to say hi.

Arco's like, "Mind is there."

Her slitted eyes dilate a little way. And where you pass, the heads of yuppies turn. Jaws thrashing, faces marked in housepaint with the blue circle. What goes out returns. Lord Darby, do you know?

"We wouldn't look to you if we didn't need to," says Raffia.

"Yeah," says Arco.

"We're still doing the show?" says Raffia.

"I think everyone already came," says Arco.

And they all crack their fingers. They crack out their fingers. It sounds like reloading a blade.

∿∿

—*Mikey of Meatheads, what is the disco-nature of existence?*

—*My child, the world is like unto a translucent darkness of jumbled shapes, mashing and grinding against each other, pushing and pushing in their blind cravement for satisfactory residues of powdered consciousness.*

—*Donn of Meatheads, what is the disco-nature of existence?*

—*I don't get it, there aren't noncontingent base particles of disco. Or maybe it's vinyls, I guess.*

—*Arco of Meatheads, what is the disco-nature of existence?*

—*Nothing's there, nothing's dancing.*

—*Raffia of Meatheads, what is the disco-nature of existence?*

Raffia?

Hey, Raffia?

—*Fuck you. Disco sucks.*

∿∿

Yeah, the world's a translucent darkness of jumbled shapes, mashing and grinding against each other. There's a round raised stage in the middle of the world, ringed with blue handi fencing. All round the edge the shadows push and push, shearing their teeth to stubs against the cheap iron bars. You're not there.

"They'll come," says Anna Complice from her lashedon armor. Diy platemail shoulderpads cannibalized from an old boiler machine, and the smashed vermillion head chalked on her back to say *SECURITY*. You're not there.

You're not there. The stage is one mound of sound gear. This tumulus of cracked amps, monitors. Ancient casings swelled taut with botulism. Their million million cords plaiting into a couple dozen white plastic powerbars down to a single outlet.

"Who's gonna come? Oh. Your band. No shit, it's her edge to do shows." Darby's sprawled cross a knoll of sunn amps, naked sept for the belted leather riding up over his belly. He's flipping a little plastic pilljar in his hand. You're not there.

Darby bites the lid off the childproof jar. Spits plastic shards all over his chest, tips pills in his mouth and chews. Before your gramma's face was known to the void these meds had expired, and the calendrical systems to fix their expiry date themselves expired yet, and the existential void expired too, and Darby Crash, who will not diy, he's like, "Dickhead, gimme a straw!"

A packet of blue bendystraws drops into his lap. There's punks somewhere screaming ready, so many, so loud, and Darby holds up his hand like motherfucking Caligula and the whole crowd hushes at once. He bites open the strawpacket and drops one in a bottle of vodka. For real. Don't even think you're there. His thoughts aren't yours, and you can't know them now.

You say you've hung with Darby's crew. You figure that could matter? Maybe a couple times you glimpsed him cross the room, his inner circle round him like his leather. Said you'd tease out his nature from the company he keeps, the stories in his wake. You'd get to know him someday, right? It's too late now, tourist, and he'll laugh as you try. He'll laugh and pinch your matchflame down, and then you won't even be a story anymore.

"These powerbars don't do shit," says Anna. She toes the little red switchlight back and forth.

"Yeah. I should of asked Pat to set up power. You need power for a show, I guess." Darby belches. "Hey, Anna? Do you still hope the right Arco shows up one day?"

Anna softly chews her lip, nodding. "That's the dumbest question I ever heard, man. And I knew Mikey D'Angelo."

Darby sucks vodka and holds himself laughing. "Hey, you know what God is, Anna? God is closure."

"There's no God," says Anna Complice.

"Yeah," says Darby. "You wonder why?"

∧∧∧

You know it's a tense show already. Nobody's outside drinking, nobody's smoking. But if you know the kid working door and you don't stop and parlay, you've got no hardcore at all.

"I saw you kill yourself," says Mikey. "Are you from Dimension X?"

"They're all X," says Pat Pending. He slaps the cowlick of matted dreadstuff at his forehead. "Oh, no, like I jumped. But just cause it was mega awkward. I thought I'd say hi again later."

"What?" says Raffia.

There's a big red plastic saladbowl full of crooked filters on the table. Beside it, the huge padlock from the story. The steel's melted in a bunch of little places, like from Siko Miko's fingertips, but it's got no forcemarks anywhere. He must of forgot to actually lock it.

"You didn't say hi either," says Mikey. "We never even saw you come in."

"Oh. I'm helping with sound." Pat looks off into the saladbowl. All the filters patchily stained the color of tea, little yellowy crustals like driedup pus. "I floated down. When I upgraded my hockeystick I put in some graviton deregulators. You guys thought I committed—"

"Oh," says Raffia.

Behind Pat Pending's table, the disco tower stands black as a blade knapped from an infinite sunglass lens. The silence gets weird between them, and the rain redoubles, pocking heavy on the building's side.

"I wanted to know," says Arco. "How long's it been since you guys got back without me?"

Pat's like, "Dude, conceptual measurements of time? Isn't that against your straight edge?" Arco just looks at him til he sighs and goes, "Three days. Tomorrow it's gonna be four."

Nobody laughs. There's this long shiver just sticks to the air.

"Same gravitation technology that keeps my lab glued to the ceiling," says Pat. "You know? When you pulled down the subsonic acoustic mikeyscope or whatever? That's cool. You can use my stuff whenever. Like, I owed you anyway."

"Nobody owes anybody," says Arco.

"Oh," says Pat. "You guys can go right in." His head dips again. "I'm helping with sound. I just had to wait for you guys, cause I'm helping with door. Can I see your wrists?"

"Why?" says Donn. Whole band's fanned out behind him, arms crossed. Behind Donn. Ever seen that before?

"Oh," says Pat. "Cause mission's your Germs burn. Just cause it's the last show. It hurts, but like I gotta pay too, right."

"You must of got a new one in this dimension," says Donn. "I burned my burn off in the museum elevator after Mikey fell asleep. Cause we read how historical yuppies had consciousness and Darby mass murdered them."

"Hardcooore, nerd!" Raffia slaps his shoulder.

"Yeah. How do you think I handled their oldschool burns? I got a zippo. You just paid mission early, that's all." Pat sighs. "Mine's the last one, then." He takes a minigolf score pencil from his dreads. Pushes the embedded filter out of his wrist and it lands in the red plastic bowl. "Go inside. Don't climb the stair, that's general mission. Take the elevator. There's no yuppies. We cleared a space."

Donn's like, "Did you ever figure out that thing bout compassion?"

"Oh," says Pat. "I needed to look at it simpler. Compassion's just when you pay really close tension to somebody and you figure out what they're thinking. I'm kind of trying to get good at it."

"No, like." Donn swallows, rubs his cheek. "Why didn't you kill yourself?"

Pat's got his thumb over the weird little hole in his wrist. "No, I opened up some clock radios and got these diodes to make graviton deregulators—"

"I'd of killed myself. It's not too late." Donn spreads his hands plainly. "Darby Crash might touch you but it doesn't mean he cares. It more means he doesn't care. His friends are all gone, man. He's like you that way."

Pat's mouth moves. Words come out after a while. "You have it easy. You know you feel stuff. You don't have to guess." His arm spazzes out and knocks the red bowl sideways through the air, dumping filters everywhere like straw. "Look, I'll see you inside. I'm doing sound but first I gotta help with fence."

"Fuck is fence?" says Raffia.

"I gotta cut the fence down. And let the yuppies in." The crystalwhite display panel on Pat's hockeystick flashes *12:00 12:00 12:00* as he stands. He's stepping through the air.

⋀⋀⋀

"Man," says Mikey. "That was intense, Donn. I thought you were all about manifesting compassion."

"I hate it," says Donn. "I think that was the best I could do."

〜〜

*B*efore anyone gets a light Donn tugs the door closed behind them. It whooshes shut like an airlock. Somebody goes, "What the fuck, Donn?" and he's like, "What?" and now it's extra extra really really dark. Drifts of sneezy dust hanging everywhere like old iron filings and the cranktorch beam's just a rusty cylinder turning in negative space, finding none of the room's edges. Mikey reaches to brush the low ceiling and there's a muffled crash somewhere above them.

"The air turned into blood." Raffia slaps at herself. "Why?"

"It's vintage blood," says Donn. "Like rivers worth. Actually it's a good sign, means tons of people kicked up dust today. So we didn't just walk into a death trap."

"No, we did," says Mikey. "Just they did too." His hooded cranktorch beam spins across the distance. "Okay, those were the stairs. I mean, they're still stairs. Am I talking too much?" Then he's like, "Where's the elevator?"

They wade through the curtainous dark. Bottleglass shards under their boots make a sound like night surf. Then there's a glossy plastic pillar with sliding doors and a tiny light the color of limeade.

"Whoa, I got the lectricity working?" says Donn. Arco and Mikey thumb the button. The doors screech open with a smell like burning chlorofluoro-carbons. Everyone gets in, and Donn goes, "Hey, hold on."

Raffia's like, "CRUH!" and swings a hammerclaw between the doors as they shudder closed. They're the same black plastic as everything. They bend, but nothing else.

"That button was just an indiglo watch glued on the wall," says Donn. But they're already rising. The glass starts raining down.

〜〜

*D*arby whips the bottle straight at heaven and it bursts against a hanging lightfixture way way up in the ceiling, and just as Raffia's tomtoms rise for one more pointless war, the glass starts raining down.

〜〜

*A*nna's wheezing like a mastiff, hauling on a huge creaky pulley. Sweat drizzles through the cracks in her armor. A grutty candlestub spins down from the gallery, pegs the side of her neck. She doesn't quit. She keeps on pulling the elevator.

Darby's still chilling horizontal. Hand behind his head, punker blows a spit bubble. "Hey, sorry. I forgot you need lectricity for those."

∧∧∧

A black plastic column rises from the hill of dead sound gear. Monitors tip and crack away, rolling to the base of the fence. The head of security's standing back, shaking out her muscles in the dingy lanternlight. There's no time passes, just four prybars shooting from the crack between elevator doors, working back and forth.

The legend slips to his feet. The doors bust off and clang on the ground. He brings up his hand but not for greeting. He grinds a handful of meth against his face, big thin flakes like borax, he's rooting in it savagely til the echo of a thunderclap explodes across the vaulted plastic sky. Half the dead light fixtures shatter in fire. The other half wake up.

Arco, Mikey, Raff and Donn. You stand together as the silver disco beams blow by. No tourist's ever made it far as this. The amps rattle under your feet with ozone and solar wind. You're that too, right? And the bottleglass fragments hanging everywhere in the dark, barely rotating, barely maginary. Their jaggednesses catching in the silver light like tiny little stars. That too, too. Fuck it. Why not. Maybe you're even the best band in the world, you're just not Darby Crash, the last first one. You think you can stand up inside the shadow of his mind? You think you can show him himself? Just for once don't try too hard. Just hang back for once, don't act stupid. Maybe it's a nuff to glimpse it. The way you got into hardcore.

You got into hardcore.

Maybe that's the joke.

All at once comes partyscreaming from the galleries. Do you see? The hollow spire of disco hell is one continuous dancefloor, winding upward from groundlevel like the ridge inside a screwhole. And this place is past capacity, everyone came out. And since they're everyone, they scream everything, they throw all things at once. Liquor and furniture, toilet bowls, they throw their friends and lengths of safety railing into the blockedoff groundlevel pit where the disco yuppies leap, dusty and blind, rubbery as dholes.

The legend smiles at something. He licks his eye with his tongue.

∧∧∧

The elevator topples sideways behind Meatheads like somebody tipped a port-a-shitter. It rolls downhill and bangs against the fence.

"Thanks for coming." Meth still drifting round Darby's face, fluorescing like a little nebula. "I know it's been weird."

"Yeah, whatever." Mikey's rocking back and forth. He makes like to push up a pair of raybans he's not wearing. "You're Darby Crash."

Donn leans on his hockeystick and talks through gritted teeth. "This won't bring the Germs back. Do you wish you didn't get them killed?"

"You're no good at this, Donn. Hurting people depends on trust." Darby's not even looking. He points at the bass case leaning against the fence and then something dark's blurring through the dark like a runaway fanblade. He only puts out his palm and the handle of Raffia's roofinghammer slaps there and stays. He's still not looking. He hands it off to Donn. There's a sooty middlefinger tied to the hatchetblade with twine.

The legend's eyes are only on Arco and she shrugs a little. Bends and touches her toes. She could be going for a run. Raffia takes the hammer and stomps to the drumkit, nothing like a ritual. Anna's already made way and now she's regarding the disco maelstrom with her palms flat on the perimeter fence. The yuppies crush and crush against the stage. Soaked in dust, formless. Almost dancing.

"I dunno why we were stressing," says Mikey. "You're Darby Crash. You're such a big influence, man."

"Nobody wants to diy," says the legend.

Mikey sweeps his hand at the climbing spiral dancefloor. "We all do."

"Youth of today." Somehow Darby's voice carries over all the screams. Above the stage and the moshfloor, broken furniture tumbles and tumbles, suspended like orbital debris. The spiel before the songs. "I mean get killed. You know there used to be a difference of words. Like before your time."

"There never was, man. You're Darby Crash." And this time he takes off the imaginary raybans, he throws them cross the floor. He turns and gives his voice to the whole giant hall.

"YOU ARE DARBY CRASH! YOU BUILT THIS SCENE AND WE'LL GET KILLED FOR YOU!"

Then all the floating junk lets go, and Darby reaches up for the first beerbottle spinning his way. He whips it back, whips it straight at heaven and it bursts on a lightfixture way way up in the ceiling and there's no sound at all. Somewhere else in time, a thunderclap already went by. And just as Raffia's tomtoms rise for one more pointless war, the glass starts raining down.

〰〰

—*He stood all night beside the drumkit Donn O'Aural of Meatheads. Bent over in the silver light with TP sticking out his ears, dreads hanging in his face and his hand like sploring the bassneck, shaking it out for acupressure points. After the first two notes it was like any show he ever played. You'd see the neck bend every way like rubber under his hands. His bassneck wasn't rubber, Donn just could do shit like that. Those riffs too heavy to hear, just a pressure. Like how you can't see the air. We knew there was low end cause we'd yell and feel nothing in our throats. Our throats were already shaking.*

That line carved in his pickguard, WE SHAKE EXTENSION. Is it fucked, nobody ever asked him what that meant?

〰〰

Fist skyward and Darby's screaming round a coughsyrup bottle jammed in his mouth. It's working as a mic so the words come out all thick and sticky with reverb. When he chomps down and whips his head side to side, bumbleberry tussin spills dark from between his lips like he got shot in the gut. He's screaming "SNAP CRACKLE POP SNAP CRACKLE POP!" like the outro for Circle One. After a while, that's even what they're playing.

〰〰

—*She played the whole night without a drumstool. Squatting on a tippedover bassamp with ears running blood, and her hair kicked sideways every time Donn dug his pick. Her arms strobed at crazy angles as she turned and turned, just blasting one drum at a time and screaming shit at Darby, not even the song. This one part she pointed her face up for the falling bottleglass, caught a mouthful of shards and swigged them round like listerine. She spat a glass stream in Darby's face and never lost the beat. She spat a lot of tongue meat too but it didn't matter. She was Raffia Tie of Meatheads. Punks could do shit like that back in the day.*

Then the feedback hisses to nothing and Darby catches his toe in the space between two amps. Falls right on his mouth and the sound of shattering teeth echoes cross the walls like a bullet into a rock face. He falls with his jacket hiked up over the notchy cheeks of his bare ass and only now, only now, the kids in the galleries cheer.

Arco just cuts into Milk Carton Angels, the long long first riff her and Mikey pass along. The notes ring up and down like sticks on broken bells and hang there for a breath til Mikey enters in. He rips into the big chunky chording and his side of the riff fits under hers, scummy and blurry, all his strings a halfstep loose. Arco moves her pickinghand away and she's practicing her next crew of notes as airguitar. Her fingers noiseless, not brushing the strings, taking the same jagged rhythm as every time they played this song. A lot of kids say they can hear the air currents, or they call this part the solo.

Darby rolls on his side. His jaw's wrecked with blood, he's already barking into his fist. Staccato yelps rising in clusters. Arco's sposed to sing this part and not til the main riff's over, the tempo's fucked too but somehow it really fits. He's slurring where she'd slur, his voice breaks in the right places. The song never went down this way, but its hardcore's still burning. You know he's listened for real. You know.

Arco's pickinghand slams back into the strings, its stuttering pattern unbroken. Airguitar congealing into regular guitar. Shit like that's sposed to happen at the end of the world.

"It's fine," he says from the spray of bottleglass. "We're with you."

Hefting the immense square of fencing over her head, Anna screams again. Maybe it's her muscles screaming as she heaves the handi barrier cross the whole length of disco hell. It flips slow and oceanic in the dark, like a panel clipped off a satellite, and crashes into the wriggling, pushing shapes near the far wall. They're smashed where they stand but no room to fall, and the whole thing hangs there lopsided with the yuppies pushing from all sides.

It rocks and sways like a floating dock in a mean windstorm. Arms shoot up and twist disembodiedly between the holes in the fence. Mosh platform. Holes in the mosh platform. Go. Go.

∿∿

*K*KTT as another femur blows open in the fire. Angular sparks whirl from the marrow and bounce cross the concrete ground. Like shit you could of been. What do you remember, tourist?

Something's soft under your head. Raise it. Coreward. Everything's always been coreward. The basement slips into its own distance like an unfinished veldt at night. The lights that stir against the ceiling's patchy ductwork, pitting into the dark, they're a numberless shrapnel of pale bonfires. Like flecks of quartz, almost, or flecks of rain on amber bottleglass. Jewelsteel through feudal-era raybans. Or tobacco spit on a flashlight lens, or sleepchunks in your eye. Bonfires all cross this windowless concrete plain colored the tawny, diluted way of cornerstore beer.

KKTT and punker snaps open a can. You can't see her face under the hood.

—*How was the show?* she says.

∿∿

*A*nna's lips grin, and her skull grins, and her head slams a little to the beat. Sometimes you can look at somebody and guess what they're thinking. But if somebody's not thinking, you can always tell what.

She pulls the little security hatchet from her bandolier and with two surgical whacks of the buttend knocks two C-pegs from the top of the handi fence segment. Know why they say your hardcore's outside you? She's not asking for you, tourist. She lifts the blue square of cheap castiron fence over her head, holding it behind her, and screams at the surging yuppie crowd. Like something newborn, skinless in its joy. The fuckedest thing in the world.

∿∿

"*H*ow long you wanna give it?" says Arco between songs.

Darby taps his wrist. He's not wearing a watch.

Hold on, he did that with only one arm, and you didn't pay tension? Fuck, tourist, you missed a fuck of a shot at lightenment.

Arco's like, "Yeah, okay."

∧∧∧

—*Then she pointed for the mosh platform and in that slice of time every punk in the universe saw her. All the kids pitching bottles, they pitched themselves off the railing instead. Stop kicking me, Raff. Kids landing crouched on the handi fence with blades and like trenchingshovels in their hands and like sporks behind their ears. It was the latest of the handi phalanxes. The kids on the outside hacked shoulder to shoulder and the kids on the inside danced. Sometimes they'd get pulled off the edge, sometimes they'd get moshed off. There was always more. Man, there's more where everything comes from. Stop kicking me, Raff. The kids on the inside danced.*

—*Put this bag on your head if you can't sleep.*

—*What, like tomorrow's a school day? Anna was stanced on the edge of the stage, in the hole in the fence she made, and they came to her. Clawing through each other toward us. The disco dead with their big red shades blown out, and like their million karat neckchains knotted sideways, their cheeks halfeaten, their chests halfeaten, their fros charged up with curdled blood. She's head of security. She's made of meat. She's so right in their way.*

∧∧∧

Mikey's like, "Arco? Play my part here."

And he throws out his guitar, and she seriously catches it by its head and the riffage coming off it doesn't even stutter, who knows, but Mikey's already vaulted shoulderfirst off the stage, he's cartwheeling right over Anna's diy rampart of amps, right into the disco horde. Tourist? If you always wanted to do something this dumb, it's probly your last chance.

∧∧∧

Up in the spiral dancefloor, doesn't matter where, kids surge and push the rail like rude engines cast of slaughterfloor steak. Go. Get up there. Jacket spikes and headbutts, yelling mouths like splits of shadow, splashed beer, blood jets, snapkicks in the air. Pick one. We're all the same in this.

Yeah, that arcore dude with his scalp tiediyed in motor oil. Sure. You're him, too. The railing in your hands, it's black plastic like everything, a waistheight barrier before the long fall. Pick a bar and kick it outa the fence, so you've got a stubby spear thick as a broomhandle. Now climb on the rail, punker. Don't jump yet. Keep your gravity low. Just love their elbows in your kidneys, the hot breath spilling on the middle of your back. Don't jump. Don't jump. Lean backward til they toss you on their shoulders.

Arms out, crowdsurf a while. Shut your eyes and go in among the chudding rhythm. Yeah. Have a deep spiritual moment. It's Arco's fingerprints, the actual ridges of them, brushing the guitarstrings like ideograms traced inside the feedback. It's Darby Crash spitting cross the stage into Donn's dreads and each drop's a separate, amplified *PLACK*. The nonymous hands pitching your shoulderblades up and round, shoving at the soles of your boots. It's like riding a rockslide. How the bass just throbs and dives and the riff turns backward under Raffia's sticks and the band's going a completely nother way, Darby's just facedown and gurgling something, but verses and choruses are just ego trippage anyway, and everything just works, everything, nothing can help itself.

Nothing, there's nothing holding up your legs, they're surfing you right over the edge. But it's like that old song of Arco's band, it's what we train for. Just tip feetfirst as they drop you, and hold hard on the spear. Now get outa yourself.

—*This is what we train for.*
—*More than the war. More than the war.*

The beefy arcore kid's falling through the strobeshot dark with his feet wide apart, hands on the plastic spear like he's sliding down it. That yuppie right beneath him with the sequined gold cowboyhat. That bobbing head. He dunks his spearpoint right there, and his boots hit its shoulders half a breath later. It's cushioning him, damping his momentum as they both drop.

They're all round you.

∿∿∿

She's pulled a bunch of amps down into the circlepit. Standing in the lee of her crude fortification she's blocking faces with her wickedly armored forearm, swinging her sledge on every downbeat. Not using the handle, the hammerhead right in her hand, like she's wielding a fucking big brick. They're pushing toward her for the stage, but no yuppie bites at Anna Complice, not once. The hammer's a hammer. The amps are amps. Silver disco light revolves against her eyes and when it's dark they're dark.

∧∧∧

"It's okay," he says from the flaming monitor stack. "We're with you."

∧∧∧

You must of put out some ego vibes while the cowboyhat yuppie crashed, cause all the nearby shapes swivel toward that beefy arcore kid. He breathes in and breathes out and lifts the spear behind his head. Step back and watch his fingers slide over the clumps and clots of gray matter fouling the spearshaft. The way you're the black spear, growing longer, shorter in time with his breath. Shattered-ended and heavy. Like a frozen shard of gravity. Be that or he's fucked.

He casts the length of busted rail cross the moshfloor. His shaved head's moving with the choppy drums, he's slipping a katana from his hipsheath, no, you're not there. You're the plastic shaft, going as he breathes. Wobble at the top of your arc like a petrified nerfdart and now the earth's pulling, pulling harder til you drop and splinter into some asshole's splintering collarbone.

While the yuppies' heads follow the dwindling spear the kid cuts once, twice. His moves strobe like animation cels in the jerking silver light. Pieces missing from a couple skulls, nothing like a circle's cleared, he vaults over the laggy shapes as they topple. Lands shoulderfirst, rolling, comes up with his back to the wall. His eyes almost unfocused, lips whispering like a tiny reverb of Darby's thunder. A couple jaws snap at the air, armslength from his brain, and then the yuppies are turned back round, pushing chaotically for the mosh platform and the spiral dancefloor and the stage.

His back to the plastic wall and his thumb stroking the blade's squarish hiltcollar. Bottleglass shards cracking under him as he stands. This one disco dude turns round, whole body nodding to the bass, and it fucking actually adjusts the lapels on its bloodsmeared white satin jacket. Then it leaps, totally vert, and comes down with locked knees to spin round balanced on one heel. Thing's pointing one finger at heaven when it's done and it grins like a split gourd, and it makes you grin the same, tourist. It's the pure spirit of disco, liberated from mind, and your jaws part and you're laughing through the kid's face, dude? Dude, it just totally smelled your ego.

You're not there. Not there not not there.

Here. Your lips open wider and now you might be laughing or making a nother sound, can't hear, but the back of your neck's prickly cold. The naked bodiment of disco-nature dives at you facefirst, cracks your head into the plastic wall. Its teeth clamp into your jawbone. Drop the katanablade, your pocketknife pounds twice in the soft flesh behind its ear, but you're fucked already, you blew it out with its jaw locked in the bone of your face.

There's bodies on you. More teeth driving into you. Tearing ragged strips from your biceps and the sides of your scalp. A yuppie's bite is painless, tourist. Like something that should matter but it doesn't. Hollowness spreading in from the places they're tearing away, washing toward your spine and it's not even cold. Like you're getting planed down to a point.

Arco would meditate right now. How they're dancing, their actual bites are dancing. They're only returning your consciousness to sweet fuckall that shat it out, nobody deserves anything anyway, and Arco's up there in Meatheads and she'll never see your face. Some punks say your last diying smells like campfire. You're arcore. You're not sposed to believe that. You're seriously sposed to smell campfire. The ground's sposed to get soft like couch cushions under your back and you turn your head and your eyes open on the House of Anything Goes.

They're pressing you breathless and your heels crash the ground. The disco-nature of existence is to suck.

∧∧∧

Mikey lands bellydown in the churning yuppie moshfloor. No, but it's like that part where Rollins jumps off the stage and stomps cross the pit of yuppies like their faces are one mcdonalds ballpit. His knees and his palms bang against heads. Something hard knocks a cough from his gut as nonymous arms scrape at him, snagging in his jacket, drawing him weird directions. Anna's bellowing something about a fucking stooge. Probly must be somebody else.

He levers himself up to an awkward handstand. Micro finger flexes to balance him on the bobbing heads, and something swipes at him and he's switched to a onearmed handplant, fingers digging in the scalp so hard his nails bleed. Balancing headfirst with Fuck It arcing beneath him, Mikey shuts his eyes and you're only with his siking, you're the meteorhammer coasting through the silvershot dark in wild loops and skips. Skulls split like plates in your wake, one-two-three-four, and then somebody leaps and bashes Mikey across the mouth.

Mikey? Your tongue presses a wiggly front tooth as you brace your hand on some asshole's shoulder. Open your eyes and check what's up. The light's all weird, steady dim yellow. You shift position, stub your extra spinalcord on the low concrete ceiling. Fall and crack the side of your head on the ground. Boots stamping all round you. You're not focusing too good, man, but at least there's no jaws ripping your face.

The ground's cracked and gray and slanted, polkaspotted with a million cigarette burns. The light's an incandescent bulb frying in a wire cage. Isn't it kinda late in the game for renos? The band's still playing No God, everyone knows that one, it's a hymn, man.

Some asshole throws a bottle. Glass sprays cross the low ceiling. Up on stage it's coming sick and sloppy, sharp riffs lifting from the churning feedback muck, and that's not Arco filling in your guitar parts. This dude's got a mega wobbly fro and a grin like a bashed-in wolf. Sleeveless tshirt scrawled in felt pen, *BESTIALITY IS THE ONLY REALITY*. And once you saw a zine of him or something. Maybe like the back of a teastained record sleeve. Or in a wall of hashsmoke once you saw the face of Pat Smear.

∿∿

"It's okay," he says from the spill of glossy bile against dark leather. "We're with you."

∿∿

Nother heavy malt bottle sails through the low basement and thocks the point of your jaw. Least that one didn't break, your eyes are blinky a nuff with forehead blood. Find the bottle sideways in your lap, tipping warm beer on your knee, and you lift it for a swig. Spit out some little crumbs of teeth.

All these weird clean mooshy punks, they're crouched against the far wall with their biggest beefers guarding in front. All their blue circles on handsewn leather armbands, Mikey, they all bear the legend, and up on stage the vortex keeps on pounding, it's so loud and buzzy you gotta close your eyes. It's not

P. 354

even chords. Are you sposed to like this? Try to close the top of your head too but there's actually no muscles for that, actually. The huddled kids shout round their cupped hands and you can't hear shit. They're wrapping their pressurecuts in rags of tshirt, actually ripping up silkscreens for medical duty, and glaring meanwhile like you started it. Looks like they're rooting through their bags for further missiles.

∧∧∧

—So then some asshole's trying to pull me upright by the protruberating spinalcord. I felt a sensation of prickling and a further sensation of consciousness. So I got up, like to keep the weight off my brain stitches, and punker's got his fist super far back. It's moving in a circle like a picture of boxing. I thought he was making a corny feint but he didn't knee me or whatever, his punch just came in. I had time actually to lick my lips and then I chopped him in the side of the elbow.

Dude released my spinal column to shake out his fractured tibia. I stepped back and scoped, it wasn't yuppies anywhere. Like a mosh pit of punks, but all soft and creamy ones, they seriously smelled like they wiped every single time they shat. They're slamdancing all slow and gentle, just rubbing up, and whoever tanned their leathers actually bothered to sear off all the little hairs. It was like Dimension Boring, sept for with oldschool Germs. But some dude's growling at me all hitting his palm with a bike chain, I'm like, Cool, and then I see punker conked against the stage holding his eye. I'm like, Wait up, did I just accidentally not purposely do his buddy's eye? And I do look down at Fuck It, there's an eyebrow stuck on.

But Darby's just leaning out over the pit staring at me. It's like baby Darby, his cheeks are all fat and shit. No white in his hair, his eye's there, his arm's there, and he looks so glad to see a little blood, it's like somebody stuffed his ass with angels. And a circle's open round me, everybody's gawking like they don't even wanna scrap, so I jumped for this pisspipe running cross the ceiling. Brought my feet up and crawled over to the far side of the pit. They didn't wanna scrap either, they were all shoving in this friendly no-elbows kinda rhythm mode. I just cleared them out with my arms and climbed on stage. Germs were pretty cool, yeah. Somebody in the pit grabbed my ankle but I didn't stomp or whatever, I was just like, Hey Darby, what in the fuck dimension's this?

Darby just applauds. Like the song's over at a nother show only he can see. He's all like, I really like your hair. Gonna call you, kay?

ᨈᨈᨈ

You just groan and spread your arms behind you. Try to lurch upright and your ass slides against the plywood stagefront. It's only kneeheight and you flop backward onto the stage, roll on your side. Belch and roll halfway cross the stage and you bang your hip on her sharp boots. No, really, man, really, man, really, it's Lorna of Germs.

Her face set like a tarotcard and she's covered in ceiling dust, her ripped black neoprene dress and her floating yellow hair. Lorna Doom weaving out and back with the one-note pulse, holding the black plastic bass so the headstock pokes the dangling lightfixture and makes dustbunnies snow into your face.

She doesn't even look at you. Her halflidded eyes flick like she's dreaming. You just stare up at her chin while the bass notes slam in through your ears and your nose and the sockets of your eyes. They're settling on the back of your skull, *DOOM, DOOM, DOOM,* fuzzy black supernovas, and Lorna of Germs doesn't even look down. Just when you're reaching up to wipe your eyes, she hawks a giant gob on your mouth. Your sleeve's over your eyes, you're floating in the smeary pulse, and you still can feel her laugh at you. It's how her thumb jitters the string.

No, you're trying to push yourself upright, but somehow you're on the edge of the stage again. All the kids there pushed back up, slamming faster, and the riff still keeps wailing. Look up and Darby Crash, that lean bloody shape in a bluedark writhing shadow, he's swinging the mic by its cord. Slaps it into his palm with a huge dense noise that blacks out the lightbulb for a breath. Then the song's gone into this stretchy, ringing silence. You're stumbled upright. Rubbing at your brains with your knuckle, feeling your short-term memory circuits vanish into white noise.

Darby's voice goes, "Nice hair, poser, but there's no room in the band."

He just glances at Pat and chops his hand a little sideways. Dismissive. Like he tossed a paper plate. Pat's unbuckling his guitarstrap as you turn your head and now he's stepping back, got two hands knotted round the neck. He spins round in a blurry circle, sweeping the whole thing in front of him and Pat Smear of Germs just guitared you right in the chest, Mikey, you fucking tourist, you're falling back into the pit.

ᨈᨈᨈ

They stop playing, guess the song's over. Darby's like, "Somebody gimme fortyfive cents? I need bus fare. If you want it can be a dollar."

Raffia rips her hihat off its mountings and flings it at Darby's jaw. He jumps and it spins into his solar plexus like a dented gold UFO, and then he's doubled over with his fists balled. But he's not coughing. Punker's seriously giggling.

And hey, some asshole's finally got past Anna onto the stage. Got a big anthill of green hair, diaperpin through her lip. She's pulling herself upright. Cheekmeat drooping open through a couple freshlooking bitewounds, you can see the wormholes in her teeth. She's rushing forward with her arms out and Mikey's ripped out this big echoing powerchord and Arco's stepped to meet her, holding Margin Walker low and horizontal like a warning.

Darby just steps in sideways, tugs anthill by the baggy armpit of her jacket. "Sellout." He's giggling and he spins her round on her own force. Falling backward he pushes her face down on his knee and there's a sound like a crack of kindling. She kicks and sags, is that it? Is her jaw still snapping?

No. Don't. Watch Donn instead. How his back's turned, his head's way down. His black dreads swinging as the powerchord reverbs and dwindles. Watch the screaming kids drop from the spiral dancefloor, wading through the air. You figured that chick was a yuppie, tourist? You thought bout thinking bout what Darby was thinking? It's all moves in a game.

He wants you trying to get inside his mind.

Don't think bout how he wants you trying to get inside his mind.

∧∧∧

Mikey goes, "Darby, like, I always wondered. Where'd you learn to fight like that?"

The legend shrugs with his one eye, he winks with his one shoulder and then Mikey's like, "Man, where'd I learn to fight even? I never practice shit."

The glass keeps hailing down.

∧∧∧

—So, okay. That shaky kid with the problematic eyesocket, they've got him propped against the far wall. Two leopardprint girls are bandaiding his eyebrow with TP, and they're burning his leg with smokes, like to take his mind off it I guess. And his buddies, they're fighting some completely different kids by now.

So I'm just like, Fuck it, show you my hardcore. And I fall backward snowangeled into the pit. When my eyes open again this giganto slamdancer's hauling at my ankle. Like, he's anchoring the front center, scratchedout zits all over his temples and his hair's diyed with bull blood, punker's all flannel and chains. He keeps tugging and I stamp out with the nother foot, but he just leans away. Like he actually knows fighting. But the glass splinters keep landing on my eyeballs so I have to blink and then he's Anna. She's crouched behind her amp fort, like pulling me out of the yuppies by my heel. Like I'm in the right part of the time stream again. So she sets me down on the stage and slaps my butt cheek. She's all like, Rad job.

—I'd of just said fuck yourself for making Arco play both guitars.

—Well, we all know Anna was more lightened than you, Raff.

∧∧∧

Mikey's bootless toes wave noncommittally, Anna's pushing him onto the stage. She's holding off a nother yuppie, fingers deep in its eyes, and she spins and socks Mikey's tailbone so hard he rolls over and over. She's like, "You're not lightened a nuff for that, asshole."

Under his breath, he's like, "Fuck if you know." But spose if you were lightened, you wouldn't need to ask.

Wait, what?

Anyway Arco's throwing his guitar at him. He stands it against some amps and starts swiping Fuck It on the fretboard, free hand tapping out a percussive solo. There's never been a solo in No God before. Now the eyebrow's stuck to the strings, and they start playing a different song halfway through his solo.

KAALIFORRROONIIAA!!

No, but you're still having a deep spiritual moment.

∧∧∧

"It's okay," he says from the yawning elevatorshaft in the mountain of amps. "We're with you."

∿∿

Did you know you were waiting? Did you know for what sign?

When the thunderflash finally hits, this big frazzous stench rolls in. Like the toner pile hit critical mass and went thermonuclear inside a xerox machine. Every lightbulb in disco hell shorts out at once, but somehow nothing's dark. Guess the silver strobes broke free, cause now they're bouncing autonomous through the venue, crawling up and down kids' faces like fuzzy caterpillars. These wriggles of light the sheerest most bloodless chromium of a blinding phosphene afterflash on a ghost's retina.

Blink.

Darby's sitting on top of the handi fence, cross from Anna's security gap. Whatever he's grinding between his teeth, wintergreen lightsavers or granny smith quaaludes, there's sharp little sparks at the sides of his mouth all drifting with the drifting bottleglass. His arms spread, both his arms spread, the meat arm and the ghost. You've seen it before. The cross he diyed on.

"You guys are all passengers," he says into his fist. Every amp carries it. "You came here cause I wanted you to."

They just cheer. The kids diying jostling in the spiral galleries, kids diying slamming on the tilted mosh platform, the kids smashed and bitten, trampled, breathing blood, they all cheer. He used to be in Germs and it never mattered once what words he was saying, but he's not talking to them. He's not talking to any of them.

On the rubble stage they're standing together. They've lain their instruments down. Their minds have their hands out, cupped. It's raining sweet fuckall.

He's not talking to them.

What, you think he's talking to you? He's not talking to you.

The disco shadows in the pit aren't pushing anymore. They're bobbing their heads like one thing, and if you can see the tiny muscle moving at the base of Darby's thumb, they're moving by that rhythm. Every yuppie in disco hell banging its head and spitting gobs on Darby Crash and it's like a river's washing on him, the river of the universe turning its stepless paddlewheel, the fuckedest thing in the world.

∿∿

Arco steps past the band, she tips up her head. The legend's up on his fence throne, soaked with blood and gray chunks of spit, and even as his lips part he's still looking nowhere but Arco.

She raises her fist to her mouth.

Wait, is there an echo in here? Or delay? Is there a reverb puddle or something?

∿∿

—I was a kid when I started this scene. I did up my hair in a fucked way and I said, I need one kid to join. And before I even said it, I had friends standing by me. But I said inside me, that's not what I asked for. Not somebody who does what I'm doing. Cause I'm fighting everything being the same, so nobody who fights with me can fight what I'm fighting.

I met a lot of posers but I got what I wanted too. Only I didn't even know. I got hung up on the posers, and whenever I gave, whenever I took something, it was cause there was posers. Not kids reaching to me. Now I'm standing in the ruins of western civilization and my hair's still up in a fucked way. And there's nothing left of what I was fighting, and I'm still fighting. Cause now I made it, but it's all still the same.

If there's an anti poseristic force somewhere I never met it. I was just trying to do something and I don't remember what. I just know all this shit was an accident. I did this for you so I'm a poser too. But you should stop doing what I'm doing. It's not working.

∿∿

So where were you, anyway?

Arco's done her spiel and she gets the first thing she ever knew she wanted?

Darby slipping forward off the fence to land there on his knees and look up at Meatheads through snotty eyes crying how he finally gets it, we're all tourists inside afraid to ever trust ourselves, and truth is Meatheads were realer without him anyway, and he's just gonna go for a walk now and process shit? And unwrapping the ribbon sword from his wrist he steps down from the stage, cuts a road of meat through the very moshfloor of disco hell? Steps out the fire door with his head down, and after that, you only hear bout his walk in spiels, and maybe a couple new Germs songs come round on a traveler's back some day?

What? That's so not how it ends.

Raspberries ate that sword, even.

∧∧∧

No, where were you, anyway?

Darby's done his spiel and he takes the final thing he ever asked for?

He falls backward with a perfect record, arms still spread and he's wearing his own grin, the same grin every dead punk's ever worn to hell? And on his siked command the million teeth of disco rive the body from the legend? But now all the rest, their hardcore's fused together cause he taught them teamwork in his passing? And burning solo, all in one, they fight free of disco hell? And then they finally get round to that system of distributed jerky drying racks?

Fuck off, tourist. This is LA.

Nothing good ever happened here.

∧∧∧

"If you want you can smoke," says Darby. "I encourage smoking." His hand's down but the amps still carry. You can hear it, whoever you're in.

The yuppies still don't stir. They chill out in the silence like this army of polyurethane servant statues in the governator's tomb. And punker, is there smoke. All the straight edge kids get coughing. As they tussle with the crash trash, punks rain over the side, profuse and slowmo, their fists still wheeling in the air.

Arco's already got her hand out stop. Meatheads looking up at her, tensing out, and she's like, "You gotta let him."

And you know what she means.

So. Darby stands on the skinny fence, turning. One hand holding his jacket open like he'd bare you what's under his lungs. "You think this was a punk show cause you never went to one. But it was only real when we used to be scared. All of us used to be more shittier at punk rock. Back in history we all had the same secret we never said aloud. We had the secret of the universe." Smoke gutters from his lips. He doesn't got a smoke. "We knew we couldn't stand gainst Ronald McReagan and the conomy and all our pissed off moms and dads. The joke would end. Man, we're not sposed to win. It just got fucked long the way. You know what, it's totally my fault. I think I'm making something when I just move my mouth with words."

It's so quiet up in the galleries. The crowd rustles and glints from its eyes.

"You think you know why I invented you. Invited you guys. But I haven't been too honest. Arco came back for real. Not just some poser from Dimension X. Now she thinks she's gonna lead core into the future. Gonna get us doing pushups. She wants to help and help us til we all exhibit maturity. And sikological growth. Look, I never meant for this thing to go on so long. I never meant for it to get fun and challenging. I miss the secret of the universe."

He slips off the fence. He's falling facefirst and his voice just carries the same. "I'm gonna kill Arco with my hands."

ᴧᴧ

The next part you can't really tell. All the yuppies rush for the stage, like Darby's thrown his whole ego down, everything. The neutron bomb, the trick you can only do once. Like there's only arms and teeth, jumping from everything. And there's your arms, too. Wish you had more. They're shooting so fast you can't aim for the brain. Just parry, just swing. There's no hardware could ever cope with this.

And behind that war a nother, with kids jumping off every edge of the spiral dancefloor. Dropping headfirst and still hucking bottles, skinheads and crash trash clobbering each other in the air. Kids slamming to the ground and rolling upright to grind the yuppies from behind. Taking sides, taking form, kids brandishing their garish compound fractures like acidtripping torchbearers recrossing this doomed and raggedy grailquest. Shirts and skins, pointlessly exchanging chi, primordial beatdown of the universe.

But there's Darby and Arco behind you.

ᴧᴧ

All round the perimeter, the disco yuppies are climbing each other, scrabbling near the top of the barricade. This pulsing mess, this thicket of jumbled bodyparts, pushing into the iron cage of handi fence as it skreaks and shudders. Broken fingers wave like crab legs through the bars, and cross the stage Anna's boosted herself up. They're four of them side by side at the fencing gap, and it's such a good fight, and they're laughing, there's never any shame in shit like this.

Darby lifts his head where he's fallen crumpled. Like some old guy wrecked on ludes and coke and vintage coughsyrup, slathered with the spit gobs of the dead. Arco stands with bent knees at center stage, leaning on her scabbard. She looks at his eyes.

"The yuppies would chill out if you wiped me first." Darby props himself up on his elbow. "You could probly handle them yourself. Is it still against your straight edge to murder people? I can't member. There's so many rules."

"No getting drunk," Arco says. "No drinking expired cough medicine. No doing coke, no doing blow." She's talking pretty quiet, but it cuts like a gong through the melee noise. "No weed, no hash, no sikadelics. No chewing pinealglands, not even if you spit them out. No keeping a secret. No itch scratching, no scab picking, no fucking." Her voice carries to the black ceiling. "No looking at ads. No looking at mirrors. No looking at words. No using perma names or measurements of time or distance or numbers your fingers can't count to." You can hear it in the plastic ventilation ducts, the bloody firedoors in the back. "No killing anybody. No telling anybody to do anything. No unshared property. No kitty petting. No turning down shows, not ever."

Arco's kicked her shoes off. Arco's unhooked Margin Walker from her belt, scabbard and everything, the long tube of bikechain and hollowed vertebrae. "The yuppies would chill if I knocked you out," she says.

Now she's on point in the camel mutilator stance, holding the whole scabbard like a club. A single bar of sweat slides from the crown of her scalp, forks between her brows, down into both eyes. Her face twists and she's padding cross the stage, fast but not too fast, taking the slope of busted amps like a gymfloor.

Then it's like Darby's trying to get up or whatever, and Arco doesn't compensate in time. Her scabbard whicks empty space under his chin. She's standing over him, tongue poking the corner of her lip, and she swings sideways. He falls back down as the stroke passes over his head. The scabbard flies right off Margin Walker and goes spinning through the dark.

Arco laughs. She steps back and tips up the blade behind her head, edge level with the steeply angled ground.

"No, not like that." Darby wobbles on his feet. The yuppies slam and pile at the fence. Metal shrieks and rips in places. Whole arms pushing through the barricade, chalky and gouged.

"I don't got to kill you, just put you down," says Arco. "I stopped your arm bleeding that time at the fire. You already took your farewell show, punker."

Arco swipes in low, twice, going for his knees. Each time he just takes a step. Over all the screaming and shoving and crunching of skulls, there's these little whistling tones. The sound of a really good blade cutting air.

"What're you doing?" Darby can hardly talk. Burbling vodka laughter, double vision of the throat. And after all this you still believe him, don't you? Maybe Darby Crash really did invent hardcore, consciousness, the Dharma. You've never seen shit like this. Arco's at the top of the slope, breathing harsh through her teeth, and Darby doesn't move at all. There's nothing in the world could untrue her aim.

So. Arco steps down the hillside, through the rain. No hurry. She's spinning Margin Walker, passing it between her two hands. Diying two blades of it, each one the other's shadow. Each edge scribing like brushwork its own negative image. Wingbeats, blurring figure eights. THIS IS NOT A FUGAZI SWORD. The last Ian McEye steel that never went out on tour, it's sailing in low, all cuttingplane, like to uncap him at the hips, and Darby puts out his hand and catches the blade.

It's the other hand.

No, but it's the other blade.

Darby of Germs reaches with the hand of his missing arm and takes Margin Walker's shadow in that fist. Her katanablade, the only one she's got, shatters from its hilt. For the first time in Arco's whole life she loses balance. A cloud of ringing shrapnel hits the stage between them and she stumbles, drops on one knee.

—But Rollins couldn't stand down without blood. He would of caught up but he slipped and crunched his ankle between some rocks. A sword cut through his guts as he fell. You know what, it could of been either sword.

"Stop fucking round," says Darby Crash. "What else you bring?"

∧∧∧

Arco looks like she's gonna say something, but she just throws down the hilt. Bows her head and breathes. Do you see it there? Curling from the broken handguard, that single broad blade of crabgrass McEye forged down the spine of his sword. Like a flat green shoelace, half crusted over with dull metal flecks.

Makes you feel like some kind of tourist.

The rest of the band, they're backed up and swinging alongside the alterna Raff. Corpse parts mounded up to their knees, constantly rolling down off the stage, and the yuppies pushing up that same meat slope like an animate wall of limbs. Nobody's started to sag yet but they're swinging way too fast, and the laughs are getting kinda forced.

Arco looks up and her face twitches one way, then another, showing only static. Like she's stopped. Like something put her down and kept moving. And the ghosts of all these distant moods are trying for her mind.

No, but now it's the sound guy. Hey, Pat. He's standing beside her, dreads brushing the ground. No, he's standing upside down in the air. He tilts his chrome hockeystick and he tilts with it. He's on his feet now, his hand's on yours. Between the oddplaced calluses, it's warm and almost gentle.

"It's okay," he says. "We're with you."

His fingers feel so weak, barely pushing your knuckles. Maybe it's the hole in his wrist. Pat's guiding your hand, tourist. On and in. There's still a nother scabbard at your hip.

⋀⋀⋀

You just kept going forward, Arco. Is it good or bad, the way you never even tried to understand? Now they're all looking at you, waiting for a sign, and here's the one thing you never practiced.

You wish you had a mirror. Maybe it would show what you were thinking. You're the only one in the whole world who's never seen your face.

⋀⋀⋀

This great height around you, this crude jumbling darkness. You stand at the foot of the rubble hill, unsheathing Straight Edge. From this far up it all seems so impassive. You're seeing yourself from the outside, so this has to be your mind.

Silver strobes of disco light slide again and again down Arco's mind, like tracking ripples on a paused videotape. She wishes she could thank the light for lending things the illusion of appearance. It's touching everything but the weightless katana in her hand.

Darby snaps his fingers and the distance collapses. He's pointing at the far wall. She sees his one eye briefly close. The eyelid muscle's flickering. All the yuppies stampede cross the moshfloor, into the dark. Every one. Sardining against the far wall, they jostle to drag their teeth on its glassy black plastic. And this wasted army of exhausted kids left on the moshfloor alone, bandoned in midswing or stompled by the yuppie lunge. Staggering, patting themselves down for bitewounds. Looking only to the stage. They're all looking at you.

The legend opens his eye. He laughs at you, Arco. "No, I changed my mind now. I don't want to fight. Let's just go have a long conversation or something. Put your sword back?"

"You think I can't just put it back." Straight Edge makes a slow patient rusping noise from Arco's hand, like a magnet drawing iron grounds. "You think I came here with Rollins steel."

"So say to them what you were hiding," says Darby. His voice carries like yours does. Lifting from all the amps.

"You think you know me, man. I'm from Dimension X." Stepping backward as you talk, stepping uphill. Your band's beside you. "We found the sword with your name. It's not the one that calls for blood. I don't have to kill you if I don't want."

"That part's bogus," says Darby. "That story? I put myself in as a joke. There's only one Straight Edge. I never made any tannablades. You think I can't member? All I ever did in history was high school."

Arco shrugs, she's got the naked sword. She turns away. Not talking to him anymore. "We got this out in the burbs. It's the blue Straight Edge from the spiel." She's walking to the top of the rubble hill. Her feet are bare. Everywhere growing between the halfburied amps there's stiff green shoots of grass. Looking out, turning, she raises her hands. Tensing the swordflat against her forearm to spell X. "I hold edge against keeping secrets and owning unshared property. But I never let anyone touch this sword even. Only my bandmates knew I carried it. I would of hid it from them if I could."

"That's all ego," says Darby. "Gonna fight me or just talk?"

Did it ever stop raining? In the sky now there's warm thunder. There's hail. She's like, "This is why it was. I couldn't face the way you all looked at me. Like you thought I was the better one. Like you thought I was just holding back from saving you. Darby Crash forged this sword under the perma name Goro Masamune in the year thirteen twentyeight. I can't say big numbers either. I can't say perma names either."

"Arco, you're so cool sometimes." Donn gets it. He actually gets it. Donn's blushing and he spreads his hands like he's brandishing the key to the city. "I hereby invite you to perform at a rock concert! On. Like. The eighth day of the second month!"

"I won't play it." He's making her grin. "Play your own show, Donn. I'm edge against turning down shows and telling orders too."

Mikey takes a few steps toward her, squats and picks through the hillside debris. Pinned half under a big flat hunk of rock there's a halfbottle of expired cough syrup. He hucks it into her hand. She chugs it down, squeezing the bottle how she's seen Mikey do, tasting Darby's grainy backwash. It clings to her gritted teeth and comes back up her throat, bitter. She gags and hucks the empty bottle over the fence. It goes skidding cross the trashcovered moshfloor and nobody even moves to pick it up. They're all looking at you.

Darby's leaning against the fence with this stupid blank grin like he got slapped. She turns away from him. "You're that too, man. Why'd you think I could save you?"

You hear Raffia yelling. "Hey, straight edge!"

Arco looks over going, "What?" and Raffia goes, "What? You don't need me pitching in. I was just gonna tell you go fuck yourself!"

She's still laughing. Wondering if this is all they'll remember. "No time, Raff. Sorry."

Then she sighs. "I've got no death song either. I totally am sorry."

So she's actually doing it. Stretching elegantly backward with her free arm over her head. Somehow the sun's on her. Arco's balanced like a sawhorse on one hand and her feet, the jersey pulling up over her hips. They must all think she practiced this part. Straight Edge lifts and it moves cross her stomach, blase beyond any point of ritual, performing the gut cut like a wind ripple through a dry stand of wheat.

Nobody says anything. She doesn't feel anything. Still balanced there, not trembling, she wipes the blade on her jeans. Both sides. Taking her weight briefly on the top of her head, she greases Straight Edge with a rag from her back pocket. Then she puts it back. She's the only one ever puts anything back.

Arco's balanced there at the very top of the hill. Nobody says anything. She doesn't feel anything. At the far edge of the moshfloor, the yuppies are just starting to move again. A tide coming in with a thousand limbs. She finally looks out at Darby, and she's smiling.

∧∧∧

No, what happened to you, tourist? How could Arco shut you out like that? The rings of her eyes blown all thin like faded yarn, and she's holding the deepest little smile. Like the weight's finally off her. Like she just woke up from her whole entire life, and now she's yawning, stretching with the stretching moment.

And what? You want to follow Arco there? Hungry ghost. All this and you still don't know. That constant weight she carried, it was you. You're left behind, you're banging the door of her smile. How can Arco look so chill? She bandoned her only friends, she only has three. Not counting you. She's gonna duck out through a slash in her own guts, break up Meatheads, leave them to fend off two feral youth crews and a host of the ravenous dead.

How can Arco look so chill? Just keep on sliding off her, tourist. You're not there, and she did it without you. She cut you out. She won, and you don't get it, and isn't that how she beat everything? And down at the foot of the hill, leaning against the fence, there's Darby Crash. Flash on the sick twist on his lips. The way he feels just like you do—

∧∧∧

I knew I'd catch you, tourist.
Old friend, best beloved.
Old joke, toy soldier
Little matchflame
my sammrye
move

∧∧∧

THIS SPACE INTENTIONALLY LEFT BLANK

∧∧∧

Where the fuck did you come from?

Ah, whatever. There's this hardlooking skinhead girl in wornout denim and an old blue jersey. Wearing two giant swords on her belt and for some reason she's bent completely backward, belly up, weight split between her hands and feet. She's just balancing there like a weirdo in the dark.

There's this bangedup old punker with one arm gone, naked under a faded black leather. He's sitting in the shadows with his legs folded under him, swigging from a carton of juice. The old guy's laughing, laughing. Did you just miss a joke?

And three more kids coming up to her, wearily ng silhouettes pumping ugly handcrank flashlights held together with t e. They're on like this big rubble hill of busted old concert speakers. No dy's moving but these three kids. There's a ragged elevator shaft sunk down the very crest of the hill, and blue handi fencing all round the hill's base, barely hanging together. And round that a huge dark hall, you can't see its edges. Looks like a show just finished up. Everything stinks like beer and ectoplasm and slaughterhouses and smouldering plastic and ozone.

You don't get it, traveler, but they already had the best week of their lives. A fucked season's coming down on Lost Angeles. There's a cellular war setting in, blowing through the bindingcracks between all the little dharmas. There's a circle always closing, a pointless compass sucking every roadtrip to its blue eventhorizon, the stars themselves already taking sides. And rising from the primordial structures at the base of every punk's spine, the old nerves that remember the amnesic sea and the House at the edge of the park, there's whispers, whispers. They say the McRib's coming back.

No, but whatever. The three kids walk up to her. This beefy guy with a mangled green bihawk and an orange bandanna, he taps the balancing weirdo a couple times on her shoulder. Like at first she doesn't notice or something.

He's like, "Dude? All that shit that just happened? I think you achieved lightenment. And the sword passed over your flesh like diet mountain dew."

There's a lot of shuffly footsteps coming in the distance. Some punk screams through the dark like his muscles are getting bitten apart.

She's like, "Really?"

He goes, "You're like the only one who didn't notice."

"Fuck this place," she says. "We're on tour. Come with me."

They jump in the hole.

∧∧∧

You can come if you want.

∧∧∧

. . . THAT'S NOT HOW IT ENDS . . .
. . . DON'T WANNA BE CONFUSED . . .